TWELVE

JASPER KENT
TWELVE

an imprint of Prometheus Books
Amherst, NY

Published 2010 by Pyr®, an imprint of Prometheus Books

Inquiries should be addressed to
Pyr
59 John Glenn Drive
Amherst, New York 14228–2119
VOICE: 716–691–0133
FAX: 716–691–0137
WWW.PYRSF.COM

14 13 12 11 10   5 4 3 2 1

Library of Congress Cataloging-in-Publication Data

Kent, Jasper.
    Twelve / by Jasper Kent.
        p. cm.
    Originally published: London : Bantam, an imprint of the Transworld Publishers, 2009.
        ISBN 978–1–61614–241–4 (pbk.)
        1. Vampires—Fiction. 2. Napoleonic Wars, 1800–1815—Campaigns—Russia—Fiction. I. Title.

PR6111.E584T88 2010
823'.92—dc22

                                                                              2010020630

Printed in the United States of America

For

S.L.P.

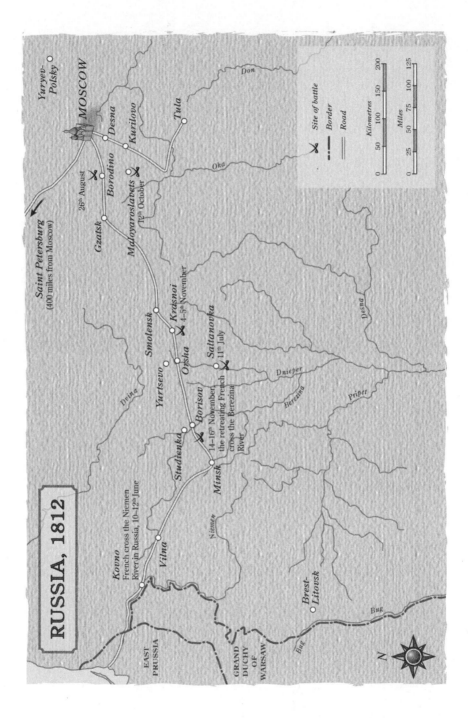

RUSSIA, 1812

Yaryev-Polsky

MOSCOW

Desna

Kurilovo

Tula

Borodino
26th August

Gzatsk

Maloyaroslavets
19th October

Saint Petersburg
(400 miles from Moscow)

Don

Oka

Krasnoi
4–5th November

Saltanovka
11th July

Smolensk

Yurtsevo

Otsha

Borisov
14–16th November
the retreating French
cross the Berezina
River

Studienka

Minsk

Dnieper

Berezina

Pripet

Desna

Dvina

Niemen

Kovno
French cross the Niemen
River in Russia, 10–12th June

Vilna

Brest-Litovsk

Bug

EAST
PRUSSIA

GRAND
DUCHY
OF
WARSAW

Bug

N

Site of battle
Border
Road

Kilometres
0 50 100 150 200

Miles
0 25 50 75 100 125

Author's Note

Distances

Averst is a Russian unit of distance, slightly greater than a kilometre.

Dates

During the nineteenth century, Russians based their dates on the old Julian Calendar, which in 1812 was twelve days behind the Gregorian Calendar used in Western Europe. All dates in the text are given in the Russian form and so, for example, the Battle of Borodino is placed on 26 August, where Western history books have it on 7 September.

PROLOGUE
A RUSSIAN FOLK TALE

Some people place this story in the town of Atkarsk, others in Volgsk, but in most versions it's Uryupin and so that is where we will keep it. All versions agree that the events occurred sometime in the early years of the reign of the great Tsar Pyetr and all agree that the town in question was infested by a plague of rats.

Rats always came to Uryupin in the summer, taking grain and bringing disease, but the people of the town, like those of any town, had learned to survive the summer months, comfortable in the knowledge that the cold of winter would kill off most of the verminous creatures—not completely wipe them out perhaps, but at least reduce their numbers so that the next summer would be no worse than the last.

But although the winters had of late been as cold as one might expect in Uryupin, they had had scant effect on the size of the rat population. The number emerging in spring seemed little fewer than there had been the previous autumn, and the number each autumn was three times what it had been in spring. By the third summer the rats were everywhere and the people of the town came up with a desperate solution. They would abandon Uryupin; leave it for the rats to feed in until there was nothing left for them to feed on. Then the rats would starve and the people, after a year or two, could return.

Before the plan could be carried out, late in July of that year, a merchant arrived in the town. He was not Russian but, as far as the people of Uryupin could tell, a European. He told the people that he had heard of their problem and that he could help. He had arrived with a simple wagon, pulled by a tired mule and covered with a great cloth, so that no one could see what was inside.

TWELVE

The merchant said that what he had in his wagon would kill every rat in the town and that if this did not prove to be the case he would not take a single copeck in payment. The leaders of the town asked what it was that the merchant had inside his wagon, but he would not show them until they agreed upon his price. Few in Uryupin had much appetite for the plan of abandoning the town and many had openly declared it to be madness, so the merchant needed to do little persuading before his alternative was accepted.

He dramatically (some versions of the story say ostentatiously) pulled off the cloth covering his wagon to reveal a cage; a cage containing monkeys— about a dozen of them. They had been placid in the darkness under the cloth, but as soon as the light hit them they began to scream and tear at the bars that confined them, reaching through as if to attack the onlookers who had crowded round.

The monkeys were not big, perhaps up to a man's knee, although their hunched posture made them appear smaller than if they had been standing fully upright. Their bodies, but for the palms of their hands and the soles of their feet, were covered in black fur, topped with a white ruff around the neck. Their heads were the heads of old men: fleshy, wrinkled skin, without a single hair. Some said they were more vultures than monkeys.

The merchant opened the cage and the monkeys ran out into the town. On the ground they moved on all fours with most of their weight on their hind legs, their knuckles barely grazing the earth, but soon they were using both arms and legs to climb up the sides of barns or down into cellars. Within minutes they had disappeared.

The people of the town waited. The merchant had warned them to keep their dogs and cats safe at home, since the monkeys were none too discriminating about their prey. Most kept their children at home too, reasoning that if one of these creatures could kill a full-grown dog, then why not a baby or an infant?

With no children playing and with the adults praying for success, the town might have been quiet, but such quietness as they enjoyed was continually broken by the screeching of a monkey as it found another rat. The ecstatic scream as one leapt upon its victim could cut through the town at any time of day or night, emanating from a cellar or from a loft or from behind a wall. No one saw the merchant's pets at work, but all could hear that they were working.

And soon, within a week, the people did begin to notice that there were fewer rats. The tenth day was the last on which a rat was ever sighted, foraging amongst the bins of pig feed, oblivious to the fate of its brothers and sisters; the fate that it was soon to meet.

The town's leaders were thankful. They offered the merchant what he had asked and half as much again. But the merchant refused to take anything.

"The task is not yet complete," he explained. "My friends have not yet returned and will not return until there is nothing more for them to eat."

Sure enough, though the people of Uryupin saw no more rats, they still heard the screaming of the monkeys at work, although now it seemed to come not from the cellars and the barns, but from the trees and the hedgerows. Rats are devious creatures, the people reasoned, and so no one was much surprised that the last survivors would find such unusual places to hide.

Midmorning of the fourteenth day after the monkeys had been released, the first one returned and settled down in the merchant's caged wagon to sleep. By early evening, all had returned. The merchant locked the cage, threw the cloth back over it, took his payment and left.

And the townspeople basked in the silence. For two weeks the terrifying screeching of the feasting monkeys had penetrated every corner of Uryupin and the relief at their departure, though unspoken, was shared by all. In their minds the people were glad to have got rid of the rats. In their hearts they were overjoyed to be free of the screaming monkeys.

But as the days went by, the silence began to weigh on them. At first they had thought the quietness had been so noticeable only in contrast to the noise of the past two weeks, but soon people began to realize it was actually more silent than it had been before; before the merchant and his monkeys ever arrived in the town. They could cover it up with the noise of speech and of their daily lives, but beyond that, there was nothing. It was an absolute, total silence.

And, as is often the case in these stories, it was a young boy, of about ten, who first noticed. There was silence because there was no birdsong. After the merchant's creatures had done their work, there was not a single bird left alive anywhere in the town of Uryupin.

Nor did any ever return.

PART ONE

CHAPTER I

DMITRY FETYUKOVICH SAID HE KNEW SOME PEOPLE.

"What do you mean, 'people'?" I asked. My voice sounded weary. Looking around the dimly lit room, I could see that we were all weary.

"People who can help. People who understand that there's more than one way to skin a cat. Or to kill a Frenchman."

"You're saying that we can't do the job ourselves?" My question came from instinctive patriotism, but I knew a hundred answers without having to hear Dmitry's reply.

"Well, we haven't done too well so far, have we? Bonaparte is already at Smolensk—beyond Smolensk by now probably. It's not about saving face any more. It's about saving Russia." Dmitry's voice showed his exasperation. Bonaparte had rolled across Russia as if the Russian army hadn't even been there. That was the plan of course, so we were told, but even if that were true, it was a demoralizing plan. Dmitry paused and stroked his beard, the scar on his cheek beneath reminding him of how strongly he had fought for his country; how hard we all had fought. "Besides," he continued, "there're only four of us. General Barclay's idea wasn't for us to defeat the French with our bare hands. We're supposed to *work out* a way to defeat them." He snorted a brief laugh as he realized he was getting above himself. "To help the rest of the army defeat them."

Dmitry's typical arrogance and his recognition of it relaxed the four of us with a ripple of silent laughter that passed around the table, but it quickly evaporated.

"You really think it's as bad as that?" It was Vadim Fyodorovich, our leader, or at least the highest-ranking of us, who asked the question.

"Don't you?" replied Dmitry.

Vadim was silent for a moment. "Yes, yes I do. I just wanted to hear it out loud."

TWELVE

"I wouldn't have believed it before Smolensk," I said.

"Perhaps that was the problem," said Vadim. "Perhaps none of us really believed what Bonaparte was capable of. That we do now gives us some . . . hope." He rubbed his face, his fingers running through his thick, black beard. "Anyway," he resumed, with a little more energy than before, "Dmitry, tell us about these people."

"A small group," explained Dmitry, "expert in working behind enemy lines. Always attacking when they are least expected. Always causing maximum disruption at minimum risk."

"They sound like *Kazaki*," I said.

Dmitry sucked his bottom lip, choosing his words. "Like Cossacks, yes— in many ways." He again thought carefully before speaking. "But not Russian."

"And how do you know them?" From Vadim's tone, it seemed clear that he knew the answers to his questions already. He and Dmitry had had plenty of time to talk on the grim ride from Smolensk back to Moscow. It was natural—certainly natural for Dmitry—to make sure he entered a debate with half of us already on his side.

"They helped us against the Turks." Dmitry's eyes fell on my diminished left hand as he spoke. My two missing fingers had long since rotted away in the corner of a prison cell in Silistria, severed by a Turkish blade. It was a wound that people seemed particularly sensitive about, although I had long since gotten used to it. The physical scars were the least of the horrors that the Turks had visited upon me.

"So does this mean that you know these people too, Aleksei?" asked Maksim Sergeivich, turning to me. Maksim was the youngest of the four of us. Just as I had noticed that Vadim was already on-side with Dmitry's plan, Maks was afraid that a three-to-one vote was a foregone conclusion. And that would be a big problem for Maks. He had a thing about democracy.

"No, no. This is as new to me as it is to you, Maks," I replied cautiously. I looked at Dmitry; this *was* all new to me, and it was odd—to say the least— that Dmitry had never mentioned it. "Dmitry and I never crossed paths in Wallachia. They seem to get about though, these . . . 'people.'" I stuck with

Dmitry's original word. "Fighting on the Danube and then travelling all the way to Moscow to help us. Where do they call home?"

"They're from around the Danube; Wallachia, Moldavia—one of *those* places. They fought there from patriotism, to defend the land of their fore-fathers. Fighting the Turks is something of a tradition down there."

"Well, the whole thing's out of the question then, isn't it?" said Maks, his eager face lighting up at being able to point out a logical flaw. He pushed his spectacles back up his nose as he spoke. "The Danube is as far away from us as . . . Warsaw. Even if you sent word to them today, Napoleon would have taken Moscow and would be warming his hands by the fire in Petersburg before they . . ."

Maks stopped before he finished his sentence. He was, more than any man I knew, able to detach himself from his own world. Most of us would find it hard to describe so glibly the realization of the horror we were all fighting, but Maks could conceive the inconceivable. It was a useful and at the same time sometimes frightening trait. But today, even he understood the potential reality of what he had said.

Vadim bridled at the image. "If Bonaparte were to make it to Moscow or Petersburg, then the only fires he would find would be the smouldering remains of a city destroyed by its own people rather than allowed to fall into the hands of the invader."

At the time it sounded like tub-thumping bravado. We little knew how true his words would turn out to be.

"Maks does have a point though," I said. "The whole thing is academic now. If we were going to use them, we should have sent word a long time ago."

"Which is why I did," said Dmitry.

He looked round the room, into each of our eyes in turn, daring one of us to object. Vadim already knew. Maks saw no logical argument against a *fait accompli*. I was tired.

"There was a letter from them waiting for me when we got back here today," continued Dmitry. "They've already set off. They expect to be here by the middle of the month."

TWELVE

"Let's just hope they don't get caught up in the French lines along the way." My comment sounded cynical, but it was a serious issue. Half of the Russian army had been dashing back from a rushed peace settlement with the Turks and had only just made it ahead of Bonaparte. Dmitry's friends would be running the same risk. But none of the others cared to take up the point, so I let it lie.

"How many of them are there?" asked Maks.

"That depends," said Dmitry. "Twenty if we're lucky—probably fewer."

"Well, what use is that?" I asked. I sounded more contemptuous than I had intended to, but no more than I felt.

"Davidov performs miracles with just a few Cossacks," Vadim pointed out.

It was below the belt; Denis Vasilyevich Davidov was something of a hero of mine. But the comparison was unfair.

"A squad from a Cossack *voisko* consists of eighty men or more; not twenty. Are your friends worth four Cossacks each?"

Dmitry looked me square in the eye. "No," he said. "They're worth ten." I felt the sudden urge to punch him, but I knew it was not Dmitry that I was angry with.

"Perhaps you should tell us what makes them so remarkable," said Vadim.

"It's hard to describe," said Dmitry, considering for a moment. "You've heard of the Oprichniki?"

Vadim and I both nodded agreement, but Maks, surprisingly, had not come across the term.

"During the reign of Ivan the Fourth—the Terrible, as he liked to be called—during one of his less benevolent phases, he set up a sort of personal troop of bodyguards known as the Oprichniki," explained Dmitry. "The job of the Oprichniki was internal suppression, which is obviously not what we're talking about here, but the method of an Oprichnik was to use absolute, unrestrained violence. Officially, they were monks. They rode around the country wearing black cowls, killing anyone that Ivan deemed should die. Although they were monks, they weren't educated, but their faith gave them the fanaticism that Ivan needed."

"And these are the guys that are going to help us?" asked Maks dubiously.

Dmitry nodded slowly. "There are similarities. My friends understand that violence is of itself a weapon. They are unhindered by scruple or fear."

"And are they religious?" I asked. "Monks, like the original Oprichniki?"

"They're not monks"—Dmitry paused, as if considering how much to tell us, then continued—"but they have their own fanaticism. Where they come from, on the borders of the Ottoman world, Christianity has always been an adaptable concept."

"Are they controllable? Trustworthy?" asked Vadim.

"As trustworthy and controllable as a musket or a cannon—in the correct hands. They just need pointing in the right direction and they get on with it."

"And you're sure they don't expect payment?" Vadim's question clearly referred to a conversation he and Dmitry had had in private.

"They enjoy their work. Like any army, they live off the vanquished." None of us quite followed Dmitry's meaning. "The spoils of war. Armies live off the gold and the food and whatever other plunder they take from the enemy."

"I'm not sure they'll find enough gold with the French army to make their journey worthwhile," I said.

"There are rewards other than gold," said Dmitry with an uncharacteristic lack of materialism. "They are experts at taking what the rest of us would ignore."

I don't think that any of us really liked the idea of resurrecting the Oprichniki, but the name stuck, even though we never said it to their faces. Once we'd met them, we got some sense of how Dmitry came up with the analogy.

It was late and Vadim Fyodorovich brought the meeting to a close. "Well then, gentlemen, we have a week or so in which to prepare for the arrival of the 'Oprichniki.' That gives us plenty enough time to work out how to make best use of them." He took a deep breath. He looked exhausted, but tried his best to instil some enthusiasm into all of us. "It's been a tough campaign so far, I know, but this time I really feel it in my water that Bonaparte has over-reached himself and that we've turned the corner. Eh? Eh?"

He seemed, against all hope and experience, to expect some sort of rousing cheer of agreement, but he got little more than a nod or a raised eyebrow as we each left the room and headed for our beds. He was not the kind of man to whom stirring propagandist speeches came naturally, nor were we the kind to be stirred by them. That's part of what had made us, until then, such a good team.

We had ridden at almost full gallop from Smolensk to Moscow, sleeping rough when we could find no convenient lodgings. The weather of early August was oppressively hot for some, but I enjoyed it; I always loved the summer and hated the winter. Even so, it was good to sleep in a real bed again. It was the same bed I always slept in—usually slept in—when staying in Moscow, in an inn just north of the Kremlin, in Tverskaya; the same inn where we had held our meeting. It was the small hours by the time we broke up, but I did not fall asleep immediately. Instead, my mind drifted back to another meeting, the first time I had met Vadim, the time when our strange little group had first begun to assemble.

"Dmitry Fetyukovich has told you what this is all about?" Vadim had asked.

Dmitry Fetyukovich, as ever, had not told me much. It had been seven years before, November of 1805; less than a month before the Battle of Austerlitz. Dmitry had said he knew of a major who was trying to form a small band for "irregular operations." I'd been interested and so the meeting had been arranged. I'd never spoken to Vadim, but I'd seen him around the camp, usually slightly dishevelled and unmilitary, but always respected by those who knew him.

"Not entirely, sir," I had replied. "Dmitry just told me it was something a bit out of the ordinary. It sounded worth a go."

"There's no 'sir's here," Vadim had told me, firmly. In those days he had been a little more austere than he became as I got to know him better, and as he became better practised at getting his way without coercion. "Respect for your superiors may be the great strength of the Russian army, but it doesn't always encourage . . ." He could not find the word.

"Thinking?" suggested Dmitry.

"Exactly," Vadim had continued. "Thinking in the army can get you into a lot of trouble."

He and Dmitry exchanged a smirk. Dmitry later told me that Vadim had once almost been court-martialled for disobeying an order. In doing so he'd captured an enemy gun emplacement and turned the tide of a battle, but the order had come from a very rich, very noble, very stupid senior officer and there were many who thought that the sensibilities of that breed of officer were of far greater significance than the winning of mere battles. Fortunately, others didn't. Moreover, and although none would have guessed it from his manner or demeanour, Vadim was also very rich and very noble, with the added advantage of not being in the slightest bit stupid. He had been promoted to major and given a pretty free rein to do whatever he thought would best harass the enemy.

"And thinking," Vadim went on, "is what I'm told you do rather a lot of."

I smiled. "It's more of a hobby, really. Like you say, there's not much use for it in battle."

"Not in battle, no. In battles you obey orders—generally. When I give orders, you obey orders; but that won't happen often. And don't imagine you'll avoid battles either. You'll still have to fight like a soldier. It's what we do between the battles that will be different."

"And what *will* we be doing?" I asked.

"Espionage. Sabotage. Uncovering information and spreading chaos. Sometimes in a small group, sometimes alone. I'll tell you what to do, then we work out how to do it. How's your French?"

Unusually, we had been speaking in Russian—something that was becoming popular amongst those who wanted to prove themselves true patriots.

"Pretty good," I said.

"Dmitry tells me you could pass yourself off on a street in Paris."

"I suppose that's true," I ventured.

TWELVE

"Well, if it's true, then say it. Modesty is just another form of lying; useful with the ladies but dangerous amongst brothers-in-arms. You tell someone you're only a 'pretty good' shot then he'll start taking risks to cover for you. Then he gets killed and it turns out you're a damned good shot, and his death's down to you. What are you like as a shot?"

"Pretty good," I replied. Vadim frowned. "But I'm damned good with a sword."

Vadim grinned. "Good. Ideally, you won't need to spend too much time using either. One last thing—for now: can you recommend anyone else for this? We can work as a team of three, but four or five would be better."

"Another thinker, you mean?" I asked.

Vadim nodded. I thought for a moment, then turned to Dmitry. "Have you mentioned Maksim Sergeivich?"

"I thought about him," said Dmitry. "He's very young and he's a bit . . . odd."

"He certainly thinks," I said.

"That's just it," replied Dmitry. "He thinks odd things."

"Sounds ideal," announced Vadim.

And so the following day Vadim had been introduced to Maks. He had required even less persuasion than I had, but then it would have been hard to find a role that was more appropriate for him. We had all met for the first time within the space of just a few months, but already our band was complete.

But now, seven years later, Dmitry had invited new members to join us—men that only he knew and only he could vouch for. Desperate diseases call for desperate remedies, but as I fell asleep I couldn't help but feel uncomfortable about these Oprichniki that Dmitry was to introduce into our midst.

Despite our late night, I woke early the following morning. We had a week until Dmitry's "people"—the Oprichniki—arrived and, with only a little preparation to be made for them, that meant almost seven days of leisure.

I walked around the still-familiar streets for the first time in nearly six months and noticed little had changed except the weather, and on this glorious summer's day that was a change for the better. The people were much as they had been. Certainly they knew that Bonaparte was approaching, but they knew too that he must stop. No emperor whose throne was as far away as Paris could ever march his army all the way to Moscow. The fact that he had marched as far as Vilna, as Vitebsk, as Smolensk, the fact that those cities were also unassailable from Paris, they fully understood. But that didn't change their belief that Moscow itself could not be reached. And I was in full agreement. Of everything I was to see in that long autumn of 1812, despite the almost unimaginable horrors, the most unreal was to be the sight of French troops on the streets of Moscow.

Was it just that it wasn't my home town that made me love Moscow? I'd lived in and around Petersburg my whole life. It was beautiful and comfortable and familiar. Familiarity didn't breed contempt, simply predictability. A knowledge of every inch led to few surprises. It was odd then that Petersburg was by far the younger of the two cities. It had been only a century before— precisely a century, in 1712—that Petersburg had replaced Moscow as the capital city, less than a decade after its foundation.

A city built as quickly as Petersburg, and built to the plans of so forceful a character as Tsar Pyetr, appeared to me to be precisely what it was— synthetic. Moscow was created over centuries by people who built what they needed to live. Petersburg was built to emulate the great cities of Europe, and so it would always seem counterfeit—only slightly more real than the cardboard frontages of the villages erected by Potemkin to give Tsarina Yekaterina a more picturesque view as she toured the backwaters of her empire. But Petersburg was the capital, and society adored it. Society had moved to Petersburg, but life remained in Moscow.

My wife, Marfa Mihailovna, loved Petersburg in a way I never could. She was just as familiar with it and used that intimacy as the basis for seeing a depth that I could never perceive. Our young son seemed to love it too, but at five years old, nothing was yet familiar to him; everything was a new adventure. So Marfa stayed in Petersburg and, however far I travelled, returning to one meant returning to the other. Returning to either or to both felt the same—comfortable.

TWELVE

As I meandered through the Moscow streets, I drank in each of the great sights of the city. I walked along the embankment of the river Moskva, looking up at the towers that punctuated the walls of the Kremlin. I turned north, passing beneath the lofty onion domes of Saint Vasily's and then across Red Square, thronged with Muscovites going about their lives. Then I continued northward, back into the maze of tiny streets in Tverskaya.

But perhaps I was fooling myself. Perhaps I was wandering around the streets of Moscow, marvelling at its people and its buildings, in order only to tease myself before I headed for my true destination, like a man who eats all his vegetables first, praising their subtle flavour while really trying to leave his plate empty of everything but the steak that is the only part of the meal he ever wanted. Or was I like a drunk who wakes early and realizes that there are times when it is too early in the day even for him and so kills time, trying to keep his mind off that first sharp, sweet drink?

It was almost midday when I reached the corner of Degtyarny Lane and sat down again on the bench where I'd first sat the previous December.

Back in the winter of 1811, I'd been there with Dmitry and Maks. Vadim had been home in Petersburg for his daughter's wedding. I'd been at the wedding too, but had returned to Moscow almost straight after, countering my guilt at the look on Marfa's face with the strange anticipation that something would happen, had to happen, once I got back to a city as vibrant as the old capital.

But little had seemed to be going on and so the three of us had, before long and for whatever reason, found ourselves sitting on that bench in the quiet, snow-covered square exchanging jokes and watching the men (and occasional women) entering and leaving the building opposite.

There had been a moment of silence as our eyes were all taken by a particularly fine-looking young lady who was leaving the building, a silence which Maks filled with an announcement made in the voice he usually reserved for describing the political affairs of nations.

"It's a brothel!"

"Of course it's a brothel," laughed Dmitry. To be honest, I hadn't noticed, but thinking about it, it seemed pretty obvious. Dmitry may have been bluffing too, but it always seemed best to appear worldly-wise in front of a young soldier like Maksim, so I laughed along with Dmitry.

"You want to go in?" Dmitry asked Maks. "It looks like it's something of a military establishment." And indeed most of the clientele did seem to be cavalry officers, just like ourselves.

"No thanks," Maks had replied, in a voice that made me wonder whether he had any human desires at all.

Dmitry turned to me. "Aleksei? Ah no. You've got the loving wife and family."

"How about you?" I asked Dmitry.

"Me? No. I don't like to play the field either." He winked at no one in particular. "There's a little place I use on the other side of Nikitskiy Street. Cheap and clean. I'll stick with that."

The girl who had caught our attention earlier soon returned, clutching tight to her body the basket of fruit and other foods she had gone out to buy. She was astonishing. Her large eyes sloped slightly upwards away from her nose and her rich lips were pressed tightly shut against the wind-blown snow through which she struggled.

I felt I had seen her before. Suddenly, it dawned on me.

"She looks like Marie-Louise."

"Who?" snorted Dmitry.

"The new empress of France," explained Maks.

"The new Madame Bonaparte," was my description.

"Ah! The old Austrian whore," was Dmitry's.

All of our comments were to a reasonable degree true. In 1810, Bonaparte had divorced his first wife, Josephine, and wed Marie-Louise, the daughter of the Austrian emperor, Francis the Second. Josephine had been unable to provide Bonaparte with children and the emperor needed an heir. How quickly the French had forgotten what they did to their last Austrian queen.

"She looks a bit like her, but not much," said Maks.

"Who knows?" I replied. "I've only ever seen one picture, but they are similar."

The picture I had seen enchanted me. It was just a print based on a portrait of her, but she seemed to me truly beautiful—much better than Josephine. But then, they said Bonaparte loved Josephine. That's why they had stayed together even without children.

"Better have him bed some Austrian harlot than touch the tsar's sister," said Dmitry. "She was too young. Very wise of Tsar Aleksandr to tell Napoleon to wait until she was eighteen."

Dmitry raised his arm. I looked up and noticed that he had made a snowball, which he was preparing to throw at the girl as she trudged her way back to the door of the brothel. However minor it was, it seemed so needlessly cruel that I shoved at his arm with my own as he threw. He was an excellent shot and, even with my hindrance, the snowball hit the wall just inches in front of her face.

She glanced towards us and, because my arm was raised, assumed that I had been the thrower. The look she gave had such a combination of anger and pride, of asking why I presumed to treat her in such a way, that I felt almost compelled to go and apologize, not just to tell her that it hadn't been me, but to explain why I hadn't tried harder to prevent it, to be forgiven for even knowing the man who had thrown the snowball.

Dmitry chuckled to himself. "Did you hear what she said to him on their wedding night?"

"Who?" I asked.

"Marie-Louise. To Bonaparte," replied Dmitry, revealing a greater knowledge of French royal marriages than he had previously shown. "After he'd screwed her for the first time, she liked it so much she said, 'Do it again.'"

I joined in Dmitry's raucous laughter, even though I'd heard the story before. Maksim didn't laugh. At the time, I'd presumed that he simply didn't get it.

"You know what *she'd* say?" continued Dmitry through his laughter, indicating the young "lady" whose resemblance to Marie-Louise had started the whole conversation. "She'd say 'Do it again—second time is half price.'"

This time both Dmitry and Maks laughed, but I didn't. It's one thing to insult a French empress, another to insult a Russian whore.

As it turned out, she charged by the hour.

CHAPTER II

TWO HOURS LATER I HAD BEEN LYING ON HER BED, WATCHING her from behind as she sat at the dressing table, brushing her long dark hair. Her name was Dominique.

"So, why did you throw the snowball at me?"

"I didn't," I replied with a self-assurance that I couldn't have expressed to her before. "My friend did. I was trying to stop him. I wanted to apologize."

"That was an odd way to apologize. You seemed to enjoy it. You must love confession."

I went over to her and kissed her shoulder. "It's good for the soul."

She pushed me away with a polite, professional firmness. "And why did you care if I got hit by a snowball?"

"I don't like winter." It was a simple answer, but the truth went much deeper, back to the cracked ice of Lake Satschan and the winter of 1805.

"Can't be much fun living in Moscow then."

"I don't live here; I'm from Petersburg. I'm just stationed here."

"Soldier, eh? Where's your uniform?" she asked, not bothering to point out that Petersburg is even colder than Moscow.

I countered her question with another. "Are you French?"

She laughed. "Do I sound it?"

"Dominique is a very French name."

"It's really Domnikiia. When I started out, everything French was so fashionable." It could not have been many years since she "started out." She smiled thoughtfully. "Less so now. And what's your name?" She saw my surprise. "You don't have to tell." But her look of childlike disappointment meant I did have to.

"Aleksei Ivanovich."

TWELVE

"Lyosha."

"Some people call me that." No one called me that any more. It was a common enough nickname for an Aleksei, but it had never seemed to suit me since I'd joined the army.

I paid and left. I used to pretend that I really had gone because I felt the need to apologize. I'd certainly felt guilty afterwards, but not so guilty that I hadn't visited her again during that winter, perhaps three or four times before we were posted out west once more in March. On many other days I had felt the desire to visit her, but had resisted, instead wandering along nearby streets, teasing myself with how close I could get without going in.

Now, in August of 1812, I was doing the same thing again. All through the retreat, from Poland, through Lithuania and through Russia, I'd known that going back to Moscow meant going back to Domnikiia.

And here I was. I'd wandered the streets and I'd sat on the bench and now was my chance to leave.

I went in.

The lounge was as I remembered it. The front door had only just been unbolted and I was the first customer of the day. Half a dozen girls were scattered about, trying to look provocative. Domnikiia stood with her back to me, talking to a colleague whilst once again brushing her long, dark brown hair. I slipped my arms around her waist and whispered in her ear, "Remember me?"

She turned round. It was not Domnikiia. Whoever she was, she tried to remember me from the dozens upon dozens of faces that must have passed before hers. She saw from my expression that I'd made a mistake and became torn between her feminine instinct to slap me and her professional instinct to offer encouragement.

"No, but I'm sure I will," she replied, the professional side winning out as she put her arms around my neck.

I pulled away from her. I tried to say something about being terribly sorry, but under the circumstances, it was quite out of place. My eyes darted around the room for help. They fell upon the real Domnikiia, who was descending the stairs.

"Aleksei Ivanovich!" She greeted me with more convincing enthusiasm than I've heard from many a hostess at many a Petersburg party. But it was, I supposed, just a skill she had acquired, much like the ability to remember my name after so many months.

She came closer and whispered in my ear, "Lyosha. Have I grown so old since last time, that you cast me aside for Margarita Kirillovna? I like my soldiers to have experience rather than youth; but most soldiers see it the other way round."

"I'm sorry, Margarita Kirillovna," I said to the girl whose back looked so like Domnikiia's. "I mistook you." I felt Domnikiia's hand leading me away and up the stairs and I gladly went with her.

Her room was little changed of itself—the same bed and the same dressing table—but summer made all the difference. The windows were open to let in the air and the shutters were closed to keep out the sun.

"You can have Margarita if you want," said Domnikiia. "She's new, but very popular."

"I'm sure any business she gets is only because people mistake her for you," I told her.

"You don't have to flatter me, you know."

Afterward, she seemed less rushed than on previous occasions. She peeped out the door as I began to dress.

"No hurry," she said. "The salon's empty. The army's out of town and the civilians are too scared to do . . . much. Why are you in town anyway, my non-uniformed officer?"

I avoided the question. "You have a very good memory."

"What? Because I remember your name and your nickname and that you're a soldier and that you don't wear a uniform and that you think you know I'm really Domnikiia not Dominique? I just give you what you want." She smirked. "You guys don't want to be fucked, you want to be noticed."

"*Think* I know? So you're not Domnikiia?"

"I might not be," she replied with the same confidence. Then her tone relented as she put her arms round my neck. "But I am." After a pause, she continued. "Trade for Dominique is picking up though."

TWELVE

"How do you mean?"

"When I started out, everyone wanted anything that was French, so everyone wanted Dominique. But over the past year nobody likes the French, so nobody wants Dominique."

I had to smile. "These politicians just don't think about the effect they have on commerce, do they?"

"Exactly. Next time you see the tsar, you tell him. But nowadays everyone wants to screw the French, so everyone wants to screw Dominique."

I laughed. "And who did I just screw? Dominique or Domnikiia?"

She giggled. "I still reckon you wanted it to be Margarita." She paused. "I don't know. What about you? Was it Aleksei or Lyosha?" I gave no answer and she changed the subject. "So what's the news from the front?"

I was astonished at her impudence. "I can't tell you that."

"Oh come on. No one would know anything if it wasn't for loose-tongued soldiers in brothels. It's tit for tat. You tell me and I'll tell you."

"And what are you going to tell me? You said yourself there are no soldiers in town."

"There are other people with tales to tell."

I guessed she was bluffing, but it did no harm to reveal what she could find out elsewhere. I told her about the defeats at Vilna and Vitebsk and Smolensk, told her the official line that the French would be stopped before Moscow, not much more.

"So, what have you got to tell me?" I asked.

"Oh, nothing."

"Tell me!" I said, rolling her on to her back.

"You going to interrogate me?"

Looking down at the tantalizing smile on her lips, it was a tempting suggestion, but the very idea brought back memories I fought to suppress. I tickled her. She giggled uncontrollably. Evidently she was very ticklish, but then, of course, that's what I would like her to be. She was, in her own way, a Potemkin village—a façade behind which I might only find disappointment if I ventured to look.

"All right! All right, Lyosha," she exclaimed through her laughter, "I'll tell you." She took a moment to get her breath back. "The only interesting things I've heard are from Tula."

"So what's going on in Tula? Something at the munitions works?" I asked. Tula was of immeasurable importance to the war. Without that city, our supplies of ordnance and ammunition would quickly dry to almost nothing.

"Not *in* Tula," replied Domnikiia. "*From* Tula. There's stories of some sort of plague. Thirty dead in Rostov. Fifteen in Pavlovsk."

Plagues were always exaggerated. When I was young, my grandmother used to tell me old folk stories about plagues, and I'd quickly chosen to be as sceptical of them as I was of the other, less earthly tales that she told. But as I'd grown older, I'd come to put more faith in my grandmother's word, on this issue at least. The last big plague to hit Moscow had been in 1771, not long before I'd been born, and a vivid memory for my grandparents and my parents, even from the safe vantage point of Petersburg. In total, a third of the people of the Moscow oblast had died. As far as I could tell, that figure was no exaggeration, though others that I had heard were. When I witnessed the plague for myself, whilst fighting south of the Danube, the mixture of rumour and fact was much the same. This new story of plague would have more than a seed of truth in it. Both towns mentioned by Domnikiia were on the river Don, one of the great arteries that run between central Russia and the Black Sea, and it wasn't unusual for disease to be carried up the river by boat. The numbers seemed unusually concentrated—but that was probably part of the process of news becoming rumour.

"I hope it doesn't come to Moscow. The plague, I mean," said Domnikiia.

"Maybe it will reach us at about the same time as the French do. Save us the trouble of killing them."

"Is that going to happen?" She huddled closer to me, her voice calling for a reassuring answer.

"No, Domnikiia," I lied. "Neither Bonaparte nor the plague will ever get as far as Moscow." But I'd seen for myself how fast both the French and the plague could travel. And what eventually did arrive proved to be more terrible than either.

TWELVE

* * *

When I returned to my room, there was a parcel waiting for me. It was from my wife. Most of the news in the accompanying letter was long out of date, but with it in the parcel was a small oval icon of Christ, on a silver chain. In her letter, Marfa explained she had heard stories that Bonaparte was the antichrist, and she asked me to wear the icon to protect myself. I felt a shiver of guilt. So far I had needed no protection from French bullets, but I had not found myself protected from temptation. I kissed the image out of habit and then put the chain round my neck, perhaps with the hope of it leading me away from any further encounters with Domnikiia, perhaps with the intent of assuaging my guilt afterwards.

Most of the letter contained nothing of special interest, just general news from Petersburg. Vadim's daughter, Yelena, was still healthily pregnant. Everyone we knew was well, but all were worried about the war and wanted my opinion on what would happen.

The part of the letter that I read again and again was about our son, Dmitry. It was nothing special, just a mother's detailed description of how he was behaving. He would be six in a few months' time and I'd probably spent less than a third of his life in his company. It was the same for so many children of soldiers. I was pleased to read that he was often asking when I would return; pleased that he even remembered I existed.

We'd named him Dmitry after Dmitry Fetyukovich. Seven years ago, Dmitry Fetyukovich had not been the tough cynic I knew today. Fighting the Turks had changed him somehow, but I had never learned precisely what had happened to him. He never learned precisely what happened to me either; no one did, not even Marfa.

I'd first met Dmitry in the June of 1805. He was passionate, radical and optimistic, as so many young, educated Russians were at the time, having heard of the freedoms that men enjoyed in the west. Despite the tsar's vocal support for the new coalition against Bonaparte, our troops were slow to move into action. Dmitry and I had both volunteered for reconnaissance work, and we spent many hours together watching and assessing enemy movements, but still our forces did not engage the French head on. England—thanks to Nelson—fought better at sea than on land and so, throughout that autumn, Austria was left alone to face the French advance, with little success. The farcical capture of tens of thousands of Austrian troops at Ulm was the pinnacle of their ineptitude. We Russians were to first see action that winter at Austerlitz; a battle of over 150,000 men.

But Austerlitz itself was not to be *our* first battle. The night before, Vadim called us together. It was our most dangerous mission to date. Vadim led us deep behind French lines, so that we could get last-minute reconnaissance of their positions. We were spotted and attacked—perhaps fifteen French against only us four.

It should have been a thrashing, but we were all strong fighters with the sword. The four of us had stood side by side, slashing and thrusting at our French attackers, who had become so pampered by the superiority of their rifles that they had forgotten how a sabre should be used. I had already despatched two when a blow from the butt of a third sword had knocked me to the ground. I saw a French sabre raised above me, poised to give a final, fatal strike when Dmitry threw himself in the way. The blade bounced off his raised arm and sliced open his right cheek. I felt his blood splatter on my face, but the wound did not hamper him. He slashed the French soldier across his belly and then struck a mortal blow to his neck. By then, I was back on my feet.

I know that at other times in other battles I have had my life saved by my comrades, and I'm sure that I have saved theirs; in the heat of battle, one does not have time to stop and notice. But on this occasion I did, and Dmitry's brave action forever held a special importance for me.

Faced with me, Vadim and Dmitry—still ferocious despite his wounds —the surviving French soon retreated. It was only then that we realized they had taken Maksim with them as their prisoner. We hoped he was a prisoner; there was certainly no body that we could see. Maksim's capture lay heavily on Vadim's conscience in particular. He had only been eighteen at the time and Vadim felt responsible for taking an inexperienced boy on such a mission, but we had little time to indulge in the luxury of regret.

TWELVE

The following day had come the Battle of Austerlitz itself—a humiliation for Austria and Russia, but perhaps Bonaparte's greatest triumph. The three of us—Dmitry, Vadim and I—were under the command, ultimately, of General Booksgevden. We were part of the force which was to take the village of Telnitz and from there, turn right to encircle Bonaparte's flank. The capture of the village was straightforward enough, but it soon became clear that we risked being encircled, not encircling. All we could do was stay there and await further orders. Elsewhere on the field, the battle had been going just as badly. The light frost and snow—which we Russians, if not our Austrian allies, should have been familiar with—was giving Bonaparte further advantage. Perhaps the frost was not heavy enough and the snow not deep enough for what Russians are used to.

It had been well into the afternoon before we at last received orders to retreat. The land behind us was a mass of bogs and lakes, but at least the cold had caused them to freeze over. I had long become separated from Vadim and Dmitry and had abandoned my horse and was, with hundreds of others, halfway across the frozen Lake Satschan when the first of the French "hot shot" landed—cannonballs heated before they were fired so that they would melt the ice when they hit. All around me, men were falling off the ice into the freezing water. Beneath my feet, through the ice, I saw bodies floating past; even living men, their numb hands searching the glassy sheets above them for a way to the surface. I tried to pull those that I could back on to the broken ice sheets, but it was not easy. Eventually, I myself fell in and only just managed to grab hold of a chunk of the floating icepack and then haul myself back on to it. Then I had possessed all of my fingers. Today, I do not know whether I would be able to achieve a similar feat.

Fear took me. I gave up any attempt to help my fellow troops out of the water and concentrated on the sole task of getting myself to the other side of the lake. I sprang from one block of floating ice to another, the constant motion being somehow more steady than my earlier slow caution. If there were other men precariously balanced on those same ice blocks, I did not notice them; my one intent was to get myself across the lake and on to solid ground. I succeeded, but looked back to see the scene of horror from which I had so recently escaped: men tottering off the unsteady ice into the water, and then attempting to swim to shore, past the drowned, freezing corpses of their comrades. It was a winter scene that was to make me abhor winter ever after.

It was two days after the battle when I discovered that Vadim and Dmitry had both safely escaped Telnitz, just as I had. On the same day, the Austrians sued Bonaparte for peace. It was one and a half years later that Russia made her peace with France—albeit a temporary and entirely strategic peace. The two emperors met on a raft on the river Niemen at Tilsit, close to the Russian border, and Tsar Aleksandr managed to fool Bonaparte into thinking that Russia would lie down for good and let France rule the entire continent.

After the peace, the final rounds of formal prisoner exchanges took place and Maks returned with a smile on his face. He had been unlucky not to be released months earlier, but the French were within the bounds of custom to hold a few prisoners until a final peace was reached. Maks did not appear to hold it against them. The wound on Dmitry's cheek healed to a heavy scar, which he hid by growing a beard. Soon after Austerlitz, I had returned to Petersburg and married my sweetheart, Marfa.

I had known her almost as long as I could remember. Her father and mine were both *chinovniks*, government officials, at the Collegium of Manufacturing. Hers had attained the rank of Titular Counsellor, whilst mine was a Collegiate Secretary, one rung lower on the bureaucratic ladder. Both had passed the grade that endowed them with personal nobility and they happily styled one another "Your Nobleness," as did anyone else who encountered them. But neither had achieved that greater honour of hereditary nobility, and so their children would have to attain their own nobility by dint of their own achievement; I through endeavour, Marfa through marriage.

And yet the idea that it would be Aleksei Ivanovich Danilov that she married did not seem to have occurred to anyone, least of all to me. It was very suddenly, only a few days before my mobilization to Austria that it occurred to me how beautiful she was. This was not the commonly accepted view, but as we stood there, at a party in her parents' house, talking, I suddenly saw her in a different light. I couldn't say what the cause of it was, but

TWELVE

I asked her to marry me there and then. Later she told me that she had loved me for years and that on that day, she and her mother had spent hours styling her hair and putting on her make-up, hoping to catch me. I never resented it—I was flattered—and never regretted it. When our only son was born less than ten months after we married, it was Marfa who suggested we name him Dmitry, after the man who had saved my life.

Over the next few years the four of us met up often, but we hadn't fought together for a long time. Dmitry and I both battled the Turk on the Danube (where it was warm), though not side by side. Vadim was in Finland (where it was cold). I was never sure exactly what Maks did.

By 1812, we had all been preparing to fight Bonaparte once again. I'd earned the hereditary right to be titled "Your High Nobleness," but I much preferred the military address of "Captain." I'd been stationed in the west of Russia as part of the First Army, under General Barclay de Tolly, along the border of the Grand Duchy of Warsaw. To my delight, both Dmitry and Maks were there too. Bonaparte chose to interpret our presence as a threat of attack, and so poured troops into the Duchy. Aleksandr had demanded that Bonaparte withdraw his troops to behind the Rhine. He had little expectation of French compliance and none materialized.

On 12 June Bonaparte crossed the Niemen. In his doing so, the Rubicon was crossed also—French troops were now on Russian soil and Aleksandr vowed not even to communicate with Bonaparte until they departed. But departure was not part of Bonaparte's strategy; not then, at least. Four days later he was in Vilna, and in the days and weeks that followed, town after town on the long road to Moscow fell under his power.

After he had taken Vilna, there was a general fear that he might prove unstoppable, and so all sorts of irregular plans were formed for ways to defeat him. Vadim volunteered himself and the rest of us, and so the old team was re-formed, though we didn't do much until after our defeat at Smolensk. Then Barclay de Tolly called us, and a number of similar small groups, to him. He knew that he was soon to be replaced as commander-in-chief by General Kutuzov and that Kutuzov would make a stand somewhere before the French reached Moscow. Barclay explained what his plan had been—very different from Kutuzov's, but one which time would demonstrate to have been appropriate. The men's physical appearance was as distinct as their tactics. Barclay was sixteen years younger than Kutuzov, but that alone could not justify the difference in their physical shape. His body was lean and his eyes and smile revealed his wisdom but hid his cunning. His bald head gave an impression of maturity. Normally, his manner of speech was clear and direct, but today, the way he described his plan seemed almost to mock Kutuzov's own euphuistic style.

"Have you ever seen children playing on a beach?" Barclay had asked us. His accent betrayed nothing of his Scottish ancestry, but hinted at his German-speaking upbringing. "They can face the tallest wave without fear; even a wave ten times their height. How? They just walk up the beach. They retreat at the same rate that the wave advances. With every step they take, the wave follows them and becomes weaker. If they stand their ground they will find the wave is far too powerful for them and will drown them. But as they calmly walk up the beach the wave gets weaker and smaller until it can barely tickle their toes. France is a great wave, gentlemen, but Russia is a very big beach.

"The plan then has been that we do nothing. The French will find that they have enough troubles simply feeding themselves, without us sacrificing Russian lives in an attempt to see them off. But General Kutuzov tells me that if doing nothing is a good plan then doing *something* must be a better one. He intends to face Bonaparte head on, somewhere before Moscow—as yet, we don't know where. Your part is to ensure that whenever and wherever that encounter occurs, the French are already weakened. Get behind their lines. Disrupt their supplies. Force them to watch their backs. Make that beach seem even bigger than it really is."

His words had made sense, and fitted perfectly with the sort of work that we knew was our speciality. Straight away, the four of us had ridden back to Moscow. It occurred to me that Dmitry must have sent for these friends of his even before that meeting with General Barclay. He seemed confident that they would arrive.

I folded Marfa's letter and put it into a drawer. I looked once more at the icon she had sent me. The Saviour's kind eyes showed no condemnation for the time I had spent with Domnikiia. Before leaving, I looked at myself in the mirror. My own eyes were not so kind.

Over that week, I spent much of my time chatting with Maks, as well as the others. Nowadays, Maks reminded me of Dmitry when I had first known him; full of ideas, full of humour. Dmitry still had humour, but it was mostly directed at other people's ideas. Dmitry was only a little older than me, but he gave the impression of having examined every idea that had ever been; and concluded that they were all rubbish.

For some reason, the subject of Bonaparte's baby son, the so-called King of Rome, had come up.

"I don't see why he needs a son. Politically, I mean," Vadim was expounding. "He had a wife that he loved, but he puts her aside for this Marie-Louise, whom they say he doesn't, just so he can have a son and heir."

I couldn't help hearing in Vadim's words some parallel with my own life. I had a child whom I loved and a wife whom I should, and off I went with a whore who, as it happened, looked like Marie-Louise. I was sure that the idea was far from Vadim's mind but, as one does in such situations, I entered the conversation with gusto before anyone could discern my guilt.

"It's a two-edged sword," I said. "He may have established a dynasty, but what's good for the dynasty isn't the same as what's good for the dynast. France's future is now assured even if Bonaparte dies, so France has less need to protect Bonaparte. Look what happened to our own tsar's father."

"But he was mad," put in Vadim.

"When the English have a mad king," said Maks, "they appoint a regent. When we have a mad king, we throttle him in his own bedroom."

"Maks!" cautioned Vadim with a growl. No one knew quite what had happened to Tsar Pavel, but it was still best not to repeat even the most widespread of rumours.

"It just shows how useless the king of England is," said Dmitry.

"But that's their strength," continued Maks. "Who have been the great Englishmen that have stood against Napoleon? Pitt? Nelson? Both dead. And yet England marches on. But if Napoleon died, would France march on?

That's why Napoleon has to found a dynasty, until France is strong enough for the emperor to be as insignificant as an English king."

"Or a Russian tsar?" I asked, before anyone else could. From Vadim it would have sounded like an accusation of treason; from Dmitry, an incitement to it.

"By the by, have you heard about these deaths in the south?" asked Maks, changing the subject abruptly. "All along the Don, as far north as Voronezh. They thought it was plague, but now the stories are changing."

There was little in Maks' account that I hadn't heard before, but I wondered where he might have picked up the rumours. It didn't take me long to find out.

Later that same day, I went to visit Domnikiia. As I was entering the establishment, I bumped into Maks, just leaving. He was embarrassed.

"Maksim Sergeivich!" I said. "I am surprised. I thought this sort of thing didn't interest you."

"It doesn't," he replied discreetly, "any more than eating or breathing interests me. But these things still have to be done." He smiled as we both realized that I, as a married man, should be more embarrassed than he. There wasn't any mockery in his expression, just an understanding of the irony. "I can see why you like Dominique so much. Please don't tell Vadim and Dmitry."

He walked away. If anyone else had said that about Dominique, their words would have been full of double meaning—of challenge and rivalry—but from Maks, they had only their face value. He said them just as he might have said, "I can see why you like vodka so much." There's enough vodka to go round, so who could be jealous about having to share? But for me, the words were devastating. My only consolation, and it was a desperate one, was that he called her Dominique, not Domnikiia.

I had to wait for Domnikiia, arriving as I did so soon after her previous client. I could have gone with one of the other girls, to show how little I cared. The problem was that I did care.

I must have been very cold. We lay side by side, not in the usual quiet embrace that followed our love-making.

TWELVE

"Are you all right, Lyosha?" she asked.

"Please don't sleep with Maks."

It was a simple enough request, but her reaction was livid. She leapt out of bed and stormed across the room. Her anger was incomprehensible to me. "Who the hell are you to ask me that, Aleksei? I'm not a serf. You don't own me—you rent me. You pay me for an hour, you get me for an hour. I'm yours. Whatever you want—I do it. You pay me for twenty-three hours, I do it for twenty-three—but that one hour a day is still mine and I'll sleep with Bonaparte himself, if he pays."

She paused for a moment, lost in her anger. "I don't say to you it's OK to kill Frenchmen, but please, Aleksei, don't kill this particular Frenchman or that particular Frenchman, or kill the French, but leave the Turks alone. It's a job. If you choose to do the job then you don't get to pick out the bits you like most." She sat down and became a little calmer. "You'd better go now; I've got clients to see."

"Can I see you tomorrow?"

"It's my job; I can't stop you," she said curtly. Then she smiled at the irony. "Weren't you listening just now?"

I left the building elated. I'd made her angry. In every conversation we'd ever had, she had kept her composure—what she said could be genuine, or it could be merely what I wanted to hear. We'd both known it, and that was part of the fun. But now, somehow, I'd got to her. She'd revealed some small, real part of herself, and what a powerful, eloquent self she had revealed.

Having said that, there was still one small matter to attend to.

"Please don't sleep with Dominique," I asked that evening when Maks and I were walking alone. "There are plenty of other girls there to choose from."

Maks seemed briefly surprised, but didn't take issue with me. "OK." He thought for a moment, feeling that more needed to be said. "She's very nice, but then I'm sure they all are."

We walked a little further until Maks filled the silence with, "We talk about you, you know."

"We?"

"Dominique and I," he replied.

He told me, I think, to be kind—to flatter me—but all it did was bring to my mind the most bizarre and unpleasant images, along with, by some unfathomable route, recollections of the story of Oedipus. "Jesus, Maks, no! Just leave it. Just don't talk about it. You've said you won't see her. That's fine. There are some things that just don't need discussing."

I marched off and went back to my room, sat down, and wrote a letter to Marfa. Almost everything I wrote was untrue, so I tore it up.

The next day, things seemed back to normal between me and Domnikiia; better than normal even. I presumed the whole thing was forgotten.

"Maks came in today, but he went with Margarita."

"OK," I replied cautiously, wondering where the conversation was going.

"He's a good friend to you. He respects you."

"You're happy with that?"

"That your friend does you a favour when you ask him? Why shouldn't I be?"

"So does that mean you're not my friend?"

"Do you want me to be?" she asked, looking directly at me. I thought for a moment about my answer, but before I could speak, she continued. "It's either/or."

I gave an exaggerated frown, and then smiled. "Fair enough." Then I changed the subject. "Maks said there were more stories of the plague along the Don."

"There are. Only it's not a plague and it's not just on the Don."

"How do you know it's not a plague?" I asked.

"The way they die. It's all rumour. Some people are saying their throats are cut, others that they've been strangled, others that they've been attacked by animals. One story is that the French have sent saboteurs to attack us from the south."

It sounded unlikely, but then it also sounded somewhat like what Vadim, Dmitry, Maks and I had been commissioned to do against the French. "How do you know all this?"

TWELVE

"Lots of traders come to Moscow from Tula, leaving their wives safely at home. Or not so safely, now there've been deaths in Tula itself."

"In Tula?"

"Yes. I looked at the places on a map. They follow the river Don. Rostov, Pavlovsk, Voronezh." She turned to me and smiled. "I looked at Petersburg, too. Is it nice there?"

"Not as nice as here," I said, somewhat dismissively, but I was too concerned by what she was saying. "And you say it's reached Tula?"

"Today someone mentioned Serpukhov; I haven't looked that up yet."

"Serpukhov?" I was shocked. "That's only about eighty versts away."

"Really? Are you worried?"

I tried to be reassuring. "No, not really. They're just rumours. You know what these peasants are like. Someone catches cold and it's a new outbreak of plague."

But as I left her, I still felt in need of some convincing myself. Any concerns were, however, soon pushed to the back of my mind. That evening, the Oprichniki arrived.

CHAPTER III

THERE WERE THIRTEEN OF THEM IN ALL. I HAD BEEN IN MY room, writing to Marfa, when I heard a knock at the door. It was Maks.

"They're here."

In the dim light of Maks' oil lamp, I saw a tall figure that I took to be their leader greeting Dmitry with the warm hug of an old friend—a hug which Dmitry did not quite return. He was an impressive man. His age could have been anywhere between fifty and seventy. A domed forehead was underlined by thick, bushy eyebrows which topped a thin, aristocratic nose. Arched nostrils were almost hidden by a long moustache of dark iron grey, which contributed to a general air of unkemptness. The moustache, like his hair, was unevenly trimmed, due perhaps to the lack of a mirror on his long journey. The general appearance of nobility fallen on hard times reminded me of the fleeing French aristocrats who had begun to arrive in Petersburg during my youth.

Dmitry introduced him to each of us in turn. In his reaction to us, he seemed to both mimic and amplify Dmitry's own attitudes. To Vadim, he showed respect and, without any explicit signals such as a salute or a click of the heels, greeted him as one old campaigner greets another. Of Maks, he was almost dismissive.

As he came to me, he took my hand in a firm grip and patted me on the back. I noticed his broad, squat fingers and coarse, dirty nails, which again contrasted with his refined demeanour. "Aleksei Ivanovich, I'm very happy to meet you at last," he said with a wide smile. As was to be expected, we all spoke in French. None of us understood the language of his country and there was no reason to suppose that he or any of them would know Russian—in that respect they had something in common with many of the Russian nobility. "Dmitry Fetyukovich spoke frequently of you as we fought side by side against the Turk," he continued. "His friend is my friend."

TWELVE

Our side of the introductions was complete, and the stranger fell silent. Vadim was the first to speak. "Forgive me," he said, "but we still haven't heard your name."

"My name?" he replied, as if surprised at even the suggestion that he might have a name. I glanced over to Dmitry, who surely must have known the visitor's name, but he was staring at the ground as though embarrassed.

"My name is Zmyeevich," announced the stranger with a sudden resolution. It was not a genuine Russian name, although somewhere at the back of my mind it struck a distant resonance with memories from my childhood. Literally, the meaning was simple—"son of the serpent." I could only guess that it was a direct translation of his name from his own tongue.

He followed us to the private room in the inn that we always used for our meetings. As they trooped in behind him, I got my first real glimpse of his twelve companions. While he had the manner of an officer who had seen better days, they seemed to me as men who had never risen above the gutter. All were scruffy and dressed without style, or at best with the style of peasants. They shuffled, round-shouldered, into the room, failing to make eye contact with any of us. They might be mistaken for a gang of convicts except that their failure to look up at us came not from respect or even fear, but simply from an utter lack of regard for our existence. Though not tall, each was broad and stockily built. I would have feared them in a contest that depended solely on brawn, but not in one of wits. They were not the type that I would expect to see in the officers' mess.

Only the last of the twelve showed any interest at all in his surroundings. He was taller than the others, though not as tall as their leader, and was marked out by his long, blond hair. The others all had their hair cut short, no doubt to reduce the numbers of lice which I felt sure would otherwise have infested them. As this last man entered, his eyes rapidly glanced around the room, taking in his surroundings and briefly scanning the faces of the four Russian officers whom he was meeting for the first time. Then his eyes dropped and he sat down, taking on the same cowed posture that his comrades had borne all along.

Maks muttered a single word in my ear: "Oprichniki." Despite their lack of character, there was still a feeling of menace about them which, Maks could see as well as I, justified Dmitry's original description.

Zmyeevich had remained standing and now began to speak in very precise, but very formal and strangely accented French. His voice had a darkness to it and seemed to emit not from his throat but from deep in his torso. Somewhere inside him it was as if giant millstones were turning against one another, or as though the lid were being slowly dragged aside to open a stone sarcophagus.

"Greetings once again, old friends and new. Greetings to you, Vadim Fyodorovich"—he turned and bowed briefly to each of us as he spoke—"to you, Maksim Sergeivich, to you, Aleksei Ivanovich and, of course, to you, our dearest of friends, Dmitry Fetyukovich.

"Dmitry Fetyukovich and I, and some of our friends here," he said, waving a graceless hand towards the twelve who were sitting around him, "first fought together some years ago against the old enemy from the east. The Turk has been an enemy of your beloved Russia for longer than any of you could remember and the first, famous battles of my own now long-distant youth were to defend my land from those same heathen invaders. But now the threat to all of us comes from where we might once have least expected it; from the west.

"While the unchristian Turk," he continued, seeming not to notice the ripple of movement that his mention of the word "unchristian" sent through the evidently pious twelve, "cannot be blamed for his heresy, having learned it from his father and his father before him, Bonaparte has led his country to an abandonment of the Christ, Whom that nation had long known and loved." I felt that Maks was about to comment on the accuracy of this and I pressed my hand on his arm to keep him silent. This was not a debating society and his point of information would not be considered in order. Even so, it surprised me as much as Maks that Zmyeevich should try to turn this into a religious conflict. It seemed to me almost that he was protesting too much.

"So now we must face the common enemy," Zmyeevich continued. "You Russians have fought more bravely than any in Europe against Bonaparte and, believe me, I have no doubt, no doubt"—he closed his eyes and gave a juddering shake of the head; he was beginning to enjoy himself in the role of public speaker—"that you will continue to do so. I bring you but twelve men. Good men—strong men, and yet I feel ashamed, ashamed that they are so few."

The rhetoric was becoming almost unbearably overblown. I glanced round at my friends. Dmitry was slouched in his chair trying to show with great effort the indifference of a man who has heard it all before. Maks was leaning forward listening intently. Had I known him less well, I might have believed he was a devotee of the figure who addressed us, but in reality I knew that he was drinking in every word only so that he might analyse it, dissect it and demolish it when the time arose. To my surprise it was Vadim who, having caught my eye, was biting his finger, trying to hold in the laughter. Vadim, who had spouted so many similar, lame platitudes in his time, who had listened in rapture to speeches by so many Russian generals, was the one who could see so quickly the shallowness of this vain Wallachian.

"They are diffident men," Zmyeevich proceeded, with a hint of emotion in his voice. "Men of virtue, men of valour, men of strength—yes, but also men of honour. They may commit great acts of . . . of (may I say it?) heroism, but still for reasons that I cannot explain, they would rather their true names remained unknown. These are the names by which you will know them:

"Pyetr. Andrei. Ioann."

As each pseudonym was called out, the man in question gave a brief nod, but still they maintained the same lack of interest; the same appearance of the belief that this whole meeting was an unnecessary distraction from some greater cause upon which they were embarking.

"Filipp. Varfolomei. Matfei."

The names he had chosen were Russian and the accent with which he spoke our own language was even less convincing than that with which he spoke French. Nevertheless, even after three names I had realized that the chosen aliases were simply the names of the twelve apostles. After six names, I think even the least religious of us had worked it out. Again, the laboured Christianity seemed intended more to mock than to glorify.

"Simon. Iakov Zevedayinich. Iakov Alfeyinich."

Vadim began to cough, which I guessed was to stifle his laughter.

"Foma. Faddei. Iuda."

When the name Foma was read out, I noted a glance between the individual so named and some of his comrades. I could imagine the scene when these names had been allocated; Pyetr, Simon, Matfei and most of the others happy with their names, but Foma feeling he had drawn the short straw, not wanting to be the Foma—the "Doubting Thomas"—of the group. I might have thought that there would also be disagreement about who got the name "Iuda," but amongst these men I could see it would be an honour, not a disgrace, to be given the name of the betrayer.

Iuda was the tall, blond-haired figure I had noted earlier.

"I am only sorry," their leader went on, "that I myself am too old and too tired to join these twelve brave men in the fight. You may doubt," and his eyes fell upon Maks, who, I'm sure, did doubt what he was going to say, whatever it might be, "that so few can do very much. But believe me, they have what is required. They have the desire—the lust to succeed."

One of the Oprichniki, Matfei, I think it was—although I was still not used to their names—made a comment in their own indecipherable language. I suspect it hinged on the word "lust." Eleven of the twelve laughed heartily, as soldiers would at some dirty joke, some not getting it, others not thinking it funny, but all laughing because that is what they ought to do. Only Iuda was different. He didn't laugh, but his face betrayed a knowing smile, just as a childless adult smiles at a child's joke, amused by its naivety, but not delighting in its innocence. He glanced at Zmyeevich and in observing their momentary connection I felt suddenly uneasy. I felt sure that whatever reasons the eleven other Wallachians had for being in Russia, these two had some greater purpose. Any mirth I might have been sharing with Vadim evaporated.

Zmyeevich continued almost instantly. "And so now I must leave you." He paused, expecting, I think, some protest from us at his departure. None came. "I have a long journey back to my homeland and you, my friends, have much work to do."

Vadim stood, remembering his duties as host. "Won't you at least stay here tonight? You can set off in the morning."

The man laughed a hearty, artificial laugh. "My dear friend, you take me too literally. I of course don't intend to travel by night in these dangerous times, but I have already arranged accommodation elsewhere in the city. I shall depart at first light, but for us, this is farewell."

The four of us stepped out into the hallway with him to say goodbye. I was glad to be out of that room for a moment, away from the strange, oppressive presence of the twelve Oprichniki. As I closed the door, they immediately began talking to each other in low, conspiratorial voices and in their own language. Even away from them, being in Zmyeevich's presence in the dark corridor was an experience I did not want to endure for very long.

He took us each in turn by the hand and kissed us on both cheeks. As his face came close to mine, a sudden miasma surrounded me, which I realized was the stench of his breath. I recalled years ago standing over a mass grave where the bodies of brave soldiers had been lying for many days. The same odour of decay rose from the depths of his stomach. I felt the same urge to run as I had then, accompanied by an even deeper sense of dread which I could not place; but I managed not to recoil.

As he moved finally to Dmitry and shook his hand, I noticed for the first time an ornate ring on his middle finger. It was the figure of a dragon, with a body of gold, emerald eyes and red, forked tongue. Its tail coiled around his finger. I suddenly doubted whether I had understood his name correctly. He could just as easily be "son of the dragon" as "son of the serpent," perhaps even "son of the viper." The ring certainly looked to me most like a dragon. I could not even be sure there was any distinction between the words in his native language.

As he stood at the doorway, Zmyeevich exchanged a few final comments with Vadim. "Now that I am gone, I leave Pyetr in charge in my place," he said in a soft, clear voice.

Maks whispered in my ear with a snigger. "Peter as his successor? He thinks he's Jesus Christ." I was in no mood now to share his humour.

The man would not have understood the Russian, even if he had heard it clearly, but he gave Maks the disappointed look of an elderly guest who has been unnecessarily and unworthily insulted. Maks became suddenly still.

"And do not be too concerned about the names," Zmyeevich continued, looking at each of us in turn with a slight smile upon his lips, as if acknowledging some ungiven praise for the humour of his choice of soubriquets. "Read nothing into the name 'Iuda.' He is not the betrayer." His eyes came to rest on Maks as he spoke the final word.

With that he left, and an iciness seemed to descend on the building. I sensed in Maks the same feeling of cold, visceral fear that I was experiencing in myself. Vadim paused for a moment and then let out his suppressed laughter. Though the same mirth had been building up in me at first, it had been replaced by something much darker. But to join in with Vadim's laughter, however little it fitted my true mood, was a relief. Dmitry smiled at our immaturity, but didn't laugh, presumably familiar with his friend's extravagant style. Only Maks remained unmoved, looking afraid and thoughtful.

"I'm sorry, Dmitry," said Vadim. "I know he's your friend and I'm sure he's a very brave man, but he does have a certain air of . . ." He searched for a polite word.

"Pomposity?" suggested Dmitry, neutrally.

Vadim smiled broadly and nodded. "And those bizarre patronymics. Zevedayinich? Alfeyinich?"

"I think he considers it his duty as a guest to make some effort with our language," explained Dmitry. "You should congratulate him for trying, even if he does get things a little wrong." Zmyeevich could not really be blamed for his inability to correctly name the apostles in Russian. I had never in my life seen a complete Russian translation of the Bible, and I doubt whether such a thing existed.

"And his own name," I added with a laugh.

"No, that's good Russian," corrected Vadim. "Zmyeevich is a character from one of the old ballads; Tugarin Zmyeevich."

That was why the name had seemed familiar to me, though I still couldn't remember the details. "And was he the hero or the villain?" I asked. Vadim shrugged his shoulders.

"I don't think that's where the name came from, anyway," explained Dmitry with a condescending calm.

TWELVE

"Are they the same men you fought with before?" asked Maks, who had recovered his power of speech, although he was still unable to share the mood of good humour.

"Four of them, I think," replied Dmitry. "Pyetr, Ioann, Varfolomei and Andrei, although they didn't go by those names before. And Foma looks familiar but . . ." Dmitry looked suddenly pale, almost as if he was about to be sick, but he quickly recovered himself. "No, he wasn't one of them. To be honest it's hard to remember. None of them made much impression on me. They're not exactly keen on conversation."

"We'd better go back in," said Vadim, who had calmed down by now.

Inside the room, the atmosphere had cheered a little. All twelve of the Oprichniki were again laughing, again in that way that groups of men do, in order to be seen laughing by the others. Our entry, if it was even observed by them, didn't immediately stop them.

We sat down again and Vadim addressed Pyetr in slow, clear French.

"We plan to head west. We will go around the French and attack their supply lines."

"We prefer to work alone." Pyetr's reply was curt, but his French was perfectly formed and quite well accented.

"You can work alone," said Vadim, speaking more fluently now he knew that they, or at least Pyetr, understood him clearly, "but you're not familiar with the land. You'll need our help with that at least."

"Agreed," nodded Pyetr. "We work at night. That way the enemy is asleep and will not be ready for us."

"That's reasonable. We can travel by day and attack during darkness."

"No." Pyetr made the explanation of his tactics sound like a list of demands. "The body must adjust to the demands of the work. We sleep by day and kill at night. If that is not comfortable for you, then we shall manage without you."

Vadim glanced around the four of us, but found no objections. "Very well," he agreed. He handed over some papers. "Here are maps of the area to the west of Moscow. Bonaparte is presently nearing the town of Viasma." He opened a map and pointed out the location. "I've also marked out possible places where we can meet if we are separated. We'll set out tomorrow evening."

Pyetr and the others showed little interest in the maps. "How many men does Bonaparte have?"

Vadim looked to me for an answer. I consulted my notes. "We estimate 130,000."

A sense of excitement ran through the Oprichniki as they heard this number, of which I could make little sense. Numbers don't matter much when one is operating by stealth. Whether they were outnumbered a thousand to twelve or a hundred thousand to twelve, they were still in a hopeless minority. A few comments passed between them and some faces broke into smiles that seemed almost lascivious.

"And how many Russians?" asked one of the others—Foma, I think—in a mocking tone.

Vadim raised a hand to stop me revealing this information, although I had no intention of doing so. Pyetr spat a single angry word at Foma, and then turned back to us. "We do not, of course, need to know that. It is just idle curiosity."

"Good," said Vadim.

Our discussions went on long into the night. We tried to give our best appraisal of the French plans and disposition. None of them asked any more about our own forces. It was agreed that they would divide into four groups. Vadim would accompany Faddei, Filipp and Iakov Zevedayinich. Dmitry would take Pyetr, Varfolomei and Ioann. Maks had Andrei, Simon and Iakov Alfeyinich and I was left with Foma, Iuda and Matfei.

It was towards dawn that they finally departed. Like their leader before them, they explained that they had arranged their own accommodation, but gave no more detail. We agreed to meet again that evening, 16 August, at nine o'clock, to begin our journey west.

I harboured no intention of following Pyetr's advice of getting used to sleeping during the day, but our late discussions had forced it upon me. It was past ten o'clock when I arose. I finished the letter to Marfa that I had been writing the previous evening. There was little I could put in it of the details of my work, or indeed of the details of my leisure time, so it turned out to be an insubstantial document. I mentioned that I was leaving Moscow and didn't know when I would return, but made no reference to the new comrades that I had met only the previous night.

I once again visited Domnikiia. My mind was on the journey that lay ahead of me and on the hollowness of my letter to Marfa, and so I said little. As with Marfa, it was wise not to discuss my work in any detail.

"I'm leaving Moscow this evening," I told her.

"Why?" She asked as if the news was not unexpected.

"The war. You remember?" I didn't need to be sarcastic.

She came over and lay beside me, stroking my hair and staring into my eyes. "Will you be coming back?"

"Of course," I replied, knowing full well that it was a question that no soldier can answer with complete certainty.

"When?"

"Before Bonaparte gets here." It was meant to be a joke, but my own belief in the possibility of Bonaparte's arrival in Moscow spoiled the delivery.

That afternoon Domnikiia was strangely distracted, strangely removed from her work, as if she had forgotten all those tricks and affectations that made her so good at her job; so able to convince that she didn't see it as a job. She was like other prostitutes I had been with; simply a compliant piece of female flesh. I couldn't tell whether she had forgotten her show because there was no prospect of repeat business with a man who was about to die, or whether the prospect of my death really had disturbed her.

As I was dressing she picked up the icon that Marfa had sent me and looked deep into the Saviour's eyes. "You only started wearing this the other day. Who gave it to you?"

It seemed somehow wrong to tell her about my wife, not because it might offend Domnikiia, who must have been used to such things, but it seemed somehow offensive to Marfa herself to mention her within that room.

"I've had it for ages. It just seemed appropriate to start wearing it, now that the danger is so near."

"Oh," she said thoughtfully, then, as if on a different subject, "Maks said . . ." She looked up at me. It looked like Maks had mentioned Marfa as the sender of the icon. If that had been what Domnikiia was about to say, she changed her mind. "Maks said you weren't superstitious."

"Maks was speaking for himself."

She put the chain over my head and hung the icon around my neck once again. "Promise me you won't ever take it off."

"Why?" I asked.

"It will protect you. Promise me!"

"I promise." It was easy enough to say. Wearing it did me no harm, though I doubted that whatever manner of god was out there would change his attitude towards me merely because of a small piece of metal hanging around my neck. But it was comforting to feel the icon hanging against my chest for a quite different reason. It acted as a reminder; a reminder of my superstitious wife who had sent it to me and of my superstitious lover who insisted that I keep it on.

As I left the brothel, a group of junior officers, about eight of them, none yet twenty years old, was loitering outside. They clearly knew what kind of establishment it was and were searching for the courage to go in. Like many young men, and perhaps particularly young soldiers, they seemed to be considering the issue in terms of their relationship with one another, rather than the more stimulating relations that they might be having with the young ladies inside. I had been about their age on my first visit to a brothel, but the difference was that I had gone alone. I had enjoyed the experience very much, but even then I had not thought it the sort of thing to discuss with my friends.

But for these boys it was about how they would be viewed by one another; a rite of passage to manhood in which it mattered what was seen to be done rather than what was actually done or how much pleasure they got from doing it. Those of them who seemed most keen still held back to keep with the crowd. Those who were reluctant went along anyway rather than be left behind. They spoke of what they were going to do in there and laughed about it, giving the distinct impression that the talking about it both before and afterwards—not even the recollection, but the talking—was where the real enjoyment lay.

It was reminiscent of something I had encountered very recently, but could not place. Then it struck me that this was exactly the same sense of hungry anticipation that I'd noted in the Oprichniki the previous night; the same way that they were all eager to go to war, but eager also to be seen by their comrades as wanting to go to war. Every soldier fights, when it comes down to it, for his brothers-in-arms—for his friends—but some, like these, do it to be accepted by their comrades, to be proved as men in the eyes of other men.

Of course the boys on their first visit to a brothel would, most likely, grow out of it. For the Oprichniki, it was too late.

Vadim, Dmitry, Maks and I met up privately a little before our appointment with the Oprichniki. We had nothing secret to discuss, but I think we all shared the same sense of foreboding and, since we were unlikely to meet again for several days, it gave us all a chance to say our goodbyes. It was typical of both me and Vadim to make something of these occasions, but even Dmitry, with his façade of jaded unconcern, and Maksim, with his of intellectual detachment, did not hold back in embracing the rest of us.

We mounted our horses and set off to the square where we had arranged to meet them. As the four of us rode side by side, the thought of another four horsemen flashed into my mind. It was laughable to decide which of us was War, Famine or Pestilence, but I felt a shiver when I noticed the pallor of Maks' horse.

As we headed through the darkness towards the western boundary of the city to our rendezvous at the Dorogomilovsky Gate, the wooden buildings that lined the streets loomed and crowded around me in a way that I had never before perceived. The twelve men with whom we were about to meet were not so mysterious as to make me afraid, but for some reason I felt that the city I so loved was itself trying to warn me of what was to come. Approaching the gate, I strove to make out from the shadows the figures of the Oprichniki, and I felt sure that I could clearly see twelve dark forms on horseback, waiting in a semicircle for our arrival. With each step closer, I tried to see if I could recognize individuals from the group, but suddenly, as we were almost upon them, I realized that it was an illusion of the shadows. There was no one there.

"Excellent!" murmured Vadim sarcastically, turning to Dmitry for a reason for the Oprichniki's absence. There was nothing that Dmitry could say, but as he took a breath to offer some form of explanation, all our heads turned sharply to the sound of a horse's hooves, back in the direction from which we had come.

Out of the gloom, a lone horseman approached. At first, we didn't identify him as an Oprichnik, but as he grew closer it became clear that his height and his general demeanour had fooled us. It was Iuda who had come to meet us.

"There has been a change of plan," he announced. "We travel faster alone, and so we're going to make our own way out to the front. There's an inn just outside Gzatsk that you marked on the map as a meeting place. We'll see you there in three days." There was no discussion to be had. After Iuda had informed us of the new arrangements, he rode off without another word.

Vadim was, I could tell, silently furious, but there was nothing to be said that could change matters, so he remained practical. "*They* may like to travel by night, but that doesn't mean we have to. We'll stay here in Moscow tonight and set off at first light. Two and a half days is plenty time enough for us to get to Gzatsk."

"I looked up Tugarin Zmyeevich, by the way," Maks announced as we cantered along the road to Gzatsk.

"And?" I asked.

"Turns out he was the villain," Maks continued.

"And so I presume he got his comeuppance," said Vadim.

"Oh, yes," replied Maks. He turned to me. "At the hands of an Alyosha; Alyosha Popovich. Shot him dead with an arrow." I was called Alyosha even less frequently than Lyosha, but I wasn't going to split hairs.

"So I guess our Zmyeevich is some kind of relative," said Vadim, concealing a smirk.

TWELVE

"I don't think so," responded Dmitry with a note of scorn. "It's pure coincidence."

"It's quite a coincidence that he should have a Russian name at all," said Maks, "given that he's not Russian." Dmitry did not rise to the bait, though it was clear to us all the leader was in truth no more named Zmyeevich than his followers were named after the apostles.

"I just hope *our* Lyosha isn't going to kill him. That's no way to treat an ally," laughed Vadim.

"Mind you," continued Maks, "Tugarin Zmyeevich was carried around on a golden bench by twelve knights, so the story goes. Twelve of them, Dmitry."

It would have been better if it had been Vadim who was Zmyeevich's friend. Dmitry was no fun to tease. He just sat tight-lipped astride his horse as we rode on.

"I expect the Oprichniki just left the bench outside the other night," I said. "It would have been tricky to get it up the stairs." Maks grinned and Vadim snorted a laugh.

"It's just coincidence!" snapped Dmitry, and spurred his horse on so that he could continue his journey away from the rest of us. I don't think the others really noticed, but for me it was just one more reason to be concerned about him—one more reason that led back to his "friends," the Oprichniki.

Two and a half days proved not only time enough for us to get to Gzatsk, but almost enough for Bonaparte to get there too. As we reached the inn, soon after nine o'clock on the evening of the nineteenth, we had already made our way through a throng of people escaping the town. The rumours were that the French would be in occupation by the following day.

This time, the Oprichniki kept their appointment. They seemed in no mood to exchange pleasantries and keen only to get on with the job at hand. We split into the groups we had determined back in Moscow. I said a far more cursory goodbye to Vadim, Dmitry and Maks than previously. I led my team of Iuda, Foma and Matfei out of the town to the south, before turning westwards towards the right flank of the advancing French.

The journey proceeded mostly in silence. Those attempts that I made at conversation with Foma and Matfei were not even rebuffed, simply ignored. Iuda was marginally more talkative, but even then only on matters directly related to our mission. It was, I suppose, wise of them. We were travelling through darkness in a direction that we knew would take us to the enemy's lines, but we had little idea of precisely where those lines were situated. It was best that we remained silent and did not reveal ourselves through unnecessary chatter. We rode on for several hours, looking and listening for any sign of Bonaparte's armies.

Some time after midnight, the crescent moon rose in the sky behind us. The light would be of little extra help to us, and might be of great assistance in revealing our presence to the enemy. Luckily, it wasn't long—much sooner, indeed, than I had expected—before we saw the first glimpse of the French campfires. The rumours of how far they had advanced were proving to be true. We dismounted and I watched the camp, about half a verst away, through my spyglass.

"How many do you see?" asked Iuda.

"There's only a dozen or so still awake, but there are several tents," I replied. "There could be over a hundred men there in total."

"Too many, I think," said Iuda thoughtfully, although to me it seemed he was stating the obvious, until he went on with, "at least for the first attack of our campaign. Probably better if we just start out by picking off a few stragglers."

I thought that this was somewhat pointless. While on the one hand, an attack on a camp of a hundred or so was impossible, attacking isolated soldiers in ones and twos would have no impact whatsoever. There were tactical problems too.

"Finding stragglers may not be easy," I told him, "They'll all stay close to their—"

I was interrupted by the abrupt French command of "Stand up!" Looking over my shoulder I saw first a bayonet, then the rifle to which it was attached and, finally, the French infantryman holding the rifle. In all, there were six of them surrounding the four of us. "Lay down your swords and guns!" continued the officer in charge.

TWELVE

The odds against us weren't insurmountable, but our survival (and, more pertinently, *my* survival) didn't seem probable if we resisted. "Do as he says," I said calmly to the three Oprichniki under my command.

I think that may well have been the first time I attempted to give them a direct order. As orders go, it wasn't particularly successful. As I began to unbuckle my scabbard, Matfei threw himself towards the nearest Frenchman. Two rifles fired at him. Whether they both missed completely or caused some minor wound, I could not see, but he did not flinch and soon had his man on the ground.

Taking our cue from Matfei, Iuda, Foma and I also attacked. The infantryman who was covering me was distracted and it was no problem to knock his bayonet to one side and get in close enough for my sword to be of use in a quick kill. I turned to the next man. He had already fired his musket and had no bayonet fixed, so should have been easy meat.

As I turned, the butt of his gun came into heavy contact with my temple. I slumped to the ground. My last vision before unconsciousness was of the French infantryman again lifting his rifle to deliver a final, fatal blow to my skull and behind him Iuda, his arm raised ready to attack and his mouth wide open in a silent scream.

CHAPTER IV

WHEN I CAME TO, IT WAS DAYLIGHT. I WAS ALONE. I TRIED to recall what had happened, but all that came to me were images of utter savagery. I had seen only seconds of the fight before I was knocked out, although perhaps I may still have been half conscious as I lay on the ground. The memories that flooded into my mind were not of any ordinary battle, but of something which felt like (and "felt" is the right word, for I could not recall actually seeing anything) a pack of wolves ripping apart its prey rather than soldiers defeating soldiers. Also blood—I remembered much blood.

I sat up, and feeling an intense pain in my head, lay down again. I put my hand to my temple where I had been hit. It was bruised, but not bleeding and not excessively tender to touch. It was the pain inside my skull that was the real problem. I sat up again, more gently this time, and looked around.

I had been right about the blood. The grass around where we had fought was covered with it. Dmitry had said the Oprichniki were ruthless fighters. Looking at myself, I saw bloodstains on the arm of my coat. I checked my body, but found no wounds to suggest that the blood was mine. There were no bodies lying around—neither of the French nor of the Oprichniki. The immediate question was who had won the battle? If the French had won, then surely I would be dead or at least a prisoner. But if the Oprichniki had won, why would they just leave me here? On the other hand, the Oprichniki hadn't been at all keen in having us along in the first place, so perhaps this encounter had played into their hands. I was alone, and by now, they might be versts away.

I stood up, trying to ignore my headache. The bloodstains and the impressions in the grass gave some indication that the bodies had been dragged away. I followed as far as I could, into a nearby copse, but the bloodstains soon petered out and the drag marks became impossible to distinguish on the rough ground. I returned to where the fight had taken place.

TWELVE

My sword and my spyglass were lying beside a tree trunk. It could not have been where I dropped them, and I could only conclude that someone had placed them there deliberately. Again, this was more likely the behaviour of an Oprichnik than a Frenchman.

I looked towards the camp on which we had been spying the previous night. The remains of the fire still smouldered, but all signs of the French themselves were gone. By now they were probably in Gzatsk.

For me there was only one option; to regroup. With that end in mind, I realized a further problem: my horse had gone. By now, I had pretty much come to the conclusion that it was the Oprichniki who had won the previous night's conflict, so it must have been they who had taken my horse—left my sword, but taken my horse. Sadly, this all seemed to fit. With a sword I could defend myself, but without a horse there was little chance that I could catch up and interfere with them. It was still difficult, however, to fathom why it was they wanted rid of me. Certainly from what I had seen they were immensely capable in close-quarter combat, but I was hardly so useless as to be a hindrance to them. There was something about them that they wanted to keep from us. Some secret way of fighting that was so effective that they had to keep it to themselves. And, as far as I could guess, Dmitry knew what it was.

Even so, there was little to be gained by standing there worrying about it. I had a long journey back east ahead of me, alone and on foot.

The first issue I had to deal with was that our next appointed meeting place (decided on the presumption that the French would still be advancing, which they were) was in Goryachkino, to the north of the main Smolensk to Moscow road—the very road along which Bonaparte and his army were now advancing and which I was currently south of. I had two options. Either I could head east as rapidly as possible and then cut across the road ahead of the French or I could go across the road west of Gzatsk, behind the French, hoping to evade their rear guard, and set off east from there.

Taking a route that would lead me well behind French lines didn't seem the best option for rejoining my compatriots, so I went for the more direct route, heading east, to the south of the Moscow road. This proved to be the right choice. Bonaparte rested his army in Gzatsk for three days and so I was in fact overcautious, keeping well away from the road which was, as yet, not in French hands, and thus delaying my progress.

The first day of my journey was uneventful. Sleeping rough was not too uncomfortable in the still-warm weather of late August. I arose early and carried on eastwards once again, making as good ground as could be expected over the rough, wooded terrain and covering about 25 versts each day.

It was just after sunset on the second day, when I heard a sound way over to my right, that I first began to suspect I was being followed. A single incongruous noise in the forest is not enough to announce the presence of a pursuer—there are natural sounds all around—but I had already heard other noises from that direction. How long ago I had heard the first of them I could not recall, but the fact that they came consistently from the same direction relative to me, even though I was on the move, told me that whoever or whatever was out there was deliberately keeping pace with me. Though the sun had already set, it still cast enough light to see by. The moon had not yet risen, and even when it did, it would be a new moon. Throughout the night there would be total darkness. I made camp and used the remaining twilight to gather some wood for a fire, not for warmth, but to give some light—and with it, some hope—in case my pursuer decided to strike.

I sat beside the fire, gazing into the flames and listening intently to the forest around me. The Russian woodlands are full of noise, although those of the night are very different from those of the day. The continuous background of birdsong, which becomes so familiar during the day that it is forgotten, had begun to quieten, with only owls remaining awake. Nocturnal animals began to move around, but they were mostly small creatures. The sound of a human skirting around my campsite, just beyond the light of the fire, watching, waiting, scheming, was unmistakable against these familiar background noises of the night.

He (I presumed it was a he, although my hearing is not quite up to making such distinctions) settled down some way ahead of me, directly on the path that I would be taking the following morning, and did not move for around half an hour. Tactically, now was the time to act, but I needed no tactics to know it. Human instinct—human fear—told me that I did not want to be found curled up on the ground, exposed and asleep and at the mercy of whoever was out there. If I was to die, I would die while conscious.

I headed out towards roughly where I believed him to be and relieved myself against a nearby tree. I stood there longer than I needed to, taking the time to let my eyes adjust to the darkness away from the fire, letting the cool air prime my body for action. Walking back, I caught a glimpse of him directly in my path, pressed into a hollow in the ground, trying not to be seen. I stepped over the figure as if I hadn't noticed him, but immediately I had passed him, I turned and gave him a heavy kick in the side of his stomach.

He groaned and rolled quickly away, but not so quickly that I didn't have time to place another boot in his ribs. By the time he had got to his feet, my sabre was drawn. In the vague light of the distant fire, there was still little to see of him, but I caught the glint of a knife in his hand. My sword seemed no deterrent to him and he threw himself at me, knocking me to the ground and pinning down my sword arm with his left hand as he raised his knife to strike. Only when he was this close did I recognize him as the Oprichnik, Iuda. His eyes showed no recognition of me, only the intensity of a man intent on another's death.

My knee connected with his groin and I managed to throw him off.

"Iuda!" I shouted at him, rising to my feet, but he still seemed not to recognize me and lunged once again with the knife. I smashed the flat of my sword against his wrist and the knife flew into the darkness. My boot in his chest forced him to the ground and I held the point of my sabre to his throat.

"Iuda! It's me. Aleksei Ivanovich." The frenzy gradually began to fade from his eyes, to be replaced by recognition. At the same time I felt a chill of fear. The last time I had seen Iuda, he had not been alone. On his own I may have beaten him, but where were Matfei and Foma? In the dark woodland, they could have been feet away and I would not have known until it was too late.

"Get over to the fire!" I indicated the way with the point of my sword. He sat down beside it and rubbed his injured wrist.

"I'm sorry, Aleksei. When you attacked me, instinct just took over."

Such an instinct to kill seemed to me to be inhumanly strong, but I let it pass. "Why were you following me?"

"I only caught sight of you just before you made camp. There are French soldiers around here. Your fire might have caught their attention. I thought I'd better keep an eye on you."

"Keep an eye on me?" I laughed. "And then try to kill me."

"It was you that attacked me." He sounded genuinely offended. "If we wanted to kill you, don't you think we would have done it while you lay there unconscious back at Gzatsk?"

It was a fair point, but his "we" had reminded me of another issue. I looked as deep as I could into the darkness around us, but saw nothing. "Where are Matfei and Foma?"

"I left them this morning," he said. As he did so, he too flicked his eyes from side to side about the woodland, as though expecting to see his friends. "They're making a few attacks on the French." He looked straight back at me, his expression giving the slightest hint that he was merely teasing me. "We're supposed to meet up again tonight."

"Where?"

"Further on." He nodded his head to the east.

I knew I wouldn't discover anything if I tackled him directly. "The countryside here must be very different from what you're used to," I said.

He considered for a moment, as if he'd never thought of the question before. "In some ways. We come from the mountains, but down in the lowlands, things aren't so different."

"You must have seen a lot of our country on your journey here." He seemed talkative, certainly by the standards of the other Oprichniki, so I hoped a few general questions might elicit a little more of their background.

"We came by boat, so there wasn't much to see," he said. In talking of his homeland, I thought I had perceived some hint of affection in his voice, but now he was once again terse and uninterested.

"I'm from Petersburg, so I know the sea pretty well." This was something of an overstatement. I'd swum in it, but I'd never sailed.

"You have family there?"

TWELVE

"Yes." I smiled, thinking of young Dmitry, and perhaps even a little of Marfa. The image of her retroussé nose and dark eyes looking up into mine filled my mind. I might have indulged myself in talking about her, but little as I had wanted to do so with Domnikiia I desired to even less with Iuda. I stuck to my line of questioning. "But you would have come from the south, of course. Where did you sail from? Constanta?"

"Varna. We sailed over the Black Sea to Rostov."

I felt suddenly cold. Rostov was near the mouth of the Don. Domnikiia's stories of death travelling upriver towards Moscow fitted neatly with the journey of the Oprichniki. "And then carried on sailing up the Don?" I asked, hoping to confirm their route.

"I should get going." He had realized I was trying to gather information. "I have to meet up with the others."

"Still doing all your work at night?" I said with a sarcasm that was born of regret. I had been trying, however obliquely, to interrogate him, and as a result I had lost him as a companion. In the dark Russian night, in woods crawling with wolves and Frenchmen, friendship might be of more value than intelligence.

"It's effective," he replied.

There was nothing I could do to keep him there. It was too late, on that occasion at least, for an olive branch. "I'm heading for Goryachkino," I told him. "I should be there the day after tomorrow. The others will be there."

"We'll try to be there too," he said as he stood to go. Then he put his hand to his belt. "My knife!"

I remembered catching a glimpse of his strange knife as we fought. It had a serrated top edge with backward-pointing teeth, like a huntsman's knife, but there had been something else—something odd about it that I couldn't quite put my finger on.

"It won't be hard to find," I said, picking a branch of pinewood from the fire to give us some light to search by.

"No, I'll go," he insisted, setting out into the darkness without me. His concern to keep me out of it naturally made me all the keener to see this knife. I ran after him, holding up the burning branch to see the way. It wasn't far to the spot where we had fought. I had the advantage of having seen where the knife fell as I struck it from his hand, but I caught sight of it only moments before he snatched it up. I had just time to notice what made it so strange.

It had two blades; not one from each end of the handle, like with some oriental weapons I have seen, but two parallel blades, as though two identical knives had had their handles strapped together. He slipped it into his belt before I could get a better look. Then he stood and offered me his hand.

"Well, goodbye then, Aleksei Ivanovich," he said as we shook hands. "I'll see you again in two days, I hope. But when we do meet, don't attack me. You may not be so lucky a second time." His final words started as a joke, but ended as a threat.

I went back to the fire, but didn't much feel like sleep. When I did doze off, it was with my sword drawn and in my hand. It was, though, I thought, unfair to worry about Iuda returning to attack me as I slept. As he had said, he'd had plenty of opportunity to kill me earlier had he wanted to. And why should he want to? The Oprichniki were on our side in this war. It seemed a long way to come just to turn on your allies. Thinking that reminded me of the route by which they had come, up the Don—the same route along which Domnikiia had described first a plague and then changed into attacks by wild animals. The Oprichniki had brought no dogs or wolves with them that we had seen, but remembering the way Iuda and the others had fought, had they needed to?

After two more days of walking and one more night's cautious sleep, I made it to Goryachkino. Our prearranged meeting place was a farm outbuilding near the main road. The French were only a few versts away when I arrived late in the afternoon, so the people of the area had already abandoned their homes, evaporating into the hinterland before the scorching wave of the French advance.

I scouted around, and soon found a message scratched into one of the walls.

8-24-18-M

TWELVE

Maks had been there, on the eighth month, the twenty-fourth day, the eighteenth hour—scarcely a day earlier. It was a system we had worked out back in Moscow, even before the Oprichniki had arrived, to cope with the problem of trying to meet up and communicate while we pursued the moving target of the Grande Armée.

The idea had been Vadim's. He had taken it from the experiences of the "little warriors" of the Spanish peninsula, who had been harassing Bonaparte's troops for years without ever forming up into an organized army. (Though the joyous news had not yet reached us, the tide in Spain had at last turned against Bonaparte. Only days earlier, Wellington had occupied Madrid.) We had studied maps of the whole area where we thought we might be operating, most of which we were quite familiar with anyway. We chose small villages, geographical features and isolated buildings and made a long list, assigning each one a unique combination of a letter and number. Thus any meeting we chose could be described simply by a date, a time and the code for the location. It took just four pieces of information: month, day, hour, location.

If one of us arrived at a meeting place, we could simply leave a message, scratched into a tree trunk or chalked on a wall, as to when we had been there, and another telling when and where the next meeting should be. A message would be signed with the author's initial. If more information needed to be conveyed, then a letter could be hidden. The character "П"—for *peesmo*—would indicate the presence of such a letter.

We had chosen meeting places as far afield as Orsha, Tula and Vladimir, but even in the city of Moscow itself, much as we hoped the French would not get that far, we had put dozens of locations on the list. Once the Oprichniki arrived, we had given them copies of the list as well.

And so Maks' message told me that he had been here, but not where he had gone. There was no sign of him now. He might have moved on or he might return, and Dmitry and Vadim could still arrive, so I waited.

Vadim arrived first, and Dmitry soon after. They had been luckier than I in keeping hold of their horses, and thus they were both less exhausted. I showed them Maks' message and briefly told them my adventures since we had last met. Vadim found much that was familiar.

"Well, at least you've seen more of yours than I have of my lot," he said. "I woke up after our first night's camp, and they'd just gone."

"What about all that 'We sleep by day and kill at night'?" I asked, badly impersonating Pyetr's accent.

"I thought I'd managed to dissuade them from that, at least until we'd got close to the enemy," Vadim replied, "but I guess they were just playing me along. They probably rode off the moment my eyes closed."

"So what have you been doing since?"

"Nothing of much benefit. Keeping an eye on the French. I could have gone back to Moscow for all the use I've been."

"And what are the French up to?" asked Dmitry.

"All set for a big battle tomorrow, around a village called Borodino—just southeast of here." He opened a map and showed us.

"And we're going to engage them?" I asked.

"Looks like it. It's all Kutuzov's idea."

"Will we win?"

Vadim shrugged his shoulders. "If we do, it will halt them. If not—well, we had to make some sort of stand before they reached Moscow."

"What about you, Dmitry?" I asked. "How quickly did your Oprichniki give you the slip?"

"They didn't," he replied. "I mean, they go off and do what they do, but they've kept in touch. I know where they are now, for instance. They're setting up an ambush on one of the roads the French are using to bring in more troops. It's not far from here." Our expressions must have conveyed scepticism. "I'll show you," he insisted.

Dmitry led us south, on foot, closer to the French lines, until we came to the edge of a small ridge. It was completely dark now, with still no moon to shed any light on what Dmitry wanted us to see, but beside the road that the ridge overlooked was a farmhouse and light shone from the window. The road was quiet.

"So where are they?" asked Vadim.

"Wait," replied Dmitry. "The road's being used by French troops. See what happens when they come along."

TWELVE

Ever since my first brief battle alongside the Oprichniki, I had wanted to ask Dmitry what he knew about them—what he had held back from us. It seemed that I would not need to ask; I would be shown. We had been waiting for almost half an hour when we finally heard the tramp, tramp, tramp of marching feet. A small group of French infantry, perhaps thirty in all, was advancing down the road. The men at the front and back of the platoon each carried a lantern, adding to the light from the farmhouse. The men marched onwards and had almost completely passed when, in total silence, a door to the farmhouse opened and out raced two dark figures. They grabbed the hindmost man—who carried one of the lanterns—and dragged him back inside. The whole incident took place without a sound and in mere seconds. It was like the tongue of a toad flicking out and grabbing an unsuspecting fly.

Someone towards the back of the platoon noticed first not that his comrade had gone, but that the light had gone. He turned, and then shouted to his lieutenant to stop.

"That was Varfolomei and Ioann, I think," Dmitry told us, by way of commentary.

"Hardly a significant loss to the French army," said Vadim sardonically.

"It's not over yet," said Dmitry.

The platoon had broken ranks to see what had become of the missing man. As we looked, we saw the same two dark figures erupt from the house again, this time taking back with them the lead man—the man with the remaining lantern. At almost the same instant, the light inside the building was extinguished. We, and the French platoon, were suddenly made blind by the darkness. But we could still hear.

The Frenchmen began calling to one another; at first, simply remarks along the lines of "What happened?" and "Are you there?" Then the shouts began to be interrupted by screams, most of them the short, curtailed screams of men taken by surprise and dying quickly. As each scream denoted the death of a man, so the number speaking to each other became fewer, but also louder and more desperate. Towards the end, only one young French voice remained.

"Are you there? Lieutenant? Sir? Who's there? Jacques? Who is there? I'm—" and then a brief yelp ended his one-sided conversation.

I have seen and heard hundreds of men die, many by my own hand, but those thirty deaths and that friendless, lone voice were as sickening as anything I had witnessed up until that time.

Dmitry, on the other hand, expressed his admiration. "Impressive, eh? Thirty men taken out by three. And in, what? Two minutes? Not enough to win us the war, I know, but it can only help."

We had only seen two figures, but Dmitry evidently knew better. Once the lights had been extinguished, there could have been any number of Oprichniki out there, attacking those soldiers, and Vadim and I would have been none the wiser.

"Frenchmen," was all Vadim could mutter grimly, but it was some consolation. They were the invaders. We could defend by any means we chose.

"Let's go down there," said Dmitry, eagerly. We followed him down the ridge and to the road. The impression that the whole scene had been presented for us—for Vadim and me—was growing within me. The Oprichniki probably did work in exactly this way at other times, but on this particular occasion they had known that they had an audience, known that Dmitry would lead us to see them at work. The intent was as much to conceal as to reveal, but I realized I would get nothing more by asking Dmitry directly.

By the time we got to the road, my eyes were becoming used to the darkness A dim light emanated from the open door. Around us there were only about half a dozen bodies remaining. A figure—I think it was Ioann—scuttled out of the farmhouse and began to drag one of the remaining dead soldiers inside. The soldier's leg twitched with some last vestige of life. Ioann shouted something back towards the house and I heard the other two laugh from within. Again I was reminded of the fresh faced recruits outside the brothel back in Moscow.

Dmitry trotted over to the farmhouse, and I saw him talking intensely to Pyetr—the third man—at the door. At something Pyetr said, Dmitry stiffened and looked over his shoulder towards us. He turned back and spoke to Pyetr, who nodded and went inside, returning with a bundle, which he gave to Dmitry.

Dmitry came back over to us. "They're just clearing them off the road so that they won't be seen by any other patrols that come by," he chose to explain, although the reasoning was obvious enough to anyone with the slightest military experience. It gave me cause to wonder if this explanation was offered only to disguise some deeper, more shameful reason, though I could not suspect what. Or perhaps not shameful, but simply, as I had suspected earlier, secret. I could understand their desire for secrecy—my own life had often depended on it—but that did not mean I was going to suppress my own curiosity.

"Pyetr's given me these," added Dmitry, holding up the bundle. Then, before we could say a word, he was scrambling back up the ridge.

None of us said very much until we were well away from what we had just witnessed. Soon we were back in Goryachkino and able to rest. Vadim's mood seemed to have lightened. His rationalization, practised over so many years and so many campaigns, that the enemy is the enemy—that their deaths were their responsibility, not ours—seemed to be winning the upper hand. I understood the arguments, I'd told myself the same story after every battle I had been in, but still something about what we had just seen made it for the first time unconvincing.

Dmitry lit a lamp and excitedly showed us the bundle that Pyetr had given him. It was made up of two French light-infantry uniforms.

"You know what you can do with these?" Dmitry tonight seemed more enthusiastic than I had seen him for many years. "You can go into the French camp—find out what their plans are."

"You're not coming with us?" I asked.

"Oh, you know *my* French. They'd spot me a mile away, but you two could wander into the Tuileries without anyone raising an eyebrow." He was almost gabbling, talking as if that was the only way to keep unwanted thoughts from his mind.

"It's either that, or go straight back to Moscow," said Vadim, soberly. "I'd rather do *something* useful while we're out here."

I thought for a moment and then nodded. "Where shall we meet up with you again?" I asked Dmitry.

"I'll wait at Shalikovo." He was calmer—perhaps as a result of our agreeing to leave him. "If we stop the French advance then that should be safe enough. If not, well, I suppose it will have to be Moscow."

"Until then, Dmitry." We hugged, but for some reason he was in a dreadful hurry. His embrace with Vadim was scarcely a pat on the back.

As he dashed off into the darkness I was almost tempted to spy on him instead of on the French, but I knew my duty. Vadim and I began to change into the French uniforms that he had provided, preparing to place ourselves deep inside the enemy's territory.

CHAPTER V

"So HOW DO I LOOK?" I ASKED VADIM AS I BUTTONED UP MY new uniform. "Do you think I'll pass muster?"

"In French from now on, if you please." His reply was, somewhat hypocritically, in Russian. I repeated my question, this time in French.

"I think you'll do," he replied, at last switching language himself, "although there's a lot of bloodstains on your jacket."

"Yours too." Around the neck, the stains were virtually invisible against the red of the collar, but on the blue of the jacket, they were easier to see. The uniforms themselves were undamaged, with no cuts or piercing that we could find.

"We'll just make up some story about holding a dying comrade in our arms," suggested Vadim. I tried to laugh, but the memory of where the clothes had actually come from was too close and too real.

We strode off towards the French encampments, without much concern for exactly where we were going or even what information we were trying to discover. For me, at least, I think the purpose of the mission was to prove myself once again a soldier and a man.

"It's a miracle that Pyetr even managed to get two intact uniforms off that lot," said Vadim.

I shivered as I felt the hug of the cold uniform, so recently the shroud of a corpse. "The little-known Miracle of the French Uniforms?" I joked.

"He *is* named after a saint."

Our mood lightened a little and our pace quickened. "You think he could walk on water then?"

"I'd like to see him try," muttered Vadim.

"Of course, the Bible gets it wrong there." It was Maks' voice, recalled into my head as part of a conversation years before on that very subject of Saint Peter walking on the Sea of Galilee.

TWELVE

"I thought you believed that the Bible gets it wrong everywhere," I had told him.

"Not everywhere. There's lots of good stuff in there, but that's just a ploy to fool people into thinking that it's all good. It's an old trick. The best place to hide a tree is in a forest. The best place to hide a lie is in a forest of truth."

"And how do we know which is which?" I had asked him.

"You ask a priest." I looked at him, stunned. He burst out laughing. "Or you could ask me," he continued. "Or you could try working it out for yourself."

"Sounds like a lot of effort. And since you evidently know the answer already, I'll ask you."

"About Saint Peter?" he asked. I nodded. "Well," he explained, "the point that they were trying to get across was one about faith. Peter steps out on the water, walks around for a bit, then loses faith and falls in. But the idea should be that faith is what gave Peter the confidence to step on to the water in the first place, not the thing that supported him once he was there—it was God Who did that. It was faith that made him trust God. But when he loses faith, God should still be there to support him, once he's made that step out on to the water.

"It's supposed to be telling us to put our faith in the invisible God, but instead, because Peter starts to sink, it just presents faith as some sort of magical mumbo-jumbo."

"So you think God supported Peter on the water?" I asked, with mock incredulity.

"No, of course not. What I'm saying is the story's about faith, not about God. The faith part is the nugget of truth and people get duped into believing the God part too."

It was lucky that we had been alone. Maks might well have got away with saying that in England or France, but not here in Russia.

"Faith's the interesting bit, though," he had continued. "Faith's what allows people to feel certain about things that they can never know for sure. And that's an important idea to get across, however much the Bible fluffs it."

"An important idea?"

"For the masses—and for politicians. For anyone who's afraid of knowledge, either in themselves or in others. For anyone who sees happiness as the be all and end all of life."

Maks' view of faith was as a fool's paradise; living in happy ignorance for fear of discovering the truth. It might work for some, but I despised the concept no less than he did.

"But isn't the story just relating the events that happened?" I asked, more to goad than to enquire.

Maks tutted. "Why is it that people believe that the Bible is the one book in the history of mankind that doesn't use allegory? Did Gulliver really go to Brobdingnag? Did Candide really visit El Dorado? It's like all those folk tales our grandmothers tell us. None of them ever happened. First you decide the point you're trying to get across, then you make up a story that gets it over. You have to look beyond the ghosts and the vampires and the miracles and see the moral message."

He had pulled up, remembering he had to breathe as well as speak. His enthusiasm bordered on anger, but the pleasure I took in listening to him was only outdone by the pleasure he took in talking. He smiled ruefully, seeing that he had contradicted himself in a way that I would not have spotted. "Well, just because some of the folk stories are made up doesn't mean they all are. Trees in the forest, you know."

Now, as I walked alongside Vadim towards the French lines, recalling the conversation, I wondered if, somewhere out there in the dark Russian countryside, Maks was regaling the three Oprichniki under his command with similar polemics. They didn't seem the type to engage in theological discussion, which was all the better for Maks—he wouldn't be interrupted.

"I just had a thought," whispered Vadim, disturbing my remembrances. We had made our way back on to the road where we had earlier watched as the Oprichniki slaughtered the French platoon. We were at most a verst beyond the farmhouse.

"What?" I asked.

"That we might be mistaken for the enemy by our own side."

TWELVE

"Or by the Oprichniki, at least," I added.

He stopped and turned to me. "They *are* on our side, Aleksei. It doesn't matter what they do; they do it for the best of reasons—for Russia."

Once again, the hackneyed, old argument reassured me, but as we walked on it struck me that while their interests might coincide with those of Russia, that didn't mean that they fought *for* Russia in the way that we did. One might as well say that we—Vadim and I—fought for England. At present we fought on the same side, but a simple signature on a treaty might in an instant change everything. And I doubted whether it would need any written treaty for the Oprichniki to change their allegiance.

The enemy seemed to have little concept of security, and it proved to be a trivial matter for two Russian officers with French uniforms and passable French accents to wander into a camp of perhaps two hundred men on the very eve of what could prove to be the decisive battle of the campaign. From experience we kept away from the tents where the more senior officers would be barracked, knowing that they would have tighter lips and sharper ears than the lower ranks. We ended up sat around a fire with four young artillery officers who introduced themselves as Stephan, Guillaume, Pierre and Louis. For the evening, I was André and Vadim was Claude.

Like most soldiers at the battlefront, they knew little of the overall strategy of their masters. They understood it at the highest level—that the plan was to take Moscow—and, even higher, that this was because the perfidious Russians were trading with the English. They understood it at the most basic level; that in the morning they were supposed to attack the Russian emplacements directly in front of them. Somewhere in between those two, in the region of how the following day's battle was to be conducted and of how the French planned to get from Borodino to Moscow, was where we discovered the gaps in their knowledge. Those gaps were easily filled with gossip and rumour.

Some of the gossip was very domestic and very French. The hottest topic was the fact that the emperor had received that very day a package containing a portrait of his young son—the so-called King of Rome. It was a pleasant conversation for me to engage in, since it reminded me of my own son in Petersburg and of my own "Marie-Louise" in Moscow.

Pierre had the same idealistic simplicity that I loved in Maks, although being younger than Maks, he had not yet found it diminished by any sense of political reality.

"Napoleon may love his son, and that's fine, but I doubt he really sees him as an heir." He looked around us for agreement. "He has made himself emperor purely as a temporary measure, to keep the Republic on track through difficult times, but he knows the next emperor, or whatever he may choose to call himself, must rise on merit, as he did, not by virtue of a serendipitous birth."

Unusually, Vadim took up the political point, although from a typically domestic angle. "But if you believe that, you're saying that Napoleon married Marie-Louise for love. From everything I've heard, he truly loved Josephine and still does."

"I agree with Claude," said Guillaume, speaking for the first time. "Napoleon has made a great sacrifice in leaving the woman he loves so as to provide the country with an heir to replace him."

"Leaving the woman he loves for a girl half his age," added Louis cynically.

I took a risk. "The same sacrifice every patriotic Frenchman makes when he leaves his wife to visit his mistress." It paid off. All four of them laughed in agreement.

Vadim, never the best at expressing his undoubted Russian patriotism, suddenly found the words to pretend he was the truest of French patriots. "And yet Napoleon is happy to leave them both to lead us here for the sake of France."

He had hit exactly the correct tone and everyone's agreement was expressed in a profusion of Gallic nodding all round the fire.

"Do you suppose he knew what the enemy had in store for us?" asked Louis after a thoughtful silence.

"They don't seem to have put up much of a fight yet," I said.

"Not the fighting," explained Stephan. "This new weapon."

"Haven't you heard?" added Guillaume. "It's some kind of sickness. They're trying to spread it amongst us."

TWELVE

"No, it's not a sickness," said Stephan. "It's animals—packs of trained wolves that they're setting upon us."

"If it had been wolves we'd have seen them," said Pierre.

"Perhaps, perhaps not," said Guillaume. "Wolves hunt at night, and there's precious little to see round here when darkness falls."

"And how would they spread any sickness, anyway?" asked Stephan.

"It only takes one or two infected corpses," explained Louis. "They don't have to be catapulted over the walls of a besieged castle—just slipped amongst the bodies of our own dead and wounded."

"I heard this morning that three of them—Russian saboteurs—walked into a camp with their pockets and their knapsacks full of gunpowder. When they were captured, they just blew themselves up, and those around them," said Pierre. "No one was hurt too badly—none of our lot, that is. The Russians were done for. But if they don't even care to protect their own lives, then how do we combat that?"

"It all sounds like the rumours of war to me," said Vadim, being both rational and trying to defend his country from the accusation. "I've heard them on every campaign I've been on. The enemy has to be made more than just an enemy. It's not enough that he opposes you; he has to be wrong as well. And if his cause is wrong, then his methods must be wrong too. And nobody likes to disagree and appear to be supporting the enemy, so the rumour grows and spreads."

All four of the French soldiers eyed Vadim intently as they listened. "So, to deny the rumours is to support the enemy, is it, Claude?" asked Pierre coldly. "As you just did?"

I resisted the urge to put my hand to my sword, but prepared myself for action at any moment. The suspense was broken as Pierre began to laugh, followed by his three comrades and then by Vadim and me.

"You're probably right, my friend," continued Pierre. "They are rumours and so, by definition, they *must* be exaggerated. It's probably just Cossacks marauding and picking off our men."

"Anyway," said Louis, "who could blame the Russians for using a new weapon if they have one? Every campaign is won by bending the rules of war just a little. There would have been men complaining, just like us, at the first use of a musket, or even a longbow—and now we wouldn't be without them."

"I'll stick with my musket, Louis," said Stephan, laughing, "and you can have your longbow."

I kept quiet through all of this, knowing that there was some truth behind these French rumours and noticing a frightening similarity to the stories I had heard from Tula. The Oprichniki were on the Don and there were rumours from the Don—and now the Oprichniki were here and those same rumours stayed with them. Towards the end of the conversation, however, I was beginning to feel more reassured. I knew that we were dealing not with a plague or with wolves, but with extremely skilful, dedicated, violent men; men whose attacks were all the more potent for the fact that they spread fear as well as death. I wasn't sure how the Oprichniki caused the rumours about themselves to be so exaggerated, but hearing the stories repeated from the mouths of these superstitious French soldiers made me realize that stories was all they were. The Oprichniki were great soldiers and they were on our side. That, as Louis himself had just said, was validation enough for us to use them.

Vadim made a move to leave. "Well, good evening, gentlemen. We must be away and prepare for the battle tomorrow."

We both rose, and there was a general shaking of hands and saying of goodbyes between us and the four of them. As we turned and walked away, a final shout came to us from Pierre's lips.

"*Zhelayoo oospyeha!*"

Vadim and I stopped still. The meaning was straightforward enough— "Good luck!" Yet it was not the meaning of the phrase that surprised us, but its language. Pierre had spoken in Russian.

CHAPTER VI

IT HAS ALWAYS STRUCK ME AS INTERESTING THE WAY THAT meaning transcends language. Recalling, for instance, the conversation we had exchanged with those French soldiers that night, I know that it took place in French, but if I were to recount it, I could do it just as well in French or Russian or even Italian. I had remembered the meaning of what was said rather than the details of the words.

Once, back in Petersburg, I had had a long conversation with an old soldier. He had received a head wound fighting the Turks during the reign of the Tsarina Yekaterina, under General Suvarov. A huge chunk of his brain was missing. It affected his ability to move and his ability to speak, but within that straitjacket of incapacity, his mind was as sharp as ever. Communication was difficult, though with practice it became easier. When he spoke, I had to listen carefully to the ill-formed sounds he produced. When he found he was at a loss to express himself, I had to guess his meaning and prompt him with suggestions until we found one with which he was happy.

And yet when I later was talking to Marfa about him, I could recall every detail of his fascinating life as if he had told me it in perfect, fluent Russian. Although I remembered the difficulties we had had in communicating, that memory was stored separately in my mind from what had actually been communicated.

Thus, as Pierre hailed us with his wish of "good luck," one part of my mind reacted to its friendly meaning. Another part screamed at me the warning that the phrase was spoken in Russian—a tongue that I should not comprehend. It was a race between the two thoughts as to which I would act upon first. In the end, the victor did not matter. Vadim spoke before I could react in any way.

"Pardon?" he said, turning back to Pierre and sticking with French.

Pierre repeated the phrase, and then explained in French. "It's Russian for 'good luck.'"

"Ah, I see," smiled Vadim. "I thought it sounded Russian."

"You don't speak it?" asked Pierre.

"Not a word," said Vadim, while I shook my head.

"Pierre here speaks it like a native," said Stephan. "He should be a spy." He paused and considered for a moment. "Unless, of course, he already is. He could be spying on us for them." Louis and Guillaume both laughed.

"Go on, Pierre," said Louis. "Hit us with some more."

Pierre rolled out a few sentences in a passable accent. They were clearly intended to catch out any honest Russian who understood them.

"Your wife is a whore, and last night she screwed my dog" was the first, followed by "Tsar Aleksandr likes to suck General Kutuzov's cock." Finally, he recounted an often told but utterly false story concerning the death of Tsarina Yekaterina. While I might have fallen for the trickery of his surprise "good luck," it was easy enough for Vadim and me now to pretend not to understand a word he said. For many senior officers of the generation before ours, little pretence would have been necessary. For a century, French had been the language of the cultivated Russian. Russian was the language of the serf. For most nations, the spies are chosen from amongst men who are fluent in a foreign tongue—men like Pierre. In Russia, spies were men such as Vadim, Dmitry, Maks and myself who, unusually, could communicate with our own populace. Only now, thanks largely to the common enemy that all Russians saw in Bonaparte, were things changing.

"And what was all that about, Pierre?" asked Louis. Pierre translated and we all laughed, particularly about Yekaterina and the horse.

We said goodbye once more and made our way out of the camp, not convinced that they trusted us, but resisting the urge to break into a run. We were almost beyond sight of the group around the fire when we saw ahead of us three French officers about to enter the camp. I readied myself to nonchalantly salute as we passed, but as they came closer, their three faces became recognizable.

It was Iuda, Foma and Matfei.

"Aleksei Ivanovich! Vadim Fyodorovich! What might you be doing here?" asked Iuda. "Surely you haven't gone over to the other side?" He had a degree of good-humoured sarcasm that I was surprised to hear from any of the Oprichniki.

"Just a little espionage," explained Vadim. "And you?"

Iuda smiled. "We come not to spy, but to kill." Matfei and Foma shuffled their feet, impatient that this needless conversation was delaying the action. "It's a good job we didn't come sooner," continued Iuda. "You make such convincing Frenchmen."

I was keen to leave, but I felt we owed Iuda some of the benefit of our research. "There's over a hundred men back there," I told him. "You don't stand a chance." Even as I spoke, I remembered what we had witnessed Pyetr, Ioann and Varfolomei achieve earlier that night, and I doubted my own words.

Iuda patted my shoulder condescendingly. "Thanks for your concern, Aleksei. See you soon."

Then they were gone, vanishing into the darkness of the night to become shadows illuminated only by the campfires, mingling amicably amongst the men that they were soon to turn on. Vadim and I walked briskly away, each of us secretly hoping to be out of earshot before the Oprichniki began their work.

Back in Goryachkino, we changed into our regular clothes. Vadim's horse was still tied up where he had left it. He mounted and set off ahead of me towards our own encampments to the east of Borodino. I continued on foot. The rain poured down on me, driven even harder by the gusting wind, and the road became muddy under my feet. I envied Vadim his quick journey on horseback, but I pressed on.

Dawn broke with no sound of birdsong. The sound of those birds that even dared to speak was smothered by the sound of twelve hundred guns opening fire as the battle began to the south. It was a beautiful sound, at least to a soldier, which was what I still liked to regard myself as. There is a simplicity to a battle that appeals to every soldier, be he the most cerebral officer or the basest *ryadovoy*. It is a suspension of morality that allows a man to act without conscience, safe in the knowledge that it is his duty to destroy the enemy. The politics, for that short duration, are the business of others. Between battles, some men suppress their doubts with unconditional love for the tsar, some with complex political reasoning, some with plain, brute stupidity.

I belonged to the middle group, and I had been a long time between battles. But I knew that I could make little difference as a soldier on my own, and so I walked on, trying to pass the battle, to meet up with Vadim, rejoin the Oprichniki and direct them to do some real damage.

To the north of Borodino, the Moskva flowed east to Moscow, but here it turned a little to the south, forcing me closer to the battlefield than my head—though not my heart—would have liked. I skirted the village of Loginovo, close enough to see that it was swarming with Bavarian cavalry, but not close enough for them to see me. My next problem was to cross the Kolocha. It wasn't a huge river, just a tributary of the Moskva, but I knew I would have to head south, towards the battle, to find a suitable point to ford it. Eventually, I found a shallow. Thinking of Maks, and musing as to whether I would simply be able to walk across the water, I stepped out into the river.

Almost as my foot touched it, the surface began to shake and ripple. It was already broken by rainfall, but this disturbance had a different pattern— one with which I was familiar. The air was still filled with the sound of cannon fire, but as I listened more carefully, I heard what I had been expecting: the sound of hooves.

Before I could turn to look, I was surrounded by horsemen; Cossacks— from the Astrakhan *voisko*, by the look of them. But they were in full retreat, almost a stampede. They crossed the river without troubling to pause, ignoring me and galloping by on either side. Amongst them were several horses that had thrown or lost their riders. They had been initially caught up in the frenzy of their stablemates, but now they were beginning to slow. I grabbed the harness of one of them and hauled myself on to it, spurring it on to catch up with the rest of the group. I glanced behind me and caught a glimpse of what they were fleeing from—a squad of Bavarian cavalry pursuing them at full gallop. I didn't pause to wait for them. Once across the river, it was easy for me to get ahead of the disorganized rabble and then turn my horse to face them.

"Pull yourselves together," I shouted, but I suspect it was more the need to avoid collision with me than any order I gave which ultimately caused them to halt. Once a dozen or so had pulled up and gathered around me, some degree of order was returned, and most of the remainder turned to join us. A few galloped off into the distance, but I had no time to concern myself with them. There were almost fifty who stayed with me. I drew my sabre, and charged back towards the Bavarians with an incoherent roar.

For a moment, I did not know if the Cossacks would follow, but I soon found myself riding with horsemen at my side, behind me, and even a few stretching out in front. Within seconds, we were upon the Bavarians. Our two squadrons clashed and then intermingled without resistance, like two droplets of water forming into one. But within that new, single droplet a battle raged. I fought with my sabre, as did many of the Cossacks, but others fired pistols at close range. The enemy was similarly armed, and whilst the two sides might have been on a level in their use of pistols, a pistol can only be fired once. After that, the Cossacks showed far greater skill—and savagery—with the use of the blade.

Even in the heat of battle, I made a comparison with the Oprichniki, or rather how I had imagined our working with the Oprichniki would be; that they would require leadership, but once given that they would fight beside their Russian leaders like heroes. But that was not how it had turned out. The Oprichniki shunned us, and when they did fight, they fought like cowards, both in their ambush at the farmhouse and later when they infiltrated the French camp. It was, in contrast, an honour to fight alongside these Cossacks, even though their customs were as strange to me as were those of the Wallachians.

I didn't hear the Bavarians' call to retreat, but in an instant the two droplets had separated again and the enemy was in flight. I charged after them, elated by the heat of the battle.

"Come back and fight, God damn you!" I heard a voice shout, and realized it was my own. At the same time, I knew that pursuit was foolish. We were heading back towards Loginovo, where I had seen so many more Bavarians; more than we could ever defeat. I turned my horse around and the Cossacks followed. Once we had crossed the Kolocha for the third time in but a few minutes, we slowed down to a canter, and I asked the sergeant to lead us back to their camp.

He pointed us to the southeast, and then spoke to me.

"That was very impressive, sir. After we lost our lieutenant, I thought we were done for."

"Thank you." I was too out of breath to say much more. There were a few moments' silence before he spoke again.

"Just one thing, sir."

"Yes?"

"Why all the swearing, sir? Fighting's a sacred business. Swearing in battle, well, it's like swearing in church."

I looked at him in amazement, and yet I already knew that Cossacks took their fighting extremely seriously.

"I'll try to keep that in mind," I said.

"God will punish you, sir," he continued, not in the blood-and-guts tone of a priest, but just as if he were reminding me that it was a good idea to keep the lock of my musket clean. His reasoning was equally straightforward. "You'll get killed . . . and so will we."

I laughed, throwing my head back, more out of the euphoria of the battle than anything else, but I admired the practicality of his piety.

Once back behind our own lines, we were passed from officer to officer until I finally faced the Cossacks' commander, General Platov. The sergeant explained what had happened. Platov stroked his thin moustache and eyed me up and down.

"And who the devil are you?" he asked.

"Captain Danilov, sir; Hussar Life Guard Regiment."

"And where's your uniform?"

"I've been on special duties, sir."

Platov knew that if this was true, then he would get little response to any further questions. On the other hand, it was an easy enough claim for anyone to make. I was about to show him my papers, but before I could he spoke briefly to an adjutant, who then rode off.

"We'll soon see about that," he said.

He didn't speak to me any further, but rode a little way away and began viewing the terrain through his spyglass. A few minutes later, his adjutant returned, accompanied by a figure that even from a distance I could recognize by his mop of thick, dark curly hair. It was Lieutenant-General Fyedor Pyetrovich Uvarov, officially my commanding officer. On seeing his arrival, Platov rode back over to join the two of us. He arrived just as Uvarov greeted me.

"Come back to join us, Aleksei Ivanovich?" asked Uvarov, with half a smile. He had not been resentful when Vadim had asked him if I might be temporarily borrowed from his regiment, but he had been sorry to see me go.

"Just passing through, sir," I replied.

"You can vouch for this man then?" asked Platov.

"As much as anyone can," said Uvarov.

"You want him back?" Platov spoke in the same tone as he would have discussed a lost dog.

Uvarov raised a questioning eyebrow at me.

"I think I'm happy where I am, sir," I said.

"Very good," said Platov, still scarcely bothering to look at me. He looked at his pocket watch. "Make yourself ready, we advance in ten minutes."

And so, a quarter of an hour later, I had led my Cossacks across the Kolocha once more, accompanied by many others. All of Platov's Cossacks, Bashkirs and Tatars took part in the attack, along with Uvarov's more regular cavalry, amongst whom I might in a different life have found myself. This time, we outflanked the Bavarians, but almost as soon as we had crossed the river, we encountered both cavalry and light infantry, which Uvarov's forces engaged, allowing the rest of us to further outflank the enemy and get behind their lines.

I charged onwards, imagining myself as my hero, Davidov, whom I had met only once, at the Battle of Eylau, but whom Vadim had known in Finland. He was famed even now—and would become more famous soon—for his audacious raids at the head of Cossack troops. We attacked whoever we saw, spreading chaos and fear, as Cossacks always do, amongst the enemy—Italians and Bavarians, mostly—who could not organize themselves into any defence. Whether we actually had any significant impact on the battle, I do not know, but there was a sense of exhilaration in this kind of fighting that I have not known before or since. Again, my sabre proved to be by far the most effective weapon, assisted by perhaps a single volley of pistol fire preceding each attack.

Eventually, the French understood the danger we posed to them. The Third Cavalry turned from the French centre and counterattacked. Once surprise had been lost, we were far less effective. The Third Cavalry held us to a more orthodox form of battle, and this in turn took the pressure off the Italians and Bavarians, who had time to organize their own defence properly. Volleys of musket fire began to decimate our ranks. Still the Cossacks unhaltingly threw themselves on the enemy, but now each attack took a greater toll on us. Men fell on either side of me long before we were close enough to use our sabres. Now I longed to be back with my comrades in the Hussars, where a few swift words from me could have organized us into lines and made us far more effective. But the Cossacks knew little of such things, and they paid the price.

The sergeant, who had rode beside me throughout, was shot in the neck. Blood cascaded from his mouth as he tried to speak, but then he fell to the ground, the hooves of his comrades' horses trampling him and quickly achieving what the bullet had slowly begun. I called for a withdrawal, but it was an order they were far less happy to obey than an attack. I rode back and forth, slapping men and horses with the flat of my blade until eventually what was left of them—perhaps thirty from the original fifty—obeyed.

It was not long after that a general retreat—for both Platov's and Uvarov's troops—was ordered. We headed back, crossing the river for a final time, to our original position on the Russian right flank. There, sitting calmly astride his horse, was a familiar figure: Vadim Fyodorovich. He said nothing, but his whole demeanour reminded me of my father, calling for me to stop playing with my friends because my tutor was waiting for me. Through the crowds of horsemen, I also saw General Uvarov. He rode over to me.

"We've been ordered to join Kutuzov in Gorki." Gorki was a village about two versts east of Borodino, where General Kutuzov had made his headquarters. "It looks like they need to reinforce the centre."

I nodded towards Vadim. Uvarov turned and looked at him for a moment, then gave him a curt salute of acknowledgement. "I see," he said. He turned away from me and surveyed his troops.

They were far fewer in number than what they had been in the morning, and many were in no state to fight. "God in Heaven!" he muttered. "We'll never keep them from Moscow now."

I thought about raising my sergeant's objections to swearing on the battlefield, but decided I was already straining my relationship with the general. Besides, the sergeant's clean mouth had not brought him any luck that day. Vadim had already turned his horse and was leaving. I headed after him.

"Any sign of Maks?" I asked, after we had discussed what we had been doing since we last met. His day had been quieter than mine. He had reported what we had discovered in the French camp, and then gone to observe the battle. Several of the Life Guards had mentioned my activities, and so he'd had no trouble finding me.

"No one seems to have heard from him, but I wouldn't have expected them to. If Maks has stuck to the plan (unlike us) then he'll be east of here. Shalikovo would be the most likely place on the list. We should head there too."

We rode to Shalikovo, with the sound of battle growing more distant, but still ever present behind us. It was late evening by the time we arrived at our chosen rendezvous—a small stable attached to an inn. The inn, like so many of the buildings along the Moscow road, had been abandoned by both owners and guests in anticipation of Bonaparte's advance. We decided to forsake the comforts of sleeping on straw for the rooms of the inn itself. Neither of us had had any real sleep for over twenty-four hours, so we took full advantage of the opportunity.

The following morning, we could hear no further sound of cannon fire. The great battle was over, though we had no idea of its outcome. We went to the stable to see if there was any sign of either Maks or Dmitry having been there before us. It didn't take long to find, chalked on to the wall, a brief but precise message from Maks:

8-26-9-M

TWELVE

We had missed him by only twelve hours when we arrived the previous evening. I noted also the shaky hand in which he had written. He had been tired or afraid—or both. There was no sign of Dmitry.

We decided to wait, partly to see if Dmitry would show up, partly to see what news there was from Borodino. We found a few bits of food left in the inn, and made ourselves a reasonable breakfast. By midmorning, the first of our retreating troops passed through the village.

The news was confused. There had been heavy casualties on both sides, although no one could give even the vaguest numbers; it was only much later that I learned the true scale of death there. Some time before dawn, after almost a full day's battle, Kutuzov had given the order for the Russian retreat. Yet still some of those who rode through claimed the battle as a victory for Russia—saying that although we had been forced to retreat, we had done enough damage to halt Bonaparte's advance and that he would never now be able to take Moscow. Others were less optimistic, but still saw some hope; Bonaparte would take Moscow, but would not be able to keep it. Still others thought that there was now nothing to keep the French from the gates of Petersburg.

Whatever the analysis of the future, it was clear that there was little point in our staying in Shalikovo. We saddled up and headed east along the road to Moscow, quickly overtaking the bedraggled, war-weary and yet not quite demoralized survivors of our glorious army. For us, as well as for them, Moscow was the obvious place to go. But whichever side it was that could truthfully claim the victory at Borodino, Bonaparte still had a hundred thousand able-bodied men at his command, and these prodigious forces were soon—like us—to descend upon the beloved city.

That night we slept rough. We arrived in Moscow towards noon of the following day. Back at the inn in Tverskaya, we made enquiries. Dmitry had arrived there earlier that day, but had already left again. Maks had not been seen since we left, a week and a half previously. Vadim went to look around some of Dmitry's more regular haunts and I said I'd do the same for Maks.

And that was enough justification for me. I knew perfectly well that Maks had been seeing Margarita at the brothel, even though I had told neither Vadim nor Dmitry. Thus visiting the brothel was an absolutely reasonable move when looking for Maks. The length of time I ended up spending there might not have been so reasonable.

I was immediately taken aback by the affection with which Domnikiia greeted me. Normal behaviour in the salon, in front of the other girls and customers, was restrained, but today Domnikiia embraced and kissed me like a wife greeting her long-lost husband, or perhaps even more like a mother greeting her long-lost son. She led me by the hand up to her room.

"Oh, Lyosha, thank God you're here. After Maks came back alone, I didn't know what was happening. I asked them to tell me the moment you came through the door." She kissed me again on the lips, her hands holding my face.

I pulled away. "You've seen Maks? When?"

She misunderstood my concern. "I literally only saw him—well, and spoke to him—but nothing more. He didn't even stay with Margarita."

I shook my head. "I didn't mean that," I said, kissing the palm of her hand. "When was he here?"

"Two days ago. He looked exhausted—he'd been riding nonstop for days—but he left again almost straight away."

"What did he say?"

"I can't remember exactly, but the important message for you was to meet him at Desna."

Desna was one of our preplanned meeting places.

"Did he say when?"

"He said he'd wait until you got there, but that only you should go. Margarita will remember more."

She went over and knocked on the door which connected her room to Margarita's. After a moment's waiting for a reply, she opened it and peeped inside. From what I could hear, Margarita was evidently busy with a client. I saw Domnikiia beckon to her and then close the door.

"She'll just be a second," said Domnikiia, and it was only moments later that Margarita slipped through the door, a sheet wrapped around her body like an ill-fitting toga.

"You remember Aleksei," said Domnikiia. Margarita gave me the brief, polite smile of someone whose livelihood is being disrupted by trivial intro-ductions. "What did Maksim say when we saw him the other day?"

Margarita reeled off what she knew with a determined accuracy that reflected both an impressive memory and a desire not to have to repeat her-self. "He said to tell Aleksei to meet him at Desna, that he'd wait there as long as he could, that only Aleksei should go, that that was why he told *us*—so that only Aleksei would find out—and that we shouldn't trust Dmitry's friends. Oh, and that we shouldn't trust Dmitry either. Who's Dmitry? Don't tell me, I'll find out later."

She made her way back to the connecting door, finding it increasingly difficult to walk as she trod down the front of her sheet. As she stepped through the doorway, she abandoned it altogether. I caught a glimpse of her naked back and heard the words "Well, hello again, Colonel . . ." uttered in a bawdy tone before she closed the door behind her.

"Who's Dmitry?" asked Domnikiia. I didn't answer. Instead I kissed her, pushing her back on to the bed.

A more comradely man than I might have galloped straight off to Desna there and then, but it had been twelve days since I'd seen Domnikiia. It wasn't that I was desperate to make love to her, just that I was desperate to be with her, and making love was what we tended to do when we were together—the only thing we did when we were together. And, to be honest, I think the sight of Margarita's naked back had inflamed my passion, if only slightly.

"Who's Dmitry?" asked Domnikiia afterwards.

"You've been wondering about that all the time?"

"No," she giggled, "but when I ask a question I expect an answer—however long it takes."

"Dmitry Fetyukovich—he's a fellow officer. Maksim and I both work with him. They're not the closest of friends, but they work well together. I trust him."

"Who? Dmitry?"

"Yes."

"And Maks?"

"I trust him too."

"And whom do you trust more, my dear, trusting Lyosha?" she asked, curling her leg around me. It was a tricky question, so I said nothing.

"What did Maks mean by 'Dmitry's friends'?" she asked.

Dmitry's friends—the Oprichniki—were what made it a tricky question. Until recently, if push had come to shove, I'd have had to trust Dmitry over Maks, but Dmitry seemed so close to those mysterious, frightening men that I couldn't now say for sure.

"They're just a group of soldiers that Dmitry fought with against the Turks. They've come up here to help us out. They're not regular soldiers—cavalry or infantry—they're more like Cossacks, but even less controllable. We call them Oprichniki."

Whether or not she knew the original meaning of the term, she didn't ask about it.

"Are they good at what they do?"

I remembered the voice of that lonely French infantryman, shouting to his commanding officer and to his friends in the dark oblivion of the night. I remembered Iuda, Matfei and Foma wandering into a camp of a hundred men without a doubt in their minds that they would be victorious. Although I had not seen them since, there was no doubt in mine that they had been. I spared Domnikiia the details.

"Very good," I replied.

I ran my hand across her thigh and she smiled at me, but her smile suddenly became a frown as she grabbed my hand and held it up to look at.

"When did this happen?" she asked in alarm.

"What?" I almost laughed, seeing no reason for her sudden anxiety.

She spent a moment searching for what to say. "Your fingers! When did it happen?"

I'd long ago become accustomed to the absence of the last two fingers of my left hand, lost under torture after I had been captured by the Turks. It was almost surprising how little I had needed them. I wrote with my right hand. I held my sword in my right hand. My aim with a musket was a little less good for having to support the stock with only two fingers, but it had never been my weapon of choice.

TWELVE

"Three years ago," I replied to Domnikiia's question. "I'm surprised you hadn't noticed," I added, pretending to sound hurt, but still genuinely surprised.

"I don't think I really noticed you at all until you left."

She ran her finger up and down between my thumb and my index finger and middle finger and then over the stumps of the other two.

"Does it hurt?" she asked.

"Not any more." I let her continue to feel the scarred remains of my fingers. Most people were oversensitive about my hand, either being constantly concerned about it or not mentioning it at all for fear they might upset me. Either way, it was better that they focused on the physical. Only one other person I knew shared Domnikiia's innocent fascination with the messy detail of what remained where my fingers had been, and that was my son, Dmitry. He liked to touch my hand in much the same way as Domnikiia was doing now and, closing my eyes, it was almost as if I was with him again. Marfa at first had told him not to, but it did me no harm, so it was allowed.

"I've never seen a picture of Empress Marie-Louise," said Domnikiia, intertwining her four fingers with my two. I was glad she had changed the subject.

"Why do you say that?" I asked.

"Apparently you think I look like her."

"Apparently?"

"Maksim told me." She spoke as if it was a confession of a sin. But that she and Maks had spoken about me was not a concern to me anymore.

"Well, you do look like her."

"So am I just a cheap substitute because you can't afford yourself a French empress?" she asked lightly.

I laughed. "She's not French, she's Austrian."

"That's not an answer."

"And you're not cheap."

"Neither's that, though I know it must be a strain on your pocket to pay for a courtesan." She paused before adding, "And a wife." She said the words with a look of petulant envy which I could only regard as a pretence. The idea that Domnikiia was in some way jealous of my marriage, whether the feeling

94

was affected or not, was flattering to me, but I was also irritated that she should attempt to bring reality into our cosy, delusional world.

"Maks again, I suppose," I said.

She nodded and then added, "You don't wear a wedding ring."

"Not a good idea for a spy," I replied. I absentmindedly rubbed the base of the ring finger of my right hand, where it should have been. My wedding ring sat, as ever, in a small mother-of-pearl box on Marfa's dressing table. I only ever wore it when I was at home in Petersburg. Marfa said that she understood my reasons.

"Oh, I see," said Domnikiia. "What's her name?"

"Whose?" I asked.

"Your wife's."

"Didn't Maks tell you that?"

"He didn't mean to tell me any of it."

"She's called Marfa Mihailovna. And we have a son—Dmitry Aleksee-vich." I sounded more annoyed than I meant to. I just wanted to get the details over with as quickly as possible so that I at least could forget that I had a wife and child.

"Another Dmitry," she observed.

"We named him after Dmitry Fetyukovich."

"Why?"

"Because he saved my life."

"I see," she said, cuddling close to me. "I think I'd like to meet Dmitry."

"Which one?"

She made no reply, but simply smiled up at me. Unwanted, the memory of Maks interrupted my thoughts. He would have been waiting alone in the discomfort of a woodsman's hut in Desna for two days. I despised myself for lingering.

"I have to go," I said, beginning to dress. "I have to see Maks."

"I understand," she replied.

For the first time, it didn't occur to me to pay her. It didn't occur to her to ask.

TWELVE

*   *   *

Stepping out into the square, I saw Vadim marching briskly towards me.

"What the hell are you doing in there?" he growled with genuine anger. "You're supposed to be looking for Maksim Sergeivich."

"I was looking for him."

"In there? That may be where you get your entertainment, Aleksei, but it's not the sort of place I'd expect to find Maks. Mind you, I'm learning an awful lot today that I wouldn't have expected from Maks. So was he in there?"

"No, but I found out where he is," I replied, unable to fathom Vadim's unusually bellicose manner.

"Good, let's go there then."

"Why the rush, all of a sudden?"

Vadim looked at me as if he thought he was about to break my heart. His tone softened, but only a little.

"Because Maksim Sergeivich is—and for all I know, always has been—a French Spy."

CHAPTER VII

I REMEMBER MY FIRST MEETING WITH MAKSIM SERGEIVICH Lukin. It was in 1805, maybe two months before Austerlitz. We were sitting in the mess, eating lunch, and I heard a confident, young voice from across the table. I looked up to see Maks, then only eighteen, in earnest conversation with Dmitry, whom I already knew quite well.

"In America, they have no king, but they have slaves," Maks was explaining. "In England, they have a king, but no slaves. In France, they killed their king and created an emperor, just so that they might not be slaves. In Russia, we have an emperor *and* we have slaves." He paused for a moment. "Of course, most Russians would say we have an emperor and we *are* slaves."

"The serfs themselves would say that, you mean?" Dmitry had interjected.

"Exactly."

I was instantly taken with Maks. I had no idea what argument he was following or what point he was trying to make, but the fresh, youthful passion of the way he expressed his ideas was striking.

"I'd hardly compare the serfs with the Negroes," I said, entering the conversation for the first time.

Maks didn't falter in his intellectual stride. "Well, no; we didn't have to travel so far to get the serfs."

It was a statement of the sort that I later found to be typical of Maks— ambiguous, detached and made with an arch glint in his eye. Was he taking a swipe at the Americans or the Russians? I remember asking him about it, or some similar issue, years later. He told me that he had no interest in nations, only in ideas.

"Aren't nations founded on ideas?" I'd asked him.

TWELVE

"Some," he had nodded, "but not many." At the time I could think of only two: France and America—and we weren't at war with America.

Outside the brothel in Tverskaya, with Bonaparte virtually at the city gates, I remembered all this and looked blankly into Vadim's eyes.

"How can he be a French spy?" I asked. "He fought against the French at Austerlitz with us. And he's been fighting them here."

"Has he?" queried Vadim. "That's not what I've been hearing. According to Dmitry, as soon as we got out to Gzatsk, Maks handed three of them straight over to the French. They were executed within hours."

"Three of whom?"

"Three of the Oprichniki: Simon, Faddei and one of the Iakovs—I can't remember which one."

"And how does Dmitry know all this?"

"Because Andrei told him. Andrei was with the other three when Maksim betrayed them, but he managed to get away." Vadim could see from my raised eyebrow that I was about to doubt the word of Andrei, a man we'd known only a few days, in condemning an old friend such as Maks. "And Dmitry spoke to Maks himself," Vadim countered before I could speak. "Maks admitted it to him."

Not long before, Maks' last message to me had said not to trust Dmitry. Now the word from Dmitry was not to trust Maks. Maks had gone into hiding—not the behaviour of an innocent under any circumstances—and had said that only I should go and see him. Was that for his protection, or was it a trap for me?

"When did Dmitry hear of all this?" I asked Vadim, but there was no need for an answer as at that moment Dmitry himself appeared on the far side of the square. He came over to us.

"You told him?" he asked Vadim.

"The gist of it, but I think you'd better tell us both again."

"How long have you known?" I asked. I was concerned at what Dmitry might have been keeping from us up to now.

"I found out right after I left you at Goryachkino. Andrei found me and told me."

"Told you what, exactly?" I was still deeply suspicious.

"As soon as they got near to Gzatsk, Maks and his Oprichniki became separated, which is to say—as it turned out—that he gave them the slip. They searched around and found that he'd been captured by the French. Of course he hadn't been captured. He'd just marched straight into the French camp."

I was about to ask how they knew, but Vadim raised a hand to indicate I should let Dmitry continue.

"They rescued him, still not realizing he was a traitor, and pretty soon he gave them the slip again. They met up with Faddei somewhere along the way, and then went on to meet us all at Goryachkino. They showed up the day before we did and there was Maks again. He told them he'd found a big, undefended French encampment, a few versts away from the main formations at Borodino. It was a sitting duck, he said, and they trusted him.

"So all four of them—Andrei, Simon, Iakov Alfeyinich and Faddei—wandered innocently into the French camp and were instantly set upon and killed. Except Andrei—he managed to escape, luckily for us—or we'd never have heard a thing about it. I guess the damned French were only expecting three of them—that's all that Maks had thought he was betraying."

"And Andrei told you all this?" I asked.

"Yes. After I'd left you, Andrei found me and told me what had happened. He told me he'd been following Maks, and knew where he was camped. When I confronted Maks, he confessed to everything—exactly what Andrei told me. We all know how he likes to talk about France and the Revolution, but I never thought he meant it for real."

"How long has it been going on?" asked Vadim.

"I don't know," replied Dmitry. "What does that matter? The point is we've got to find him and deal with him. Have you found out where he is?"

"Aleksei knows," said Vadim, and he and Dmitry turned to me.

I thought for a moment. If Dmitry on his own had denounced Maks, then I might have trusted him, but the fact that it was Dmitry and Andrei—one of the Oprichniki—made me doubtful. Since their arrival, Dmitry's allegiance had seemed far more with them than with us. Of course, they were supposedly on our side, but now was the moment when we had to know that for sure.

TWELVE

"I'll go and find him myself," I said. "I'll bring him back here."

"You damned well won't," Dmitry told me. "We're all going to go and make sure he comes with us."

"I'll go alone," I replied firmly. "He's only expecting to see me. If we all go, he may run. He'll come with me. If he doesn't then we'll know for sure he's a traitor."

Dmitry sneered.

"Believe me, Dmitry Fetyukovich," I told him in cold earnest, "if Maksim is a traitor then he has betrayed me as much as any of us. I'm not going to let a man like that get away with it."

"I could order you to tell us where he is," said Vadim, but I could tell from his voice that he wasn't going to risk seeing his squad further eviscerated by having his orders disobeyed. He looked at me, then to Dmitry, then back to me. "Very well, Aleksei. You go. Bring him back here and we'll decide together what to do with him—if he's guilty." But his last words were an afterthought—he had already decided.

I saddled up and began my journey south out of the city. Desna wasn't far, but I wasn't eager to get there, and so I proceeded at a gentle canter. Whether or not I trusted Dmitry's word on what Maks had done, I didn't entirely trust him to follow Vadim's orders and leave me to do my job alone. Along the journey, I kept one eye over my shoulder and turned off the main road to double back a few times, but there was no sign that I was being followed. It had already been dark for some time when I arrived at the woodsman's hut, just north of the village.

I had not seen the place before—I think it had been Maks' own suggestion originally to add it to the list—and I was surprised by its size. It was big enough for one or two men to sleep in relative comfort if required.

I knocked on the door and spoke softly. "Maks! Maks, it's Aleksei."

The door opened and I saw Maks' face, pale, unwashed and frightened. "Are you alone?" he asked. I nodded. He took a paranoid glance around before opening the door fully and letting me inside.

"How long have you been here?" I asked.

"Two days," he replied. The inside of the hut was barren, but for a simple clay stove against one wall and a single small chair. "Sit!." he said to me, indicating the chair. I picked up the chair and moved it to the centre of the room.

"No, you sit," I said. I tried to sound generous but, in reality, I was preparing for an interrogation, and I would be in a better position if I were to stand and walk while he was forced to remain seated and look up at me. He did as I had said.

"I've spoken to Dmitry," I said.

Maks looked to the floor. "Good," he muttered.

"Is it true?" I asked.

"Is what true?"

I lost my composure and spoke to him more personally than I had intended to, breaking out of the role of interrogator. "This isn't a debate, Maks. This isn't even a trial. This is about our friendship. Just give a straight answer."

"I can't." His reply was completely genuine. "You know me, Aleksei, I just don't think that way. I don't speak that way." I knew what he meant. Some men put up an intellectual front to give a veneer of profundity to their gut feelings. Maks did not deal in gut feelings. He had them and—I had realized when he had explained away his visit to the brothel—he understood them, but he didn't care for them or rely upon them. His sincerest expressions were always constructed through a process of reason. "But if you talk specifically of friendship, that's one thing I haven't betrayed. I wouldn't betray anything that counted."

"But you've betrayed your country."

It wasn't put as a question, but he answered it anyway. "Yes."

"And you sent Simon, Faddei and Iakov Alfeyinich to be slaughtered by the French."

"Oh yes, and Andrei too if I could have—although we could argue about the 'slaughtered.'"

"What do you mean? Are you saying they're not dead?"

"No, no. They're dead. I was just questioning the rather evocative choice of word." Anyone who didn't know Maks might have thought that he was trying to be confrontational, or perhaps that he was trying to be affable—to make a friend of his interrogator—but I knew that he was simply being his usual, honest, precise self. His mind dealt with what he must have realized was the imminent prospect of his death as a traitor with the same detachment that he viewed a discussion on literature or a new political theory.

"So you're not making any attempt to deny that you've been spying for Bonaparte?" I asked him directly.

"No. Why should I?"

I bridled at this sudden show of apparent honesty. "Would you have denied it a month ago?"

"Of course."

"So what is it that makes you so keen to be honest with me now?"

"The fact that you know everything. I'm not going to make the effort of lying to a man who knows the truth," he replied with absolute simplicity. If only one of us then had comprehended that I didn't know everything, that there were explanations that desperately needed to be made, then things might have turned out very different. But Maks, for all his articulacy, had never been one to readily understand that the thoughts that were so clearly laid out in his brain had not yet managed to find their way into those of other people. The fact that my horror at his being a traitor to his country was so great, even though that crime to him meant so little, perhaps confused him into thinking I knew about the greater horror he had discovered.

"So how long have you been working for Bonaparte?" I asked him.

"You know I've always been sympathetic to the Revolution."

I nodded. We all had been, until the Revolution had turned into an empire and the empire had invaded our country.

"It was when I was captured at Austerlitz," Maks continued. "They have experts who can spot potential recruits: the young, the politically avant-garde. The only way that they changed my mind was to point out that Napoleon would either be the master of Europe or would be defeated. There can be no happy compromise that leaves a free Russia—the British wouldn't allow that, for a start, and who can blame them? They have their own interests to consider.

"But I had to choose. Did I want a world in which the ideas of the Revolution flourished or one in which they perished? You know what I would have chosen, Aleksei, without even having to ask."

He was right. I couldn't accuse him of inconsistency. Everything he ever did was a predictable conclusion of his beliefs and his circumstances. It had been my mistake not to take what I knew of him to its logical end.

"And so, after a few years' indoctrination, they released you like any other prisoner?"

"'Indoctrination' is another of those evocative words, like 'slaughtered,'" he replied, "but that's the general idea of it."

"And what 'services' have you done for Bonaparte since?"

"Very little, to be honest." He smiled ironically. "Vadim had seen in me exactly the same potential for 'irregular' operations as the French did, so almost everything military I've done has been with you, him and Dmitry, and even then there's not been much. I've reported back what I've known about general troop movements and so forth, but it's always seemed too immediate, too personal, to tell them about anything *we've* done. It turns out to be a lot easier to betray a country than a person."

"Until last week when you knowingly sent three brave men to their deaths."

"Again, we could quibble over words there, but that was different. That was for the good of humanity."

"Humanity?" I scoffed. "It's always for humanity, isn't it? But tell me, Maksim, what makes French humanity more important than Russian humanity? Or British more important than Austrian? We can't fight for the whole of humanity, because humanity has no enemies but other humans." He was about to object, but I was in no mood to yield. When I'd arrived at Desna, I had been urgently hoping that Dmitry had somehow been wrong—that Andrei had lied—and as Maksim had confirmed everything I'd been told I had tried to sympathize, tried to understand why he had done what he had done. But now, as he tried to justify the deaths of three of our comrades on the basis of the good of humanity, that was when I saw him for the traitor that he was and felt as Dmitry must have done when he first found out.

TWELVE

"You say that you protect your friends while you abandon your country, but your country isn't just some arbitrary tract of land decided by forgotten generals a hundred years ago. It's your friends' friends and your friends' families. But I suppose you have a bigger intellect than I, Maksim Sergeivich. I can't cope with loving the whole of humanity. I just love what I know."

I paused, hoping my words had struck home, though to what purpose I didn't know. Maks sat silently in his chair, not even looking at me. Suddenly I saw what he had seen. I don't know how they had entered or how long they had been there, but I now perceived in the dim candlelight that standing around us in a circle were Pyetr, Iuda, Filipp, Andrei, Iakov Zevedayinich and Varfolomei.

With regard to Maks, the Oprichniki had their own plans for justice.

Chapter VIII

"I THINK YOU CAN LEAVE US NOW, ALEKSEI IVANOVICH," said Pyetr. He stood directly opposite me, with Maks sitting halfway between us.

"What do you mean?"

"It is three of our fellows who have died at Maksim Sergeivich's hand. It is for us to punish him."

"Maksim Sergeivich is a traitor to his oath as an officer in the Russian army. I am to take him back to Moscow for court-martial," I announced firmly, despite the fact that I was in no position to enforce my will on them.

Pyetr was resolute, speaking almost in a whisper. "He is *ours*."

A thought occurred to me. "How did you know we were here?"

Pyetr didn't have the presence of mind to ignore the question; instead he answered with an obvious lie. "We followed you."

"No, you didn't," I told him. "Otherwise you wouldn't have arrived such a long time after me."

"Dmitry Fetyukovich told us," said Iuda.

"And how did he know?"

"I've no idea. Why don't you go back to Moscow and ask him?" replied Iuda.

"Why don't you go back and ask your whore?" said Filipp, and a few of them laughed the same, grubby laugh that I'd heard before.

Iuda came over and took my arm, leading me aside. I glanced down at Maks and saw that he sat in a petrified silence, smart enough to know that he could not run and could not fight and so frantically searching for an alternative way to escape.

"This is really much the best solution, you know, Aleksei," Iuda said to me smoothly. "You know that he's a traitor and you know that he deserves to die. But do you want it on your conscience that you killed your friend—or even that you took him back to Moscow to be killed?"

I made no answer.

"Do you doubt that he's a traitor?" continued Iuda.

"No."

"So he deserves to die."

"He does."

"And if you leave him here with us"—Iuda's voice had dropped to a whisper—"then you'll always be able to say that you were outnumbered; that whatever you believed to be right didn't matter because if you had resisted, we would still have succeeded by force, and you would both be dead." It was both a cajolement and a threat and it succeeded. I didn't care to ask myself which of the two was the more persuasive.

I went over to Maks and drew his sabre from its scabbard. He was condemned to death and it somehow seemed to lessen the reality of the fact by going through the ritual. I stood in front of him and held the sword above his head, my hands spread wide apart. Maks looked up at me, tears showing behind the lenses of his eyeglasses.

"Please don't do this to me, Aleksei."

"This is what happens to traitors, Maks. You know that," I replied quietly, trying to fill my head with such hatred for his treachery that it would drive out all sympathy.

"Not the sword. I mean, don't leave me with them."

"One death is much like another, Maks," I told him, though I knew even then it was a lie. "Would you prefer it to be done by friends?"

He smiled resignedly and then looked away.

I'd never intentionally broken a sabre before and there was no training for this sort of thing given in the army. The sword bent and bent and bent still further, until the blade was almost doubled back on itself, and yet still it would not break. With my arms outstretched as they were over Maks' head, I was at the limit of what strength I could apply. My muscles began to ache with cramp, screaming at me to relieve them of the strain. It took all my energy to keep the blade at the angle I had achieved, but I was rapidly losing the strength to do even that, let alone to bend it further to its breaking point. Suddenly, with a dissonant chime that reminded me somehow of the hissing of a snake, the steel shattered. Both my arms jarred excruciatingly as the release of the metal's stress echoed through them. My left hand, clutching the sharp blade tightly with its two remaining fingers, began to bleed from a cut across the palm.

Two of the Oprichniki, Filipp and Varfolomei I think, took a step forward to assist me, but Iuda raised an arm to hold them back, understanding that this was something I must do alone.

I remembered what I had been about to say minutes earlier, when the Oprichniki arrived. "How could you of all people, Maks, justify the killing of your fellow man by saying it was in the name of humanity?" I took the two halves of the broken sword, placed them side by side and tossed them dismissively into Maks' lap. Then I turned and walked into the darkness of the night outside.

"But that's the point, Aleksei," screamed Maks after me in desperation. "I thought you understood. They're not—" Whatever they were not (and whoever "they" were), I did not hear. Maks' voice was cut off by a brief, startled yelp as one of the Oprichniki either hit him or . . . I didn't like to think. It was only hours later that I realized that that final sound from Maks was exactly the same cry I had heard from the French soldier, victim of that same terrible group of men, less than a week before in Goryachkino.

Half of my mind had no regrets, and I consoled myself with the knowledge that it was the half with which Maksim himself would have agreed. Taking a step back, I couldn't pity Maks or that French soldier for the way they died, nor could I pity the death of a Russian traitor more than that of a French patriot, nor a foreign mercenary more than a friend of seven years' standing. There's no good way to die and no good reason to die. Death is momentarily unpleasant for those who experience it and often expedient for those who cause it, but the details of the moment of death are not worth worrying about.

The other half of me knew that I had only left Maks there with the Oprichniki out of cowardice. Practical, rational cowardice to be sure (is there any other kind?), but still the fact remained that my intention had been to bring Maks back to Moscow and the reason I hadn't was because of a risk to my own life. Wouldn't that risk have been worth it to give Maks one more hour or one more day of life? Mightn't it have given him one final chance to explain himself in a way that I hadn't so far been able to understand?

As my horse followed its nose and headed back to Moscow with little guidance from me, my mind was filled only with happy memories of the beautiful young man I had just left to die. His treachery, which had concerned me so obsessively for what?—six hours at most—and which had been the cause of his death, was totally forgotten amongst remembrances of his wit, his exuberance and his sparkling cynicism.

In the early hours, as I finally reached the outskirts of Moscow, I realized that although he had been alive when I left him, and though he was, beyond any doubt, dead now, I had no idea of the precise time of Maksim's death, because I had not been there. I recalled the death of my father and my similar ignorance then of its exact moment. I had been scarcely more than a child and my mother had, for what she saw as my protection, kept me out of his room through the last hours of his illness. I remember, as I sat and waited, I had repeatedly wondered how I should be feeling; whether I should be praying for him to survive or mourning the fact that he had not. I had no real concern that getting it wrong would have any practical effect on the fate of my father, but it certainly had an overwhelming bearing on how I felt.

I had vowed then never to make the same mistake—never to walk away and be absent at the moment of a friend's death. And yet here today I had failed to keep that vow, as I would fail again. I could excuse myself of the practical cowardice of allowing the Oprichniki to take him, but there was no defence for my moral cowardice in not staying with him until the end. In any sense that mattered, I had left him to die alone. Worse still, he had known it.

It was morning when I arrived back in Moscow and, in the hours that I had been away, the mood of the city had changed beyond any imagining. The remnants of our army, which Vadim and I had overtaken so easily on the road from Borodino, were now arriving in the city. They were not arriving to regroup, not arriving to make a stand, but arriving because they had nowhere else to go. If they had feared that extra tens of thousands of soldiers would make the city overcrowded, they need not have. As the soldiers were entering, so the civilians were leaving—their confidence of months before in the unreachability of Moscow now vanished. The streets were awash with movement, always from the west, always to the east. Carts piled high with furniture, with fabrics, with silver and with gold, headed out of Moscow, their owners riding up front and keeping a careful eye on their possessions. On some, I could even see the owners, or as often their servants, spread across the goods on the cart like some many-legged spider, trying to keep a hand on every item, so that none might fall by the wayside to be gathered up by the advancing French, who, they were now certain, would soon arrive.

Behind the carts of the people of Moscow came the wagons carrying their wounded defenders. The casualties of Borodino filled any street of the city that was not already occupied by the departing citizens. As one lavishly appointed cartload of property left to the east, it made room for another to enter, loaded with the dying or even the dead. Where the two strata met, there was sometimes a mixing, sometimes a separation. Some of the citizens were repelled by the sight of those who had so bravely fought to defend them, others gladly unloaded their most treasured possessions to make a little room for one wounded soldier to be taken to safety. But while such self-sacrifice might save the life of a single man, it would remove only a drop from the ocean of humanity that was now pouring into the city.

And yet it was one more drop of humanity than I had managed to save that day.

I had no immediate desire to find Vadim and Dmitry. I would have no problem explaining to *them* why I had returned, against Vadim's instructions, without Maks, but I did not relish the doubting voice in my own head that I knew I must hear as I told them. Though why should I listen to that voice now? It had been happy enough to keep a cowardly silence back in Desna. A man's conscience shouts so much more loudly in the past tense than it ever manages to achieve in the present.

If I was not to see Vadim and Dmitry immediately, then there was only one other place in Moscow that I could go. My intention was simple enough. However cowardly and however shocking it might seem, those souls that were now fleeing the city were acting wisely, and I was going to ensure that Domnikiia would be one of them; to ensure that she had a safe place to go and to give her enough money to provide for her food and travel as she made her way there. At the back of my mind was the fear that the abandonment of Moscow might be the furthest thing possible from her inclination. As I pushed my way through the crowded streets, fending off those citizens unfortunate enough to be travelling on foot and pushing away the blindly searching hands of soldiers who lay dying on open carts, I realized that the city would soon be full of French soldiers; rich, victorious and, above all, amorous French soldiers. Domnikiia could make more from them in a day than she had done of late in a week from the crushed Muscovites. Would she, I wondered, find more popularity as the homely, French Dominique who could remind them of their sweethearts back in Paris or as the exotic, erotic and, most importantly, vanquished Russian Domnikiia? But I was, as I knew well by now, no judge of a Russian's patriotism. When I arrived, she was preparing to leave.

Although it was past one o'clock, well into the brothel's normal trading hours, I arrived to find the door closed and locked. I stepped back into the square and threw a stone up at Domnikiia's window. The window opened and out popped the head of Margarita Kirillovna.

"We're closed," she snapped.

"Margarita!" I called. She screwed up her eyes as she tried to recognize me. "Is Domnikiia there?"

Her head disappeared and the window closed again. I waited. Minutes later, I heard the bolts being drawn back at the door. This time, the face that half peeped outside was Domnikiia's. I went over and tried to kiss her, but she smoothly avoided it, beckoning me hurriedly inside and bolting the door behind me. Within, I encountered one of the most beautiful visions of chaos I could ever have imagined. The salon was a mélange of beautiful girls packing their beautiful clothes into trunks, which, though relatively plain, somehow managed to assimilate the beauty of what was going on around them. There were eight girls working at the brothel, and although I had a heart only for one, I had eyes for them all. In their demure, controlled, professional allure they were a temptation to the most puritan of men. In their natural, girlish panic their charm was only augmented by their vitality.

I followed Domnikiia up to her room, where a large trunk took centre stage, half filled with clothes. Margarita came back and forth from her room, adding new layers of attire to the trunk, and as soon as we entered the room, Domnikiia strode over to her wardrobe and began to do the same. She had not spoken a word to me since I had arrived.

As she passed me, I grabbed her wrist and pulled her to me, but this time it was I who aborted our kiss. I had not seen before, since it had been hidden by the door earlier and by her avoiding my direct gaze since, that she had bruises on her right eye and on her high, round cheek. Her upper lip was split just below her right nostril and though it was not a fresh wound, it still oozed blood from where she had reopened it trying to smile. On her jaw I could also see, now I looked closely, the faint bruising of where she had been held by a large, brutal hand.

Although the very conception made me for a moment despise myself more even than I did her assailant, I felt a thrill of attraction for her run through me that was greater than anything I had felt towards her before. Her beauty was accentuated, not hidden, by the vulnerability endowed upon her by those wounds.

I kissed her lips as lightly as I dared, not wanting to hurt her physically, but neither wanting to suggest any diminution of my passion for her as a consequence of these blemishes.

"Who did this to you?"

"I asked you who Dmitry was," she replied acerbically. "I found out."

"He did this?" I tried to sound disbelieving, but just as I was in my heart of hearts unsurprised by the discovery that Maks had been a spy, so I was unsurprised to find that Dmitry could treat a woman like that for his own ends. I'd never known him do it in the past—but there was no inconsistency I could find between the action and what I knew of his character. "He wanted to know where Maks was, I suppose."

TWELVE

She didn't answer, but buried her face in my chest and began to cry. Her self-imposed silence so far had been out of fear that she would be unable to control herself. Now she had told me the one important fact that she had to convey, she indulged herself in the pleasure of the abandonment of self-control, and indulged me in the pleasure of being her comforter. Yet she still had one more thing to tell me.

"But I didn't tell him, Lyosha," she let out through her sobs. "I didn't. I didn't."

I could find in my heart no blame for her for having betrayed Maks to Dmitry, and so I was happy to allow her the deception, both to me and to herself. For me it was a relief that she had had some unarguable justification for telling Dmitry. I had pushed to the back of my mind the suggestion made in Desna by Filipp that Domnikiia had helped them, but it had worried me. Even now, though, I had underestimated Domnikiia.

"*I* told him," said Margarita, still shuttling back and forth between her room and the trunk.

"Why?" I asked.

Margarita looked up from the trunk, slightly surprised. Then she gestured towards Domnikiia with her eyes before looking back at me. "Wouldn't you?"

After a few moments, Domnikiia pulled away from me and continued with her packing.

"Where are you heading to?" I asked.

Domnikiia was still unwilling to talk, so Margarita answered for her. "Yuryev-Polsky." It was a sound choice; 150 versts to the northeast and well off the route that the French would take even if they did march beyond Moscow. If they were to go any further, it was generally assumed, it would be northwestward, towards Petersburg. If the fall of Moscow did not precipitate the fall of Russia then the capture of Petersburg—so the French would reason—most surely would.

"Do you need money?" I asked, taking from my pocket a wad of bank-notes, which I had intended to give to them—well, to Domnikiia at any rate.

"No," Margarita replied, then, realizing she sounded ungrateful, added, "but thank you. Pyetr Pyetrovich is taking care of all of us."

I tried to show no reaction to the name. Pyetr Pyetrovich was the owner of the building in which I now stood and—in effect, if not in law—the owner of Domnikiia, Margarita and the other girls. On the few occasions when I had met him, he had seemed most amiable and to be completely understanding of my reasons for visiting Domnikiia. But, just as the girls themselves would change their personalities to please the tastes of the client at hand, I'm sure that he would be all things to all men, so that he might gain their custom.

"Protecting his business?"

"I suppose," replied Margarita.

Domnikiia came away from her packing and, with a murmured "thank you," took two of the banknotes from my hand. It wasn't a huge amount, but it was strange how the significance of money in our relationship had become so inverted over the past few days. When I paid her for sex, it had been a symbol of our distance—our independence. Now she took it from me for nothing, to show that she would rather be dependent on me than on Pyetr Pyetrovich. That, at least, was my interpretation.

"When are you leaving?" I asked.

"Tomorrow," Margarita told me. "First thing."

"I'll come and see you again this evening," I said and made to leave.

"I'll have to let you out," said Margarita.

"No, I'll go," Domnikiia told her, her voice now returning to something of its familiar brightness.

"Are you going to be all right?" I asked her at the door.

"We'll be fine," she said casually. "Yuryev-Polsky is a nice long way away."

"No, I meant you." I raised my hand to stroke her bruised cheek, but refrained for fear of hurting her. She took my hand in hers and pressed it against her face, caressing it and once again running her fingers over what remained of mine.

"These wounds will heal," she said. "It was just that . . . It's been a long time." She smiled, almost nostalgically. "I'd got used to not being beaten. That's what makes it worth working for Pyetr Pyetrovich."

I felt her fingers on mine and I knew what she meant. Even wounds like mine, which would never heal, can be forgotten. But the terror of how they were inflicted cannot. A deep hatred for Dmitry welled up inside me. In my concern for Domnikiia, I'd almost forgotten that it was my friend who had done this to her; my friend and therefore my fault. And since there was little I could do to physically punish myself, all my anger became focused on him. *He* had caused her this pain, *he* had sent the Oprichniki after me and Maks and *he* had torn apart my world by exposing Maks as a spy in the first place.

"I'm going to find Dmitry," I said, making it clear from my tone what I intended to do when I found him. Then I kissed her. "I'll see you this evening."

I had half expected her to make some plea for me to be lenient on Dmitry, but none came. I admired her all the more for her desire for retribution. As I walked away, I heard the sound of the heavy bolts being drawn across the door behind me.

I went back to the inn and still found no sign of Dmitry or Vadim, but there was a note slipped under my door. It read simply:

8-30-11-Ч7-ВД

We would meet the following day, the thirtieth of August, at eleven in the morning at location Ч7. This meant on the south bank of the Moskva, opposite the Kremlin. The initials "В" and "Д" indicated that it was from both Vadim and Dmitry. With the enemy almost upon us, it was a wise precaution for us not all to be billeted in one place. I was lucky that they had already made the decision and thus I was the one who did not have to relocate—at least not for the time being.

That afternoon I wrote two letters. The first was to Marfa. There was not much of importance to tell. I mentioned the Battle of Borodino—skipping over my small part in it—and the debate as to whether it was a defeat or a victory, and then went on to downplay the evacuation of Moscow. It was all really just padding before I got on to the subject of Maks. Maks had stayed with us in Petersburg for several months after his repatriation in 1807 and Marfa had met him a few times since, becoming quite fond of him.

I told her as close to the truth as I dared; that he had been a French spy, that he had sent some comrades to their deaths at the hands of the French, that he had confessed it and that he had been executed. Reading back through my sanitized account, I could see that no one could have any reason to feel sympathy for Maks. No one would question that he deserved to die for his treason, or even blame me for letting the Oprichniki carry out the sentence. So I added a few words in defence of Maks, the same defence which still led me to question my own actions. I wrote of his idealism, his admiration for the Revolution and for Bonaparte and of his refusal, in spite of all these, to do anything that would betray his true friends.

The second letter was to Maksim's mother, Yelizaveta Malinovna. I had never met her—she lived far away in the south, in Saratov—but Maks had often spoken of her, not with fondness (that was not his style) but with, I suppose, loyalty. I laughed to myself as the word entered my head, but I had to admit that Maks was no less loyal than most, his loyalty was simply placed elsewhere. Maks' father had died of dysentery when Maks was very young. His only other close relatives were two sisters, but I didn't know where they lived. Yelizaveta Malinovna would forward the tragic news. In my letter to her I made no mention of treachery. Maksim had died like a hero fighting the French. I was unable, I explained, to give full details for reasons of national security, but I gave enough background for her to infer, once the histories of the war had been published, that he had died bravely at Borodino.

After I had written the two letters, recounting Maks' death to both my wife and his mother, I realized that I had completely forgotten to tell Domnikiia. In hindsight, it may have been a wise decision. She had to be told, but the timing and the approach had to be well considered. That, however, hadn't been the reason for my not telling her. It had simply slipped my mind. The death of one of my closest friends, with my collaboration, at which I had wept all through my journey back from Desna, had been pushed out of my mind by the sight of a few bruises on my lover's face. I was a very fickle man.

True to my promise, I returned to see Domnikiia that evening. As I made my way through the city, the streets still pulsated with the flow of people and their possessions and of retreating soldiers. The proportion of soldiers was increasing as more and more wounded came into the city. Some could walk, others were carried on stretchers by their companions and still others lay, conscious or otherwise, on flat wagons, the dying mixed indiscriminately with the dead. It may not have been that all of the 30,000 Russian casualties came through the city over those few days, but it seemed very close to it.

When I arrived, the brothel was still closed and the door bolted. This time, a stone at the window attracted the attention of Domnikiia herself. She came down and I suggested that we should walk for a while. We were away from the main thoroughfares of the city and so the streets and squares were a little quieter. We were not the only couple that wandered the streets of Moscow that night, hand in hand, knowing that they would soon be parted.

After some talk and some silence, I came to the point.

"Maks is dead," I announced quietly.

"I didn't like to ask."

We walked on in silence for a little longer. "Don't you want to know what happened?"

"Yes," she replied, "but you don't have to tell me."

"He was a traitor." I didn't offer any more detail and I felt confident she wouldn't ask.

"I liked him," she said after a pause. To her, as to me, liking him was quite orthogonal to his being a spy. There are likable traitors and hateful patriots.

"So did I."

"Did he know that?"

"Yes," I said with a misunderstanding laugh. "We'd known each other seven years." Except, of course, I hadn't completely known him.

"I mean at the end. Did he know that you *still* liked him?"

Did it really matter what a man felt in the last few minutes of his life, compared with all the things he's felt in the years leading up to that? Perhaps now, less than a day after Maks' death, those final minutes mattered more than they would in ten years' time when his whole life could be viewed from a distance. Mattered more to me, I meant, not to him. I doubted whether I could have gone through with it—gone through with leaving him to the Oprichniki—if my final thoughts or my final words to him had been of friendship. I had pushed all such ideas out of my mind with thoughts of him as a traitor. Although our liking of Maks could be quite independent of our knowledge of his treachery, in the final reckoning of him, one had to be counted as outweighing the other. In Desna, Maks' treachery had been the weightier matter, but the scales still fluctuated hour by hour, reluctant to reveal the side on which they would finally come to rest.

I said nothing in reply to Domnikiia's question.

"What are *you* going to do?" she asked after a while.

"About what?"

"Are you going to stay in the city?"

"I don't know. I'll talk with Vadim and Dmitry tomorrow."

She stopped and turned to me, speaking with a new intensity. "Why don't you leave with me in the morning?"

It was tempting, but I knew my cowardice and my self-centredness could only reveal themselves in more subtle situations, where they could hide within a maze of soul-searching analysis. To abandon my fellow men and my country to an invading enemy for the sake of a woman—that would be too blatant a betrayal of my duty.

"Russia needs me more than ever now." It sounded pretentious, but I meant it genuinely. "There's a lot we can do to undermine Bonaparte's army once it gets here."

"So you're staying?"

"That's my guess."

"And if you have to leave?"

"I know where you'll be."

"And if you're killed?"

Again, Domnikiia had asked a question to which I could find no reply.

We were back at the door of the brothel. We stood facing one another, her hands in mine, with nothing more to say, but not wanting to say what could well be our final goodbye.

We heard the sound of the bolts being drawn from inside. The door

TWELVE

opened to reveal Margarita, who must have seen our approach. She pulled the door open further to reveal another figure—tall, blond-haired and pale.

"Good evening, Aleksei Ivanovich," he said.

It was Iuda.

CHAPTER IX

IN MY SHOCK I SQUEEZED DOMNIKIIA'S HANDS SO TIGHTLY that I made her flinch. The surprise at seeing Iuda there was quickly followed by questions. Why was he there? How had he known where to find me? The answer to the latter came to me easily—Dmitry. I felt more than ever that Dmitry's feet were both far too firmly planted in the Oprichnik camp.

"Aren't you going to introduce me to this delightful young lady?" Iuda continued with a smile. It had taken me a moment to realize that he was speaking Russian, and extremely fluent Russian at that. Previously, we had communicated with the Oprichniki in nothing but French. I scoured my memory for any conversations that we—Vadim, Dmitry, Maks and I—might have had in their presence under the assumption that we would not be understood.

"I'm Dominique," Domnikiia told him, holding out her hand. As he kissed it, gazing throughout upward into her eyes, I once again felt a certain secret pride that to others she was still Dominique. I was one of the few who knew her by her Russian name.

"People call me Iuda," he replied. "I was just saying to my old friend, Margarita Kirillovna"—Margarita giggled as he spoke—"how much I've come to admire Aleksei since we've been working together."

"Old friend?" I asked with a raised eyebrow.

"Of all of five minutes," said Margarita. "He said he'd come here to find you. It didn't seem right to let him wait outside. He says he's going to save us from the French."

"Not by myself," protested Iuda, falsely it seemed to me, but others might have been convinced. "I am merely a tool to do as Aleksei Ivanovich wishes."

"Did you know Maksim as well?" asked Domnikiia. She wanted to talk about him, but knew that it was difficult for me.

"Not well," replied Iuda, "but what I knew I liked. I can't agree with his reasons for turning to France, but I'm sure he did what he did with an honest heart and for what he thought was the good of humanity."

I was astonished at his duplicity. It was he who had forced me to hand over Maks to him and the others, and here he was quoting Maks' own words back at me. What was more, he had completely boxed me in. If I were to take a contrary position now, then I would be attacking Maks. I realized how much wiser it would have been to tell Domnikiia every detail in the first place.

"I know that you had a dreadful decision to make, Aleksei," he continued, putting his hand on my arm and displaying a look of intense sincerity in his eyes, "but I know too that, deep down, you feel that you were right in what you did. It's never easy to place one's country above one's friends. I too have lost some dear friends in this war, Aleksei. My heart goes out to you. Your friend Maks"—and now he was addressing Domnikiia directly—"was a brave man until the end." The pause between "man" and "until" was heard only by my ears.

She took his hand and held it in hers. "Thank you, Iuda," she said. "Thank you for saying that about Maks." He lifted her right hand and kissed it again. Then he raised his hat to both Margarita and Domnikiia.

"Goodbye, dear friends. I hope you both enjoy your time in Yuryev-Polsky. If Aleksei is half the soldier I know him to be, we'll soon have the city safe for you again." Then, turning to me, "I'm sure you have goodbyes to say, Aleksei. I'll wait for you." He walked away, over towards the bench from which I'd first seen Domnikiia, almost a year before.

I noticed both women following his departure with smiling faces. I raised my hat to Margarita, feeling that the gesture would be seen only as a pale imitation of Iuda. "Goodbye then, Margarita Kirillovna. I hope we shall meet again soon."

Margarita smiled and then, after a moment, realized that it was she that I intended to be the one to depart. "Oh, right," she said. "Don't leave the door open for too long." She went inside.

"I should have known you wanted to talk about Maksim," I said to Domnikiia.

"Oh, that's all right"—she spoke with concern at the thought of having caused me any worry—"I know you don't want to. But it was good to hear Iuda say such nice things about him. He seems like a decent man to have on your side. That's not his real name, is it?" It took me a moment to realize that the question was in jest.

"No," I laughed. "No, it's not, but I have no idea what his name really is."

"You'd better go. He's waiting."

We kissed for what seemed like only a moment, although no length of time could ever have been enough, and then she went inside, the sound of the bolts bringing home the truth of a separation that, for all I knew, might never be ended.

I went over to Iuda. Sitting next to him on the bench, after a covert, silent arrival, was Matfei.

"What do you want?" I asked, failing to disguise my hostility.

"Firstly," said Iuda, "I wanted to confirm for you that Maksim Sergeivich is dead. I know that in these situations any slight doubt can be cankerous."

"Did you bring him back for burial?"

"Hardly practical, I'm afraid, in these dangerous times, but trust me, the body was dealt with properly." He saw my expression. "Remember, Aleksei Ivanovich, we too come from a Christian country," he said, with a genuine desire to convince me.

I realized I was being churlish. We were still on the same side. "Thank you," I said. "And the second thing?"

"To decide what we're going to do next; militarily."

"I don't know. I've got to discuss it with Vadim, Dmitry and . . ." it was a reflex . . . "with Vadim and Dmitry."

"We have, to be honest, already spoken with Vadim. We think it would be best if we were to stay hidden in Moscow when the French arrive. Then we can cause the maximum disruption. We can either weaken them, so that they dare not carry on to Petersburg, or even force them to leave Moscow altogether."

"Just the twelve of you to liberate Moscow? Nine of you now." I suddenly noticed the equal ratios of our losses and remembered that they too were men and would be grieving the loss of their friends no less than I did that of Maks.

TWELVE

Iuda became colder and spoke like an artisan whose workmanship has been insulted. "You have already seen what just a few of us are capable of."

"True enough." In all honesty, it sounded like a good plan. The sort of tactics that I'd seen the Oprichniki use weren't best suited to attacking an army on the march. But an army at rest, far from home in a strange city—that was another story. "Where do we come in?" I asked.

"We know Moscow as little as the French do. You can tell us where to hide; where to find the enemy. You can pass yourselves off as residual Russians or as French officers—as I have already seen. We are neither Russian nor French. Most of us would soon be found out." He glanced towards Matfei as he spoke. Iuda knew well enough, as I had heard, that his Russian would convince most natives, let alone the French invaders. It was for his less accomplished confederates, such as Matfei, that he was concerned.

I considered for a moment. "I'll discuss it with Vadim and Dmitry tomorrow. Where shall we meet?"

"We've already arranged such details with Vadim. He'll tell you."

With that they both rose and walked off into the night. Through the darkness I could see that Matfei soon turned off the street and the two of them went their separate ways. It occurred to me that Matfei, who had said nothing during the conversation, could only have come along to offer Iuda protection. I could not see Iuda bringing him for the pleasure of his company. Clearly, the only person that Iuda might need protecting from was me.

And so I had discovered two things. Firstly, that Iuda appreciated that, after what had happened to Maks, he could not entirely trust me as an ally. Secondly, that if it were to come to a clash between us, Iuda was not completely convinced he would win.

I had said goodbye to Domnikiia, but it was not to be the last time I saw her before she left Moscow. Iuda and Matfei's appearance at the brothel had filled me with concern. It was clear enough that Dmitry had told them that it would be a good place to find me and, once there, Iuda had observed for himself my relationship with Domnikiia. It was also evident that he had found out from Margarita that they were travelling to Yuryev-Polsky. It could all, of course, be put down to paranoia. Iuda had no argument with me and, even if he did, that would not mean he would try to get to me through Domnikiia. On the other hand, I was unable to sleep until I had at least seen her safe departure.

The streets were quieter than during the day. Those carts and carriages that were about were mostly tied up for the night, their occupants sleeping in them ready for the day's journey ahead. I found myself a vantage point some way down the street from her door and waited, looking out for any sign of the Oprichniki as well as for Domnikiia. It was just after six o'clock when, lit by the sun's early rays and heralded by the dawn chorus, three covered wagons pulled up outside the brothel door. The door opened and the three coachmen went inside, returning with trunks and bags, which they loaded on to the rear wagon. They repeated their journey again and again, until the wagon was almost full. Then out processed eight girls and a man. The man was Pyetr Pyetrovich, a personage of ostentatious but undeniable wealth. How else could he afford three coaches when members of the richest families in Moscow were trading in their most valued heirlooms for a single seat on a hay cart?

I felt a thrill of satisfaction as I focused upon Domnikiia amongst the girls. It was an inexplicably exciting sensation. I could have gone up to greet Domnikiia face to face if I had wanted to. If she had known that I was there watching, she would not have minded in the slightest. And yet for some unknown reason, I gained a far greater enjoyment from viewing her in secret.

Pyetr Pyetrovich locked his door with a large key. Four of the girls climbed into the front wagon and four into the middle one. Domnikiia was the last to clamber into the middle wagon. I realized that any fears I had about Iuda and the Oprichniki were just self-delusion. All I had wanted was one more momentary glimpse of her.

Pyetr Pyetrovich got on to the front wagon beside the coachman, and the convoy set off. As the carriage turned the corner I caught one brief final sight of Domnikiia sitting there, calm and, little though it suited her, demure.

She was safely on her way out of Moscow, and of the Oprichniki there had been no sign.

I returned to bed and managed a few hours of thankful sleep before setting out for my appointment with Vadim and Dmitry. Progress was slow, as in daylight the streets once again thronged with people, horses, carts and wagons. On one corner, a crowd was gathered around a man who was tied to a tree and being flogged. Although it was not they who were being flogged, fear showed on every face in the crowd—a fear of the coming invaders which they tried and failed to forget by gazing on this spectacle. Amongst them was an artillery sublieutenant, relaxing with a clay pipe and watching the beating with a smile.

"What did he do?" I asked.

"He was a footman," came the artilleryman's incongruous reply.

"I mean, why is he being flogged?"

"Oh, I see." He tried a clearer explanation. "He's French."

"How did he get here then?"

"He's lived here for years. They dragged him out from over there." He indicated a large, well-appointed house of the type one would expect to have French servants. "They say he's a spy."

"Has he been tried?"

"Nope." He drew deeply on his pipe. "That's why they're only flogging him." I couldn't help but wish that other suspected French spies had been treated with such leniency.

"Shouldn't you do something to stop them?" I demanded.

He turned to me and I saw for the first time that his right eye was missing, the socket scarcely beginning to heal over the all-too-fresh wound. He spoke with passion.

"Stop them? I stood and watched as half my platoon was blown to pieces by a single French shell. You think I had this done"—he gestured towards his missing eye—"just so I could look like General Kutuzov? When civvies like this lot decide to take some revenge on my behalf, you think I'm going to do anything when a damned civvy like you asks me to stop them? You go fight for yourself before you tell a soldier what to do."

As usual, I wasn't in uniform, and though I could have shown him my papers to prove my rank, what business was it of mine? From stories I heard later, the man was lucky he was only being flogged.

I carried on towards the Moskva. The crammed streets became even more slow moving. Whatever desperation had inspired the people to flee the city had failed to translate into any keenness in their actual progress. Crowds like the one that had gathered around the flogging did not help, since even those people who didn't stop and cause the obstruction slowed down to get a view of what was going on as they passed.

Along Nikitskiy Street, I came to another constriction in the flow of traffic. A small, flat cart pulled by two grenadiers from the line infantry had come to a halt. On it, lying crossways, side by side, were three of their comrades, their uniforms tattered and bloody. There was an argument between the two men—boys really—who had been pulling the wagon, and two other soldiers—both dragoons, forced to travel on foot. Of these two, one—the one who was in reality doing all the arguing—was in reasonably good shape. His friend was in a sorry condition. His head hung limply, without the desire to look again on anything above the ground. He supported himself on a makeshift crutch; just a conveniently sized branch with a fork in it, which was crammed into his armpit. The need for his crutch became all too apparent as I scanned down his body. His left foot and lower leg hung loosely off the rest of him, just below the knee. Of the shinbone, there was clearly nothing left, and it was only flesh and skin that kept the limb attached. As the cart moved on a little and he took a few steps to keep up, his leg trailed behind him uselessly, dragging in the dirt like the tails of an adult's coat worn by a child. Most likely, the wound had come from a cannonball, bouncing inexorably towards him across the battlefield of Borodino. Whatever the cause, the leg should have been amputated at a dressing station in the field, but at that great battle, the demand for surgery had far outstripped supply, and it looked as though the injured soldier's comrade had helped get him all the way to Moscow in hope of finding room in a hospital. Now, the argument was over a place on the cart.

"But the man's dead!" said the limping dragoon's friend, indicating the middle of the three men lying on the cart. "Throw him off and give his place to someone who still has a chance."

"He's not dead," insisted one of the cart-pullers. "He's been like that for days, ever since we picked him up. If he was dead he'd be rotting by now. Your mate smells worse than he does."

TWELVE

It was sadly true. The gangrene that had set in to the man's wound had most likely already spread far enough to take his whole leg, if not his life. I pushed my way forward to examine the man on the wagon.

It was plain enough to see; he was most certainly dead.

His face and arms and neck bore many cuts and scratches, but none that seemed to be the cause of his death. His dark green uniform was stained with unimaginable amounts of blood, which may well have belonged to others, but, if it was his, explained not only his death, but also the terrible pallor of his skin. There was no sign of breathing, no hint of a heartbeat and his body was as cold as water. I lifted his eyelids and looked into his dead, threatening eyes. The huge black pupils—grown so large that his irises were obliterated—gave no response to the light of the sun.

"He *is* dead," I announced, trying to convey an authority which would achieve the end of getting that poor, limping man on to the cart.

"So why doesn't he rot?" asked one of the men who had been hauling him across the city. It certainly was an odd phenomenon. It might have been the case, of course, that he had been alive when they started out and had only died recently, though to judge by his temperature, not all that recently—at least a day ago. But he was undoubtedly dead now.

"I don't know," I said, giving the accurate impression that I didn't much care either. I began to drag the body from the cart.

"Wait!" The voice belonged to a priest who had emerged from somewhere amongst the onlookers. He spoke softly, but thanks to the resonance of his voice and the eminence of his occupation, he commanded immediate respect from the crowd.

"There may be a reason for this," he said, approaching the body. He gave it much the same examination as I had done, but with a little more of the showmanship that, I am sorry to have to say, one expects from a priest. "He is dead. The gentleman is quite correct." People looked at me and nodded, happier with my conclusion now that it had been confirmed by someone they could trust. "And he has been dead many days." This was more than I had been prepared to venture. "And yet the body does not decay."

The priest lifted the corpse's hand and kissed it. He then took a step back from the cart and closed his eyes for a moment of silent prayer, opening them again to make his pronouncement.

"When a holy man dies—a man who is without sin or a man whose sins have been forgiven—then there is no need for his sins to leave his corporeal remains. The putrefaction of a man's body is caused by the departure of his sins. If there are no sins to depart, then there cannot be decay. I have seen this in the bodies of many departed priests and monks, but to see it in a common soldier is rare. And yet there is no reason why a soldier cannot be without sin. This man must have led the most saintly of lives."

I missed the point completely. "But now he's dead, he can still be removed to make way for the living," I said.

"No, no, my son," explained the priest, shaking his head with a paternal smile. "The body of a man like this deserves greater respect than that of any living sinner. Leave him there. His blessings will spread to the two men who lie on either side of him. And to you too," he added, turning to the two men pulling the cart.

Once the priest had spoken, there was no room for argument. The two men heaved and the cart trundled along down the street, accompanied by a swarm of believers, interested to see more of the miracle that the priest had just described. They would have been more at home on the streets of Nazareth than on those of Moscow. The wounded man and his companion continued on foot. His footsteps repeated in turn the abrupt click of his crutch, the firm tread of his booted right foot and then the long, pointless scrape of his dangling left.

I walked with them for a while, away from where I should have been heading, stopping every cart and wagon that came past to see if it had any room for an extra, wounded man. It was about the tenth one I asked that did and so we hauled him aboard. His friend thanked me profoundly and walked alongside the wagon with a new spring in his step. The wounded man didn't understand enough even to raise his head and look at me. Whatever last vestige of life remained in him had been wholly focused on walking, on keeping on walking, as he had done all the way from Borodino to Moscow. Perhaps now he was being carried, his last reason to stay alive had been taken from him. I doubted that there would ultimately be much difference in the fate of a dead man whose body did not rot and a live one whose leg was rotting away beneath him.

I turned around and headed back the way I had come. It was already past eleven, so I hurried to make it to my meeting with Vadim and Dmitry. I crossed the once beautiful Red Square which, now deserted, could be seen in all its glory. Yet that glory was reduced to almost nothing by the absence of any people to enjoy it or even to ignore it. Red Square was near the very centre of the city; a city that everyone was trying to leave. And so, like the eye of the most fearful storm, it was the quietest place on earth.

As I passed Saint Vasily's and moved on to the Moskva Bridge, which stood beside the Kremlin spanning the river, the swarming crowds began to increase again. All were heading in the opposite direction from me, slowing my progress. Amongst them were a hundred soldiers with a hundred stories, each as pitiful as that of the men I had just encountered, but none of whom I could help. I realized suddenly how pointless it was for me to fret over issues that affected me and only me when all around the life of every one of my fellow countrymen was in turmoil. My concern for Maks and my concern even for myself seemed to become lost in this sea of faces. What observer, seeing the bridge with any degree of perspective, could single me out from the crowds through which I pushed my way? To any outside viewer, the global impact of this migration of a city's populace would have far greater significance than not just my own story, but the story of any one of us. Moscow was dying, and what was the fate of any single Muscovite against that? One might as well consider the fate of the individual cells in that poor soldier's gangrenous leg and forget the impending death of the whole man. Even the Lord God, Who could see inside the soul of every man on that bridge, would surely see in mine no greater cause for interest than in any other.

The temptation struck me to just lie back, to let the flow of the crowd take me in a direction of their choosing, not of mine, since whichever way I went, no one would notice. But someone, I knew, *would* notice. God might not be able to act as a constant sentinel in each of our lives, but He appoints as His deputy ourselves. In the very act of asking who cares what happens to me or to Vadim or to Domnikiia or to the memory of Maks, I provided at least one answer: myself. And by even mentioning those names, I reminded myself of others who, if they were to view the Moskva Bridge from the surface of the moon, would still pick me out from those around me.

I pressed on. Looking across the river to the far bank, I saw Vadim and Dmitry waiting for me. I raised my arm to greet them, but I was not sure whether they had seen me. At that moment, a hand grabbed my coat.

I turned and saw that it was a wounded soldier, lying on one of the open wagons which had been rattling past. The traffic had stopped moving once again and the man pulled me towards him.

"You!" He hissed at me with unspeakable hatred. "You fiend! You monster! You devil!"

He lay back again, exhausted by the effort of speaking, but the fact that he had said all this to me in French reminded me of who he was; for, the last time we had spoken, he had revealed to me an expert knowledge not of the French language, but of Russian. It was Pierre, the young French officer whose camp we had infiltrated, and whom we had left to the absent mercy of the Oprichniki.

CHAPTER X

"FOR GOD'S SAKE, SPEAK RUSSIAN IF YOU WANT TO LIVE another five minutes," I whispered to him fiercely.

"What do you mean?" he said, continuing to speak in French. He had acquired a Russian cuirassier's uniform from somewhere and so clearly had at some stage been trying to pass himself off, but it seemed to have been temporarily forgotten.

"You're in the centre of Moscow, Pierre. Speak Russian," I continued under my breath, hoping that even if he didn't understand where he was, he would instinctively respond to my Russian with the same.

"Why am I in Moscow?" he asked, at last using the vernacular.

"You must have been taken for a casualty." I still spoke quietly. Although he no longer spoke in French, anyone overhearing might soon work out his true nationality. No one seemed much concerned with our conversation however. Most of the crowd was pushing forward to see what was the cause of the latest holdup. "Where did you get the uniform?"

"Uniform?" He looked down at his body and saw what he was wearing. Even then, he seemed to think my question trivial. "I took it from a corpse after I escaped from you." He looked at me again and his earlier vitriol reemerged. "You! Why did you do that? We may be the enemy, but we're not *animals*."

He had a wound to his right cheek which made each word an agony to him. This at least meant that he was unable to raise his voice. The cheek was not quite cut through, but most of the skin was missing, carved away by two jagged, parallel score marks. Whatever had done it had both cut the skin and begun to flay it in a single stroke. He had a similar wound on the side of his neck—any closer to the front and it would have been fatal.

"It wasn't me," I told him. "When I left you, you were well. You'd just insulted the tsar," I continued, encouraging him to remember. I was desperate to hear how the Oprichniki operated.

He raised his hand to his wounds as if trying to recall. His forearm bore an injury similar to the others. Clearly, Pierre had tried to fend off his attacker. Again a chunk of skin and flesh had been scraped off in a strip about the width of two fingers. It could have been inflicted by claws or teeth, but, knowing who it was that had attacked him, I immediately recalled the glimpse I had seen of Iuda's strange, double-bladed knife.

He peered at me closely. "You're right," he said. "You and the other one did leave, and then some more of you came. But you must have been there!" He tried to raise his voice. I shook my head and put my hand on his shoulder to calm him. "Or at least you paved the way for them." That I couldn't completely deny.

"What happened when they came?" I asked, urging him on.

He fixed his eyes upon mine, but in his mind he was seeing that campsite near Borodino, five days previously. His description flickered between lucidity and incoherence. "We didn't see them. Men started vanishing—over minutes, not hours. We were eating at the same time as they were. You'd turn away to get something and turn back and your neighbour was gone. Not everyone ate. Then Louis found them. And the bodies—among the bodies. We were so few left. They circled us. Stalked us. Weren't they satisfied? They moved so quickly. And killed. They could see through the darkness. I fought one off. Louis fought. It took two of them. I ran. They chased me. Spread out like wolves. Calling to each other like huntsmen. But I was fast—so fast—so afraid. They gave up. Louis screamed, but I was fast."

He seemed proud of his speed. He had the build of a runner, and the Oprichniki looked to me the sort that would soon give up a chase if it became too swift.

Pierre's eyes focused on me once again. He shook his head, almost imperceptibly. "You weren't there. You couldn't have done that. But you knew. You must have known." A realization dawned in his eyes. "You sent them! They weren't Russian. We weren't *their* enemy. They had no reason to do that—not once they were satisfied."

It was the second time he'd used the word. "What do you mean—
'satisfied'?" I asked him, but he had collapsed back on to the wagon. His eyes
were still open, but his breathing was shallow and he showed no sign of
recognition of the world around him. "Pierre," I persisted, "what did you
mean?" There was no answer. How could the Oprichniki be satisfied? What
had he meant by that? A soldier isn't satisfied until the enemy is defeated—
or surrenders. Did he mean that they wouldn't accept surrender when it was
offered? Or had he meant that the Oprichniki had been after some sort of
information—that they were satisfied once they'd been told what they
wanted to know? I tried to imagine what the Oprichniki could possibly want
to discover from the occupants of a French encampment—and what they
would do with the information now they had it.

There was a slight commotion amongst the crowd and I saw that the
traffic ahead was beginning to move again. It was clear that I would get no
more from Pierre. I bent over and whispered in his ear, not knowing whether
he could hear me. "Next time you wake up, remember to speak Russian."

The wagon began to roll away. It hadn't even occurred to me that this
was a French soldier disguised in a Russian uniform—an infiltrator and a spy
who should be arrested and executed as such. But I had felt no personal
betrayal, as I had with Maks. It became clear again that there was no line of
thought I could take that did not, eventually, end in Maks.

"Aleksei!" Vadim's voice was full of enthusiasm, and he grabbed me in a
hearty, embrace which I gratefully returned. It had been a long two days since
I had seen him last. Dmitry stood beside us. He might not have shown his
affection in that way at the best of times, but today he was wary of me. We quietly assessed each other; he trying to judge how much I knew; I trying to decide
how I really felt about him. Initially he was just Dmitry—the same Dmitry I
had known for years; slightly distant, sometimes selfish, sometimes blinkered,
but fundamentally reliable. I had to remind myself that he had sent the
Oprichniki after me to Desna and that was why Maks was dead, or at least dead
sooner and less properly than he might otherwise have been. I had plenty of evidence now of how the Oprichniki worked. I could hold out little hope that they
had treated Maks any differently. I had to remind myself that it was Dmitry

who had left Domnikiia bruised and bleeding in order to get the information that he couldn't get from me. As we spoke, I let the memories and the images of Maks and Domnikiia flow over me in a rising tide of venom that I knew I would need if I was to take any action against Dmitry.

"So where's Maks?" asked Vadim.

"Why don't you ask him?" I replied, nodding towards Dmitry.

"No, Aleksei," said Vadim sternly, sensing that order needed to be maintained, "I'm asking you."

"I went to Desna—that's where Maks had gone—and found him there." I was looking at Dmitry throughout, trying to gauge his reaction to each thing that I said, searching for something that would help me to hate him. "We talked for a while."

"Did he confess?" asked Vadim.

And that of course was the reality of it. However much I might bemoan the injustice of what had happened, there was no doubt as to his guilt. "Yes, he confessed. You know Maksim. He wouldn't waste time lying about what we already knew."

"Was he ashamed? Repentant?" Vadim could tell that my story was not going to be completely straightforward.

"No." I would have smiled at the memory of Maks' consistency, but I knew that I could allow myself no such self-indulgence that would soften me in my resolve against Dmitry. "For him, it was just the logical conclusion of a long chain of reason. To dissuade him from his path, you'd have to dissuade two and two from being four."

"So where is he, Aleksei?" Vadim was now overtly suspicious. "I appreciate it wouldn't be wise to bring him here to Moscow. Did you manage to find some gaol that would take him?"

"No, Vadim. He's still in Desna. He always will be."

"Still in Desna?" Then he cottoned on. "Aleksei, you didn't . . . ?"

"No, Vadim, *I* didn't." My voice became harsh and I paced around them until I was behind Dmitry. "But Maks and I weren't alone for long, were we, Dmitry Fetyukovich? Soon your friends the Oprichniki showed up, didn't they? And they wanted to exact vengeance for themselves. And how did they know where we were?" I was shouting in Dmitry's ear by now. "Because Dmitry Fetyukovich told them. And how did he know? Because he beat up a mere girl to make her tell him. And so the Oprichniki made it very clear that either I left Maks with them, or I wouldn't leave at all. And so I left— not to save my own skin, but to give me a chance to get hold of Dmitry Fetyukovich and do this!"

I punched him sharply in the kidney. He bent forward, clutching his side. I placed my hands on his back, pushing him down on to my knee as I raised it sharply into his chest. He gasped, but still offered no retaliation. He was a bigger man than I and, from what I knew, a better fighter. I guessed that he had decided to take what was coming to him like a stoic. If he expected compassion from me at this reaction, he was to be surprised—as indeed was I. I had soaked myself in the anger generated by what he'd done to Domnikiia and Maks and, now, for one of the few times in my life, I was beyond my own control. I kicked his legs from under him and he collapsed to the ground, leaving himself prone for my repeated sharp kicks to his chest and stomach. As each blow connected, I thought to myself alternately "Maks!" and "Domnikiia!" and felt the same joy each time, as if I had been with them instead of here. I felt an energy throbbing through my leg as I kicked at him; an energy desperate to get out of me and into him. My entire mind and body abandoned themselves to the sensation. I no longer saw anything and no longer sensed anything except the feeling of exhilaration each time my foot pounded into his torso. It flooded my entire being, not as a pleasant sensation, but an all-consuming one. It was like the spasm that rips through one's body whilst vomiting, as I regurgitated on to Dmitry the hatred for him that I had nurtured within my belly.

"Aleksei! Aleksei! Captain Danilov!" I must have heard my name shouted half a dozen times before it penetrated my consciousness. Vadim had dragged me away from Dmitry, though I still tried to kick towards him. Something of a crowd of passersby had gathered round. Some were bent down over Dmitry, seeing if he was all right.

I breathed deeply. I felt satisfied—physically satisfied. Every extremity of my body felt that it had done its job and now, as a whole, I—almost as if it were "we"—began to calm. I looked over to Dmitry's aching body and felt a pulse of guilt pass through me. Not guilt—pity. I pitied Dmitry's pain without feeling guilt at causing it. The glance from Dmitry's anguished eyes, as well as my own rational mind, told me that what I had done was allowable. Vadim himself confirmed it.

"That's enough, Aleksei Ivanovich. You were owed that—Dmitry knows it too—but we still have a war to fight. The next time you do that, do it to a Frenchman."

Dmitry was rising to his feet. He lifted his hand for me to take and help him up, but I couldn't. I'd been in the army long enough to see many savage brawls that might have terminated with the death of either man, and yet seen those same men laughing and drinking together hours later. In this and many other things, I could not be as trivial as that. I couldn't belittle my own loss of control with something as easy as a handshake. It had frightened me and it should frighten Dmitry, and anyone else who saw it, to deter them from raising that wrath in me again. At the same time, I realized that the possibility that I hadn't lost control frightened me even more than the belief that I had. If the unrestrained violence that had just ejected from my body had been under my conscious control, guided by my intelligence and yet untrammelled by my conscience, then I was a dangerous creature indeed. But if it had been an uncontrollable frenzy, why had I only kicked his torso, where I could hurt him, and not his head, where I might kill? Perhaps there is some visceral, primeval instinct that tells a man how to hurt another man, without causing his death. Perhaps I'd learned it in that Turkish gaol in Silistria.

Dmitry had stood himself up without my helping hand. "Are we all right, Lyosha?" It was almost an entreaty. He hadn't called me Lyosha since we had first met and I'd told him it made me feel like a kid. I looked through his beard to the scar on his cheek—the memento of where he had saved my life—and good memories of him came washing through my mind, rinsing away the rancid taste of the thoughts of Maks and Domnikiia that had come before.

"No," I replied, "but we will be, Mitka. We will be." I never guessed how long it would take.

*   *   *

The three of us walked off the bridge and on to the river's southern bank, where we could talk freely, away from the hubbub of the fleeing soldiers, citizens and socialites.

"So what's the plan now?" I asked.

"Didn't Iuda speak to you?" asked Vadim. "He said he would."

Dmitry did not seem keen to make any comment. He hugged his bruised ribs and did his best to keep his breathing steady. My sense of pity now was increasing to complement my lack of mercy earlier. The real source of my rage against Dmitry was that he had forced me to allow myself no vestige of forgiveness when I had confronted Maks. Who would be next in turn to suffer at my hand for what I had done to Maks? Vadim? I caught Dmitry's eye and responded likewise to the smile in it. It had only been minutes, and yet despite myself I began to understand how those young soldiers could be drinking together, so soon after being at each other's throats.

"Yeah, I saw him last night," I replied to Vadim. "You're happy with his plan?"

"His plan?"

"For them to hide in the city. Wait until the French arrive and then demonstrate to them that Moscow can be . . . inhospitable—for an unwelcome guest. Isn't that the plan Iuda explained to you?"

"No," chuckled Vadim, "that's the plan that *I* explained to *him*. Iuda wanted to keep attacking their supply lines. That's not unreasonable, but he can't see what it will mean to have them in Moscow."

"It's odd for them to fuss about who gets the credit for the plan. They don't seem like the sort to worry much about their social standing."

"That Iuda is different," wheezed Dmitry, "very different. When I was with them in Wallachia, there were only ten of them—and, like I said, only four of those are amongst these—but all of them had that same subservient quality that these have; with the exception of Iuda. That's what makes them such good killers—like cannonballs—you aim and you fire, and anything that doesn't get out of the line of the shot is ripped apart. But not Iuda; he has his own desires—even vanities. He takes his own aim. I'd have thought it would lessen his ability to kill, but it makes him better. He can choose when to care and when not to. That's the most dangerous combination of all."

We sat quietly and considered Dmitry's words. There was little comment to be made on them.

"So are we happy with the plan?" pressed Vadim.

"Yes, of course," I said. Dmitry nodded. There was, once again, silence for a while.

"There's another odd thing about Iuda," I said.

"And what's that?" asked Vadim.

"Well," I said, "Iuda seems to take all the decisions, but I thought Pyetr was supposed to be in charge."

"Funny," responded Vadim. "I thought I was."

Vadim was always in charge—always utterly in charge—when he needed to be. As Bonaparte had taken Vilna, we—the Lifeguard Hussars under General Uvarov, along with the whole of the First Army of the West—had retreated to Drissa. As they took Drissa, we retreated to Polotsk. Two months earlier, during a hot, sticky July, I had been lying on my bed in a room at an inn in Polotsk—a room which I was sharing with four others—when I heard a familiar voice.

"On your feet, Captain Danilov!"

He stood, leaning against the doorway, his face neither smiling nor stern, but his eyes confidently expressing the affection that we both knew existed between us. I raced over to greet him.

"Vadim! How are you? It's good to see you. Where have you been?"

He smiled. "I've been a bit south of here, with Bagration." He spoke the great general's name as though he knew him personally, which was quite possible. Vadim was the kind of officer who seemed to know everyone. He had connections in Petersburg society that most could only dream of. But unlike many other well-connected officers, Vadim chose to use those friendships to genuinely achieve military objectives, not simply to advance his own career. The favours he would quietly ask of Bagration would be for more rations or more arms for his men, not for promotion or a safe posting, well away from the front line.

"So how did he manage to get rid of you?" I asked.

"I told him I had some work to do. Speaking of which, are you busy?"

"Busy retreating," I said bitterly. "What did you have in mind?"

"Saving Russia."

"As easy as that?"

He shrugged, taking my agreement as read. "I'll meet you here tonight at eight. Oh, and see if you can bring Maksim Sergeivich along."

I knew where Maks was billeted. He was easy to find, but surprisingly difficult to persuade to join us.

"It's been a long time since we worked together, Aleksei; back before Austerlitz, and I didn't manage too well then, did I? I think I'd do better just to stick with regular soldiering. I'd be putting you at risk."

I realized now exactly how he, as a traitor in our midst, could see himself as a risk, but at the time it seemed quite uncharacteristic.

"You, Maks? A regular soldier?" I laughed as I spoke. When I had first met him, he had seemed the most unlikely of warriors. Only once he had joined up with Dmitry, Vadim and me that first time did he really begin to fit in. "You'd be bored rigid."

"True enough, but that doesn't make it the wrong course of action." This was more like classic Maks.

"But we need you."

He said nothing. He looked torn. I could tell that in his heart there was nothing he would like more than to rejoin the old team, but something in his head held him back.

"Vadim told me to bring you," I said.

"He ordered you?" A fleeting look of pride crossed his face at the mention of Vadim's name.

I pulled a face. "You know Vadim," I said.

"I'll see you at eight, then," replied Maks.

Maks arrived first that evening, soon followed by Vadim, who had brought Dmitry with him. Dmitry was also in Polotsk with the First Army, so Maks and I had seen plenty of him. The only reunion was between Maks and Vadim.

"Back to the fold then, eh, Maksim?" said the latter, shaking his hand.

"With you the watchful shepherd?" I asked, looking at Vadim.

"More the wolf than the shepherd," murmured Dmitry.

"We'll all be wolves, and pity the poor little French lambs," said Vadim.

"So it's more like back to the wolf pack?" asked Maks.

And so, seven years after we had first formed, the wolf pack had regenerated. Soon Polotsk had fallen, and we had once again retreated. It wasn't until Smolensk was taken that Barclay de Tolly had spoken to Vadim (or perhaps the other way round) and we had been set on our present course. And now in Moscow, in September, the pack of four was down to three. Maks no longer suffered any risk of being bored.

Standing beside the Moskva River in the heart of Moscow, the three of us—Vadim, Dmitry and I—made a few more detailed arrangements. During his earlier discussions with Iuda, Vadim had selected seven meeting places from our list of those within Moscow itself. The easiest arrangement was to have a different rendezvous for each day of the week. The time would always be the same; nine in the evening.

"And we meet every night?" I asked.

"Iuda said that at least one of them would try to be there every night," replied Vadim. "As for us; I think we should all three try to make it whenever we can. We won't be seeing each other the rest of the time."

"Why not?"

"We all need to stay under cover—and stay separate. It's up to you what you do. You can be a French officer or an escaped Russian convict—I don't need to know. We've got to be the eyes and ears of the Oprichniki. We need to see where the French are going and what they are doing. Then we need to tell the Oprichniki where to strike."

"Or strike for ourselves," I put in.

"No!" said Dmitry with sudden vehemence. Vadim and I both looked at him. "That's not their style," he added. "They'd rather we left it to them." I would have pressed him, but Vadim agreed with his conclusion, if not his reasoning.

"Dmitry's right," said Vadim, "regardless of their 'style,' our style is not to get ourselves killed. To put it crudely, the Oprichniki are more expendable than we are. I'm sorry, Dmitry, I know they're your friends, but that's the way it is."

Dmitry smirked painfully. "Oh, you know me, Vadim. Everyone is more expendable than I am."

"So do we start meeting from tonight?" I asked.

"No," said Vadim. "Well—not necessarily. We can wait until the French actually arrive. I don't think that will be tonight. Take these." He handed Dmitry and me each a purse. Inside was a small fortune in gold coins. "This is not your money or even my money—it's the tsar's money. We may encounter expenses in the course of the next few weeks. If you don't need to spend it then don't. I'll be expecting most of it back once we've kicked out Bonaparte."

We sank into silence, realizing that we might not see each other for many days, and that when we did, it would be in a city under French occupation.

"I wrote to Maks' mother," I announced.

"Thank you," said Vadim. "I trust that he died a hero."

I nodded. "Any news from Yelena Vadimovna?"

"Last I heard she was well, but that was almost a month ago. She's due in a few weeks."

"So we can't call you 'granddad' yet?"

"Not yet," replied Vadim levelly, "or ever."

Again we lapsed into quiet contemplation, sitting on the low wall and gazing into the river, reluctant to say our goodbyes. We were like three old men who have said, over the years, everything that could possibly be said, who sit outside all day, watching the world as it passes by them, fearful of leaving lest one of them never comes back again; three men who remember that in their distant youth they had been, and had forever expected to be, four. In such times as these, we couldn't even be sure of the luxury of getting old.

"Who were you talking to on the bridge?" asked Vadim.

TWELVE

"When?"

"When we found you—the wounded soldier."

"Didn't you recognize him?"

Vadim shook his head. "I barely saw him."

"It was Pierre." Vadim looked blank. "The Frenchman. You remember, he told us all about Tsarina Yekaterina and the horse."

"Passing himself off as a Russian?" Vadim asked, mildly angry. "Why didn't you . . ." but I think he realized that I wasn't in the mood for unmasking any more French spies just now, and left the question unasked.

"Did Vadim tell you about the camp?" I asked Dmitry. "And about Iuda, Matfei and Foma showing up?" Dmitry nodded.

"The interesting thing is, of course," I continued slowly, watching Dmitry to gauge his reaction, to see if he would reveal anything, "that he escaped—Pierre, I mean."

"So the Oprichniki are not quite so infallible as we thought," said Vadim.

"No indeed," I went on. "Not like them to leave a survivor who can go on and tell everything that happened to him."

Dmitry turned to me with a look of searching horror in his eyes, straining to turn his battered body. There was something that Pierre might have told me—something terrible—and Dmitry was scrutinizing my very soul to see if Pierre *had* told me; to see what I knew. Of course, all I'd heard from Pierre were his confused, delirious ramblings, but now I knew from Dmitry that there was something I might have known—something that I now planned to find out.

Soon after, we took our leave of one another. This time there was little expression of emotion. We were all too intent on our personal plans for the next few days. Vadim had one final thing to say.

"We may not do this, you know. It's not something I want to face, but that's a big army out there. I just want to say that if any of us gets wounded, or if things get too hot for us in the city, then we shouldn't be afraid to leave. If we can let each other know, then all the better, but survival is just as important as heroism. All right?"

Dmitry and I both nodded in sombre agreement, and then we parted. Vadim had told us that it was our own affair where and how we hid ourselves, but by some instinct that we had established over years of working together, we headed off immediately in different directions. Vadim went west along the river bank. Dmitry and I walked the opposite way in silence, but it was less than a minute before Dmitry turned north, back over the bridge.

I continued east. My plan of action had been, somewhat obliquely, inspired by the sight of the French footman being flogged. I soon turned south and headed over the canal into the region of Zamoskvorechye. It was easy enough to find an abandoned house, with planks nailed hastily over the windows and doors, and even easier to break through these naive defences. Whoever had quitted the house had been generous enough to take their servants with them, but not, fortunately for me, generous enough to take all their servants' possessions. It was no trouble for me to find a butler's uniform that fit. I reckoned that, once the French arrived, a Russian servant would be able to move around the city relatively unmolested. If not, it would be the work of an instant to transform myself to a French émigré servant, welcoming with open arms the liberating army that had freed him from his cruel masters.

The empty house would also make a good place for me to stay, at least for the time being, although I would have to be wary, since the invading masses would also be looking for abandoned buildings where they could be billeted. There were plenty of alternative exits if I needed to leave in a hurry.

And so I waited. Moscow became quieter and emptier as those who had lingered finally left, but still the French did not come. I wandered the streets of my beloved city for the next few days, astounded by the horror of its tranquillity. A few people remained, perhaps one fiftieth of the population, and all were sapped by the distance that separated them from the next person they might see. A week earlier, Muscovites would have had to push and jostle to make it through the busy streets—and would have complained about the overcrowding too—but now it was almost like living in the countryside, but without knowing the rules for such a life. In the country, one can go for hours without seeing another human soul, but when one does, they are always a friend, always someone to converse with. In this deserted Moscow, other people were just such a rarity, but those who were left were used to ignoring the thousands of individuals that they might pass within the space of a single hour, and so they ignored the few that they saw now. Thus even those who remained, that fiftieth of the population, were weakened by their isolation to a further fiftieth of their usual vitality.

It was as if the entire city had ceased to breathe. The physical entity that was Moscow still existed, but the spirit that had made it live was gone. As yet the body that was left showed no sign of decay, but even the most imperceptive of observers would soon be able to see that it was dead. Soon the maggots of the French army would arrive to feast on the remains.

Strangely though, it was a full three days before they arrived. From what I could gather later on, Bonaparte had expected Kutuzov to make a further, final stand at the gates of the city and so had hesitated. Kutuzov made no such defence—it would have been futile—and by the evening of 1 September, it was clear that French troops would be entering the city the following day.

That night, I had a dream.

CHAPTER XI

I WAS IN MY BEDROOM—THE BEDROOM I HAD SLEPT IN AS A child. I was well aware that this room was nothing like the room I had as a child but, as is often the case in dreams, I knew as an indisputable fact that this *was* the bedroom of my childhood. Two beds lay, quite incorrectly, along opposite walls of the room, with space between to walk. In the far wall, which the heads of both beds abutted, was a window. The curtains were drawn shut, but one could perceive that outside it was a bright, sunny winter's day.

On the left-hand bed lay a boy, sleeping on his side with his face to the wall so that only his back was in view. It was—and again I knew this for a fact without seeing his face—myself at the age of five or six. On the same bed, with her back to the boy, sat my wife, Marfa, showing polite interest in what she saw on the other side of the room.

Standing at the foot of the other bed was the Emperor Napoleon. He faced the woman who sat on the bed, his wife—the Empress Marie-Louise. In her lap she held a large bowl, and in the bowl there were figs. She held up a fig to the emperor, who took it in his hand. He raised it to his mouth and bit into it and, as the green skin ruptured, the red flesh and seeds oozed out around his lips. He licked his lips clean and then took four more bites from the fig until only the stalk was left. He popped this into his mouth and swallowed it, as if that had been the tastiest part of the whole fruit, and then he licked his fingers.

He held out his hand—his left hand this time—towards his empress for another fig and I noticed for the first time that his hand was missing its last two fingers, just like mine. I looked at my own left hand, cradling it in my right as I considered my disfigurement, and wondered how it was that I had never before remarked on the coincidence of Bonaparte having the same injury I did. I looked up again and found the emperor had gone, or at least he had gone from my view, for I was now looking through his eyes, although I did not know whether the others in the room were seeing Bonaparte or Aleksei Ivanovich standing before them.

I looked towards my empress to find that she too had transformed— though little transformation was needed—from Marie-Louise into my own Domnikiia. I sat down on the bed close beside her, glancing over to Marfa, who still displayed the same inquisitive equanimity at what was going on. Domnikiia still held the bowl on her lap, but now, rather than figs, it contained grapes. The fruit, I suddenly knew, and knew also that I had always known, was poisoned. Domnikiia proffered the bowl across the room to Marfa, silently inviting her to take one of those delicious grapes. Marfa presented the palm of her hand in polite refusal.

Looking once again at the boy behind her on the bed, it occurred to me that I had been mistaken in thinking that he was my younger self. Just as any father would know his son from a single hair of his head, I recognized the boy as my son, Dmitry Alekseevich. At the same moment, I understood that he was dead; poisoned by Domnikiia's grapes. The knowledge saddened me, but I would express the emotion no more deeply than that. At his belt he wore the little wooden sword that I had made for him the last time I had seen him.

The door, next to the foot of the bed on which the boy's body lay, opened and my mother walked into the room. She had died when I was twenty-two, and although, even in my dream, I was well aware of this, it seemed perfectly reasonable to now see my dead mother entering my childhood bedroom. Almost as soon as she had come into the room, she went across to Domnikiia, who once again held out the bowl to offer her a grape.

My mother declined with the polite warmth with which I felt distantly familiar. "No thank you, my dear," she said, smiling at Domnikiia. "I'm already dead." These were the only words that anyone spoke throughout the entire dream.

Then she went and sat on the other bed, next to my wife. They greeted one another with courtesy, but with no curiosity.

Domnikiia held the bowl out to my mother again. As she did so, I saw on her hand a ring. It was the figure of a dragon, with a body of gold, emerald eyes and red, forked tongue; the same ring that Zmyeevich had been wearing that night when we met. Around the ring, Domnikiia's hand looked old and pale. Decaying skin was flaking away from her shrivelled fingers. I looked up to her face and saw that it was not her hand that wore the ring, but the hand of Zmyeevich himself. He was leaning over her from behind, holding and covering her hand, and guiding her as she offered the bowl of grapes. He looked older than when I had seen him. His grey hair had become white and his skin was decrepit and terribly wrinkled. His eyes were the eyes of an old man, begging to be remembered as he was in his youth.

Still my mother and Marfa maintained their polite rejection of the grapes. Zmyeevich left Domnikiia and went over to the door through which my mother had entered. He opened the door and, with a gesture of his hand, ushered in the Oprichnik Pyetr. Pyetr crossed the room to stand behind Domnikiia. At his entrance, Domnikiia had glanced towards the door to see who it was, but having seen, indicated no further interest and returned her gaze to me. Pyetr bent forward. As he did so, his hand slipped under her arm and around her, coming to rest upon her breast. His head hovered above her shoulder for a moment as he paused to lick his lips, then he bent down further, gently kissing her neck, and at the same time, noticed by no one else in the room but me, he squeezed her breast in his hand.

Domnikiia maintained her gaze on mine. As Pyetr kissed her and caressed her, her eyes widened very slightly, like a woman who has just seen her lover across a room of friends and tries to hide her reaction from those around her. Pyetr stood up and removed his hand and, as he did so, Domnikiia reached into the bowl and took out a grape, which she held out towards me. I opened my mouth, in full knowledge that the grapes were poisoned, and let her slip it inside, closing my lips quickly so as to briefly feel her fingers between them as she took her hand away.

Pyetr left, although I have no idea how, and at the door, Zmyeevich let in the next Oprichnik, Andrei. His behaviour was identical to Pyetr's; the kiss on Domnikiia's neck and the hand on Domnikiia's breast. Her response was once again the same and I once again greedily consumed the grape as she gave it to me, aware that I would be poisoned in the same way that my son, lying lifeless on the bed across the room, had been poisoned, but still eager to eat the grapes because of the slightest of touches of Domnikiia's fingers that accompanied them.

And so the story retold itself over and over for each of the Oprichniki. Zmyeevich showed into the room next Iakov Zevedayinich, then Ioann, then Filipp, Varfolomei, Foma, Matfei, Iakov Alfeyinich, Faddei and Simon. Each one kissed and fondled Domnikiia, and each time she responded by feeding me another poisoned grape. I swallowed each grape gladly, with an increasing sense of sorrow that they would cause my death, but with no desire to do anything to prevent it.

After Simon had come and gone, I knew that there was just one more Oprichnik left to arrive. I glanced over to the other bed, where my wife and my mother still both sat with the same look of docile curiosity on their faces, knowing in their hearts the danger of what they were witnessing, but too indulgent of my eccentric whims to criticize these people, whom they took to be my friends. Behind them, I noticed that the little wooden sword at my son's side was broken in two. And my son was bigger, much bigger—but still dead. It was now Maks, and I understood then that it always had been, although I could still not see his face.

Zmyeevich had one final guest to invite into the room. It was Iuda. He walked up to Domnikiia, but did nothing more than bow slightly and tip his hat. Then he went over to the window and flung the curtains wide open, filling the room with light. Through the window I saw the winter scene outside. A small pond sat in the middle of a snow-covered garden. A wide, jagged crack split the sheet of ice that lay on top of it. Iuda turned away from the window and towards me with a triumphant smile on his face, his arms still raised in the air from where they had clutched the curtains, accepting the cheers of a crowd that I could not hear or see, but that I knew was there.

He stood behind Domnikiia and bent over her, not to kiss her or caress her as the others had done, but simply to take a grape from the bowl in front of her. He walked over to me and casually offered me the grape, which I took in my hand, but did not eat. I held it between my thumb and fingers and offered it back to Domnikiia, but she refused, shaking her head and backing away from the death that she was well aware the grapes would bring and which I had so calmly accepted. Iuda again stepped behind her and held her head still, allowing me to hold the grape up to her lips, but still she kept them tight shut, squeezing her eyes shut as well, as if to add to her impregnability.

I crushed the grape against her lips and, though she tried to turn her head away, she could not. Iuda's grip held her firm. I saw my two remaining fingers rubbing the skin and crushed flesh of the grape against Domnikiia's lips, trying to force her to accept even the slightest morsel of the poison. I looked at the stumps of my two missing fingers and thought how much easier it would have been, had my hand been complete, to force her lips open and make her taste the fruit.

And then I noticed, curled around my middle finger, a ring shaped like a dragon, with a body of gold, emerald eyes and red, forked tongue.

I woke up.

Whether a dream is a nightmare is a question not of content, but of mood. Nothing in my dream had been conspicuously horrifying, but I awoke with the feeling—as certain as any knowledge I have ever had—that something irredeemably awful had taken place, something that had destroyed my whole world. Had I been asked what that thing was, I would have been unable to say, and in the time it would have taken me to recall what it was, I would have woken up enough to realize it was nothing. But for a few seconds after waking, I had no doubt as to either its existence or its enormity.

At the moment of waking I leapt out of bed, instinctively feeling that my fear would require a remedy of physical action. My surroundings were strange. I had to do something to fight off the terror that confronted me. But I couldn't remember what I had to do—or even what that terror was.

Within seconds, wakefulness returned to me fully. I was in a bedroom in the abandoned house in Zamoskvorechye. This was the fourth night I'd been there. I recalled my dream, and could have recited every detail of it. Rationality took control of me as I understood that the fears were in my own mind—that they had no other reality. The sense of relief permeated both mind and body like a warming glass of vodka. But still it had been a nightmare. Still I was haunted by the childlike fear of going back to sleep and possibly returning to that horrifying place from which, by waking, I had just escaped.

I lay back down on the bed. I had no idea what time it was—outside, it was still dark as pitch and I felt no urge to light a candle. I wondered whether I would be able to return to sleep. As a young child, when I'd had a nightmare, my mother had sometimes let me sleep in her bed until morning. My father would not hear of such mollycoddling, so it was only when he was away that it was allowed. After he died, I grew up very quickly and so the need no longer arose. Even then I would fail to go back to sleep, but I would lie awake in terror in my own bed, like a man.

And now I *was* a man, and still I lay awake. I went over the dream again and again in my mind, trying to determine which specific element it was that had turned it into a nightmare, or to fall back to sleep in the attempt. It was something about the grapes that seemed most resonant with the sense of fearfulness that still lingered in me; something in the act of Domnikiia's offering them, of my taking them, although the prospect of my death from the poison held little apprehension for me.

I may have dozed as I lay there, yet I would swear that I was wide awake throughout; just as curled up in the safety of my mother's bed I had still never felt safe enough to slip back into the world of unconsciousness. The horror would always be ended by the sound of birds. As dawn broke, birdsong would hail the resurrection of the sun and the beginning of the new day. Time—which had stopped in the continual, unchanging darkness of the early hours, when there was no way of telling whether one's last thought had occurred a second ago or an hour ago—would begin again.

And so there in Moscow, the dawn chorus, which I still, as I had since childhood, associated both with being terrified and with the termination of that terror, eventually heralded the new day. Time began again and the night, and the nightmare, could be forgotten.

As rationality at last became fully resurgent in me I realized that a rational man should find much more to fear in that particular day than there had been in the night before it. That was the day that the French would enter Moscow.

It was well into the afternoon when the French finally arrived from the west, even as the last brigades of what remained of the Russian army scuttled away antipodally to the east. Amongst the last to leave, so the rumourmongers would have it, had been Count Rostopchin, the city's governor. Fearful that the Russian mob would not let him depart, he had delivered to them a restaurateur by the name of Vereshchagin who was accused of being a French spy. The mob had torn Vereshchagin to pieces, while Rostopchin slipped away to freedom, unmolested. It was not the only time that I would find parallels between myself and Moscow's governor.

When they did arrive, the invaders were led not by Bonaparte, but by his brother-in-law, Marshal Murat, whom Bonaparte (ashamed, as any republican would be, of having a common soldier marry his sister) had elevated to the rank of King of Naples. Bonaparte himself was to follow Murat into the city the following day. I secreted myself among a small crowd of inquisitive Muscovites who witnessed Murat's arrival with more curiosity than fear or respect. Many thought that they were seeing Bonaparte himself, but I had seen enough pictures of the Little Corporal to know that this was not he. The flamboyant uniform and loose, curly, almost feminine hair were styles that Bonaparte would have abhorred, and left me in no doubt as to which one of France's marshals this was.

French troops spread in waves across the deserted city, showing little concern for the few Russians that remained. I was stopped occasionally, but there were far too few Russian speakers amongst them to accompany every platoon. When challenged I, like others I saw in the city, had merely to reply with a stream of suitably grovelling Russian babble and I was allowed on my way.

That day was a Monday, and our arranged meeting place for Mondays was Red Square itself. In more conventional times, it was an ideal location for a covert meeting, thronged as it was with crowds from which two or three figures in conversation would not stand out. Today, however, the crowds were crowds of French soldiery. To meet there would have been brave, and when

TWELVE

carrying out acts of sabotage in an occupied city, bravery is not a quality that goes hand in hand with success.

I skirted around the square, returning three times that evening, but saw no sign of Vadim, or Dmitry, or of any of the Oprichniki.

I returned to the house that I'd been staying in only to discover that it was already a temporary barracks for a dozen or so French officers. Wisely, I had not left those few possessions I had inside. Climbing up to the roof, I found the small bundle I had hidden there, along with my sword, safe and intact. None of those inside heard me as I retrieved them. I headed further south and found somewhat less luxurious, but still serviceable accommodation, which the French had decided was beneath them. I was not the first man in history, nor would I be the last, forced to sleep in a stable.

The following day, there was little I could do but wander around the city. Food was still reasonably abundant, but at a price. Those Muscovites who had stayed behind may have had numerous reasons for doing so, but for some there was a profit to be made. An invading army could, of course, simply requisition every item of food, every bottle of vodka and any other victuals that they desired, but though they would get what they consumed for nothing, it would also be the last they would get. A moving army can pillage, but a resting army must trade. It must employ others to go out of the city and resupply what it requires. This, at least, was the conventional wisdom. I believed it and, to my best estimation, Bonaparte believed it too. As ever, we had both underestimated the resolution of the Russian peasant. A few fresh supplies found their way into the city, but precious little. The French—and their horses—in the end had to survive on what was already stocked up in cellars and storehouses. It would not be enough. Had the French realized this, their stay in Moscow might have been even shorter— and that might indeed have saved them, if they had left in time to get out of Russia ahead of winter. Not all of the French army did understand the need for trade, but the few remaining Moscow tradesmen supplied those who did as well as, conveniently, supplying me. I suspect that, had I chosen to disguise myself as a French officer while I stayed in Moscow, then I could have fed myself at half the price. There were few discounts offered to an abandoned Russian butler.

Compared with two days ago, Moscow was once again teeming with life. Bonaparte's army was, at this stage in his campaign, perhaps 100,000 strong—appallingly fewer than the number that he started out with, but enough to give the city some pale shadow of revivification. Still they were fewer than half the true population of the city, but they spent more time out on the streets than had the real Muscovites, who had homes to go to, so Moscow seemed busy, superficially.

I remember once, when fighting south of the Danube, I surveyed through my spyglass an abandoned battlefield, scattered with the corpses of both friend and foe. Suddenly, I had seen movement. A soldier, lying on his back, his face covered with blood, whom everyone had taken for dead, was moving his hand. It had been the slightest of motions, made through the terrible pain of his injuries, but the fact that he could confront that pain and vanquish it sufficiently to make that feeble signal showed how much he wanted to indicate that he was alive—how much he wanted to live.

The field had still been under Turkish fire, but I had dashed out, oblivious to the shouts of my commanding officer, bending low as if it might save me from enemy gunshot. I had to rescue that poor, injured man. I made it to where he was and threw myself to the ground. I could hear the whizzing of bullets around me, but I don't think that they were aimed at me. My first intention was to murmur some words of encouragement into the soldier's ear; to let him know that if he wanted to live, then I was there to help him. Then I had to find a way to drag his weak body across the vast expanse of land that separated us from our own lines.

And then I saw his hand.

It was still moving, but the movement was not a desperate signal for assistance—the last plea of a dying man clinging to life—it was simply the wriggling of a hundred maggots. They had eaten most of his hand away, but their gluttonous writhing had, to the eyes of a man who had wanted to see life where there was none, seemed like a coherent motion; a twitching of the fingers that the maggots had long since assimilated.

In just such a way might the casual viewer conceive that life had in fact returned to Moscow. The streets were once again filled with vitality, with bustle, with commotion. But looking closely they would see that those figures that filled the streets, though they might on the surface look like the city's former inhabitants, were living on the city, not in it. Their purpose was to consume what they found (notwithstanding that trade rather than pillage might be a more efficient approach to the task of consumption), not to nurture for the benefit of their successors or for the benefit of the city itself.

Moscow was as full of life as a cadaver on the embalmer's table. The fluids and chemicals that had been introduced into its veins can engorge it sufficiently to give it some vague semblance of the living creature that it once was, but they would never have the ability to provide the vital essence that once made that body a man. The image brought to my mind the Oprichniki. They passed themselves off physically as men, but I had never seen in any one of them a hint of the desires and loves and anguishes of living beings.

Did the French occupiers, I wondered, perceive themselves as parasites feasting on the corpse of a once-great city, or did they believe that they were the vanguard of a new wave of life that had revitalized all the rest of Europe and was now supplying the physical reality of the Enlightenment to Russia? I think that Bonaparte himself probably believed that, but I also think he was deluding himself. Maks had shared Bonaparte's delusion.

It had been almost four hours since I had thought of Maks.

It was in the midafternoon of that day, the third of September, that I heard the first stories of fires raging in Moscow. I had invested in a substantial quantity of tobacco and was furtively offering it at an entirely unreasonable price to any French officer or soldier that I came across. The most unanticipated thing that I learned from this was that I had missed my calling. By the time I had sold scarcely a third of my stock, I had more than made back what I had paid for it. I understood how those few thousand who had remained in Moscow, however much they feared for their lives, must have been tempted by the profit that was to be had.

The profit which I was seeking was in the currency not of gold, but of knowledge. I still maintained the simplistic façade of a man who spoke no French, and so I was able to pick up all the news of plans and deployments that the French were discussing, as well as the gossip and tittle-tattle.

Fires were springing up all over Moscow. The French stories were that former convicts in the prisons of Moscow had been released and instructed by the departed governor, Rostopchin, to burn down the city, rather than let the French occupy it. The Muscovites I spoke to told, predictably, a different story: it was the French who were starting the fires, intent not just on occupying the city, not just on raping it, but ultimately on destroying it. This made little sense to me; no maggot could ever be pleased to see the corpse on which it fed cremated. Another point of view was that the fires were simply accidents. The French cared less for the city than did its inhabitants, so they would be less concerned about a toppled candle or a leaping cinder. In addition, with no civil authorities in place, there was no organization—nor any impetus—to put out any fire caused in such a way. Formerly, Moscow had been well stocked with hoses and pumps and men who knew how to operate them, but all had vanished with the evacuation. The Russians and the French stared at one another over the blazing city, each blaming the other, and neither was prepared to blink.

Among the stories about the fires, there were other rumours that I picked up; rumours that were frighteningly familiar; rumours that there was a plague in Moscow. And as I heard more of these rumours, the idea of a plague began to transform. The French were beginning to talk of strangulations, of disappearances, of a pack of wild animals.

The Oprichniki were doing their work. And yet I wondered if the two phenomena might not be related. The Oprichniki had no preconceptions of war, found no barriers of convention or custom that they would not cross. Perhaps the fires too were part of their unconventional solution to the goal of ejecting the French. I doubted whether I could have sacrificed the city itself to that goal, but the Oprichniki, as outsiders, had no such scruples. And so I might have failed where they would succeed. With the Oprichniki it was very easy (and very pleasing) to mortgage one's scruples, knowing that after the battle those scruples would be returned to one untouched—neither diminished nor consulted.

*   *   *

TWELVE

Tuesday's rendezvous was the church of Saint Clement, in the suburb of Zamoskvorechye, not so far from my new residence. Its priest had, it seemed, abandoned it and left Moscow, convinced that it was beyond his abilities to convert these invaders from their atheism to godliness, let alone to Christianity, let even more alone to the Orthodox religion.

I felt a chill as I gazed up at the church's red walls, feeling a sensation of menace that I imagine is not uncommon in even the most pious of men when encountering the overawing physical presence of such a building. A church, we all know from our earliest years, is the house of the Lord; a place of love and sanctuary. And yet the presentiment of horror and menace that I felt, huddled in the darkness of the gateway, lit only by the setting half-moon, must surely be one that is shared by all. I suppose it is because a church, however much we associate it with the love of Christ, is a place that we also associate with the dead. It cuts to the very heart of our belief. The bliss of paradise is the ultimate reward towards which the life of every Christian is directed, and yet how much do we all fear death? We fear death so greatly that we even fear those most incapacitated of creatures: the dead themselves.

I glanced around, but still saw no sign of Vadim or Dmitry, or indeed of any of the Oprichniki.

It seemed like only moments later when I looked around again, to find I had been joined by Ioann and Foma.

CHAPTER XII

I FELT A SENSATION OF SELF-LOATHING AS I DISCOVERED HOW
pleasant—I'm afraid that *is* the correct word—it was to see these familiar
faces. Without doubt, I wanted to meet with Vadim, or even Dmitry, but to
be able to speak freely with people that I knew, be it for only a few weeks,
was a relief. The constant pressure of pretence as a covert patriot amongst a
swarm of invaders is debilitating. Despite the fact that somewhere in my
mind I had been hoping that if it had to be an Oprichnik it would be Iuda
who came along, I think that my smile was genuine as I shook both Foma
and Ioann by the hand.

"I'm glad to see you," I told them. They smiled and nodded as if they
hadn't quite followed the detail of the French I had spoken to them, but
appreciated the sentiment.

"Where have you been staying?" I slowed the pace of my speech and, I
fear, introduced the tone of condescension which one uses when speaking to
people who understand neither French nor Russian.

"We have found a cellar," said Foma. "It is a perfect lair." I forgave him
his odd choice of words. I had learned French from an early age, in parallel
with learning Russian itself. For someone who learned it later in life, the
subtle ambiguities of meaning are easily overlooked.

"Have you seen any of your comrades?" I asked.

They discussed the issue amongst themselves, using their own language,
before Foma replied. "We have seen one or two, but more importantly, we
have seen their work."

I understood that he meant by their "work" the deaths of French soldiers.
At the time, more than on any occasion before or certainly since, I felt complete accordance with their achievements and complete indifference to their
methods.

"I have heard of your work too," I told them. "The French are quite afraid of you."

"As far as I know, we have only killed twenty so far," said Foma. He quickly followed up with an explanation of this small number. "It is better to keep the numbers inconsequential. Even with so few deaths, you have already heard rumours; any more and there would be mobs rampaging the streets in search of us."

"It's a lesson that we have learned at the expense of fallen friends," interjected Ioann. "We will have plenty of time in the city. We do not gorge like dogs, forgetting tomorrow."

"Do you have anything to tell us?" asked Foma, cutting his friend short.

I briefly summarized what I had seen and heard of troop dispositions, but it, and I, felt superfluous. Moscow was full—full to bursting—of Frenchmen and their allies. The Oprichniki needed no more directing than a reaper needs pointing towards a field lush with wheat or than a fox needs to have a particular chicken marked out as his prey once he has found the henhouse. On the other hand, despite their revolutionary slogan, not all Frenchmen were equal, certainly not in terms of their threat to us. Officers were obviously more fruitful targets than men, and specialized officers—in the artillery or on the general staff—would be the greatest loss to the French military machine. So it was towards such locations, where I knew them, that I directed Foma and Ioann.

"Where are the fires at present?" asked Foma, when I had finished.

"See for yourself," I said, pointing. "All along Pokrovka Street, and other streets too." Looking north over the city, the night sky was reddened by the glimmer of fire. The fires themselves showed up as glowing arcs that silhouetted groups of buildings. "I suspected that you might have started them yourselves," I added.

"Us?" Foma was taken aback, almost insulted by the suggestion, and also strangely afraid. "Fire's no use to us." He showed no inclination to explain further what he meant by this.

"We will go now," he continued. "We, or some of the others, will do our best to meet with you again tomorrow." They both nodded a brief farewell to me and headed back to the street. Once there, they exchanged a few words with each other before separating, Ioann heading south and Foma north.

I knew that now was my opportunity. I had heard reports of the Oprichniki's work, and seen a choreographed display of it on the road near Borodino, but now was my first, irresistible opportunity to see them work for real. Foma was alone, and I took my chance.

I had tracked men in the past across vast distances, through woods and across mountains, and rarely been caught out by them. Pursuit through a city was somewhat different but had many principles in common. Out in the wilderness, one can sometimes track at a distance of a verst or more, knowing that any traces one's quarry leaves will remain for a few hours, and knowing also that he is most likely the only other human soul in the whole area.

In the city, one must keep closer. If Foma were to get far enough from me to turn two corners, then I might lose him. If I got so close as to be on the same stretch of road as him, he had only to glance over his shoulder and I would be seen. I had the advantage, however, that I knew Moscow intimately. If he went down one street, then I could slip down a sideroad, cover three sides of a square in the time it took him to cover one, and be at the next crossroads before he was.

He headed quickly north. Although he might not know Moscow in any great detail, he knew where he was going. When I had briefed the two Oprichniki earlier, I had told them that many of the French had billeted themselves in the north of the city, and so it was towards there that Foma was heading. Pursuit was made more difficult by the regular patrols of French soldiers, although they were a hindrance to Foma's progress as well. Since few of the French spoke Russian, his lack of the language would probably not be his undoing if he were stopped. He could simply jabber at them in his own tongue, which I guessed was some form of Romanian, and their ears would hear no distinction between what he said and the equally incomprehensible babble of genuine Russian. To me, the language that the Oprichniki spoke seemed to have more in common with Italian and French than it had with Russian, but that was to make a similar mistake. Whatever one's nationality, be it French, Russian or Japanese, there is an instinct not to bother with sub-classifications of things that have already been classified as foreign.

TWELVE

Foma still ran the risk, however, that he might meet a patrol which did have a Russian speaker in its ranks, and then he would be found out. Whether through this reasoning, or out of instinct, his approach to avoiding the problem was to avoid being seen. As a patrol (or indeed anyone) came near he would step into some dim doorway or alley and wait for them to pass. His skill at hiding in darkness was remarkable. At one point, when I was watching him from the far end of the street, he heard approaching footsteps and flung himself into the shadow of the wall at the end of a block of houses. It was as if he had vanished before my eyes.

I watched for several minutes as first an organized patrol and then a rowdy group of off-duty soldiers came past, and still he remained invisible. I got out my spyglass and looked again at the place where I had last seen him, but I could make out nothing but the vague shapes of dark shadows cast against the wall. Then, suddenly, what I was looking at transformed; not through any intrinsic change in itself, but simply by my unconscious reappraisal of what I was seeing. I wasn't staring at a shadow, but at the side of Foma's face, pressed against the wall in utter and complete stillness. It was that ability to stay quite still that somehow allowed him to disappear. His dark coat hid most of his body. Looking around further, I could also make out his hand, pressed against the wall as if reaching out to those who were passing by, but again implausibly still. Of the arm that I knew must lie somewhere between his hand and his face, I could make out nothing.

Looking back to his face, I noticed that there was one minuscule hint of movement. His eyes were flicking back and forth. They say that when a man dreams his body remains quite still and yet his eyes continue to move, indicating physically to the real world in which direction the dreamer is looking in his mind. The only difference was that Foma's eyes were open, following the stragglers of the off-duty soldiers as they tottered past.

After the last trailing man had gone by, his footsteps fading into the night, Foma moved and was suddenly quite visible once again. But he didn't continue on his way. He liked what he had seen and began to follow the soldiers back up the road. This time it was my turn to step back into the shadows as he passed.

Foma followed the soldiers, I followed Foma and we all headed gradually eastward into the outskirts of Kitay Gorod. Fresh flames shone to the southeast, but the area in which we found ourselves remained untouched, not just by fire, but by the French. Beyond the small troop that we were following, we saw no other patrols. Soon the soldiers came to their destination—an abandoned school building that they were using as their barracks. With the same laughter and jokes that had accompanied their entire journey across town, they made their way into the building and closed the door.

Foma was only a short way behind them, but again he had stood stock-still, with his back pressed to the wall, and had remained unseen by anyone but me. Hiding myself at the end of the street, I watched Foma to see what he would do next. Now that the boisterous revelry of the soldiers had ceased, my own breathing sounded deafeningly loud. Foma passed back and forth outside the school, gazing up at the high windows, reminding me of a cat pacing up and down beneath a caged bird, never doubting its ability to climb up and take the puny, twittering creature, but simply looking for the best route to ascend—the best route being that by which the cat is least likely to be found out.

After a little consideration, Foma stopped beneath one of the windows, deciding that it was the easiest one to reach, or perhaps noticing some slight clue that suggested he would be able to break it open. Without hesitation, he began to climb the wall. It was an astonishing feat, one which I could not have achieved, and neither could any but the most expert of climbers. He found every tiny crevice and fissure in the wall and somehow managed to insinuate his fingers or toes deeply enough inside to gain some purchase. Just as when he had been hiding, his body clung inseparably close to the wall, and as he moved each limb in turn, sliding it across to its next grip, his body flowed like water across a rock, never venturing away from the precipice he scaled in case it unbalanced him. The impression was of some sort of lizard or insect—no, neither of those, instead a spider—climbing up that wall, but I realized that Foma's achievement was not in truth inhuman, but superhuman. Any man with the strength and skill and experience—and, it has to be said, daring—could have achieved it. I was not such a man, and it was difficult to conceive that a man so unprepossessing as Foma could in any area of activity be so exceptionally talented.

He reached the window and opened it without trouble, scuttling into the building with a swiftness that almost made it appear he had been pulled from inside. There was no way that I would be able to follow him, nor had I any desire to find myself trapped in a room with him as he discovered that I had been following him.

I crept up to the school building and listened. All was silent within; no hint of what Foma might be doing inside, nor any reaction from any of the soldiers who slept there. There was little I could do but wait, and hope that Foma would leave by the same window he had entered, or at least from the same side of the building. The house opposite had a rather grand portico and so there I sat, leaning my back against the wall and hidden from the school by one of the pillars.

I suspect I may have dozed off, but it felt like only seconds later that I was being challenged, in heavily accented Russian, by the commanding officer of a small squad of French troops.

"What are you doing here?" he barked.

"Sleeping, sir!" I leapt to my feet in an effort to show respect, but I realized that if I wasn't careful, I might betray my military background.

"Don't you have a home?" As the lieutenant spoke, I noticed behind him the window of the school across the street swing open once again.

"It's been occupied, sir," I replied, trying not to look at the window and thereby betray Foma, "by your compatriots."

"And where was that?"

This was a tricky question. I tried to recall somewhere close by where I had seen French soldiers billeted.

"Kolpachny Lane, sir." Behind him, the figure of Foma slipped to the ground, not quite jumping, not quite climbing; flowing—slower than water but faster than honey—like blood. He passed across the wall as the shadow of a stationary object cast by a moving light.

"I see," continued the officer. It looked like he believed me and had some sympathy for my predicament. "But I can't help that. The men have to sleep somewhere."

I nodded. Foma walked silently away down the street, almost swaggering compared to his earlier furtive gait, as if proud of what he had achieved within the temporary barracks. Whether he glanced over towards me and the French soldier, I don't know. Even if he had, he may not have recognized me. He certainly made no action to come to my assistance.

"I have to sleep somewhere too," I told the lieutenant, trying not to appear so submissive that I might arouse suspicion.

"That's as may be, but you can't sleep here. That's a barracks over there." He glanced over his shoulder, but Foma had already vanished into the night. "We can't have the natives loitering around here."

"I'm sorry, sir," I said. Anger began to well up inside me as he spoke, particularly at dismissive words such as "native," but it was not the anger of Captain Aleksei Ivanovich Danilov—he understood that this was just the bluster of a frightened junior officer in a foreign country. It was the anger of the homeless Russian butler that I had become, much as I always became whoever I had to pretend to be. It would not convince this lieutenant if the Muscovite before him simply stayed calm. I had to stay calm, but to do so in spite of myself, and make it clear to him that I was angry and urgently containing myself so as not to show it. So many layers of deception are too difficult to juggle. It is better simply to believe it oneself, then one cannot be doubted by any man.

It was beneath him to dismiss me, but he said nothing more, and so I scurried off in the direction that Foma had gone. The trail was, however, now cold. Foma had been scarcely half a minute ahead of me, but already he would have had a choice of ten or more roads to take. I didn't give up—I'd always play a ten to one shot—but on this occasion it proved to be that he had taken one of the other nine.

I headed back to my stable in Zamoskvorechye and went to sleep.

The following day, I returned to the school. By that time, I looked pretty rough. I hadn't actually been sleeping out of doors, as had some of the people of Moscow, but I was still dirty and dishevelled and smelled of the streets. This struck me as a good pretext for starting a conversation with the two guards who now stood outside the schoolhouse.

TWELVE

"Excuse me, sirs," I said to them in Russian, "would you have any food?" They looked at me blankly. "Some bread, perhaps?" Still they didn't understand. I switched to French. *"Du pain? Du pain?"* I pleaded, as if it was the only phrase I knew in French, and trying to speak it with a Russian accent. There were real tears in my eyes and one of the guards went inside, returning moments later with a dirty crust. "Thank you, sir," I continued, in French, presuming that most Muscovites would know at least that much.

I crouched down on the pavement with my back to the wall and gnawed hungrily at the stale bread. They showed little inclination to move me on. A third soldier joined the two guards.

"Any news of Albert?" the first guard asked him.

"Still nothing," he replied.

"I'm certain he came back with us last night," said the second.

"Oh, he did. His bed was slept in—and bloodstained—but there's no sign of him. Even if he'd been murdered, there'd be a body."

I immediately recalled to mind the scene days ago near Goryachkino, when the Oprichniki had been so fastidious in removing the bodies of all those soldiers that they had slaughtered outside the farmhouse.

"One of the patrols last night came across a Russian sleeping rough—or pretending to—just over there." The first guard nodded towards the doorway where I had been found the previous night. "Maybe he was a lookout."

"Maybe," mused the newcomer, then, to give vent to his frustration, he mounted a hefty kick to my leg as he snarled at me, *"Bistro! Bistro!"* The accent was almost impenetrable, but it was the only word of Russian that most of the invaders had bothered to learn: "Quickly! Quickly!" It was used in any circumstances; whether, as now, to send me hurrying on my way, or to clear the path in front of them, or—with, as time went by, greater and greater urgency—to procure themselves a meal. In this case, it was my opportunity to escape. I gladly complied.

I spent the day much as I had the previous one, wandering the streets, picking up scraps of information from both the French occupiers and from those remaining Russians whom they repressed. I avoided Kitay Gorod, which was now almost completely ablaze, though there were few places that I could venture in the city where I would not see flames nearby, or come across the devastation left behind where fire had already exhausted itself. Before the occupation, the main enclave for French émigrés had been in the area round Kutznetsky Bridge, spanning the river Neglinnaya; now diverted from its natural course into a part-covered canal, before acting as a moat beside the western wall of the Kremlin and finally flowing into the Moskva. Though the inferno reached the very borders of this area, it went no further. Some of the French I spoke to believed that it was the will of God that "their" part of the city had been saved. The will of Bonaparte also made a contribution; he had ordered that a picket of men should stand around Kutznetsky Bridge, ensuring that if ever the flames did encroach, they would be beaten back.

The fires and stories of how the fires had begun and discussions of when they would end were the main subjects on everyone's lips. Hidden amongst them were tales of other mysterious deaths and disappearances that could not be put down to the conflagration. These, I had little doubt and took some pleasure in knowing, were the work of my friends the Oprichniki. Other news was more political. Bonaparte had abandoned the Kremlin, for fear that the fire would reach it, moving to the Petrovsky Palace on the outskirts of the city. Furthermore, the French were beginning to discuss what Bonaparte's next step would be. The previous day there had been an air of if not euphoria, at least proud achievement in their conquest of a foreign city, but now they were wondering what they were actually going to do with it. Few relished the prospect of marching on to Petersburg, but there would be no safety or comfort in remaining in Moscow over the winter. There was still a general expectation that Tsar Aleksandr would soon give up his pride and begin to negotiate some sort of peace, but that would still leave the Grande Armée isolated and far from home.

That evening, being a Wednesday, we were due to meet on the Stone Bridge, west of the Kremlin. I didn't attend, but watched from well away to the west, on the south bank of the river. My plan was to follow one of the Oprichniki again. If I spoke with Vadim and Dmitry, it might slow me down. I couldn't even be sure that Dmitry wouldn't try to stop me. The moon was high and three-quarters full when I arrived, somewhat earlier than scheduled. Before long I saw a figure walk to the middle of the bridge and gaze down into the river below. It was Dmitry. He was soon joined by Vadim. They spoke for a moment and then walked together to the south side of the bridge. Some five minutes later they returned. Clearly, they didn't want to be seen lingering in one place for too long and were patrolling the bridge so as to encounter any Oprichniki that chose to show up.

I felt an enormous urge to go over there and speak to them. It had been five days since I had exchanged a word with either of them, and in that time I had not had a single, honest, straightforward conversation with anyone. My brief exchange with Foma and Ioann the previous night counted for nothing. I realized that I felt almost homesick, not for a place—I felt Moscow to be my home now far more than Petersburg—but for people; for my friends. Five minutes of conversation with either of them would give me the same relief as plunging into a cool river in sweltering weather. Just as I have in the past been gripped by the eccentric inclination on a hot day in a public place to rip off my clothes and bathe before all in some cooling pond, I felt now the desire to indulge myself in the comforting conversation of my friends. On those occasions, as now, I resisted the temptation. I had a greater task than the alleviation of my own discomforts.

I watched Dmitry and Vadim pacing back and forth with a certain unwholesome pleasure—like the true, unknown father of a child might watch that child as it played with its mother's husband, or as a spurned lover might watch his beloved through her open window—pretending I was there, imagining the conversation as if I were taking part, but unable to step out of the shadows and join in. It was only now, when its relief was so tantalizingly close, that I comprehended the depth of my loneliness. Although I had been pleased to see Foma and Ioann the night before, I had soon become reacquainted with their absolute lack of character. They were not merely sullen; they were simply nothing—soulless portraits of men from a distant land whom I felt I had never met in person.

Vadim and Dmitry were passing across the bridge for the fourth time when they encountered two more figures coming from the opposite direction.

One was Varfolomei; the other I could not make out. It was not Iuda, who was easy to recognize by his height alone, if not by his hair and his posture. The two Oprichniki spoke a little with Vadim and Dmitry, but for no longer than five minutes, then my friends departed, both heading north. The Oprichniki waited a short while to be sure that they had gone, and then set off themselves. Varfolomei headed north whilst the other, once he had stepped off the southern end of the bridge, turned right and proceeded along the embankment where I was hiding.

As he passed, I saw that it was Matfei. I pressed back into the bushes and he walked past, unaware of, or at least unresponsive to, my presence. I followed him, much as I had done Foma the previous night. It looked to me as though he was keen to get back to the north side of the river, but he was still unfamiliar with the geography of the city. The river curved south and we had to cover nearly two versts before we came to the Crimean Bridge and were able to get back across. Almost immediately, Matfei spotted a French patrol which, like Foma, he followed from a safe distance. We continued for about half an hour, but Matfei made no attempt at any attack on the patrol. For all I could tell, this was still early in their watch, and they might not return to barracks for several hours.

Eventually, Matfei must have come to this conclusion as well, for he was distracted by the sound of a pleasant French baritone emanating from one of the grander houses that we passed. There was a light at the window, but I could not see who was inside. Matfei crept up and peered closely through the glass. Suddenly, he started. Once again, as I had been with Foma, I was reminded of a cat, tensing as it catches sight of its prey. Either the door was unlocked, or he had some way of opening it, for he was soon inside the house, leaving me to watch and wait in the shadows outside. And to listen.

The Frenchman's pleasant voice continued to serenade the night. On our arrival, he had been singing an aria that I recognized to be from Beethoven's *Fidelio*. At Austerlitz, tunes from this then-new opera had been on the lips of French and Austrian soldiers alike, and on those of some of the more cosmopolitan Russians. Now the unseen singer had switched to that old favourite (in certain quarters) "La Marseillaise." I smiled to myself; I could well imagine Vadim incensed by the singing of that song in a house in Moscow, though I think it would have been bluster. In his heart, I'm not sure Vadim loved his country any more than I did, or than Dmitry or . . . well, no more than Dmitry or I anyway, but Vadim did like to make his patriotism clear for everyone else to see. He loved the emblems of Russia and hated the emblems of the invader. How I would have loved to have him beside me then, huffing and puffing at the outrage of hearing the air of Moscow polluted by such a tune. In truth, Bonaparte himself would have been little happier. He found "La Marseillaise" a little too redolent of revolution for his new imperial dynasty, but it remained popular amongst the men.

For my part, I loved the tune. I lay my head against the wall behind me and enjoyed the rendition. The Frenchman inside the house sang in a fruity tone and had just got to the bit about the bellowing soldiers coming to cut the throats of his sons and his consorts when he too was cut short. The song ended in a curt, startled yelp, with which I was becoming all too familiar. I continued the song under my breath, choking back a tear whose cause I could not quite determine:

> *"Aux armes citoyens.*
> *Formez vos bataillons.*
> *Marchons, marchons!*
> *Qu'un sang impur*
> *Abreuve nos sillons."*

It was inexplicable to be so overcome with emotion at a foreign anthem—far from the finest music, or verse, ever written—but for the man inside the house, whose death at Matfei's hand I had just listened to, it had meant everything. I had witnessed many deaths over the past decade, and if he had been stood on the battlefield, supporting to the last a tricolour, then his death would have been . . . respectable—both to me and, I believe, to him. But ever since we had begun to work with the Oprichniki, there had not been one single honourable death amongst the whole lot of them. Maks' death, the deaths of the uncounted French, even the deaths of the Oprichniki—Simon, Iakov Alfeyinich and Faddei—betrayed by Maks to the French; none of these fitted into the mould of the regular deaths of war. Perhaps in years to come, such ways of dying would become commonplace and acceptable, as the Frenchman—Louis, I think it was—had suggested back at that encampment we had infiltrated, but just then I yearned to witness a straightforward death by cannonball or sword. When I had chosen my path, away from the regular army, I had thought espionage was about information; about discovering what lay in the enemy's mind. I soon learned that it was simply about terminating those minds—about finding new and more unusual ways to carry death to our foes.

The door of the house opened and Matfei emerged once again. Glancing from side to side, he headed back up the street the way we had come. A coldness gripped me as, for the first time, I noticed something tangibly vile in one of the Oprichniki. Up until then, their methods and their manner were distasteful—distasteful to me and hence the problem was as much mine as theirs; no more than a clash of cultures. But what I now saw took a step beyond distaste, into abhorrence. I noticed—and at that distance I could hardly see, yet I was nonetheless certain—that he had blood on his lips.

Still, there might be nothing untoward in that. The Frenchman might have put up a fight before his death, laying a punch on Matfei's face, and so the blood might simply be Matfei's own.

After a few steps, the Oprichnik stopped and raised his hand to his mouth, wiping the stain away. He looked at his fingers, considering the blood that he found there. I couldn't help but remember the blood on my own fingers, as those fingers were one after the other removed from my hand. Perhaps Matfei had not realized that he had been injured, and now, on seeing his own blood as confirmation of the wound, he would merely wipe his fingers clean on his coat. He did not. He raised his fingers back to his mouth and licked them delectably until the blood was gone. Then he set off once again on his way. Memories of long-forgotten stories forced their way into my mind, but I repressed them. I continued my pursuit.

As we travelled back northeastward, Matfei's stride was now less surreptitious—more the step of a contented gentleman returning to his home after an evening's revelry. Indeed, the directness of his motion suggested that he was no longer meandering through the city in search of targets, but was heading for some specific objective, which could only be his lodgings.

The fact that he had done his work for the evening and was heading for home, however, did not deter him from keeping an eye out for any other opportunities to kill that might arise. We had been travelling for about half an hour, always in a roughly northeasterly direction, when Matfei suddenly pressed himself against a wall and vanished, much as I had seen Foma do. His hearing was clearly sharper than mine; it wasn't for several seconds that I heard the regular footfall of a patrol.

I ducked into an alleyway, watching the point at which Matfei had disappeared, hoping, if not to see him as he hid, at least to have my eyes focused on the right place when he eventually moved. The patrol marched past him, close enough to feel his breath on their cheeks, if he was in fact breathing at all, such was his stillness. And even now, just two days into their occupation of Moscow, I think "marched" was too flattering a word for the French troops. Over the weeks that the French remained in Moscow, the behaviour of the average soldier was to deteriorate beyond all military decorum, but already their marching was slack and ragged. They chatted and laughed as they went by, and the last of them paused to light a cigar that he had, no doubt, stolen from some empty Muscovite home, part of the pillage that the French termed the *"Foire de Moscou"*—the Moscow Fair.

I held my breath, though in anticipation of what, I could not tell. Did I fear that the French would see Matfei, that the French would see me or that Matfei would see me? The actual outcome was, I think, the one that I had really been afraid of. The hindmost, straggling man, lighting his cigar, stood unwittingly at the very point in the street where Matfei had thrust himself, camouflaged against the wall. He had fallen ten, perhaps fifteen paces behind his companions.

Matfei pounced. In a single motion he stepped to the soldier's side and flung his tightly clenched fist back against the man's larynx. The blow itself could have caused fatal damage to the soldier—though not immediately fatal—but additionally, it bashed his head back against the wall behind him with a damp cracking sound. Matfei's action had exhibited enormous strength, but also an indolent casualness, like a child cuffing aside a ball as he runs in for his dinner. The soldier crumpled unconscious to his knees, dragging in scraping breaths through his shattered windpipe.

Before the man's comrades had even the first inkling of his disappearance, Matfei had found the street entrance to the cellar of a nearby tavern, and had slipped down inside, dragging the dying soldier with him.

I crept up to the trapdoor, which Matfei had left open, not daring to go too close, as though it were the entrance to a bear's cave. For all I knew, Matfei could be sitting there in the darkness, looking out at me, waiting until I had moved near enough for him to swoop upon me and drag me back inside. I stood a little way away from the open cellar, trying to make out any hint of movement from within and listening closely. I heard only the vaguest sounds of movement, and then a crash of breaking glass, followed by an exclamation that I took to be a curse.

Suddenly, a dim glow could be seen at the opening to the cellar. Clearly, Matfei was as blind as I was in the pitch dark and needed additional light. I moved closer to the entrance, remaining standing so that I might be ready to run and also so that I wouldn't peek around the edge of the trapdoor to find myself face to face with Matfei. This way I could see deep into the cellar from some distance, and when I finally saw him, I would still be far enough for him not to reach me.

The first thing I saw was the sparkling remains of several broken vodka bottles, presumably those which Matfei had smashed in the darkness. Behind them was a small lantern which lit the room—Matfei had either been lucky in finding it there, or well prepared in bringing it along with him. A pool of spilled vodka was spreading out from the bottles and gradually soaking into the compacted earth of the cellar floor, but still I could not see Matfei or his victim. I took another step, to improve my line of sight, and a foot came into view—Matfei's from the look of it. He was kneeling or even on all fours and so the sole of his boot faced upwards. Beside it, the clear puddle of vodka was mingling with another, darker spillage, whose source I could not see.

With one more step towards the cellar door, the full picture was revealed.

TWELVE

Matfei was on his knees, crouched over the body of the French soldier. One hand was on the man's chest, pressing him down in case he tried to struggle, although he appeared little capable of it. Matfei's other hand was under the soldier's chin, pushing back his head at a macabre angle so that his neck jutted enticingly outwards and upwards. At a first glance, one might have thought Matfei was kissing him, or trying to revive him, but it was not on the soldier's mouth that Matfei had placed his own lips, but on his neck.

The dark puddle that I had seen was a pool of blood, dribbling from the soldier's throat beneath Matfei's mouth. It was unthinkable, but it could only be that Matfei was drinking the man's blood. Even so, he was wasting an awful lot of it. This was not, however, I recalled with a shiver, his first meal of the evening.

Matfei adjusted his position slightly and the soldier's previously motionless legs began to thrash in a pathetic, strengthless, final attempt to resist the assault on his body. Matfei pressed down harder on the man's chest and began to raise his head, satisfied, I thought, with what he had drunk and pausing in his foul imbibement.

But as Matfei raised his head, so the neck and the head of the soldier began to move with it. Matfei pushed against the body beneath him and I saw that his teeth were still sunk deeply into the man's throat. As he strained upwards, the skin suddenly ruptured and gave way and Matfei's head rose rapidly, a lump of flesh trailing from his bloody mouth.

Chapter XIII

"*V* OORDALAK!*"

The word had found its way from my deepest childhood memories to my vocal cords before my adult mind had time to pour scorn upon it. I heard the whispered sound and only then realized that it was I who had spoken it.

Voordalak—the vampire. Now I remembered the word in the voice that had first spoken it to me. It was an instantly vivid memory: the old house in Petersburg that belonged to my grandmother and in which she had in her old age and her diminishing wealth retreated into just a few rooms; the taste and the texture of the sweet *pirozhki* of which she maintained a seemingly unending supply; the children gathered around her—myself and my two brothers and various cousins whom I could never quite keep track of—listening to her stories.

My grandmother was the dichotomy that lay at the heart of the Russian spirit made flesh. That at least, and using somewhat different words, was what my father, her son, had brought me up to believe and what I did believe. Despite the dilution of her family's capital over the generations, she maintained an unshakeable belief in etiquette, in the keeping up of a demeanour that fitted one's station and in the God-given order of society and of the world in general. And yet beneath that outward pride lay the intellect of a peasant. There was no stupidity to her, merely a complete lack of any useful education, and worse than that—far worse—a lack of any hunger to be educated. She had inherited her wealth from her parents and they from their parents and her knowledge of the world came to her, unamended, by the same route. Just as she, sitting in the few habitable rooms of her once grand house, with only one ageing maid to serve her, failed to realize that wealth did not last forever but must be continually renewed, so she failed to understand that knowledge itself must be renewed, and not simply kept. The two concepts—

in both success and failure—were inseparable. It was not for nothing that Christ had chosen the word "talent" in His parable.

And so it was entirely in keeping with her own upbringing that my grandmother passed on her knowledge to her children and later to her grandchildren. From her I learned vast amounts of the history of the empire which I have never doubted, and even more about religion, which I constantly and fruitlessly have. But her greatest joy, her greatest expression of love for us, was in her attempts to terrify us. She told us stories, with the same personal confidence with which she described Tsar Pyetr or Jesus, of all the horrors—both natural and supernatural—that could ever be expected to keep a child awake at night. She told of witches, of wolves, of plagues of rats and, which scared me most of all, of the *voordalak*—the undead vampire.

My father quickly put me straight on the matter. Long before I was born—having seen the luxury in which some of his more distant cousins lived, while he had to work to maintain the most modest of households—he had realized the flaws in his mother's view of the world. He knew that his family would have to create its own wealth and that to do so, it would have to acquire an education. He had put the stories of vampires out of his mind, and when he discovered that I had heard them too, he put them out of mine. He found money to pay for some sort of education for me and each of my brothers, and I was the one who was lucky, or unlucky, enough for that education to be a military one. All thoughts of vampires, and witches, wolves and plagues of rats disappeared from my mind and I became a man.

My grandmother had died when I was seven, but it seemed she had been better read than I had given her credit for. "Give me a child until he is seven and I will give you the man." St. Ignatius had said it and, it seemed, my grandmother had known it. For in that instant when I had seen Matfei down in the cellar hunched over the soldier's body, everything that my grandmother had told me had flooded back into my mind like an invading army. Now I had seen it with my own eyes, the conviction I had had as a child, the conviction that my grandmother knew she had instilled into me, came back to me with renewed strength. These creatures truly existed. I had seen it. And with that knowledge came another certainty—again imbued in me by my grandmother as an indisputable truth—that such creatures were evil and must be destroyed.

And all that memory and all that knowledge returned to me in the moment it took me to listen to a single word, whispered on my own lips.

"*Voordalak!*"

Matfei heard it too. He raised himself from his grisly meal and looked towards the open trapdoor. I took a rapid step back into the shadows. I could still see the bottom half of Matfei's body, but not his face. He hesitated, wondering whether he truly had heard a noise and whether it posed any danger to him. He quickly chose the path of discretion and I saw his feet heading up the cellar steps and into the tavern above. He slammed the door behind him.

I dropped down into the cellar and examined the soldier's defiled body. He was most certainly dead. His wide eyes gazed unseeing at the ceiling above him and in the murky half-light of the lantern his skin was ashen, its colour drained from his body into the pool that stained the floor around him—and drained too into Matfei. The wounds to his throat were horrendous. Only gaping red caverns remained where there had once been flesh. His crushed voicebox remained *in situ*, but on either side the muscles of the neck had been wrenched away so deeply that the two cavities were joined together—I could, had I so desired, have placed two fingers in one wound and seen them emerge from the other.

I heard footsteps in the room above and remembered that the creature that had done this was still in the building. There was nothing that could be done to assist the dead man with whom I shared the cellar, but plenty I could do to avenge him, for vengeance was my immediate thought, driven into me by my departed grandmother, regardless of the fact that he was a Frenchman—my enemy. I climbed back out of the cellar and scampered across the street to hide. I watched the tavern and did not have to wait long to see Matfei emerge cautiously through the main door. He glanced from side to side and then took a few steps towards the open cellar, casting his eyes inside for a moment, but seeing only the remains of what he had left there. It might have been opportune to attack him there and then, but I could not see myself being victorious in such a battle. I was not armed with my sword—that would not have been compatible with my guise of being a butler—and only had a knife, which I had concealed in my coat. Besides, in all of my grandmother's stories, the *voordalak* rarely responded to the simplistic methods of killing that are so effective on humans.

He set off along the street, heading again to the northeast. He seemed to travel more warily than he had before, though not now concerned for anyone that he might run into ahead of him, but with an eye over his shoulder for fear that he was being followed. I don't think that he ever saw me or heard me, but he knew that there had been someone watching him in the tavern cellar. He also appeared now to be in more of a hurry—his pace was brisk, occasionally breaking into a stumbling run. At first I thought that this was in an effort to escape his pursuer, but as such it seemed ineffectual. Then I realized that it tied in with another piece of folklore that my superstitious grandmother—and how wrong I now knew I was to regard her in that way—had poured into me as a child. Dawn was approaching. The dull red light of the burning city which had filled the sky all night was now being replaced by the half-light of the as yet unrisen sun. Could it be that, as in legend, Matfei had to make his way to some dark resting place; that he would perish if as much as a glimmer of the sun's light fell upon him? "We sleep by day and kill at night." Those had been Pyetr's words at our first meeting, three weeks before; words that could easily have come from the lips of my grandmother or of any grandmother as she gave a description to her darling grandchildren of ancient encounters with the dreaded creatures of the night. As a military tactic, it had much to be said for it, imitating the lifestyle taken up by many predatory creatures in the wild. Now it seemed that Matfei and his friends chose that existence not in *imitation* of the wolves and the bats, but because they—the Oprichniki—*were* creatures of the wild, bound by nature itself to follow that nocturnal doctrine.

We were now in an area very familiar to me; only two blocks from the house on Degtyarny Lane where I had spent so many happy hours with Domnikiia. I thanked the Lord that she was no longer in the city. But Matfei carried on, through streets already consumed by the great fires, past others that were still ablaze. It was in Gruzinskaya Street, well outside the main sprawl of the city, that he finally showed signs of being home.

It was a small house, far more humble than most of those occupied by the French. From outside I could see the narrow, low windows that let some little light into a cellar for which there was no entrance from the street. Matfei flung himself over the fence into the back yard and, listening to his footfall, I could hear that his path was downwards to the cellar and not upwards to the house. I tried to look into the cellar through those small windows at the front, but could see nothing. They were painted over from the inside or covered with curtains.

I paused for a moment, for the first time since I had seen Matfei in the cellar. What I had seen him doing to that man—and I pushed the image from my mind immediately as I recalled it—was certainly abominable, inhuman even, but I had seen enough of the world to know that humans were quite capable of carrying out inhuman acts. I had witnessed that during those few hours I had spent as a captive of the Turks. But what they or I might be driven to *in extremis* was not the same as what I had seen Matfei do. And yet in the encroaching light of dawn, the memories of my grandmother's tales began to recede once again. My father's rationality reasserted itself. Perhaps my grandmother was right; there were creatures which drank the blood of men. Perhaps? It was now beyond question—I had witnessed it. But that did not mean that a special word like *"voordalak"* needed to be conjured up to describe them. Matfei was just a man—however warped and vile a breed of man he might be. A cannibal is no less of an abomination than a vampire, but it is a much easier concept to handle.

Whatever his nature, it would make no difference to his fate. He had to die, and I would kill him. It did not matter that he was my ally; this was now an issue beyond mere war. That much at least remained from what my grandmother had taught me—a certainty as to what was right and what was wrong, a sense shared by the whole of humanity that in whatever squabbles we have between each other, there are some boundaries that are not crossed. But Matfei's nature did affect the question of how easy he would be to despatch. If he was merely some degenerate specimen of humanity, I would have little trouble with him. If a vampire, then I would have to be more wary. I tried to remember more of the folklore, but I knew that even if I could recall my grandmother's words, I would have no way of separating the kernel of fact from generations of embellishment. I did not want to find myself Matfei's prey simply for believing in some storybook method for despatching a vampire. Nor did I want to hold back from a conventional attack which might in reality prove to be perfectly effective. As so often, I wondered what Maks would have done.

Maks! For him too it did not matter as to the nature of these creatures. I had left him with them, and having seen the way that Matfei had done his work in the cellar, I had no reason to suppose they would have treated Maks any differently. Be they vampires or men, they would have ripped the flesh from his body and devoured it while he still lived. But then another part of the folklore emerged from my memory, and I prayed to God that either my grandmother was wrong or that the Oprichniki were mere men.

I vaulted the fence. The dawn was becoming ever brighter and the birds sang their song of salutation to it with all their might, but it would still be a good five minutes before the sun actually rose. And yet, I wondered, how much reliance could I place in the old legends that these creatures must shrink throughout eternity from the sun? Ultimately, it did not matter. Matfei had to die. All nine of the Oprichniki that remained had to die. And to kill nine I first had to kill one, and Matfei now awaited me at the bottom of those cellar stairs. At least, I hoped it was only Matfei. Did these creatures sleep alone? Might I go down there to find all nine of them waiting to welcome me, aware after my inept attempts the previous night to follow Foma that I was pursuing them? Had Matfei's long journey of butchery across the city been simply a lure to get me to this point so that I might be removed once and for all as an obstacle to their activities?

Beyond the fence, inside a small courtyard, a flight of stone steps led down to the cellar. At the bottom, a closed door hid from me what lay inside. Matfei, for sure, but who else I did not know. I descended on tiptoe and listened at the door. All was silent. I turned the handle and stepped inside.

It was dark, but not pitch black. Some light shone through the open door and the roughly torn cloth that I could see draped across the small, high windows did not completely obliterate the glow of the day awakening outside.

The atmosphere was stale and dank, and colder than the air in the street. Within moments my eyes had adjusted to the dim light and I saw what lay in the cellar.

There were two coffins. I call them coffins because of their present usage. They had not been built to be coffins, but simply as large packing cases of the sort often used to transport muskets and other armaments to the front lines. By virtue of their size and shape, however, they sufficed as resting places for these dead creatures. The one furthest from the door was empty. Its lid lay untidily across it, reminding me of an unmade bed and making it easy to see that its owner had not yet returned. The other was neatly closed and therein, I concluded in the absence of any other hiding place, lay Matfei.

I took hold of the lid. It was not locked or restrained in any way and it lifted easily to reveal Matfei's recumbent body. To anyone who did not know the nature of this creature he would have appeared as though dead. Even a physician, who might test his heartbeat or his breathing, would have found no conventional sign of life. Any doubts I might have had now fled. This was no man, however depraved. This was the *voordalak*. This was the terror of my childhood become real. He lay quite still, his eyelids closed, his arms by his side. He was in many ways much like the soldier whose body he had left in another cellar less than an hour before, but the one difference was in his complexion. Whereas the soldier had been pale—deathly white as is fitting in the dead—Matfei had a warm and ruddy hue. All the colour that had been taken from the soldier had been transferred, through his blood, into the creature that lay dormant before me. And with the colour, the life was also transferred. In nature, one animal may feed on another's flesh; the taking of life is an inevitable consequence. But here in Matfei was a creature that fed directly on the life of others. The eating of flesh and drinking of blood may have been a necessary mechanism—a repugnant mimicry of the Eucharist—but the nutrient that was required was life itself.

I couldn't return that life, or the countless others that Matfei had taken in his time, but in ending his I could at least ensure that there would be no more deaths at his hand. I had with me still, in my pocket, a large folding knife. I took it out and opened it. The blade was easily long enough and strong enough to pierce his heart as he lay there, unaware of my presence, but I hesitated. I had no compunction about taking his life—if it could be so called—but I remembered again the stories of how difficult such monsters could be to kill. A metal blade was useless; every story I had ever heard agreed on that. Or would silver perhaps work? It didn't matter; my blade was made of steel. It had to be a blade of wood—a wooden stake.

I looked around me and my eyes fell upon the lid that I had moments earlier removed from Matfei's coffin and leaned against the wall. Would that do? Didn't I recall that it couldn't be just any wood, but had to be hawthorn? The packing case lid was certainly not made from hawthorn. And how could I get a usable stake from the flat lid? And where should I stab Matfei? My grandmother's words began to come back clearly—too clearly. I could remember with certainty that in some stories the *voordalak* had to be impaled through the heart, in others through the mouth. Could both be right? Was either?

I looked down again at the knife in my hands. It felt solid and comforting. I had used it to kill in the past. Surely, whatever manner of creature Matfei was, he was subject to nature's laws. To have his heart pierced, whatever the material that did it might be, must destroy him. I raised the blade and turned back towards my quarry.

Matfei's fist came down sharply on my hand, knocking the knife to the ground. He was standing beside his coffin, just inches from me, evidently awakened by my presence. He shoved my chest with both hands, exerting a herculean strength which flung me across the room and into the coffin lid, smashing it into pieces. I struggled to my feet and stood, leaning against the wall, gasping to recover the wind that had been knocked out of me.

"So," he said in his thickly accented French, "the Russian commander has decided he's had enough of his underling, has he?" He strode towards me menacingly as he spoke, imbued with a new self-confidence that I had not seen in any of them before. His eyes were filled with a fire of sneering hatred which was directed solely at me. "I'm surprised you'd stoop to getting your hands dirty." He was in front of me again now and grabbed my lapels, hurling me across the room and into another wall. "Why not just hire somebody else to kill us once we've killed the French for you? I saw the way you and your friends sniggered at the master when he spoke to you—like he was some old fool—some foreigner who didn't deserve to be in your beautiful city."

He had crossed the room to me again and this time he struck me across the jaw with the back of his hand. The blow had the same casual might that I had seen him display earlier. It knocked me back into the corner, amongst the shattered remains of his coffin lid. In the face of his strength, I was helpless. At the farmhouse near Borodino, I had witnessed the Oprichniki use speed to capture their prey. In the streets and houses of Moscow it had been stealth. Here I found that Matfei needed neither; his physical power alone was more than enough for him to subdue me. But as if to prove that even this would not be the ultimate instrument of my death, he bared his teeth, still stained with the blood he had drawn at the throats of his earlier victims. His canines, as folklore tells, were bigger than those of a human, but were not, as I had imagined in my childhood, the sharp, precise tools of a surgeon. They were the teeth of a dog, designed more to tear than to pierce.

"You people think you are so refined, with your beauty and your love," he continued as he approached me once again. I was surprised by this unsuspected feeling of pent-up loathing he had for me. "But Dmitry Fetyukovich was right; you don't have the stomach to do what we do and you don't have the guts to stop us."

A tiny part of me wanted to hear him out, not out of politeness, but out of a desperate hunger to discover what could be in the mind of a creature such as this. The struggle for my life, however, was of a greater importance, and now seemed to be my best opportunity. My aim was no longer to kill, but simply to survive; and survival meant flight, for which I needed to get him as far away from the door as possible.

I picked up the broken half of the coffin lid and held it in front of me with both hands, as if intending to use it as a shield. Then I dropped it downwards so that its jagged broken edge pointed towards Matfei as a single row of sharp, wooden teeth. At the same instant I launched myself up off the floor and out of the corner towards him. The upward impact of the serrated edge of the heavy lid into his chest caught him off balance and actually lifted him from the floor momentarily. I carried on running, gathering momentum and pushing him across the room. Had he once found a foothold, he might have been able to use his huge strength against me, but with his feet trailing along the ground, unable to find a purchase, there was nothing he could do.

His back hit the opposite wall and he came to a sudden halt. The coffin lid, and myself with it, came to a halt a fraction of a second later, but in that fraction, the heavy wooden board had travelled far enough to crush his chest. Splinters of wood had penetrated between his shattered ribs and into the organs beneath. Every sense told me to flee, but instead I stood there panting, leaning against the lid with all my weight to pin him against the wall. His head was slumped on to his chest and for a moment I thought he was dead. Then with a swift movement his head snapped upward and I again saw the glare of his hate-filled eyes. He pressed his arms against the wall behind him and, despite all the force I could summon against him, began to push his body away from it. Then, with a look of sudden surprise, he weakened and fell back. The wooden shards that permeated his chest embedded themselves just a little further as the heavy lid followed the motion of his body. I wasn't sure whether his final spasm had been the writhing of a dying animal or that as a result of his movement some tiny splinter had penetrated that vital fraction further into his heart, but now he hung limply and moved no more.

I held my breath, fearing that he might once again revive and avenge himself, and unsure of how to determine if he was truly dead. My uncertainty was unnecessary. Proof of his death soon came in an unexpected but unmistakable fashion. His whole body underwent an almost imperceptibly gradual transformation. One could more easily have captured the movement of the hands of a clock than to have noted any specific event of change in him. And yet within two minutes, the corpse had dehydrated before my eyes. The texture of his skin altered from marble to chalk; his hair from silk to cotton; his eyes from glass to ice. Every physical quality became an unconvincing imitation of what it had once been, just as in his undead life, his whole existence was an imitation of the man he had once been. At the moment of his death the creature before me, however gruesome and horrific, had displayed the richness and vibrancy of an oil painting. But now, though it was of the same scene, it was as though the oil had been replaced by watercolour. The subject was identical, but the medium had changed.

I relaxed my pressure on the wooden lid between us and the depth of penetration of the desiccation became clear. The body had no integrity left in it whatsoever. Every bone, every hair, every sinew had become dust. The dust had remained at the same point in space as the element of the body from which it had decayed, since it had had no impetus to move, but at that slight movement of the wooden guillotine that bisected the body, it began to fall away. His legs and arms and the lower half of his torso crumbled to the ground in an ashen pile, spilling out of his now shapeless garments like flour from a ruptured sack. I was left face to face with the parched bust of Matfei. A head and shoulders that rested on top of the instrument of his death, as true to life as any marble Caesar that has ever been unearthed, but nothing like as permanent. It took me a few moments to relax, to realize that he was dead beyond any resurrection, but finally I stepped back and let the wooden lid drop to the floor. As it fell, so did the last remnants of Matfei, not to shatter as they hit the ground, but before even reaching it, dispersed by the air through which they fell. As the last of his clothing hit the ground, a final puff of dust erupted from the chimney formed by the collar of his coat and then he was, beyond any doubt, no more.

I sank to the floor, flinging my head backwards with an urgent requirement to breathe deeply. The tension in my muscles hesitantly began to die away as my body came to understand that the fight was over. I looked across to where Matfei had perished, to where the body would have lain had this been any ordinary death, and as I did so I felt uneasy. Something was missing. Something that should have been there was not there. The body itself was obviously one thing that should have been there, but that was not it. It was not something missing from the room, but something missing from me. I felt absolutely no sensation of regret. One might expect that a soldier of more than ten years' standing, used to killing, has long passed the stage in his life when he regrets the death of his enemy, and to some extent this was true. In battle, when the enemy is remote, separated by the range of a cannonball or a musket shot, then killing is a mechanical action—the pulling of a trigger or the lighting of a fuse. Sometimes those actions cause death and sometimes, when the shot misses, they don't. Even when swords are drawn in battle, the enemy is faceless and it is difficult to say, at the end of it all, whom exactly one has despatched.

But that was not the kind of soldiery in which I had become involved. Many of the deaths I had caused had been personal, as this had been. Some had been men that I had been spying on, who had turned round to discover me following them and against whom I had to defend myself. Others I had marked out to kill, studying the details of their lives and their routine before striking. In every case I had known what I had done was right, that their deaths were necessary to my survival or for the benefit of Russia, but always I had regretted that there had not been some other way, that years before some twist of fate had not put the man in the situation where I had to kill him.

With Matfei, however, the killing had been a pleasure. There was no niggling wish that fate might not have caused our paths to cross, but quite the reverse. I was glad to have been there; glad to have been the instrument of his death. The inhumanity that I had perceived in the Oprichniki now made complete sense.

Inhumanity was their most telling quality—and it cut both ways. It was inhumanity that allowed them to kill with such ease, with such determination and without scruple. They had at some point in their lives found a way to amputate their humanity, seeing it as a hindrance to what they desired to achieve. But having lost the restraint of humanity, they had also lost its protection. They had lost that secret Masonic sign of recognition that one human sees in another and gives him pity—holds him back from killing if there is any other way. Matfei may have been freed from any qualm about killing a man, but with it he paid the price that any man who knew his nature would have no qualm about destroying him.

Perhaps it was less complex than that. Perhaps the reason that I did not regret Matfei's death was simply that I had not witnessed it. Matfei had died many years before and far, far away, when he had first been transformed into what he had become. The rapid physical decay of his remains, to which I had just been witness, was merely the instant release of the years of accumulated decay since he had first died. Whether at his true death he had willingly chosen the undead path that his body had taken, or whether it had been forced upon him, I did not know. On that issue hinged the whole question of whether he merited any pity at all.

A sound above me interrupted my contemplation. A booted foot smashed through one of the high, narrow windows that opened on to the street. A voice shouted inside. It was one of the Oprichniki. I did not know which—I found it hard to tell some of them apart by sight, let alone by sound—but he was calling to Matfei. The Oprichnik—the *voordalak*—slithered through the smashed window feet first, but rather than jumping to the cellar floor (which was more than the height of a man below the window) he hung there, supporting his entire weight on one arm and using the other to grab hold of something he had left outside. I could see now that it was Varfolomei.

Having found his grip, Varfolomei finally dropped to the ground, bringing with him through the window the inert body of a soldier. The dark green uniform revealed it to be an Italian—one of the many non-French nationals that made up almost half the Grande Armée. Varfolomei grasped him firmly by the collar of his coat. As the body fell, Varfolomei lost hold of it, and the soldier (a Carabinier, if I judged right, who could not have been more than seventeen) slammed to the ground. He groaned and tried to turn on his side. As I had seen before, the Oprichniki preferred their meals still to have a little life remaining in them.

Varfolomei knelt beside his prey, running his eyes up and down the young man's body and rubbing his own face and neck with a sense of urgent yearning. Again he called out to Matfei, generous enough to share his trophy with his friend.

"Matfei can't hear you, I'm afraid, Varfolomei." I spoke with a confidence born out of my earlier battle, but not justified by the luck of my victory.

Varfolomei turned and rose to a crouched position, poised for an attack. He was, I think, the youngest of all the Oprichniki. That is, the youngest in appearance and therefore the youngest when he first met his death. Once preserved in that state he might have wandered the earth for centuries—longer even than any of the others—or for mere months. It was impossible to tell—and all guesswork on my part.

"Where *is* Matfei?" he asked.

I nodded towards the mound of clothes that lay discarded against the wall, coated in the powdery residue that was all there was of Matfei. "Don't you recognize him?"

Varfolomei walked over and examined what remained of his comrade. His lip curled in an expression of distaste that was just what one might see when a human comes across the rotting carcass of an animal. There was a visceral disgust, but no sense of spiritual sympathy with the living being out of which those remains were formed. To me Matfei was merely dust; a dry powder that would soon be dispersed by the wind. To Varfolomei it was a *memento mori*, and his mood suddenly changed to one of devastation. He sank to his knees and picked up a handful, letting it run away through his open fingers as he inspected it in a hopeless search for some hint of remnant life.

"They told me I would live forever," he announced.

"Is that what attracted you to it?" I asked him.

"No. They said I would know no fear. Fear was my worst enemy." He glanced towards me. I could not have been a very intimidating sight. I was unarmed and exhausted, my body slumped forwards and my arms resting on my knees. I could scarcely lift my head to speak to him.

"Fear of what?" I asked. Behind him, I saw the Italian roll on to his front and raise himself to his knees.

"Of consequence," replied Varfolomei, with an ambiguity that implied he had thought about this many times before and chosen the word with care. The Italian was on his feet and was creeping towards Varfolomei with drawn sword.

"So you fear consequences?"

"I used to fear the opinions of my peers." He raised his eyes from the dust in his hand and looked at me. "Now I have new peers." His hand slammed out to his side, hitting the Carabinier's chest and knocking him to the floor. It was a moment's distraction for Varfolomei, but long enough for me to shoot out my hand and grab what I needed.

"People like you used to despise me," continued Varfolomei, rising to his feet, "and I can tell you still do. But do you know what's changed? I don't care any more." Behind him the soldier had risen to his feet. He did not bother to recover his sword, but began to shadow Varfolomei's steps as he approached me, always keeping a safe distance behind.

"You talk as if you care," I said, rising to my feet. The reason that the soldier had not picked up his sword became clear. He was not stalking Varfolomei, but creeping towards the door. Now that he was within reach, he made a dash for it. He made his escape without interruption and we heard his feet race up the steps to freedom.

In his hurry, he had neglected to shut the door behind him. A fragile beam of the dawn's earliest sunlight shone through the door and into the cellar, a little way behind Varfolomei. He glanced behind him and his jaw tightened slightly, almost imperceptibly.

"And there seems to be something else you're frightened of," I said, taking a step towards him. He could not move away from me for fear of stepping into the sunlight. There was, of course, little reason why he should move away. I could present no threat to him, but the army whose retreat is cut off will always have a greater fear of its attacker.

"It is nothing in comparison to what you have to fear." There was no false bravado in his voice. He believed it and he was right. I could feel my own pulse in my neck as my heart attempted to prepare me for what was about to come. I took another step forward. Varfolomei could either retreat or attack—and he could not retreat. I had deprived him of choice, and choice is a potent weapon of war.

Trapped, he launched his attack and threw himself at me with all his strength. I fell backwards, but as I did so, I raised my hand, presenting to his chest the sharp, pointed splinter of wood that I had snatched up earlier.

I hit the floor heavily, banging the back of my head against the ground hard enough that I feared I might lose consciousness, but throughout I kept the wooden stake pointed towards him. He fell upon me like a wild dog, his eyes ablaze with hatred and craving. I saw his mouth wide open, his fang-like canines descending towards my throat, preparing to rip it out, as I had seen Matfei do earlier. Then I felt an aching thump against the right side of my chest, almost like a stab wound, as the momentum of his body imparted itself to the stake and thence into me. But I had the blunt end of the stake to my chest, and although it might bruise, it did not pierce.

Since my body would not yield and nor could the wooden splinter itself, there was only one alternative. Varfolomei's body continued to descend towards me and I felt the wind punched out of me as his full weight landed, but his teeth made no attempt to connect with my throat; his eyes no longer looked on my face with either wrath or hunger. He was already dead. For his body to reach mine, the stake which I held out had been forced to pass through it. I had already learned by Matfei's death that the stake didn't need to be hawthorn; it just needed to pass through the heart. Varfolomei's death was mere confirmation.

I felt the weight of his lifeless body draped on me like an exhausted lover. Almost immediately, the load began to lighten. I heard a hissing sound, like running water—the dusty remains of Varfolomei's decayed body cascading off mine on to the floor. Just as they had with Matfei, the years of decay since his first, true death had come to his body in seconds. His head remained intact for a brief moment longer, his face staring into mine without even those basest and most basic of emotions which the Oprichniki could display in life. Then it collapsed, leaving only his empty clothing clinging to my body and filling my mouth with a dust that I leapt to my feet to spit out, wishing that I had a canteen with me to rinse away the taste. Not that it had much taste. It was the concept that I needed to wash away.

I left the cellar quickly, walked up the stairs and climbed back over the fence and on to the street. I walked a little way until ahead I saw a patrol of about half a dozen French heading towards me. At their head was a dishevelled young man who was shouting at them in an Italian which they little understood.

"It's this way. There were two of them. They were fighting over who should kill me." It was the young infantryman who had just escaped from the cellar. I slipped down a sidestreet. As for the two that he thought had been fighting over him, I had escaped, and of the other he would find little but dust.

CHAPTER XIV

I WAS ABOUT AS FAR FROM MY BED AS IT IS POSSIBLE FOR ONE thing to be from another in Moscow. As I headed back across town, the air was heavy with the stench of smoke. Buildings were ablaze everywhere—perhaps half of the city was burnt or burning. Even south of the river in Zamoskvorechye, houses were on fire.

The flames had not reached the stable where I had been staying, but I felt no inclination to be caught asleep in a wooden building if the fire did reach it during the day. I was desperately tired, having been up all night, and I suspected that the night that was to come would require similar exertions of me. Across the street was a small church, abandoned by its priest and his entourage before the French arrived and, crucially, made of stone. I gathered up what few possessions I had left in the stable and made my way over. It was a matter of little trouble to break into the crypt and I slipped inside.

It was cold and dark. Outside, even though it was now midmorning, the city basked in an eerie twilight caused by the thick smoke that hung over it. Somewhere through it, I could just make out the disc of the sun, shining brightly, but lessened in its power by the smog that the fires all around constantly replenished. Within the crypt, it was darker still. It was an ideal place for anyone who wanted to sleep undisturbed during the day.

I paused, remembering that there were still seven others in the city who needed a dark, secluded place to sleep through the hours of daylight. What if, by some unlucky chance, one or more of the Oprichniki had chosen this very place to secrete their coffins? Would I awake to find that I had slept alongside the very creatures that I hoped to destroy?

On the other hand, there were many, many churches with crypts in Moscow, and many other similarly safe places that weren't crypts at all. It would have surprised me if the Oprichniki could even go near a holy place such as a church, although I immediately remembered that Foma and Ioann had met me outside one less than two days before. But I was very, very tired. For all I knew, the smoke outside was so thick that the Oprichniki might be able to wander around in the open without need to fear the sun. I lay down, using a stone step as a pillow, but despite my exhaustion, I could not sleep.

Since I had last closed my eyes, my whole conception of the world around me had been ripped apart. So many things that had seemed mysterious about the Oprichniki could now be explained: their enormous strength, their avoidance of daylight, the tales of death that had followed them on their journey up the Don. Most of all, I now understood their motivation. They did not fight for their country or for my country, but for the most primitive instinct of all; they fought for food. But even that did not quite fit. They killed more than they needed, surely, for food. At the farmhouse in Gory-achkino, three of them had killed thirty men. Did they need ten each for their cravings to be satisfied?

"Satisfied." It was the word Pierre had used when he was describing their attack on his camp. They had continued to kill even though they were satis-fied—even though they had eaten all they could. So perhaps they killed for other reasons beyond food—for pleasure, much as rich, idle men (and I must include myself at times amongst them) hunt animals that they could never eat. Or perhaps they killed so many for much the same reason as the Russian army did—because they were enemies on our soil. Perhaps they were merely doing what we had gladly asked them to do—helping to kill our enemies. Could I really blame them for doing what I had asked and for getting some enjoyment out of it? I had chosen to join the army, so many years before, because I wanted to travel. I had killed, I would guess, one man for every twenty versts of Europe I had crossed. Was not their justification—that they needed to eat—better than mine, which was, to reduce it to its most basic, that I was curious?

I cast such thoughts from my mind. I knew in my gut that these crea-tures were evil. There was much in the knowledge of past generations that an enlightened man of the nineteenth century could regard as primitive—in sci-ence, warfare, literature and music—but that did not mean it should all be dismissed. I'd been arrogant enough to laugh at my grandmother's stories—laughing to hide my fear—but now she'd been irrefutably proved to be right. I still had to discover some of the details, but she had been right about the existence of vampires, and I was not going to dispute their vile nature. I would not disagree with centuries of accumulated wisdom on what is good and what is evil; on what is right and what is wrong. Every atom of my experience and of the wisdom handed down to me from my forebears told me how I should regard these creatures, and there was no amount of logical, rational consideration of their behaviour that could change that. They were abominations against God and they had to die. I had begun the task the previous night and I would continue the next night—and the next and the next until the job was complete.

I tried to sleep once again and this time found that drowsiness quickly overcame me. I thought of the seven other figures lying elsewhere in the city in similar dark places also seeking the reinvigoration of slumber. As I dozed off, it occurred to me to wonder how they had managed to sleep out in the countryside as we had headed out west to meet the advancing Russians, with no permanence as to where we would be from one day to the next. The question did not occupy my mind enough to keep me awake.

Nor did the implications of what Maks had done, or of what had befallen him. I had realized almost as soon as I had discovered that the Oprichniki were vampires that Maks might well have had Simon, Iakov Alfeyinich and Faddei killed not because of his loyalty to France, but out of his loyalty to humanity. "Humanity." It was the very word Maks had used the last time we spoke, moments before I abandoned him to those creatures. It seemed almost certain that he had known what they were. Beyond doubt was the fact that his death had been the most gruesome imaginable. And yet I managed to sleep.

When I awoke it was into total darkness. I leapt to my feet, afraid that I had slept all day, but as consciousness returned to me, I realized it was dark simply because I was still in the crypt. A heavy, throbbing ache gnawed at the right side of my chest. The events of the previous night came back to me in an engulfing wave of remembrance. The pain in my chest was where the stake that had penetrated Varfolomei's body had merely bruised mine. I went over to the door and looked outside to find that it was still daylight—the middle of the afternoon. The smell of a burning city hung in the air.

There was little that I could do until that evening's meeting. I would arrive early and hope that Vadim and Dmitry were there early too—before any of the Oprichniki arrived. Three of us against seven would be better odds. It was something of a blessing that my mind was occupied by the night ahead, else I might have broken down at the state to which the city had been reduced. Whole blocks of once grand buildings lay in smouldering piles of charred remains. The leaves of trees, some already turning brown with the onset of autumn, had become grey from the thin layer of ash that coated them. Was any of that ash, I wondered, in fact flecks of the dust into which Matfei and Varfolomei's bodies had corroded, swept up by the wind into the air and mixed with the smoke from the fires? How long would it take for their remains to be spread thinly across the whole city; the whole country; the whole planet? How much of the dust that fills our homes, that is beaten out of our carpets, that we inadvertently inhale every day, comes from other such creatures, killed long ago by righteous men, their residue spread to the four corners of the earth?

Here and there amongst the burnt-out buildings mementos of the souls that once inhabited them had survived the conflagration. China bowls and plates scattered the floor where the cupboards that had held them once stood. In one house a heavy oak table had survived unscathed while all around it had been consumed. In another lay a pile of empty book bindings, their paper contents burnt away while they had somehow survived. There were few that died in the fires. Even if Moscow had not already been abandoned by its people, fire in a tightly packed city is always more of a danger to property than to life. The fire is seen at the end of the street. The neighbours shout. People flee their homes and stand out in the road to watch. And still the flames have moved up the street by less than the width of a single house. The inferno moves as slowly as the tide, but with the same determination. The greatest risk to the onlookers is not the flames or the smoke, but the chance that an entire building might collapse outward into the street, crushing those who stand and gawp.

Where I was now, amongst the ruins, that scene of conflagration had been played out hours or even days previously. Elsewhere in the city, it was at that moment taking place. In the remains of some of the grander houses—grander before the fire levelled the homes of both the rich and the poor—crouched figures poked among the debris, scavenging for anything that might be of value. Some rich families had left their finest jewellery behind, hidden beneath floorboards or behind panelled walls. But they could not hide it from the fire. With the floorboards and the walls gone, all these things fell to the ground. Precious stones survived the flames intact; precious metals melted and reset, but lost little of their value for it. Those who scavenged risked burning their fingers on the still-glowing embers, but they thought it a worthwhile price to pay. Others were wiser, and sent their children to do the foraging.

Still wiser were those who foraged not for wealth, but simply for sustenance. In kitchen gardens—accessible from the street now that the houses to which they once belonged had been razed—men, women and children scrabbled for the few rotting cabbages and potatoes that remained, which they either ate raw immediately, or hid inside their coats to savour later. Whilst Russians scavenged both inside for jewels and outside for food, the French troops had no concept of the possibility of starvation, and concentrated in their looting only on what was traditionally valuable. In the weeks that were to come, many would discover that they would gladly exchange a ruby for a beet root, or a diamond for a potato. A few would cling to their spoils forever, deluding themselves to the last that a rich man can never go hungry.

It was Thursday and so our rendezvous was at the Resurrection Gate, the northern entry to Red Square. I arrived soon after eight, almost an hour before we were due to meet. The sun had already set and, as I stood and waited, looking at the weather-beaten mosaic icons above each arch of the gateway, I was thankful that the fires had not got this far—at least, not yet.

One icon depicted Saint George, the city's patron saint, running his lance through the mouth of his monstrous foe, the dragon that lay spread-eagled, almost in supplication, beneath the hooves of the saint's steed. It seemed indisputably final—good, as is right and proper, vanquishing evil. But was there more to come? The dragon had its long, serpentine tail wrapped around the horse's hind leg. Was this just a last contortion of the beast's death agonies, or had the dragon conceived a plan whereby it might dismount its foe and, against probability and against legend, devour the saint? The icon illustrated just a single moment. We could see neither how the dragon and saint had arrived at this confrontation, nor how it was to be resolved. To find out, we have only the mythic tales—written by men, not by dragons.

With a smile, I allowed myself the indulgence of picturing me—Aleksei Ivanovich Danilov—as a modern Saint George, saving Moscow from a new spawn of monsters that were threatening it. They were not dragons but, it occurred to me, they had been brought here by Zmyeevich—the son of the dragon. Had it been his father that George had killed? Had he brought the Oprichniki to Moscow for revenge? I laughed out loud at the path my imagination had chosen, then glanced around; no one was there to have heard me. I wondered how an icon of me might look, doing battle with Matfei and Varfolomei in that cellar. Again, the iconographers would be able only to capture a moment. They would not show that it was I who, in part, had invited the monsters into the city, nor could they show, as yet, the final scene of the story. When and how would I feel the serpent's tail wrap around my ankle and drag me to my doom?

"It feels like it's been a long time, Aleksei Ivanovich."

I turned. It was Dmitry. It had been six days since I had spoken to him and then I had felt a hatred towards him that I thought I could never overcome. It had begun to fade almost immediately but it had been a long six days, and now my opinion towards him hinged on one simple question: did he already know? I had worked alongside the Oprichniki for a few weeks and, although there had been many small things that had made me feel uneasy about them, it was not until I had seen Matfei in that cellar—in fact later, when I had seen his body crumble to dust—that I had known for certain what they were. Dmitry had known them for much longer. Could he possibly have avoided finding out? I had suspected right from the beginning that there was something about the Oprichniki that he was keeping from us, but never something like this. Perhaps he just had his own suspicions and had dismissed them as ridiculous. If he did know, then I had no idea what to say to him. If he didn't, then he had to be warned.

But when I looked at him, I felt another certainty. He was simply familiar old Dmitry; a man of reliable, almost mundane, simplicity. He was not a man who existed in a world of vampires. If he had known of it, it would have changed him, and I would have known. I stepped towards him and embraced him heartily.

"Oh, Dmitry!" I muttered into his shoulder. He flinched. It seemed that six days had done more to heal my mental attitude towards him than they had done to heal the physical injuries I had inflicted on him when we last met.

I took a step back. "Are you all right?" I asked him.

"It still hurts a little," he replied, without bitterness. "You knew what you were doing." I think it was meant as a compliment. He looked at me intently and his face showed concern. "I think the question is better aimed at you. Are *you* all right?"

"I've been . . . busy."

"You look terrible. Have you slept? Have you even eaten?"

Over the past days, I hadn't thought to consider my own circumstances. I had bought food, at preposterous prices, from marketplaces when I had had the opportunity. I had slept, but my rest had been disrupted as I had adjusted my sleeping pattern to synchronize with that of the enemy; not the French, but my new enemy, the Oprichniki. My body still ached with the bruises of my encounters with Varfolomei and Matfei. I had not washed. I had not changed my clothes. I had been sleeping first in a stable and then in a crypt. There had been no mirror for me to see myself in for days, but Dmitry's expression was mirror enough.

Dmitry fished into his pocket and brought out a block of something, wrapped in paper. He offered it to me. It was cheese. I sat down with my back against the Resurrection Gate, and ate it with a hunger I had not known was in me.

"I don't like to gloat," said Dmitry, sitting beside me, "but I've found this one of the easiest jobs I've ever had. Meet up with the Oprichniki of an evening, have a quick chat, and then let them get on with it. They're causing more havoc than we could ever do."

"Yes," I said forcefully, through a mouthful of cheese, "and I've found out why."

"Why"? How is there a 'why' about it?"

I looked at him gravely, wondering whether I had the words to explain what would be—and had until recently been to me—unbelievable. The words that we have to talk about these things are the words that are used to recount stories, not to convey the truth. I remembered how Vadim had broken to me the news that Maks was a spy. All I could do was speak directly.

"They're not human, Dmitry. They're monsters. They kill so that they can feast on the flesh of their victims." It was a delight to speak about it. While what I knew remained simply thoughts in my head, my sanity had hung solely on the flimsy thread of its truth. By giving voice to it I became once again sure that the knowledge was real; a passenger in my mind, not a creation of it.

Dmitry was unmoved—neither shocked nor disbelieving, and yet apparently comprehending. In case there was any doubt, I decided to make things utterly clear for him, using the word that my grandmother had spoken with fear, my father with scorn. I used the word with precision.

"Dmitry, they're *voordalaki*."

Dmitry shook his head, as if in a momentary spasm. "So?" he asked. "We fight alongside Prussians, Austrians, Englishmen. We don't care who they are as long as they are on our side."

He hadn't even bothered to ask me how I knew. What I had told him was preposterous superstition and his reaction was not to deny it but to belittle it. He was not saying to me "don't be ridiculous" so much as "don't be sentimental." It was at once obvious that I had been mistaken about him.

"So you knew?" I asked him.

"Yes, I knew." His reply was dismissive, but that he needed to say more showed that he was also defensive. "I knew that they are the most accomplished killers I have ever met. I knew that my country was threatened with invasion. I knew that they could kill a dozen Turks where all our guns and cannon might have killed one. I knew that we needed them and, most importantly, Aleksei, I knew that we could trust them. This is our country we're fighting for; it's not a time to be picky about how we fight. The French would do the same, but we're the lucky ones—they're working for us and they do what we tell them. If we ask that they kill only the French then they kill only the French—and by the hundred."

We were interrupted by a third voice. "They killed Maksim." It was Vadim who spoke, stepping out from the shadows. I don't know how long he had been listening. "He was Russian."

I wished it were not the case, but the argument was far too easy to answer. "They killed Maksim with our consent," I replied. "He was as good as French."

Vadim nodded grimly. "Perhaps you should tell me everything you've discovered," he said. "Dmitry Fetyukovich may have his own reasons for believing in the . . ." he hesitated to use such a superstitious word, ". . . voordalak, but I need a little more persuading."

Vadim's arrival had so quickly transformed into a discussion that I had no opportunity to greet him, as I had Dmitry, with the affection that had been building within me over the past few days. But had there ever been an appropriate moment, it had now passed.

"I'll tell you," I said, "but we had better walk. The Oprichniki may arrive here at any moment." We walked across Red Square. When almost empty, as it was now, it is the perfect place for a private conversation, if one stays close to the middle of it. No one can approach without being seen; no one can get within earshot. The nearest hiding places would be amongst the market stalls and simply constructed shops that ringed the perimeter of the square and—to my mind—detracted from its grandeur. No one was trading at this hour and those stalls which had not already burnt were abandoned. We were free to talk in private. A raised voice could echo from one side of the square to the other, but a whisper dies away unnoticed by any but those for whom it was intended.

I realized that I had to be careful of what I told them—more specifically, of what I told Dmitry. If it was no great surprise to him to discover the true nature of the Oprichniki, then that would make it even more of a shock to him to discover that I had killed two of them. I wasn't so sensitive as to worry about shocking Dmitry, but I felt fairly sure that he would sooner or later be telling the other Oprichniki what I had done. That I could do without.

I told them of how I had followed Foma. There was not much in that to contribute to my condemnation of them, but it established the pattern that I was later to see Matfei follow. Then I told them of my pursuit of Matfei, and told them what I saw beneath the tavern—of how he tore out the throat of that Frenchman with his teeth and of the wounds I found on the body when I got closer. Then I had to stay close to the truth, but not reveal all.

"I followed him further," I continued, "to another cellar, north of Tverskaya. I waited outside and soon I saw Varfolomei arrive. I was already pretty sure about what we were dealing with, so I waited until it was fully daylight before following them down. Inside, I saw them. They sleep in coffins. I could look close enough even to see their teeth. The stories you hear are true—they have fangs like wolves."

The most unambiguous proof as to what these creatures were lay, of course, in the manner of their deaths, but I was unable to reveal that part of the story. Instead, I extemporized. Matfei and Varfolomei were in no position to contradict me.

"They awoke and came towards me. I don't know if they were going to attack me, but I backed away; back out of the door, into the light. They stopped, as if the doorway was a barrier to them. They dared not step into the light." Still I faced a problem. Their fear of the light was not enough to convince Vadim as to what manner of creatures they were. I had seen them face to face—that had been enough for me—but without describing how they actually died, what proof did I have? I realized the best way to condemn dead men was also the most traditional—to claim that they confessed to me.

"So I felt a little safer and we began to talk," I continued. "They're not ashamed of what they are; they freely admitted it. They couldn't see why I should be shocked at it." The reaction I was describing was in fact close to the one that Dmitry had displayed moments earlier, but it seemed the safest bet for how they might have reacted if I had given them the chance.

"And you believed them?" asked Vadim, as if I were a fool. I turned to him, my face expressing something of my outrage. "I wouldn't have expected such credulity in you, Aleksei."

"I wasn't being credulous."

"Oh, come on!" Vadim raised his voice, and then lowered it, looking around in case he had been heard. "Either I can accept that all that rubbish the peasants believe about the dead rising from their graves and drinking the blood of the living—things that no intelligent man has countenanced for centuries—is true, or I can believe that one of my officers got hoaxed by a couple of foreign mercenaries with a twisted sense of humour. That's hard enough to swallow, but it's the better option."

"But I saw Matfei, tearing the flesh from a man's throat with his teeth!" Now it was my voice that was raised.

"You could have seen anything."

I took a breath. It seemed I would have to tell them the evidence of my own eyes, whatever the risk. Before I could speak, Dmitry came to my rescue.

"It's true, Vadim. I've seen far more than Aleksei has. Not here, but back in Wallachia. I knew what they were when I called them here."

"And you decided not to tell us," said Vadim.

"I had promised them that I would keep their secret."

"That wasn't your decision to make."

"It was part of the deal. They wouldn't have come otherwise." He could see that Vadim was still unconvinced. "We need them, Vadim. When it comes down to it, they are very proficient soldiers. They have killed who we wanted them to kill. They will help us to drive out the French. You're not going to throw all that away, are you?" He was talking only to Vadim. There was little point in trying to persuade me.

"Forget about them," said Vadim. "I don't have any quarrel with them, Captain Petrenko." He was at his most formal and therefore his most irate. "My quarrel is about why you chose not to tell us what you *claim* to know."

"Then quarrel with me later. We're in the middle of a war." I had never heard Dmitry—or any of us—speak to Vadim in such an openly rebellious tone before. Vadim was not one to lord it over his subordinates, but Dmitry was crossing into unknown territory as to what he would put up with.

TWELVE

Vadim covered his face with his hands and breathed deeply. "This is madness," he said. "Arguing as to whether you should have told me they were vampires. I should be dressing you both down for being so gullible."

"Perhaps we had better postpone this," I interrupted, nodding across the square to where I had seen two figures approaching. At a distance it was unclear who the shorter one was, but they were undoubtedly Oprichniki and the taller one could be no one but Iuda.

Vadim and Dmitry stepped apart, trying to look somehow nonchalant for the benefit of the creatures that approached us.

"We'll speak of this later, Dmitry Fetyukovich," muttered Vadim through a false smile. "If what you say is true, then that was no way for Maksim to die."

"So what's a good way for a traitor to die?" came Dmitry's reply. Before anyone could add anything else, the Oprichniki were with us.

It was Ioann that accompanied him, but as usual, Iuda did all the talking.

"Good evening, Vadim Fyodorovich, Dmitry Fetyukovich, Aleksei Ivanovich."

We each acknowledged his greeting.

"How is your work progressing?" asked Vadim.

"According to plan," replied Iuda. "We are restraining ourselves so as not to give too much alarm. At present the fires are causing as much trouble for the French as we are."

"I think they've nearly run their course now," said Vadim. "The French have organized themselves enough to deal with them. On top of that, there's not much left to burn." He said it with a casualness that belied how deeply we all felt for the devastation of the city.

"Good. They have been a cause of much concern to me and my friends. Indeed, we have not seen some of our friends for several days," said Iuda. "Have any attended your meetings?"

"We saw Matfei and Varfolomei last night," said Dmitry.

"We?"

"Vadim Fyodorovich and myself."

"So you were not at that meeting, Aleksei Ivanovich," said Iuda, turning to me. I wondered if he already knew about what had happened to Matfei and Varfolomei and whether he was trying to read my mind. I was relieved that Dmitry had not mentioned my following them.

"No, I didn't make it. But the previous night I saw Foma and Ioann," I replied, nodding towards Ioann, who still stood tacitly beside his taller comrade. "It's not always easy to travel across the city, even at night. I'm sure the others are perfectly safe."

"You are no doubt right, Aleksei Ivanovich—those whom you have not seen are quite safe, I'm sure. I myself saw Pyetr and Andrei only last night."

Ioann shuffled his feet impatiently and looked around him.

"I think we had best be about our work," said Iuda, noting Ioann's nervousness. "I'm sure we shall all meet again soon." He glanced at each of us in turn, in case we had anything more to say. Seeing that we had nothing, they turned and walked away.

Once they were out of earshot, I heard Vadim's voice in my ear. "So, which one do you want to take?" The thought of pursuit that had been on my mind had evidently been on Vadim's too.

"You choose," I said.

"You're going to follow them?" asked Dmitry, as if astonished that we could consider something so underhand.

"I would like to see for myself what Aleksei has described," said Vadim. "Then I might be convinced. I'll take Iuda."

"Fine by me," I said. My plan was not simply to follow, but to follow and to kill. To that end, I would prefer it to be Ioann. Strange though it was to admit, Iuda managed to carry some vestige of personality about him—relative at least to the other Oprichniki—that would make his death less of a pleasure. "I'll take Ioann."

"You don't have to join in if it goes against your conscience, Dmitry," said Vadim with a knowing smile. It was unthinkable that Dmitry would allow himself to be left out of it.

"No, I'll tag along. I'll go with Aleksei."

"It's all right," I said, not wanting Dmitry to interfere with my true purpose. "I'll be fine. You go with Vadim."

TWELVE

"No, Aleksei. We're the old team. We work best together."

I couldn't make any further protest without it being too obvious, and Dmitry knew it.

The two Oprichniki were still just visible, leaving the square to the right of Saint Vasily's. The three of us scurried through the burnt remains of the square's shops and then skirted around the left-hand side of the cathedral. Iuda and Ioann had separated, with Iuda heading in our direction. We ducked back into one of the many columned archways beneath the cathedral's steps. Iuda passed by without seeing us. With a brief smile and a wave of farewell, Vadim set off in pursuit.

Dmitry and I headed off in the other direction and soon caught sight of Ioann once again. He had turned west along the embankment between the Kremlin and the Moskva.

Ioann's travels of that night were not much different from those of Matfei the previous night, or of Foma the night before that. His chosen prey—like Foma's—was from a concentrated group of soldiers. During the night he found three separate barracks, two of which I'd mentioned when I'd briefed him and Foma a couple of days earlier. He slipped quietly into each one, making no sound as he entered or as he killed. We made no investigation ourselves of what he had done or whom he had killed. We both knew full well what had taken place—unlike Vadim, we required no further physical evidence.

Waiting and watching as Ioann went about his activities summarized for me the ambivalence of my attitude to the Oprichniki. My intent was to kill Ioann as soon as the opportunity arose and I should have been mortified at each killing that my delay allowed him to perpetrate. In reality, I could only be happy at those deaths. They were the deaths of French invaders. Their deaths were the very purpose for which we had summoned the Oprichniki to Moscow. My desire to kill Ioann was based solely on what he was, not on what he did. I supported him in his actions and condemned him for his nature. It was the exact opposite of why I had allowed Maks to die.

After his three repasts, Ioann's movement had become less stealthy. As I had observed in Matfei the previous night, once their hunger had been sated, then the Oprichniki became a little less feral in their movements. His walk was more upright—more proud—and, were it not for the circumstances in which the city found itself, he might have been mistaken for a Moscow socialite returning from a night of gaming or dancing.

With Dmitry's assistance, following was far easier than it had been alone. In a city, there is an established way for two men to follow another. The pursuers never need get near their quarry; they never even have to take a single step along the path that he has trod. While one remains stationary to watch where the target is going, the other runs down a sidestreet to get ahead of him. Once he has made it to a new viewpoint, the roles are switched. The man who is being followed never sees movement and never knows that he is being pursued.

This approach was complicated by the fact that I was urgently trying to evade Dmitry whilst still keeping track of Ioann, because I knew that Dmitry would try to thwart me in my goal of destroying at least one more of the repulsive creatures that night. Dmitry seemed to guess that I was planning something and so he spent as much of his time pursuing me as he did helping me to pursue Ioann.

Despite these intricacies, and the steady rain that began to fall during the night, we did not lose sight of Ioann. His resting place turned out to be not far from where we had first met him and Iuda earlier that night; close to Kutznetsky Bridge, the French quarter that had still managed to escape the flames. It was an address in a tightly built area, where the boundaries between separate properties within a block were so indistinct that one front door could have led to any one of three or more homes. Remarkably, these buildings too were as yet untouched by the fires which had already consumed many of their neighbours. Ioann crept up the steps to a door and slipped inside.

"Any more you want to see?" asked Dmitry, unenthusiastically.

"Yes," I replied. "I want to see where he goes."

"He went in there. He's not going anywhere else tonight. It'll be dawn in an hour."

But I was already setting off to see precisely where in the building Ioann lay. The fact that I had not been able to shake Dmitry off my back was not going to be a permanent impediment to my goal. If I could see where he slept, then I would have the benefit of a full day of sunlight to come back and slaughter Ioann in a manner of my choosing.

I reached the doorway, still ajar as Ioann had left it, and peeped inside. Within, I could see nothing but an empty hallway. I heard footsteps behind me. It was Dmitry, clearly (and wisely) unwilling to leave me alone with Ioann for even a few minutes.

"You see anything?" he asked. I shook my head and pushed open the door. There were three doors off the hallway, plus a flight of stairs. Beneath the stairs, open, was a fourth doorway which, undoubtedly, led down to the cellar. That surely was where Ioann would have gone.

More prepared than the previous night, I had brought with me a candle, which I lit. I held it ahead of me as we descended the stairs. Dmitry was close behind me, his hand against my back. A sudden fear possessed me. If we were to encounter Ioann—and maybe other Oprichniki as well—on whose side would Dmitry place himself? Was that hand on my back there to steady and reassure me, or would it be the case that if I turned to flee the *voordalaki* we encountered, Dmitry's hand would thrust me pitilessly into their midst? Dmitry had saved my life seven years before. We had been the closest of friends before that and ever since. I had named my son after him. It was a shocking reflection on one or both of us that at this moment I could doubt him.

At the bottom of the stairs, my candle illuminated on one side an archway into a small cellar and on the other a closed double door. A brief glance through the archway proved that there was nothing there. The ceiling was partially collapsed and no one had bothered to repair it in years. It was a miracle that no dinner party from the room above—tables, chairs, tureens, plates, servants, guests and all—had ever fallen through and landed in there. None had, nor had Ioann made his bed there.

Dmitry remained on the stairs, again almost deliberately blocking my exit. I pulled open the left-hand door and peered into the darkness beyond. This cellar was larger than the other; less dilapidated but still unused by the occupants of the house. No windows shone any light into it, and there were no other exits but the one at which I stood. Much as I had seen twenty-four hours previously, in the centre of the floor lay two coffins. This time they were not the makeshift crates of the night before. Whoever slept here slept in luxury. The coffins were solid oak, with brass handles. Where the vampires had obtained them, I could not guess.

I walked over towards them. Halfway across the room I heard a sound at my back. I had just walked into a cellar with only one exit. Anyone who had been expecting me could easily have hidden beside the doorway and stepped out only now to seal the trap. I turned. It was Dmitry, peeping through the doorway. For a man so familiar with the ways of the Oprichniki, he was remarkably timid about encountering them in their own environment. I beckoned to him to follow me, but he stayed where he was.

I took a step towards the first coffin. It was empty. Stepping over that, I looked into the second. There lay Ioann, his face the same rosy flush of repletion that I had seen in Matfei. Ioann had not even bothered to pull the coffin lid across him. In that windowless cellar, there was little chance of any sunlight disrupting his sleep.

"What's in them?" hissed Dmitry from the door.

I dared not make even that little noise. I simply mouthed to him. "Ioann's in this one. The other's empty."

"Then let's get the hell out of here before the other one comes back." Dmitry spoke louder this time, and once he had spoken, he was gone. I could only defer to his experience and assume that these creatures did not like their slumbers to be disturbed.

I went back up the stairs to the hallway and then out of the front door, looking around to see where Dmitry was. I heard a hiss and looked to its source. It was Dmitry, settled atop the low roof of a building on the other side of the street where he could observe this building unnoticed. I ran across and climbed on to the roof to lie beside him.

"Not a moment too soon," he said, pointing towards the far end of the street. The unmistakable form of Iuda had appeared. Unlike Ioann, he had retained his stealthy creeping posture. Perhaps he had not eaten. Perhaps he was wise enough to understand the continued need for caution once he had. Whatever the reason, he kept to the walls and to the shadows throughout as he progressed down the street.

TWELVE

"No sign of Vadim, though," whispered Dmitry smugly. "Evidently he lost track of him."

"Either that or he's so good at avoiding detection that he's keeping hidden from us as well as Iuda," I replied. For my part, I wasn't sure which was more likely. Vadim was a little older than the rest of us, and his skills in this sort of work had never been quite up to the abilities of me, Dmitry or Maks. Maks had always excelled at it—both in hunting and in avoiding being hunted. No one could get close to Maks unless he wanted them to— unless he trusted them. I pulled myself up. It was another train of thought that I did not wish to follow.

Iuda had reached the steps of the house. With a swift glance around, he went inside.

"I trust you don't want to follow him too, and check where he's going, Aleksei?" said Dmitry.

I smiled. "No, I think we can make a guess on that one."

We climbed down from the roof and headed back up the street.

"Well," said Dmitry, "if Vadim's out there, he's bound to see us now."

But of Vadim there was no sign. "Iuda must have given him the slip," I said.

The sun was just peeking over the horizon as we turned the corner into the next road. Iuda had left his homecoming to the latest possible moment.

"Shall we go and steal some breakfast then?" asked Dmitry, in a manner so casual one might have thought that the mysteries of the past few days had never occurred.

"No," I said. "I'm tired. I'll see you tonight." With that I parted company from him, heading in whichever direction he wasn't.

I meandered through the city streets for about an hour. I had all day to return and destroy the creatures that slept in that cellar, but it would feel better to get it over with sooner. Turning back to the blocks of houses to the east of Red Square, I saw the now all too familiar glow of flames. The fires, thanks to the rain of the previous night, were generally dying down. But the rain had now stopped and there were still areas of Moscow that remained untouched by the flames and so were still ripe for the burning.

I began to run back to where Ioann and Iuda lay. Although I had slightly less stomach for killing Iuda than for the others, I still knew that it had to be done. The fire in this area, however, would make my job much easier. Even so, I had to make sure the vampires found no route of escape.

When I got there, half of the block beneath which the two Oprichniki lay was already ablaze. Within five minutes their cellar too would be a furnace. I couldn't remember the folklore in detail, but I did remember the slight fear that Foma had shown when I mentioned the fires to him. I felt quite confident that fire was one of the ways by which vampires might be destroyed. Even if they tried to escape the fire, they would have to leave the safety of the cellar to do so. If the flames did not destroy them, then when they came out into the street, the light of the sun would.

It was still not certain enough, however. Their cellar lay beneath a massive sprawl of buildings. It was conceivable that, with a degree of luck, they might find their way to safety without ever having to expose themselves to daylight. It was a risk I did not want to take.

I raced into the house and down the cellar steps with none of the trepidation that I had shown during the night. The doors behind which the two coffins lay remained closed. Already I could smell smoke creeping in from the neighbouring houses. I looked around me. In the collapsed cellar opposite I saw a short beam of wood. It was perfect. The cellar doors had on them two large handles through which the beam would fit, barring the door securely.

I turned and lifted the wooden beam. When I turned back, I saw that the doors had begun to move. Somebody was beginning to push them from the inside. The vampires were awake and were about to make their bid for freedom. I flung myself against the door, the beam stretched out in front of me with my full weight behind it. Whoever was pushing the doors open was taken completely off guard and they slammed shut. I had only moments before he recovered. I could not both lean against the door and use the beam to bar it permanently. I took my weight away and slipped the beam behind the two iron handles, fearing at every moment that the doors would spew open before I had made them safe. They did not, and now that the beam was in place, they would not. I breathed again.

TWELVE

I knew that I should leave, that I had as much to fear from fire as the vampires did, but I felt the urge to wait, to make certain that they perished. I sat down on the steps. Almost immediately, heard someone banging against the doors. At first it was the rapid beating of someone demanding attention, then it was the slower, heavier thud of a shoulder trying to break down a barrier. The door held. Soon there was coughing. I could see smoke beginning to seep under the door. I remembered one of my grandmother's stories, wherein a *voordalak* could transform itself into mist or smoke at will. Could that be true? If it was, then I might have expected to see evidence of them doing it already. And still the coughing and the banging continued, so I felt I was safe.

With the fire so close upon me, I decided it was time to leave. As I began climbing the stairs, the beating on the doors returned to the rapid pounding that cried attention. Now, between coughs, it was accompanied by an excruciated scream.

"Help! Help!"

I could not resist smiling at the thought of Iuda or Ioann, whichever it was, dying in such pain after what they had inflicted on others. At a conscious level, it never even occurred to me that the cry was in Russian. Soon the voice lost the strength even to scream. I heard the sound of a body slumping to the ground and the voice relaxed from a scream to a prayer.

"My God, have mercy upon me."

It was only then that I recognized the voice as Dmitry's.

CHAPTER XV

I THREW MYSELF BACK DOWN THE STAIRS AND LIFTED THE bar from the doors. Immediately they swung open and Dmitry's semi-conscious body spilled out on to the floor. At the same time, I was hit by a wall of smoke and heat which combined to make breathing an impossibility.

The cellar beyond was in flames. Fire licked across the wooden ceiling and the supporting beams were almost charcoal. Within moments the roof would collapse. One of the coffins was completely ablaze, the other, in which I could just make out Ioann's still-dormant body, was already beginning to blacken in the flames. It had been dragged from its original position towards the door, so that Dmitry's feet almost rested against it.

I bent down over Dmitry. He was breathing shallowly. The backs of his hands and his forearms were burnt. On the right side of his face, his beard had withered away to reveal his scar, surviving intact as the rest of his cheek had blistered under the intense heat. I would have slapped his face to try to bring him round, but given his injuries, I chose to shake him by the shoulders.

He soon began to cough and open his eyes.

"Can you walk?" I asked.

"Yes, yes!" he insisted, pushing himself up to a sitting position.

"We have to get out, and fast." I went back to the doorway. The stairway down which I had descended was beginning to smoulder.

In places its ceiling was already alight. It was still passable and, anyway, it was the only exit we had.

"Come on," I said, turning back to Dmitry.

"Give me a hand!" Dmitry was further into the cellar than where I had left him. His hands were clasped around a handle on Ioann's coffin and he was straining every sinew to pull it to the door. In his weakness, Dmitry was unable to move it even an inch. "We have to get them out of here."

TWELVE

Even if I had wanted to save the Oprichniki—rather than leave them there to be reduced to nothingness by the all-consuming flames—it would have been impossible. Ioann showed no sign of regaining consciousness and there was little hope for even the two of us to manhandle his coffin up the blazing stairway.

"Leave him, Dmitry! You've got to come now!" Dmitry ignored me and continued to haul pathetically at the coffin. I dashed back over to him and pulled him away. He could offer little resistance. I pushed him towards the door, and he seemed then either to bow to my stronger will or realize that his rescue attempt was hopeless. I herded him in front of me up the stairs. When he was almost at the top, and I was about halfway up, the step beneath my foot gave way. The fire below the wooden stairs was intense—enough to eat away at them without actually sending them up in flames. As my leg fell through the gap, up to my thigh, I felt immediately the heat of the cavity below. My leg began to roast with a pain such as I had never before experienced.

My body twisted and I found myself looking back down the stairs into the cellar. Through the smoke and flame I saw Ioann, awake now and fighting his way towards us. His eyes fell upon me and, with a leap that was unmistakably similar to the movement with which Varfolomei had launched himself on me the previous night, he attacked. He seemed not so much concerned with saving his life as with avenging his and Iuda's deaths, or at least with having one final meal.

As he leapt, the ceiling above him gave way. Burning beams crashed to the ground and took Ioann with them. They would have fallen on me too, pinning me to the steps and trapping me in this inferno, had I not felt Dmitry's strong arms at that moment lift me from where I lay and out into the hallway above. Even there, we were not safe. The whole house was ablaze and on the verge of collapse. We made a dash for the door, one of us supporting the other, though which was which I could not say, and made it outside to the cool, life-giving Moscow air.

The fire had now attracted some attention. A French captain was attempting to organize a human chain of both French soldiers and Russian civilians to get water to the fire. The task was hopeless, but they were intent on it and paid little attention to the two figures that had just bolted out of the house and lay gasping for breath in the street outside.

At length I heard a voice ask, in genuine Muscovite Russian, "What were you doing in there?"

I raised my head. It was a girl of about fifteen, scruffy, with a dirty face and tightly curled black hair. She was leaning over Dmitry to see if he was unconscious or dead, but speaking to me.

"We were sleeping in there. Our house has already been burnt down. This time it almost got us." I rolled on to my side towards Dmitry. "Is he all right?" I asked.

"He's badly burned, but he may live," she replied, and then went over to the captain who, I presumed, had sent her to find out what we were about. She spoke to him briefly and then returned to us.

"Come with me," she said, trying to lift Dmitry. I put my shoulder beneath Dmitry's arm and together we managed to raise him to his feet. With whatever slight consciousness he had about him, he managed to take some of his own weight on his legs and so we slowly made progress away from the burning buildings. My own leg continued to feel as though it was roasting within my breeches, but the pain remained constant whether or not I put any weight on it, so it was little hindrance to our progress.

"What's your name?" I asked the girl as we walked.

"Natalia," she replied.

"I'm Aleksei. This is Dmitry."

"Why have you stayed in Moscow?" she said.

"Our household packed up and left us behind. He's a chef." I nodded towards Dmitry. "I'm a butler."

"No you're not," she laughed. I don't know what gave it away, but it was evidently easier to fool dozens of French officers than a single Russian child. "I reckon you're soldiers." I made no reply. "Are you going to kill all the French for us and make the city ours again?"

I smiled to myself. "That's the plan."

"Did you start the fires?"

"No," I replied. "The fires don't do Moscow any good."

"They don't do the French any good—that's what matters."

"You were talking happily enough to that captain."

"I'd have pushed him into the flames if I could. Not too far in. I'd rather he burned slowly. I'd hold him down and let my own hand burn if I needed to."

"So for you it's any price to defeat Bonaparte?"

"They killed my brother. He was a soldier, just like you. Well, not like you. He was just a *ryadovoy*, not an officer." How she knew we were officers, I could not tell.

"Where did he die?" I asked.

"At Smolensk."

"What was his name?"

"Fedya. He said the tsar would never let them take Moscow." She paused for a moment before adding, "He was wrong about that."

"No, I think you just misheard. The tsar will never let them keep Moscow. That's why he sent me and Dmitry here."

"Just you?" she asked derisively.

"And others."

"I hear they've let loose a plague that only affects Frenchmen. Is that true?"

"Would you be happy if it was?"

"I'd be happy to pay any price to get rid of them. I was happy to lose Fedya." She became suddenly silent. I sensed a tear rising inside her as she comprehended what she had said about her brother. "Not happy," she managed to force out with a choked voice, desperate for me to understand what I found so obvious.

"I know what you mean," I said.

"So remember me when you kill them. And Fedya too. Think of us and don't show any mercy."

I had no time to reply. We had arrived at her "home." It was a shantytown, founded in a churchyard a few blocks to the north of where Natalia had found us. Rough tents and awnings had been set up to accommodate perhaps fifty or sixty people. Around the periphery, a sort of market had formed, selling basic foodstuffs and clothing along with more prestigious items that had no doubt been pilfered from nearby houses. While I could not begrudge them the sale of the valuables left behind by evacuees who had no further use for them, I had seen in Natalia and saw now in the others an emaciation which told me they should not be storing up gold in exchange for food, but quite the reverse. Clothing too, though now it seemed like a source of income, would be sadly missed in the winter months in a town two-thirds consumed by fire, even if the French did leave.

She led us through the marketplace to a central area divided up into small cells by rough curtains of thin linen. She took us into one of them, where a man, aged around fifty, sat cross-legged on the muddy floor, tapping nails into a pair of boots. Around him were scattered a few rudimentary possessions, and on the other side of the cubicle a sheepskin marked the position of their bed; a roughly tied bundle of cloth serving as a pillow. On this, we laid Dmitry.

"This is my father," said Natalia. "He's a cobbler," she added unnecessarily.

I held out my hand. "Aleksei Ivanovich."

He held out his in return. "Boris," he said. "Boris Mihailovich."

"Aleksei is an officer," said Natalia proudly.

"Then I'm sure he would prefer it if you did not announce the fact too loudly, my dear," replied Boris Mihailovich. He held out the boots to her. "Now take these back to Lieutenant . . . whoever it was, and make sure you get from him what he promised."

Natalia took the boots and scurried off. Throughout my life I had, I hoped, served my country and served my superior officers, but I had never had to work in the way that a valet serves his master or a cobbler serves his customer. The contrast between Natalia's desire for the death of every Frenchman in Moscow and her willingness to take money off them was one that I had not experienced; at least not from that side of the deal. Did Domnikiia, I wondered, harbour the same ambiguous feelings towards her clients? I hoped that, with one exception, she did and I believed truly in that one exception and in its being me, but I would have given much to be with her then and to hear her reassurance that it was so. I would have given much to be with her, whatever she chose to say.

TWELVE

"How's your friend?" asked Boris, inclining his head towards Dmitry. His face was filled with warm curiosity. The whites of his eyes were a jaded yellow and he had to squint to focus on me, but I have rarely looked into a face in which I felt such an immediate trust. The question was not conversational, but asked out of genuine concern for a man to whom he had never spoken. He had picked up a new pair of boots to work on and sat hunched over them, his eyes close to his work with the short-sightedness that is the mark of expertise in a true craftsman. When he spoke to me, he glanced upwards, the wrinkles gathering across his forehead like waves in the sea, stopping at an abrupt line to leave the bald dome of his head smooth and unperturbed.

"He's badly burnt, but I think he'll be all right." I leaned over to Dmitry. He was breathing more normally now. The burns to his face, hands and forearms were painful, but not deep enough to kill. "We will leave you before nightfall."

"No, no, no. Leave us when you will, but there is no rush. I love my Natalia as much as I did her mother, but a daughter can never be a son. My son, Fyodor Borisovich, was a soldier too. He died at Smolensk. He was eighteen." He paused, lost in the memories of his son, then he reached over to a pile of rags beside him, slipping his hand underneath.

"Here," he said, pulling out his hand and bringing with it a bottle of vodka, half full. "I cannot drink with Natalia like I could with Fedya." He opened the bottle and put it to his lips, drinking no more than a gulp. He wiped the top. "I'm sorry I have no glasses," he said as he handed the bottle to me.

I sat down on the ground, stretching my burnt leg out in front of me in hope of easing the continuous, dull pain. I deliberately drank as much from the bottle as he had; no more and no less. I offered the bottle back to him with a smile and an utterly heartfelt "thank you."

"No, you drink as much as you please," he told me. "I'm sure my daughter has been too polite to tell you, but you look appalling; worse than your friend over there." I recalled how Dmitry had been shocked at my appearance the previous evening. The night's activities could have done me no favours. But at his mention of Dmitry I remembered that my friend was in greater need of a drink than either myself or the old cobbler. I held the bottle to his lips and he swallowed the few drops that fell into his mouth. He coughed a little and muttered something under his breath. I tried to force some more of the spirit between his lips, but he held them shut and turned his head away.

Once more, I offered the bottle back to Boris Mihailovich. He took another small swig, before handing it back to me. "You drink it, Aleksei. Fedya can drink no more, so you should have it."

I took a gulp, taking more pleasure in it than I had the first, feeling the fire trickle down my throat and through my chest before spreading like a fountain around the walls of my stomach. I took a second gulp and felt the same feeling of refreshment. I knew that the man was giving me the last of his supply, that I should be grateful and abstemious, but I could not. I took gulp after delicious gulp until the bottle was dry.

If he was upset to see the last of his vodka drunk, he did not show it. He merely smiled the smile of an old man who enjoys seeing in others the enjoyment of pleasures that he can no longer appreciate for himself.

"Were you at Smolensk?" he asked. I nodded. "Tell me about it."

And so began a long day of me recounting every war story that I knew. I told him of distant campaigns, like Austerlitz, and of the more recent battles at Smolensk and Borodino. I always spoke as if I had been just a regular soldier. He needed no stories of espionage and the Oprichniki, simply good honest tales of soldiery of the sort that he knew his son had been involved in.

As I spoke, he continued to mend boots, able to listen and to work without one activity in any way interfering with the other. Sadly, he had only three pairs in his pile and, once they were mended, there was no more work for him to do. During our conversation Natalia returned. She had the money she had received for the one pair of boots that he had given her, plus two more for him to deal with. He made quick work of them, listening throughout to my stories, and as I spoke, Natalia also sat beside us on the floor, enraptured by my words, basking in the illusion that her brother was once again with them.

Towards midafternoon, Boris sent his daughter away to fetch some food. She returned with a loaf of bread and, miraculously, some butter. Dmitry was in no condition to eat, but they shared the food with me as though I was a part of their family. Once again, my heart told me to restrain myself, but my hunger was victorious.

My leg, it turned out after I had gingerly rolled up my trouser leg to inspect it, was not too badly burnt. Dmitry had snatched me out from the burning stairway after only seconds, so the heat had not penetrated too deeply. All the hairs on my shin and calf had shrivelled to nothing. The skin was red, but still intact. It would easily heal. I was certainly in a far better state than Dmitry.

By evening, I had shown my missing fingers and told them a much sanitized version of how I lost them. I had turned Dmitry's head to show them the scar on his cheek and tell them the story behind that. I would have loved to tell them of the brave heroics of a young *ryadovoy* I had met at Smolensk named Fyodor Borisovich, but I could not. Even if I had met him, I doubt I would have remembered him, and I could not bring myself to lie to these people—even to flatter them—on a matter so close to their hearts as that.

As night fell, I realized that I had work to do. I took my leave of them, but told them I would return.

There was a freshness in the air of Moscow that night which seemed familiar and yet which I had so quickly forgotten. The last of the fires were dying away and there was nothing new to burn and so the air once again smelled normal. Better than normal. In purging the city of so many buildings, the fires had left behind them a cleaner city; a city with less waste and less sewage. Perhaps the shortage in the city of every item that might support life also meant that there simply was less waste. No one would throw out the driest of bones or the most rotten of vegetables at a time when they did not know where their next meal would come from. The rats must have been having a hard time.

Personally, I preferred the traditional stenches of the city. Some slight alleviation would be pleasant, but not to this extent. The smells were the smells of life. The cleanliness was the cleanliness of an empty desert.

That night's rendezvous was in Tverskaya, at a tavern not far from the inn where we had stayed in Moscow in happier times. It wasn't clear to me whether we were meant to meet inside or outside. Inside is clearly the obvious place when meeting at an inn, but the risk was that it would be swarming with French soldiers looking for any place where they might relax. When I arrived I saw that the issue was beyond debate. There was no inside and no outside, because there was no tavern. It, along with every other building in the block, had burnt to the ground.

I stood and waited on the other side of the street, which was less damaged, leaning against the wall and scanning the wreckage of buildings opposite. I was suddenly hit by how tired I was. It had been before nightfall the previous day that I had last slept, deep in the crypt of that church in Zamoskvorechye. My eyelids began to droop. I tried holding them half open, then closing just one, then the other, then I decided to allow myself a few seconds' rest by closing them both.

I awoke with a jerk. I didn't know how long I had been asleep, but I was still on my feet, so I doubted it could have been more than a few seconds. Something was moving in the dark, charred shadows opposite me. As I looked, the movement stopped.

"Vadim," I hissed, more in hope than in expectation. There was no reply. It was only Vadim that I was hoping to see, but I was well aware that my appointment was with the Oprichniki as well. It was a risk that I had to take, but I suddenly realized how foolish I was being. I had killed four of them now. How was I to know that none of the others had been silently watching as I acted? Even if they didn't have the evidence of their own eyes, they could easily become suspicious. And I knew all too well how they had taken their revenge on Maks for his offences against them.

There was movement amongst the rubble again, this time to the right; I only caught it with the corner of my eye. I pressed myself back against the wall, but I knew I could still be clearly seen. I had been a fool to come. There were still five vampires abroad in the city with good reason to pick upon me as their prey. Even if I hid away in the deepest crypt they would eventually find me, but I had made it easy for them and kept our appointment. Perhaps I had hoped that they would give enough credit to my guile that they would assume I wouldn't show up. But had I been in their shoes, I would have gone even for a long shot like that.

I saw a glint of light, a reflection from an Oprichnik's eye, and then heard a movement from further down the street. My hand reached to my chest and I felt the comforting hardness of the icon of the Saviour. I offered Him a silent prayer. It would have surprised Him; He had not heard from me for many years, but I had been brought up to believe that He wasn't one to hold a petty grudge. I edged down the wall towards the end of the street, hoping that they hadn't posted a guard there, but knowing that even if I ran, they would quickly catch up with me. They might toy with me. Let me flee tonight only to strike some other evening. Nowhere would be safe in a city that was now theirs to plunder—a city I had brought them to.

Suddenly, there was a squeal, and the sound of falling rubble. I looked and saw a cat bounding from the ruined tavern and into the street. It turned and stood its ground as another cat leapt at it in pursuit. Both were scrawny, but the first had some morsel of food in its mouth. The second wanted it.

I fled. I had gone fifty paces before it became clear to me that those cats were all that I had seen and heard amongst the charcoal, but I didn't stop running. Just because the Oprichniki weren't there now, they might be there later. If Vadim showed up, then that was his look-out. He was smart enough not to, anyway—smarter than me. I ran back to the shantytown where I had left Dmitry with Natalia and her father. I was calmer than I had been, but terror still pervaded my body; a terror that should have struck me when I first saw Matfei's teeth at that soldier's throat, but which now took hold of me with a vengeance. Dmitry still occupied what served as the only bed. Natalia and Boris lay sleeping on the muddy floor, wrapped in each other's arms for warmth and comfort. There was an empty strip of earth between them and Dmitry. I lay there, but sleep did not come to me quickly. When it did, it was a welcome oblivion.

I awoke late the following morning, and by then I had decided on the course that Dmitry and I must take.

I smelled tea. I sat up and immediately found Natalia's hand offering me a cup. I took it and drank gratefully. Her father still sat in his usual place, quietly sipping his.

"Good morning, Aleksei Ivanovich." It was Dmitry speaking. He was sat up on his makeshift bed, also drinking tea and with a half-eaten apple in his hand.

"How do you feel?" I asked. He looked at his blistered hands and arms. I noticed that while the palm of his left hand, in which he held the tea, was normal, his right was red raw, burnt as badly as the rest of his arm. He could hold the apple only by the extreme tips of his fingers and I could see it would be many weeks before he would be able to hold a sword again. He put down his tea and held his left hand to the right side of his face. Without even touching, he could sense in the heat from his hand that he was burnt there too. He looked at his blistered hand again.

"Does my face look the same?" he asked.

"It's not quite as bad," I told him. "Once your beard grows back, it will hardly show." That was, of course, if his beard could grow back.

"What happened?"

"We were in the cellar. We were caught in the fire."

"The cellar where . . ."

"The cellar where we were sleeping," I interrupted firmly, not wanting Natalia or her father to know any more than they had to. Dmitry nodded, understanding.

Boris seemed to understand too. "I think we have things to do," he said to his daughter. She looked at him in surprise, then realized what he meant. They both rose and went out of the cubicle.

"I remember being trapped in the cellar," said Dmitry. "You dragged me out. Iuda and Ioann were in there. Did they . . . I shook my head. "They didn't wake up," I lied. "The coffins were too heavy to move. We barely made it out."

Dmitry nodded contemplatively. If he had worked out that it was I who had locked him in the cellar in the first place, he showed no signs of mentioning it, but then again, there was plenty he had been keeping from me recently. "How long ago was that?" he asked.

"Only a day ago."

"Did you try to meet with them last night?"

I nodded, remembering my terror. "None of them showed. Nor did Vadim."

TWELVE

"I'm not sure they'd have been in the best of moods if you had met them." I felt the urge to laugh, but resisted. I didn't want to have to explain my fears to Dmitry.

"I think we should leave Moscow," I announced. It was pure cowardice, but I knew that Moscow now contained too many threats for me to have any desire to stay there. And, of course, Dmitry needed time to recover. Dmitry did not answer. "You're in no state to do anything," I explained, to my conscience as much as to him. "The Oprichniki can handle things fine by themselves. And if they're not happy with our spying on them, then this isn't a safe city for us to be in."

"They wouldn't harm us, Aleksei. They might be angry but, well—you were angry with me, and I only got a few bruises for it."

I said nothing. Dmitry was probably right, assuming that they knew only as much of what I had been up to as he knew—and until they had no more use for us.

"What about Vadim?" asked Dmitry.

"I'll try to find him tonight. If not I'll leave a message." Dmitry looked doubtful. "He can look after himself," I assured him.

"How are we going to get out?"

I'd thought about this. "Do you have any left of the gold that Vadim gave us?" I asked.

Dmitry put his hand inside his coat and then withdrew it, remembering that his burns made him unable to manipulate anything. "Could you?" he asked. "It's in a money belt."

I pulled up his shirt and undid the belt. It felt heavy. "I didn't have cause to spend much," he explained, then the obvious question occurred to him. "Anyway, where's yours?"

"I stashed mine," I said. "I'm off to get it now."

I made my way past the dozens of similar compartments that made up the settlement. At the perimeter, I found Boris and Natalia waiting, quietly. Although it would have been quite easy for them to hang around and eavesdrop on our conversation, they had not, as I had trusted they wouldn't.

"I'll be back this evening," I told them. "Look after Dmitry for me."

*   *   *

My first port of call was the crypt where I had been sleeping earlier in the week. There I had left my few possessions and my share of the gold. None of it had been disturbed. It was risky to carry my sword with me through the occupied city, but even more so to travel outside the city without it. I ripped off a strip of cloth from my shirt and made a sling which I could use to hang it from my shoulder under my coat. It would not fool any French guards who chose to search me, but it would at least pass a visual inspection.

My next task, which I thought would be my hardest, was to find transport out of Moscow. The sight of even a few pieces of gold seemed to bring forth resources that I would never have dreamed existed in the city. I picked up food, tea and vodka and, eventually, having been passed from one entrepreneur to the next, found a man who said he could provide a wagon and horse for me. The price was high, but the down payment was relatively small, so I had some confidence that he would fulfill his side of the deal. We arranged to meet just east of the city, on the Vladimir road at dawn the following day.

Now I travelled round the city to all seven of our daily meeting points. At each I left the same message:

9-10-12-И9-АД

И9 was Yuryev-Polsky. It was an overly precise message to say that Dmitry and I would be there at midday in three days' time, but it was all that could be expressed within the confines of our code. It should at least, I hoped, give Vadim the idea that we had left Moscow. Yuryev-Polsky was far enough away that we would not just be nipping over there for a twelve o'clock meeting.

At most places it was easy to chalk or to scratch a message in a position where it would be found but not so obvious that it might be accidentally destroyed. In doing this, I had the opportunity to check for any message that Vadim might have himself left, but I found none. At the burnt-down tavern in Tverskaya, there was nowhere that I could leave anything for Vadim. If he had been there and left some scrawled note for me, then it had already been lost to the flames.

The final meeting place to which I went was the one for that evening itself. It was the site of the Petrovka Theatre, one of the few locations in Moscow guaranteed to be safe from the fires that had destroyed two-thirds of the city, having been burnt to the ground in another fire some seven years earlier. We were to meet at the northwest corner of the ruined site. I chalked my message on a low wall and then waited, watching from a distance, hoping that Vadim would arrive—praying that the Oprichniki would not.

I waited two hours before I felt certain that Vadim would not show. Almost throughout, I had the sensation of being watched. I looked around repeatedly and saw no one of note—certainly no vampires. I still had no reason to suppose they had any suspicion of me, but it was a risk turning up at a meeting place that they knew about, whence they could follow me and discover where Dmitry and I slept, along with the innocent cobbler and his daughter. It was, however, a risk I had to take. It was betrayal enough to abandon Vadim in the city, despite the fact that that was precisely what he had said we might have to do. I had at least to make some effort to contact him, even though the attempt had failed.

I headed back the short distance to the shantytown by a circuitous route. I don't think I was followed. As I approached the tiny space, I heard Dmitry and Natalia talking. Dmitry was lying on the area of ground designated to be the bed, lit by the guttering flame of a candle. Natalia sat beside him. Boris was asleep in the corner.

"There you are, at last," said Dmitry as I entered. "Where have you been?"

"I was waiting for Vadim," I explained, "but he wasn't there."

"Do you want to give it another day?"

I didn't feel inclined to give it another minute. "No, it's too late. I've arranged transport for tomorrow. We'll have to leave here before dawn."

"Where will you go to?" asked Natalia.

"Yuryev-Polsky," I replied.

"Why there?" asked Dmitry, although I suspect he knew quite well.

"Why not?"

We sat in silence for a while, accompanied only by Boris's shallow breathing.

"Will you come with us, Natasha? You and your father?" It was a surprising request to come from Dmitry's lips, as surprising as his use of the familiar "Natasha" instead of the more formal "Natalia." She had nursed him for two days—only one of which he'd been conscious for—but clearly it had had an effect on him. I never recalled Dmitry being dependent on anyone before. Now he had his first taste of it, it seemed he liked it.

The girl laughed. "Leave?"

"We can take you to safety," Dmitry went on.

"We're safe here. We could have left a week ago when the French came if we'd wanted to." Then she turned to me. "I thought you were going to kill all the French and drive them from the city," she said admonishingly.

"Dmitry needs to be taken somewhere safe. I'll come back," I said, but I knew that I didn't mean it.

I awoke early and gently shook Dmitry. Natalia and her father lay together, sleeping soundly. From the food I had bought the previous day I left them some tea, two bottles of vodka, two of wine, some bread and some honey.

It was about two versts across the city to where the wagon was, I hoped, waiting for us. Although Dmitry was weak, he could just about walk with my support and, although the journey would be slow, I felt we would make it. My only concern was that we might arrive well after dawn and, if we were too late, our contact might not wait.

We had not gone far when I heard footsteps running behind us. For a terrible moment, I felt sure it was an Oprichnik preparing to pounce on us at the very moment of our escape. It didn't take long for me to realize that the footsteps were too light for that, and approached us too directly.

It was Natalia. She put herself under Dmitry's other arm and the three of us made swift progress through the silent streets, in much the same manner as when we had first met her, two days before.

TWELVE

"I said I wouldn't come with you," Natalia explained, "but I'll come as far as the edge of the city."

We walked in silence for a while. I saw sweat breaking out on Dmitry's brow. Even with our support, the effort was exhausting for his weakened body. The sweat must have stung horribly as it ran down his burnt cheek, but he did not complain.

"Do you have a wife, Captain Danilov?" asked Natalia, breaking the silence.

"That's very formal. You were calling me Aleksei yesterday."

"Which do you prefer? I like 'Captain.'"

"It's a shame you didn't meet Vadim. He's a major."

"That's better, isn't it?"

"It's more senior," I told her, knowing that Vadim himself was all too well aware of the distinction.

"So are you married?"

"Yes I am. And we have a son, called Dmitry."

"Just like Captain Petrenko."

"He was named after Captain Petrenko."

"Why? No, I remember. He saved your life at Austerlitz."

"That's right."

"And now you've saved his life, so you're even."

"I don't think it works quite like that."

The conversation lulled and we carried on walking. Again it was Natalia who broke the silence.

"So is that why you're going to Yuryev-Polsky; because your wife's there?"

Despite his discomfort, Dmitry managed to emit a short cynical laugh.

"No," I replied, "we just have friends there."

"Is Captain Petrenko married?"

"What Captain Petrenko really likes to be called is Mitka," I said, taking petty revenge on Dmitry's cynicism.

"Really?" I nodded. "So, is Mitka married?"

"No, he's not."

"Why is that?" she asked.

"I think that's one you'd better ask him." Dmitry was, I'm sure, relieved just then to be unable to speak.

We arrived at the edge of the city about ten minutes after dawn. The man with whom I had spoken the day before was there, with an open wagon to which was harnessed a mule, rather than a horse, but it would suffice. There were no signs that he had brought anyone with him or that he planned to ambush us and take the money. There was no haggling over the agreed price. It was all done with the simple trust of one man in his fellow countryman that can only emerge at a time of war.

He headed back to the city on foot, and Natalia and I loaded Dmitry up on to the wagon, along with our few possessions.

"Goodbye, Captain Danilov," said Natalia, taking my hand. Then she went over to Dmitry and leaned forward, kissing him on his uninjured cheek. "Goodbye, Capt . . . Mitka," she said with a giggle.

She began to walk away, then she turned. "And thank you for the food—from me and from my father."

I went over to her and pressed a few of the gold coins I had left into her hand.

"What's this for?" she asked.

"To repay your kindness," I said.

"Kindness doesn't need any repayment." She was not insulted at all, only uncomprehending. "It doesn't work like that." She tried to hand it back.

"It's a gift," said Dmitry as loudly as he could manage.

"Why should I get a gift?" she asked, with a voice that clearly expected an answer, as if the right answer were more important than the gift.

"What's the date today, Aleksei?" Dmitry asked me. I had to think for a moment.

"The eighth—the eighth of September."

"And why is that important?" asked Dmitry. Natalia grinned a childish grin that told me she knew full well what Dmitry was getting at. Still though, *he* had to say it. For my part, I was completely lost.

"You tell me," she replied playfully.

TWELVE

"It's the feast of Saint Natalia—your name day. That's why you get a gift," Dmitry told her.

"Thank you," said Natalia, giving a beaming smile and clutching the coins to her chest as though they were the most valuable things she had ever owned (which, in fact, they probably were). She turned and ran gaily back towards Moscow.

I mounted the front of the wagon and we set off in the direction of the rising sun.

"So have you memorized all the name days, Dmitry?"

"Yes." There was no reason to doubt him, but it seemed astonishingly out of character.

"Why?" I asked.

His reply was simple. "You saw her smile."

Chapter XVI

IT TOOK US THREE DAYS TO GET TO YURYEV-POLSKY. I WAS surprised how soon out of Moscow the country began to return to normal. We saw serfs working in the fields and wagons taking goods to local markets. Some were even travelling in the opposite direction to us, back towards Moscow, where they knew they could get the best price for what they had to sell. Nowhere was there a French uniform in sight.

I slept more comfortably than I had for many days, and not just thanks to my receding fear. For inns along the road it was business as usual, so we were well fed and well looked after. Prices were back to normal—a joy after the exploitation of occupied Moscow—and because Dmitry was seen by all as an heroic wounded soldier, we always got a little more of everything than we might otherwise.

Dmitry and I spoke much on our journey and our friendship became cemented once again. We didn't discuss any weighty matters, such as the war, and we certainly never got on to the Oprichniki, but through normal conversation we remembered who we were and managed to forget—or at least suppress—the events that had forced us apart over the past weeks.

Yuryev-Polsky was packed with refugees and with wounded soldiers. Finding care for Dmitry was no problem. He was given a bed in a makeshift hospital—formerly a convent—and medical opinion was that he would recover. The scars would always show, but even the use of his right hand should return to him eventually.

I left him and went to look for Domnikiia. It turned out to be easier to find Pyetr Pyetrovich, whom everyone in the town seemed to know. If you needed something, anything, Pyetr Pyetrovich could furnish you with it—for a price. Food, alcohol, ammunition—he was the man to get it for you. I found him in a tavern. He was unmistakable as one of the courageous few who still opted for elegant French fashions; though that appeared to be no obstruction to his businesslike discussion with a colonel in the artillery. When he had finished, I approached.

"Pyetr Pyetrovich?" I said, offering my hand.

"Yes," he replied, taking my hand and trying to remember where he had seen me before.

"I'm Captain Danilov," I told him. "I was hoping you could help me, I'm looking for Domnikiia Semyonovna." He looked at me blankly. "For Dominique."

"Ah!" he exclaimed, recognizing me at last. "For Dominique."

He lowered his voice. "I'm afraid, captain, that for the time being, that side of my business is closed—not that I have had any problems with it, I assure you. It's just that at the moment there are far better ways to earn a living. But once you boys can clear Bonaparte out of Moscow, then it will be business as usual, don't you worry." He winked.

"I simply want to see her," I explained with some restraint. "She is a friend."

"Really? A friend?" The concept appeared new to him. "Well then, you'll find her in the hospital next to the church of Saint Nikolia. She's a nurse there."

"A nurse?"

"They all are. There's a lot of sick soldiers in town."

I headed for the hospital. It wasn't large, consisting of just two long rooms running at right angles to each other, with about twenty beds in each. I looked into the first and instantly recognized Domnikiia, bending over the bed at the furthest end of the room. I waited, my hand resting on the door post as I attempted to look relaxed. In fact, I was gripping it for support.

She stood up from the bed and began walking to the next one. She looked towards me. She was too distant to make eye contact, but as her eyes fell on me, her footsteps faltered slightly, as though she had turned an ankle. She recovered instantly and continued walking only as far as the next bed. She bent over the patient, spoke to him and fluffed his pillows. Then she moved on to the next patient, and the next and the next. As she approached she never looked directly at me. Though she moved so agonizingly slowly, still the force of her approach felt to me as if I were being charged down by a galloping stallion. A feeling of dreadful anticipation built up in me the closer she got. I could not step away and yet the prospect of her finally reaching me filled me with a sense of some great impending impact.

At last, having done her duty by each of the twenty men in the ward, she arrived at the door. She looked up at me with her beautiful slanting eyes and smiled her professional smile—as useful to her in her current profession as in her former.

"Good afternoon, Aleksei Ivanovich," she said, giving away no hint of emotion. I merely smiled in reply. "Step outside with me for a moment," she continued.

She led the way out to a quiet courtyard. I felt my heart beating in my chest, begging to be set free. She turned and put her hands to my head, pulling me down on to her lips. We kissed so ardently, but also so briefly, before she pulled away and put her lips first to my forehead, then to my eyebrows, then to my eyes, then my cheeks, then my ears, then my chin, my neck, my hands, my palms and my fingers. I was for the moment a passive, compliant body as her lips marked out every piece of me as her territory. Finally, she raised my left hand to her lips and kissed the tiny webbing of skin between my middle finger and what remained of my ring finger. Then she leaned into my chest, her arms not embracing me but held up in front of her, crushed between us. Now she was offering passivity, and I held her tight to me with all my strength.

"I feared you were dead, Lyosha."

"Why would you think that?"

"I didn't think it, I just feared it."

"I watched you leave Moscow," I told her. "Early that morning."

"Good," she smiled up at me. "I didn't see you."

"I'm a professional," I replied.

We began to walk, hand in hand; finger woven with finger.

"Why have you left Moscow so soon?" she asked.

"Dmitry was badly burnt in the fires. I brought him here."

TWELVE

"You should have let him burn." She changed her mind, almost without pausing. "I'm sorry, he's your friend—important enough for you to bring here."

"He wasn't for a little while, but I think we're over that now."

"Why weren't you? Because of Maks?"

"And you."

"So why did you come here to Yuryev-Polsky?"

"Dmitry suggested it. I wasn't too keen," I said with a smirk. She made a tight little fist and jabbed me in the ribs.

"And your other friend, Vadim; is he here too?"

"No. As far as we know, he's still in Moscow. I'm hoping he'll join us." It sounded hollow, even to me.

For the next couple of weeks, our relationship was the least physical it had ever been. I had found accommodation in a barracks near to where Dmitry was recovering, and Domnikiia was living in nurses' quarters. In the time that we had together we were forced to behave much like any other courting soldier and nurse thrown together by the forces of war. We spent our time talking and holding hands and walking round the town, and though it would be nice to say that through these conversations we learned to understand one another better than we ever had before, it simply wouldn't be true. Our conversations were no more and no less intimate or stimulating than those we had had naked and entwined in her bed in Moscow. For me, at least they had the benefit of being cheaper.

I told her much of what had happened since we had parted in Moscow; of the state of the city under French occupation and of the destruction brought by the fires. I told her of Boris and Natalia and how they had cared for us before we left, but I told her nothing of the Oprichniki and what I had discovered about them. I knew that I would have to tell her, but whenever an opportunity arose, I shied from it. My silence assisted the cosy delusion of safety which I had deliberately built for myself, but underneath, the terror was never far from my mind.

"You never ask about me," she said one day from nowhere as we walked through a late summer's evening.

"I ask you every day what you've been up to," I replied, mildly offended.

"I mean about who I am—about my life before you knew me."

"Oh, that," I said, and after a moment's pause, "So tell me."

"What would you like to know?"

"Everything" would have been the true answer, but specifics would be easier. I started with, "Where were you born?"

"Moscow," she replied. "I've always lived in Moscow."

"Never been outside?"

"I don't think I'd ever been three versts from where I was born, until I came here."

"You must find Yuryev-Polsky very exotic," I said.

"It's small and boring," she said. It was an accurate summary.

"So where is your family?"

"I don't know," she replied. "My father owned a shop—a milliner's. We lived above it—him and my mother and my brother and me. We weren't rich, but he had ambition. He believed the best route to success was to make friends of his customers, if they were rich enough or important enough. But the rich get rich by not paying their bills until they have to, and he didn't feel he could ask people so much above him for something so grubby as payment of a bill."

"So you've learned from his mistakes?" I said lightly.

"Too right. But my customers tend to pay pretty quickly anyway. No one wants his wife to come across an unpaid bill from me at the end of the month."

"So what went wrong?"

"Who says anything went wrong?" she said, surprised. "I'm here, now, with you, aren't I?"

"You could have got here by an easier route."

"Could I? The only other route into your trousers would be to become some stuck-up society girl in Petersburg, and that was never an option."

I stiffened. It wasn't an accurate description of Marfa in any way, but from the deliberate little I had told Domnikiia about her, it was to be expected.

"I'm sorry," continued Domnikiia. "That wasn't fair."

TWELVE

"That's all right. So what did happen?"

"I was swept off my feet by a customer. One of my father's customers, I mean—at least at first. He used to come into the shop and buy his wife the most lovely hats. Then he bought me a lovely hat. And then he got what he'd expected in return. Soon he would just give me money. But then his wife found out, and she told her friends, and suddenly husbands weren't allowed to come to us for their wives' hats.

"My father knew what had caused it. We had an argument and he hit me, so I left. I rented a room and got by the only way I knew how. Only now the men I saw weren't the sort who tended to buy hats for their wives, even if they could have afforded them. Before long, one of them hit me, so I went back home."

"I see," I said.

"Except that there was no home. The shop had closed down and my family had gone. I guess I'd spoiled his reputation. And so I went back to work, and more men hit me, but most men paid, so I survived. Then I met Pyetr Pyetrovich. And he knew how to get the men to pay more, even though I was paid less. But I have a roof and a bed and a . . . home."

"Didn't you ever look for your family?" I asked.

"I will do," she replied, "but not just yet. It's not been long enough yet."

The way she told the story made it sound as if it had all happened a long, long time ago, but she was still too young for anything to have happened to her so very long ago.

"How long has it been?" I asked.

"Three years—since I left home."

"You've been lucky, I suppose."

"Luckier than most," she said. "I'm pretty. Men like that."

"And you're smart. Men like that too."

"No, Lyosha," she said condescendingly, "that's just you." We walked in silence for a little. "So, are you going to tell me all the secrets of *your* past?" she asked eventually.

"Best not, I think. Besides, it shouldn't make any difference."

"How do you mean?"

"It's the same as the reason I never asked you about yours; I know you," I said. "You don't need explaining." I might once have said the same thing about Maks.

"Life must be very dull for you, Aleksei Ivanovich," she replied haughtily, "knowing so much. Perhaps one day I shall surprise you."

She never stopped.

Towards the end of September, Dmitry was sufficiently recovered to be moved from the hospital to a regular barracks. The risk of his burns becoming diseased was past, the doctors said, and it was now simply a question of waiting until his skin grew back fully.

"Does this mean you'll be going back to Moscow?" asked Domnikiia when I told her. It wasn't until I had been sitting on that wagon with Dmitry laid on the back, riding away from the city, that I had realized how truly terrified I had been in Moscow. The discovery that the Oprichniki were vampires had been one that I had first reacted to with immediate action. But as the need for action had abated, my fears had found room to float to the surface. I had seen how the Oprichniki killed—seen their strength and seen their savagery. I knew that I did not want to die like that, and that knowledge made me realize that I did not want to die at all. I wanted to live and enjoy life. I wanted my wife and my son and my mistress and to have more children and, damn it, more mistresses. I wanted to read books and drink wine and play cards and die when I was very, very old.

"Not yet," I replied. "The word is that Bonaparte will have to leave soon, whatever happens. He's wasted too much time. He could have gone for a final victory in Petersburg, but he went on thinking that Moscow was the key—that it would break Russia's heart to see her captured. Most of us thought the same, but we all turned out to be wrong. The tsar has made no peace, and the French will have to winter in a safer city than Moscow. The longer they leave it, the more they risk getting cut off when winter comes."

"So we didn't need you to save Moscow after all?" I had no answer. "Oh, Lyosha, I'm sure you helped a little." Her tone was supremely patronizing. "Is your friend Iuda still in Moscow, sorting out the French?"

"No, he's dead."

"You don't seem too sorry. What happened to him?"

Again, I should have spoken; again, I didn't.

"The same fire that Dmitry got injured in—Iuda wasn't so lucky."

Dmitry leaving the hospital meant that I too could look for better accommodation. I was lucky enough to find myself a fair-sized room at a reasonable price and so, once again, I had the privacy I desired.

Domnikiia the mistress was a very different lover from Dominique the prostitute. Which I preferred is hard to say, because the difference between the two came in the absence of deceit. To be told as a willing listener by a convincing actress that one is the world's greatest lover is a very pleasurable experience. But once the actress's mask has been dropped it can never be credibly raised again. Knowing the truth, that one's lovemaking could be improved upon, is not as pleasant as the delusion of perfection, but it is more pleasant than the exploded delusion. And there is always the pleasure of knowing that regular practice leads to improvement.

As I realized that there would soon be no avoiding my return to Moscow, I realized too that one day I would probably have to face the five remaining Oprichniki: Pyetr, Andrei, Iakov Zevedayinich, Filipp and Foma. I knew that they could be killed by fire. At least, I believed it; I had no solid evidence that Iuda and Ioann were dead. I knew for certain that they could be killed by a wooden stake through the heart, and that was the method that I could better control. I began to whittle for myself a stout wooden dagger—almost a small sword—that I could wield with the same skill as I did a sabre and thus, with a swift lunge, despatch a vampire in much the same way as I could a man.

One afternoon, while I was sitting on my bed, working on my new weapon, Domnikiia came into my room.

After we had greeted each other, she asked about the sword. "Is that for your son?" It was very like a wooden sword that I had made for Dmitry Alekseevich a couple of years before, the one I had seen at his side in my dream, but this had a much more deadly purpose. I knew then, as I had always known, that it was my duty to tell Domnikiia what I had discovered. Her connection with me might bring her into danger and she at least deserved to be aware of the nature of that danger.

"No, it's not," I replied. I put the sword to one side and lay back on the bed. She lay beside me with her head upon my chest. I stared up at the small window above us as I told her, trying to hide the terror in my heart as I spoke.

"You remember the Oprichniki?"

"Of course," she said. "I met Iuda, remember."

I nodded, pausing to give myself time to think how I could best convey what I knew. Directness was the only course I could take. "You know what a *voordalak* is?" I asked.

She looked at me. Her expression showed mild surprise at the turn the conversation had taken. Then she looked at the wooden sword, and back to me. Her face transformed. She understood—but she didn't believe.

"You shouldn't joke about that," she said.

"Don't you believe in vampires?"

She stood up. "Oh, *I* believe in vampires, Lyosha," she said, a hint of anger in her voice, "but *you* don't, I'm pretty sure. It's not fun to be teased for not being as smart as . . ."

I interrupted her. "Didn't," I said.

"What?"

"I didn't believe in them. I do now."

She smiled a little. "Well, that's one small victory for the peasant mind." Then she shook her head. "But they can't be. Why do you think they are?"

"You see," I said. "You have doubts."

"I suppose. I don't know. Just because you believe in something doesn't mean you think you'll ever see it. How do you know?"

"I've seen them kill," I said. "I've seen them die."

"My God," Domnikiia murmured.

Suddenly, she got down on to her knees and started to frantically undo my shirt. Then, just as suddenly, she stopped.

"Thank God!" she exclaimed.

"What?"

"You're still wearing it." She was staring at the icon that lay on my chest—the one that Marfa had sent me and that only now I remembered Domnikiia had insisted I wear.

"Will that help?" I asked.

"That's what they say. It has done so far, hasn't it?" She pulled from the neck of her dress a small silver crucifix on a chain. I had noticed it many times. "I always wear this." She kissed it and put it back. "So it's not true that they live forever?"

"No," I replied. "Seven of them are already dead."

"Did you kill them?"

"Some of them. They're harder to kill, but they're mortal, like the rest of us."

"I was always told they never age," she said, her eyes gazing blankly at memories of childhood. "They can't die, they can only be killed. Sunlight does it. Or a wooden stake, piercing their once-human heart." It was astonishing how quickly we could both be taken to a world where such things were commonplace.

"What about fire?" I asked, still aware that I had no certainty in believing that Iuda and Ioann were dead.

She thought for a moment, then nodded. "Yes, I think I heard that works too." Then the reality of what we were discussing seemed to dawn on her. "Is that how you did it?"

"Two of them," I said. "Maks killed three."

She lay her head back down on my chest. "Good old Maks," she said quietly. I hoped that she would raise the question of how Maks had died, knowing that I never could, but she remained silent. I watched a tear creep across her cheek and become absorbed into her skin. When she spoke, it was not to discuss Maks.

"It would be lovely to never age," she said. "To always be young and have the vitality of youth."

"And to watch all of your friends age and die around you," I added.

"It wouldn't have to be like that. What if we were both vampires?" Her mood was almost deliberately lighthearted. "We could live forever together. If we did no one any harm, they'd leave us alone. Don't you think you could love me forever?"

"They have no life and they have no love," I said with all the gravity I could muster. "They have hunger. They have to eat and they enjoy causing pain as they do it."

"But that's probably just what they were like in life. We'd be like us. Do you think any man would refuse to have his blood drunk by a vampire as pretty as me—and then be made immortal by it too?"

This was too much. I leapt to my feet, causing her to fall to the hard wooden floor. I grabbed the dagger I had been carving and held it out to her, simply to show to her, not to threaten, but I don't think she saw it like that.

"Do you know what this is for?" I shouted. "This is to kill them—to stab them in the heart, because that's the way to destroy them. They can't be killed like men because, as men, they died a long time ago." Without getting up off the floor, she backed up against the wall with a look of fear in her eyes which, I'm sorry to say, I enjoyed seeing. "If you were a vampire, people would hunt you down and kill you in just the same way. And they'd be right to do it, because these things are monsters—animals—worse than animals, because they once had souls enough to know right from wrong."

I flung the dagger back across the room and threw myself on my bed. She sat huddled in against the wall, right next to the bed, silent and thoughtful, but showing no sign of moving from the uncomfortable position. It was an hour before either of us spoke.

"I didn't *mean* it," she said moodily. "It would be a fantasy to have you to myself for a year, let alone forever."

I should have replied, but I didn't. Five minutes later she stood up and left the room.

Domnikiia never visited me again in Yuryev-Polsky. While he had been in hospital, and after, she had taken to calling on Dmitry. She did this, I think, largely for my sake, since she had no reason to like him, and also out of some sense of duty as a nurse. Even after we argued, she continued to visit him, and so our paths still crossed occasionally; she was always polite, but always devastatingly formal. No more "Lyosha"s emanated from her lips.

I occasionally came across Margarita too. Like Domnikiia, she was working as a nurse, although the rumours from some of the soldiers under her care were that she was still keeping her hand in at her former trade. I begged her to talk to Domnikiia for me, or to tell me what I should say to her myself.

"Can't you even work that out?" she said with an uncalled-for hostility that I felt came to her from Domnikiia.

"If I knew what to say, I'd have said it."

"But you didn't."

"So what should I say?"

"What would you say to your wife?" replied Margarita acidly.

"I can't help being married," I explained, but evidently I had missed the point. With a sharp "tut," she turned and left.

The day after my argument with Domnikiia, it had snowed for the first time. It was early—October had only just begun—and the snow was very light, not even trying to settle. Many versts away in Moscow, that same snow must have placed a chill in Bonaparte's soul. He had not planned to spend the winter in Russia.

Just over a week later, news came that the Grande Armée had at last quit Moscow and was heading out of the city to the southwest. Bonaparte had stayed for five weeks—just as the wave stays for a few moments at the top of the beach—before understanding that he had won a worthless trophy. Now his starving army had to flee for safety, with a reinvigorated Russian army in full pursuit.

I went to see Dmitry. His hands and arms were, though scarred, almost fully usable. His beard was not growing back. He did not shave it off completely, but left the smooth, ruddy bald patch so that all could see the long straight scar from a French sabre that the flames had been unable to erase. We discussed the news from Moscow.

"So what do you plan to do?" he asked.

"Get back as soon as possible. Half the town will be setting off there in the next few days."

"Wouldn't it be better to join up with the regular army? Moscow's no longer the battlefield. We should be chasing the French."

"We have to try and make contact with Vadim. And let the Oprichniki know what's happening." The first half of what I said had been honest.

Dmitry thought for a moment. "We can't be sure that he or they are still in Moscow. I'm planning to go south and join up with the main body of the army. If Vadim's there, I'll get word to you. You go to Moscow."

I decided to test the water. There had been a thousand opportunities in the weeks since our departure from Moscow, but, as with Domnikiia, I had always put it off. Now was my last chance, at least for a while, and I knew that if there was any hint in Dmitry of the loathing of the Oprichniki that dwelt in me, then there was a chance that he could once again be turned into a formidable ally.

"Do you trust them?" I asked.

"Trust them?" He tried to pretend he didn't understand, but we knew each other too well for him to bother for long. "It's different for you, Aleksei."

"Different?"

"They deceived you—*we* deceived you. We didn't tell you what they were from the start. That wasn't fair."

Wise though, I thought.

"That's no basis for trust," he continued, "especially given your—everyone's—natural fear of them. But I always knew, right from the very start."

"What happened?" I asked. "Right at the start?"

"It's a long story, Aleksei, from a long time ago."

"What happened?" At first I had asked idly, but now I was insistent. Whatever he had to tell me could be of incalculable help in fighting the Oprichniki, and might even help me to understand how Dmitry could be so accepting of them.

Dmitry looked at me and understood that I wasn't going to let him run away from this one. He took a deep breath.

Chapter XVII

"**I**T WAS BACK IN '09," HE SAID, "WHEN IT SEEMED LIKE THE Turks were our only problem—and what a problem! You must have been down in the southeast then, across the Danube, but in the west, we were having real trouble. The Turks were way further north and I was trying to organize Wallachian peasants to do some of the fighting for us—to save their own country."

Dmitry walked over to stare out of the window, the cold sunlight causing the burnt skin of his cheek to glisten.

"But it was useless," he continued. "They had no more wits than the serfs, and they were a darned sight slower to take an order. Still, I suppose they'd learned over the years that driving out the Turks just made it easier for *us* to move in—us or whoever happened to be fighting the Turks at the time. Anyway, things had gone badly and we'd been pushed right back up into the Carpathians. There was me and about fifteen locals—only one of them spoke any French—cut down from a force of over a hundred.

"It was late winter—you couldn't call it spring yet—and though the winters are nothing like as cold down there as they are here, we were high up in the mountains, so we felt it. Darkness fell, and we could see the torches of the Turks on the foothills below us, climbing up after us. There must have been ten of them for each one of us and, although it was going to take them a good couple of hours to reach us, reach us they would. And you know what they're like with prisoners."

He turned slightly and nodded towards my hand and its missing fingers. I said nothing.

"I was all for carrying on up the mountain. At least then there might be some hope that they'd give up pursuing us, especially with the cold, but the others had lost it. They just sat around the fire muttering to each other and wouldn't move. The one I could understand said they were waiting for the 'saviour.' I said we'd all be seeing Him soon enough, but it turns out they were talking about some local mythic hero—though it might as well have been Christ, judging by the way they crossed themselves whenever this 'saviour' was mentioned.

"It was some local warlord from the Middle Ages; a ruthless type, but pretty handy at dealing with invading Turks. A genuine figure, if they were to be believed, which was all very well, but not much use to us four hundred years later. The idea was, of course, that he would 'rise again,' much like Christ, when the country was in its direst need. Nothing very original; you'd get the same basic plot from peasants anywhere in Europe."

He paused briefly and I could see his shoulders stiffen.

"But there was a slight difference. This redeemer lived and died not five versts from where we were camped. His castle was still there—in ruins, of course. Two of the Wallachians wanted to go up there—to beg for help—but the rest were scared, the one who'd been translating for me included. I went along with the two of them, not that I thought we were going to be saved by a four-hundred-year-old ghost, you understand, but I hoped these ruins might turn out to be defensible.

"The three of us clambered over steep, rough ground for ten minutes until we unexpectedly—for me, though not for the other two—came to a road. There was a bright moon to guide us and so, what with the road, we moved much more swiftly. I began to think that if the castle did turn out to be something we could use, then we might really have some chance of holding out until the Turks got bored. But as I cheered up, the two Wallachians' mood darkened. They muttered to each other and began to walk more slowly until eventually they stopped, and seemed to be discussing whether to go on at all.

"I thought, to hell with them, and just carried on down the road. It did the trick because before long, they'd caught up with me again. It was odd, though, the way they'd hang back a little way behind me, but always stay close. I couldn't tell whether they were looking to me for protection, or just making sure that I was delivered up to whoever we might find at our destination."

Again Dmitry paused, lost in thought as he stared out into the distance.

"It was the reaction of the two of them that first told me we'd arrived. I didn't even see it, but suddenly one of them pointed and they both froze, looking. It must have been in plain view for ten minutes already but it wasn't until I looked that I saw. It was built into the mountainside—almost growing out of it—and it suddenly became clear to me that it was not a line of rocks that overhung the road we'd been walking down, but the walls of a vast, ruined castle, from whose tall black windows came no ray of light, and whose broken battlements showed a jagged line against the moonlit sky.

"We went up to the gateway of a courtyard. The whole place was utterly dilapidated, but it must have been unassailable in its time. I could certainly believe it dated back to the Middle Ages. Even so, it wasn't completely decrepit; across the courtyard I could see, set in a projecting doorway of massive stone, a great wooden door had survived—old, and studded with large iron nails.

"My two companions were muttering amongst themselves. As they finished, one of them made visible efforts to compose himself and then he marched hesitantly into the courtyard. The other raised a hand to tell me to remain where I was, though I needed no prompting. Inside the courtyard, the first one was staring up at a high window, his eyes fixed on an occupant that I could not see, and that I doubted he could either.

"He threw himself to his knees in front of the door and raised up his hands and shouted out what I took to be his plea for help, always staring up at that window. He continued to cry out, now beating at his breast, now tearing his hair until finally he flung himself forward and I could hear his bare hands beating against that heavy wooden door. At length the sound stopped and we waited. The Wallachian inside the courtyard just lay still, slumped against the door. The one with me glanced nervously around, his eyes coming to rest on each of the windows above us in turn, looking for someone who would answer his countryman's plea. But answer came there none.

"After perhaps ten minutes, the one inside the courtyard pulled himself to his feet and came back towards us, shaking his head dolefully as he looked at his friend. With no words passed between them, they turned and headed back down the road from which we had come. My plan had been that we might make some use of the castle, and though it had the makings of a strong position, I was in no mood to remain there alone. I briskly caught up with them.

"Our return was much quicker than had been the journey up to the castle. I might have become lost, but the others had no problem finding the camp. Those who had remained had sunk into a fatalistic silence, and it took no words from us to convey the failure of our mission. Ridiculous as it had seemed to me both before we set out and after we returned, there had been a moment when I had been half expecting to see their saviour emerge from the castle and come to our aid.

"The Turks were much closer now, and soon, as well as being able to see their torches, we could hear their shouts from one to the other as they spread out to surround us. We knew the time was close. I rose to my feet, and the others did likewise. I was armed with a musket, a pistol and a sword. Some of the others had swords, some merely knives. Through the trees I could now begin to make out the shapes of men, each in a pool of light cast by his own flame. And then we heard the sound.

"It was not an unfamiliar sound—the sound of horses' hooves galloping—but on that cold, barren mountainside, it was incongruous. The Wallachians with me were as bewildered as I as to its cause, but it soon became clear that it came from behind us—from further up the mountain—and that it was coming closer.

"The Turks hadn't heard it, or didn't care, and had continued to advance. Now they were in range. Shots fired out and two men near to me fell. I fired back with my musket and brought one down. All the time, the sound of hooves became more thunderous. I turned to look for what was causing it, but still there was nothing to see. The Turks were well armed and had no need to engage us hand to hand. They had stopped and begun to pick us off with their muskets. A Wallachian in front of me was hit and fell back on to me, knocking me over. I twisted and was facing back uphill just as the horsemen leapt into view.

"Zmyeevich came first, clearing the ridge that had hidden his approach atop a white stallion. He was terrifying—his eyes filled with hateful lust and his fangs bared. Immediately on his tail came ten others; Oprichniki, as we've called them—vampires of a lower caste than Zmyeevich. They galloped past—in some cases over—the Wallachians and down towards the Turks, and I remember noticing that, terrifying though the horsemen were, they carried neither swords nor spears—nothing with which they might attack the opposition as they charged them. It was only later that I made the association with Zmyeevich's wolf-like teeth. The Turks themselves might have laughed. Mounted though these new arrivals were, they were utterly outnumbered— and outgunned. You wouldn't have expected more than two of them to make it across the open space between us and to penetrate the enemy line. I certainly didn't, but then I didn't know them.

"The first volley from the Turks ripped through their bodies, but had no effect on their charge. More guns fired, but still the lesson hadn't been learned. Then some began to believe the evidence of their own eyes and realized that bullets would do nothing to stop these creatures. Now they aimed at the horses—flesh-and-blood horses that fell quickly under the hail of musket shot. But it was too late. The horses had done their job and carried the vampires into the midst of the enemy. As each horse fell from under its rider, the rider would land on his feet and continue to run, falling upon the Turks in front of him.

"I couldn't see what they were doing. We could hear men screaming, but as each was attacked, his torch was dropped or extinguished and so we could see nothing of their fate. The men around me cowered in fear, and I decided that there was little to be gained by being heroic. Much like that time we watched the Oprichniki at work on the road to Borodino, weeks ago, we heard the shouts and screams of the Turks become fewer and more desperate. I expect you felt as I did, Aleksei, a mixture of horror and awe at the brutality and efficiency of the killers."

I said nothing. Perhaps he was right. Perhaps I had felt both those things, but any such emotions had long since been replaced in me by the purest form of loathing.

"With practised speed, the few remaining cries faded to nothing. The surviving Wallachians and I stayed frozen in terror, their superstitious fear infecting me and leaving me bewildered as to what to do. I soon overcame it and tried to find out from the others what they knew of what had happened, but it was useless. The French speaker among them lay dead, a Turkish bullet through his eye. Even if I had been able to communicate with the rest of them, I doubt whether I could have broken through their terror. Although, as I was already beginning to sense, the horsemen we'd seen were in some way related to the saviour they had spoken of, these peasants seemed to greet his arrival more with fear than with joy.

"I strode out on my own towards where the Turks had been. Amongst the trees ahead, I caught sight of crouching, scurrying shadows and heard sounds that lay halfway between the language of men and the grunts of animals. Then I heard a loud cry. I was sure it was in Turkish, but it was quickly silenced, to be replaced by more of the snorting and sniggering that I had heard before. I wandered through the trees for several minutes, stumbling across dozens of Turkish bodies, each with the same bloody wound to the neck—many with other wounds beyond that—but still I came face to face with none of the horsemen. Then I stopped and listened.

"The noises I had been hearing had subsided and all I could now hear around me was the hoarse, shallow breathing of animals preparing to attack—*all* around me. I had walked into their midst and now I was encircled. I put my hand to my sword, knowing even then that it would be of little use. There was the sound of a footstep close behind. I turned and found myself face to face with Zmyeevich.

"He spoke, but I didn't understand the language. I did notice the foulness of his breath; like a swamp. He spoke again, in a different language, but again, not one I understood. Then he spoke in English: 'Good evening.' I rolled off a stock English phrase to say that I was Russian. He paused, trying to formulate a sentence, then smiled and said in fluent French, 'In that case, you speak French.'

"I told him I did, and he led me away. Only then did I notice that he was dragging behind him, like a cloak that he was too lazy to throw over his shoulder, the inert body of a Turk. As we walked on, he turned and casually discarded the body behind him, into the centre of the circle of creatures that had surrounded me. Behind us I could hear them closing in on what their master had flung them.

"We went back towards where I had left the Wallachians. In the time since I had left them, they'd plucked up some courage and were now standing, discussing what to do next. On our arrival—on Zmyeevich's arrival—they flung themselves to the ground once more and cowered. Zmyeevich paid them no attention. We sat some way away from them and talked.

"Fascination overcame both fear and good manners, and I asked him the most obvious question directly: 'What *are* you?'

"'You are Russian,' he said, 'and so you will understand these things. We are vampires—*voordalaki*, in your tongue.' I had no need to express surprise. 'And we are patriots,' he continued.

"'You're all Wallachian?' I asked him.

"'Mostly, at the moment; a few from Moldavia. We are an ever-changing band—except in terms of leadership,' he added, with a slight bow. 'But at the moment, we are all from . . . around here.'

"By now, his comrades had begun to emerge from the forest. The ten of them had formed a low, huddled group, not unlike the formation of my own Wallachian comrades, but there was something in their midst that was catching the attention of this new group. I could guess only too well what it was.

"'They don't all seem like you,' I said.

"'And they don't seem like you,' he replied, wafting his hand towards the Wallachians. 'There are different classes of men in all societies.' He turned to face me directly. 'And that is why it is such a rare privilege to sit here and talk with you.'

"'So I presume you saw us at the castle,' I said.

"'I did, but I had already known you were here and known what we would do.'

"'And you've lived there four hundred years?'

"'Not quite yet,' he replied with a wistful smile that little suited him, 'but soon.'

"'And the others—are they all as old?'

"'Oh, no,' he replied scornfully. 'To live to my age requires skill, intel-

lect, foresight. These are not the abilities one finds—or seeks—in a foot soldier. They are older than you to be sure, but not by a great deal.'

"'And you created them?' I asked. 'Made them vampires, I mean.'

"'Again, no. Who could be proud to claim such creatures as his sons? They tend to perpetuate themselves. Occasionally a stranger may join us—a vampire whose ears our fame has reached. Generally, they are welcomed.'

"One of the Wallachians—the one who had gone up to the door of the castle—had sidled over to the group of vampires, trying to see what they were about. As he got close, one of them turned and pounced. Within seconds the Wallachian was pinned to the floor, with two more crouching over him. Zmyeevich shouted at them and they stopped to look at him. He shouted again and they reluctantly returned to the pack. I could almost see their tails between their legs.

"Zmyeevich and I talked some more, though I noticed him becoming distracted, glancing over to where his underlings were finishing off the remains of various Turkish corpses which they dragged from out of the woods. It was at his suggestion that we decided to work together, at least to clear the Turks out of his area of the Carpathians. We would work much as we had planned to in Moscow; *we* would scout by day to locate the Turks and then *they* would come out at night to destroy them. He said he would have no trouble finding us on the mountains. He even went over and explained our plans to the six surviving Wallachians.

"'And now it is nearing dawn, and you must excuse us,' he said to me as he returned from speaking to them. 'But first, might I borrow your sabre?'

"I handed it to him, not knowing what use he could possibly have for it. He took it and strode towards the other vampires, who were still huddled around the body of one of the Turks. I couldn't make out what he did with the sword, but soon he was leading his band away, back uphill towards his castle. As they came close, I could see he was holding the tip of my sword to his mouth. On it was a chunk of bloody, raw flesh, which he tore at with his teeth until he had consumed it all. Then, with a smile, he threw the weapon back to me. As I caught it, he gave a casual salute and carried on up the mountain. Within minutes, they were out of sight.

"I sat down, looking at the remnants of the night's battle and considering our bizarre conversation. In the cold light of day, all that I had heard and seen would be strange and unbelievable, and yet I had no sense of doubting it—no sense of shock, even, at the discovery. I suppose that, because I had no personal apprehension of danger, I had no feeling of horror. Then I looked at the ravaged Turkish corpses that lay around us, looked at my huddled, frightened comrades and looked at the blade of my sabre, caked in blood in a way that was so familiar and yet, on that day, so repellent. I turned and vomited."

He stopped and for several seconds we were both silent.

"So did you meet him again?" I asked eventually.

"It was just like he'd suggested. We'd comb the mountains by day, locating the Turks, but we wouldn't engage them. At night, Zmyeevich and the others would appear, and that particular band of invaders would be destroyed. They must have killed hundreds in total. Zmyeevich was good company—you may laugh, but he was better than anyone else I'd met in that damned country. And I talked to the other vampires a little too. They weren't quite as subhuman as Zmyeevich made out. Well, you know what they're like; you've spoken to the Oprichniki. And remember, they were my brothers-in-arms; at least for the duration. They didn't use those names, but Pyetr, Varfolomei, Andrei and Ioann were the only ones in common with now."

Dmitry turned and looked me in the eye, considering what he was about to say. Then he shook his head dismissively, as if waking from a dream.

"As far as I can remember, at least," he said. "It was a long time ago."

"How long did you stay with them?" I asked.

"Not long. Eventually, after about a fortnight, we caught sight of a Russian battalion and I decided to return to the familiar. I waited until Zmyeevich met up with us that night to say goodbye. He understood why I'd made my decision, and told me with all sincerity that if I ever needed help I should not be afraid to ask."

"And he was as good as his word," I said. Dmitry didn't catch the bitterness of my tone.

"Exactly, Aleksei. Exactly. You may not like what they are—God knows, I don't either—but they *can* be trusted. They've proved that."

TWELVE

And in my own mind, I couldn't fault him. The Oprichniki had answered our call for help; they had done what we had asked them to do. Dmitry and I both knew it, and yet we appeared to have come to very different conclusions. I searched for the distinction between us, and soon found it. God might know that Dmitry did not like what these creatures were, but I remained to be convinced. My visceral, instinctive hatred of them, simply for what they were, seemed missing—or at least hidden—in Dmitry. His view of them as being like cannon that simply had to be pointed towards the enemy was quite, quite logical. It would have surprised Maks, as it did me, to find Dmitry the more rational of the two of us.

Yet, if that was rationality, it could go to hell. Love was irrational, yet it was both right and beautiful. Couldn't hatred be just the same? My experience of the Oprichniki had convinced me that it could.

I had further questions for him, but no stomach to ask them. I changed the subject. "When are you leaving?" I asked.

"I'm ready now." He smiled sheepishly. "I'd already made plans. I'll leave today." Then he added, "Look out for Natalia and Boris for me."

We embraced. There were no words with which to say goodbye, and yet as I walked away I knew in my heart that there was still a more honest conversation to be had between us. Dmitry, I was certain, was lying—or at least not telling the full story. His account of his first meeting with Zmyeevich was too tidy; too much designed to make Dmitry himself happy. There was more that he had wanted to tell me, but had not.

And why not? Because I was a liar too. Dmitry might not have the insight to guess what exactly I was holding back, but he had known me long enough to see that there was something. That something was that I had made it my quest—a quest that I would continue now that I had no more excuses for not returning to Moscow—to destroy every one of these abominable creatures. And why did I not in turn tell him my secret? Because I did not trust him. I deceived him because I knew he was deceiving me. His behaviour was identical. Neither of us could break the deadlock with a leap, or even a small step, of faith.

How much easier it had been when Maks was the only deceiver amongst us. His presence had sown no seeds of doubt into our midst. Perhaps he had just been a better liar than either Dmitry or I, so much so that, even now, even after he had been exposed, even now he was dead, I still felt a greater degree of trust in him than in the living comrade with whom I had just parted.

Two days later a great convoy of coaches, trucks and wagons left Yuryev-Polsky. It was the fourteenth of October—over a month since we had said goodbye to Natalia and departed the city. It turned out to be the last day before winter truly fell upon us. On the second day of our journey, the temperature dropped suddenly. Our ride to Moscow would be colder than anyone had planned for, but it would only last three or four days and then I would be back. Bonaparte's retreat through the Russian winter would take much longer.

Looking behind me along the great train of vehicles, I caught sight of the three covered wagons that Pyetr Pyetrovich had used to evacuate his "assets" from Moscow. He sat at the front of the first coach, next to the driver. Behind him, in the shade of the canopy, I could just make out a face that I knew to be Domnikiia's. I spent most of the long journey simply staring towards her.

My own carriage contained quite a mixture of people—old and young, some families—none that I felt much urge to converse with. I remember on the afternoon of our fourth day of travel, as I caught my first glimpse of the towers and domes of my beloved city, a mother sitting next to me was just finishing off telling a folk story to her two young children, bringing back memories of my own childhood. I looked at the approaching city for only a few minutes before turning back to gaze once again at Domnikiia.

The story that the mother was vividly telling her children had been one of my grandmother's favourites, and one of her strangest and, despite its simplicity, most frightening. It was about a town in the south called Uryupin, and I listened idly, comforted in the memory of my fears as a child which now seemed so utterly insignificant.

"After the traveller and his creatures had gone, everyone rejoiced," she recounted, her voice rising to match the rejoicing, "but soon people began to notice that something was wrong." She bent towards her children conspiratorially, and her voice lowered.

TWELVE

"The town was quiet—so quiet that you could have heard the sound of a farmer sowing poppy seed." The children smiled up at her, anticipating the ending of a story they had heard many times before.

"In the end, it was a little boy, just about your age, Grisha," she said to her son, "who understood what was wrong. It was so quiet because there was no birdsong. The traveller's pets had eaten not only the rats, but all of the birds in the village too.

"And to this day, you know, not one of them has come back."

PART TWO

Chapter XVIII

IT WAS A SUNDAY WHEN I ARRIVED BACK IN MOSCOW. I WAS glad to have seen the city at its worst, for now, although it was still in a sorry state, I could at least see that there was some improvement. For those like Domnikiia and most of the populace, who had left before the French had even arrived, the contrast with now must have been heartbreaking. They had last seen a city still at the height of its physical splendour, still with the lifeblood of its people flowing through its streets, even though at that time they were flowing out of the city. When I had last seen Moscow, two-thirds of it had been razed by fire, a fraction of the population remained and the streets were filled only with occupying French soldiers.

Today, two-thirds of the city was still destroyed by fire. No surprise for me, but a horror to many others who returned, particularly if they returned to find it was their home that had been destroyed. Today, there were no French in the city, neutral for those who had never seen the French, but an improvement for me, who had. Today, the population was still small, but larger than at its worst and increasing all the time. For those who had seen it full, the city was still empty. For me, it was not yet full, but at least it was filling.

Thus I must have cut an eccentric figure that day. While most of the returning Muscovites wore faces of haggard shock and shuffled around contemplating the enormity of the task of rebuilding—both personally and civically—that lay before them, I strode about with the evident pleasure of a voyager revisiting a beautiful town that he has not seen for many years.

Even so, my face must have become indistinguishable from those around it when I first laid eyes on the horror that had befallen the Kremlin. It had been spared the fires of the first days of Bonaparte's occupation, thanks largely to the efforts of the French themselves to protect it as the richest jewel in the crown that they had captured. But on his departure, Bonaparte had instructed that the citadel should be mined and destroyed so that we could not reclaim that which he could not keep. There could be no military justification for it, as there might possibly have been for the fires that dogged the French when they first took the city; it was mere petulance.

Luck, however, having chosen that autumn of 1812 to desert Bonaparte, had deserted him completely. The Kremlin was not destroyed. Perhaps his subordinates had been half-hearted in executing so churlish an order. Perhaps the rain had dampened the fuses. Whatever the cause, few of the charges had ignited. But whatever relief Muscovites might have felt that the Kremlin was saved, it was still a misery to see the damage that had been done. Facing Red Square, everything between the Arsenal and the Saint Nicholas Tower was gone, along with several other towers stretching down towards the river. Venturing within, I saw that the Palace of the Facets had collapsed. Worst of all, the great golden cross that had once topped the Ivan the Great Bell Tower was gone. It had not been destroyed in any explosion, but dragged to the ground and carted off as part of Bonaparte's plunder.

Sad though it was to witness the mutilation caused by the departure of the French, I counted myself as fortunate to have missed the brief trough of anarchy into which the remaining population of Moscow had descended in the twenty-four hours after the French had left. What I heard of it was disheartening enough. A crowd had marched on the Foundlings' Home, where there were no longer to be found orphans, but hundreds of French wounded who were too weak to be moved. Few survived the wrath of the mob, though their deaths were quicker than those of many of their comrades who *had* been able to walk out into the slow, freezing mortality of the Russian winter. Had the mob's only actions been those of vengeance, then they might have been attributed to some misplaced sense of patriotism, but, so I was told, looting had become more rife than ever. Those supplies that should have been eked out between all Muscovites were grabbed by the strongest and most selfish. Fortunately, there were Russian troops under Prince Khonvansky near to the city, waiting for the French to leave, and so the period when no law—neither French nor Russian—reigned was mercifully brief. By the time I returned, civilization—if not civility—had long been restored.

The inn in Tverskaya where I usually stayed (when I wasn't frequenting stables and crypts) had at least in part survived the fires. Flames had consumed much of the block, and as many as half of the rooms had been destroyed, but its proprietors had already returned and were attempting to resurrect their business using those few rooms that remained habitable. I chatted to the innkeeper as he led me up to a dispiritingly humble room. (The set which I used to occupy was no more—the stairs that had once led up to it now led only to a precipice overlooking a wasteland of detritus and rubble.) He asked after Vadim, Dmitry and Maks. I told him they were all well, finding it easier simply to lie about Maks, but I gathered that he had not seen Vadim any more recently than I had.

There was little I could do to track down Vadim. When the French arrived he, like me, had gone underground. His skills at hiding himself from view might not have been the greatest in the world, but in a city the size of Moscow, there was nowhere I could even begin to search for him. All I could do was attend the same daily meeting points that we had arranged weeks before. It was a dim hope, but that was the last plan of action we had. However slim the chance, it was the best I had of finding him. On top of that, there was also the possibility that one or more of the Oprichniki might show up—a prospect that I viewed with some ambivalence.

Sunday's meeting place was the Church of Fyodor Stratilit, beside Menshikov's Tower, east of the Kremlin. I took a slight detour to revisit the place where I had spent my last night in the city, in Boris and Natalia's tiny dwelling within the shantytown. When I got there, nothing remained of it—a few possessions of little value were strewn about, and I could see the remains of the homemade tents that the people had built. I even managed to find the precise spot where, I estimated, Boris and Natalia's particular compartment had been. They had left nothing of value. A broken bottle stuck half out of the mud. Whether it had been the one I had drunk from, or one of those I had given them, or some other stray, discarded bottle, I could not tell.

Asking around, I heard that the encampment had been broken up by the French only a few days after we left. There had been no bloodshed—the people there had simply dispersed to other locations in the city. There was little hope that anyone would know where a specific cobbler and his daughter had gone. I carried on to the meeting which I hoped Vadim would attend.

He was not there when I arrived, a little before nine. It took me but a moment to find the message I had left for him, scratched against the soft stone on a low part of the wall. My heart beat faster in the anticipation that he might have followed it up with a subsequent message in response, but there was none. I waited for an hour, but Vadim did not come. I headed back to my bed.

The following morning, I made a tour of the six remaining meeting points, much as I had done on my last day before leaving Moscow. My purpose was, as it had in part been at the church the previous night, to check whether Vadim had left any responses to my messages. Most of my messages remained intact. One of the chalk ones had vanished completely, presumably washed away by rain, and another had been half rubbed off, but was still essentially legible. However, at none of them did I find any corresponding reply from Vadim. I even checked the burnt-out tavern, where I had not left anything at all, in case Vadim had written a message there, but there was nothing.

If he had read any of the messages, he would surely have replied. Even if he had decided instantly on joining us in Yuryev-Polsky, he would have at least indicated that he had been at the rendezvous. It was, of course, possible that he had been at the place but not seen the message but, on the other hand, I had put them in conventional places—places where Vadim, with his years of experience, would certainly have looked. I could only conclude that he had not attended any meeting since we had last seen him, under the archway at Saint Vasily's. Like us, he must have left the city soon after. But even then, wouldn't he have left messages for us as I did? The other possibility was that he had never left the city and never would.

It seemed increasingly likely. If Iuda had realized that Vadim was following him, he would have had no qualms about ridding himself of his pursuer and indulging in a good meal at a single stroke. Vadim would have put up a good fight, but his scepticism was obvious even at the mention of the word "*voordalak*," and so he might not have been as wary as he should. Moreover, it was Iuda, not Vadim, that I had seen more recently. And who was to know that they hadn't run into one of the other Oprichniki, and then Vadim would have been beyond hope. It was an irony and a very small comfort that, if this was the case, Iuda himself had perished only hours later in the inferno of the cellar.

But though I feared, I did not know. It was just as likely that Vadim had fled Moscow. If that was the case then, with the city coming back to life, now was the time when he would be most likely to return, just as I had. All I could do was turn up at the appropriate place at nine o'clock each evening and hope.

That afternoon, I paid a visit to Degtyarny Lane. I hadn't completely abandoned hope on Domnikiia, but if she was lost to me, then I at least wanted it to end on an amicable footing. I also wanted to throw myself at her feet and tell her I loved her, but she was well aware of that—saying it wouldn't change anything.

I was not entirely surprised to find that the brothel had not only survived the fires, but was already open for business—although business did not yet seem to be booming. That the building had survived the flames could only be put down to good luck, but Pyetr Pyetrovich was a man who knew how to be lucky.

Domnikiia was not in the salon. The other girls sat around languidly, tired already of waiting for clients who did not arrive. None of them came up to me; they knew my face well enough to know whom I had come to see. On the stairs, I met Margarita.

"Oh, it's you," she said inhospitably.

"I've come to see Domnikiia."

"I can't stop you," she replied, and continued down the stairs.

"Sorry the nursing job didn't work out," I muttered, just loud enough for her to hear.

I knocked on Domnikiia's door and entered on her reply.

"Oh, it's you," she said, in a tone with far less passion—of any kind— than that with which Margarita had just uttered the same words.

"Yes," I said. "I wanted to see you."

TWELVE

"Well, you know me, Aleksei. A job's a job and I won't refuse a man with money."

"That wasn't what I came to do."

"So what did you come to do?"

I thought about it for a moment, and found that I didn't know. I knew full well what I wanted to achieve, but I had no real plans for how to achieve it. I realized there was one thing that needed to be said whichever way I was to leave her—be it as her lover or as her former lover.

"I came to say I'm sorry," I said.

"Sorry for what? For shouting at me when I said I wanted to be a vampire?" She spoke dismissively, as if such an apology could have little importance.

"No," I replied, knowing that only complete honesty would suffice. "I was right to do that. I'm sorry for not accepting your apology afterwards."

"Why didn't you?" Her voice was suddenly full of humility. I could boast about my sensitive appreciation of the subtleties of the female heart, but in reality it had been only by luck that I had stumbled upon saying what she wanted to hear.

"I didn't think it needed saying. It was obvious."

"Was it?" She spoke almost in a whisper now. "Why?"

"Because . . ." But I didn't have an answer. It was obvious because *I* knew exactly how my mind worked and how I felt about her. She did not.

She took a step towards me. "Is there anything else obvious that you haven't said to me?" she enquired tantalizingly, standing so close that she had to crane her neck upwards to look at me. I leaned forward to kiss her. She held her fingers to my lips to stop me. "Uh-uh," she said, shaking her head. "You have to say it."

"Isn't it obvious yet?"

"Say it, Lyosha!" she murmured, more mouthing than speaking.

I bent down to her ear and whispered it to her. Straightening up, I saw in her face a smile even more radiant than that I had seen on Natalia's when Dmitry had remembered her name day. I bent forward to kiss her and this time she offered no objections. I pushed her towards the bed, but now she did stop me.

"Not here," she said. "Not if we don't have to. Where are you staying?"

"At the inn, where I used to."

"It will have to be late; maybe after midnight."

"That's all right."

"If I can come at all."

"It would be easier for me to see you here," I told her.

"No, I don't want that. I want it to be like it was in Yuryev-Polsky—like when I was a nurse."

"OK," I said and kissed her again. Then I left.

I waited again for Vadim that evening. It was Monday and so the venue was Red Square. I paced about for an hour or so. Autumn had given way to winter and I had to keep walking just to keep warm, my hands buried deep in my pockets. The square was far from bustling and those who were there walked across it briskly and purposefully, not wanting to spend any more time than necessary in the cold night air. Vadim was not among them.

I returned to the inn. I had told the innkeeper that a lady might be visiting me, and so a raised eyebrow to him as I entered was question enough for him. A brief shake of the head was his reply. But it was still early.

I had fallen asleep by the time she entered my bedroom. It wasn't until I felt her cool, naked body press against my back and wrap itself around mine that I knew she was there. I rolled over to face her.

"Do I need to say anything now, Domnikiia?" I asked her softly.

"No," she whispered, with a smile I could not see. "It's obvious."

The following morning, I walked her back to Degtyarny Lane. It was almost midday. We had lain in bed for a long time—neither of us having occupations in which early rising was a requirement—talking about very little.

Then I was free until my appointment—and how I wished that I could really use a word that gave it such certainty—with Vadim. I found myself some lunch and then wandered around the streets, judging the degree to which Moscow was recuperating from its occupation.

It would, I believed, recover. Petersburg had become our capital only a hundred years ago. Nine years before that, it had been a swamp. It had taken the determination of a great man, the greatest in our history, Tsar Pyetr the First, to build the earliest structures on that swamp and then to make it his capital within so short a space of time. Today, there was no man alive that was his equal, not just in Russia but in the whole world. Bonaparte had aspired to inherit those laurels, but long ago he had proved himself unworthy of them. His retreat from Moscow was the final evidence of his failure to attain such status.

So today, we had no Pyetr to rebuild our city for us, but we had thousands—hundreds of thousands—of Petrushkas; little Pyetrs, who by themselves could no more raise Moscow from the ashes than I could raise the dead from their graves, but who together could restore it to its former greatness, so recently lost. And they did not even have to build it from nothing. They had their memories and, despite what had been lost to the fires, they still had the essential shape of the city. You can burn buildings, but it is harder to burn streets. Thus the plan of a city may survive.

And, of course, a third of the city had survived intact. I was walking down one of these undamaged streets when I noticed three cobbler's shops, huddled next to each other as one often sees with rivals in the same trade, sharing each other's warmth, but envying each other's custom. I peered through the window of each one. Not seeing what I was looking for, I went into the third and spoke to the shopkeeper.

"Have you ever come across a shoemaker by the name of Boris Mihailovich?"

"Boris?" replied the man. "Yes, I know him."

"Is his shop around here?"

"No. No, it's not."

"Do you know where it is?" I asked.

"It's not anywhere. It was burnt down on the first night of the fires."

"But he survived, I know that. Have you seen him recently, or his daughter?"

"Ah, so it's Natalia you're interested in, is it? Well, I saw them both about a week ago—after the French had gone—but not since."

"Maybe they've disappeared," suggested his assistant, who had been sweeping up around us, "like the rest of them." He emphasized the word "disappeared" as though it were new to him, or had taken on a new, more specific meaning.

"Disappeared"?" I asked.

"People have been coming into the city, but not staying," explained the shopkeeper without much concern. "I think they've just decided that there's no business to be had here and have gone off somewhere else. Oleg Stepanovich, the baker from up the street, is the only one I've known personally. Came back to Moscow, opened up his shop, closed it in the evening and didn't open it the next day. I reckon he's gone chasing after the army because they'll pay more for his bread, but he didn't tell his wife, so it may be more than just the army he's chasing."

"*I* reckon Bonaparte's left some of his men here, hidden, to pick us off one by one as we come back," suggested the assistant, leaning on his broom.

"Well, if they pick you off, Vitya," said the cobbler, "it'll be a long time before anyone notices much difference round here." The sweeping was quickly resumed.

I thanked the men and went on my way, knowing from what they had said that the Oprichniki were still in town. What had been said was vague, but it was also chillingly similar to the stories that had emanated from wherever the Oprichniki happened to be. It was, of course, an assumption to suggest that that was what had happened to Boris and his daughter, but I knew then that, for them and for anyone else, the city was not safe.

That evening's rendezvous was at the Church of Saint Clement. As I waited outside, I recalled the last time I had been there, exactly six weeks before, and my encounter with Ioann and Foma. Ioann was now dead, I knew—deader even than he had been when we had met—but I still felt the dread that Foma might return that night to take his revenge. By now they must have been aware that four of their fellows had died within the space of a few nights. It would take little genius—and they didn't have much, particularly now there was no Iuda to do their thinking—for them to deduce that I might in some way be responsible. But whatever they had deduced, none of them showed up. Neither did Vadim.

TWELVE

To make matters worse, Domnikiia did not visit me that night. It is remarkable how quickly one can become accustomed to not sleeping alone.

In one way, Domnikiia staying away had been a good thing. The next morning I received a letter from Marfa. It was dated over three weeks earlier, but in the confusion of the French occupation and retreat, it was a miracle that it had made it through to me at all.

While in Yuryev-Polsky, I had sent her several letters, but they had evidently crossed with this one. Her concern for my safety showed between every line she wrote. She told of the news that they were hearing in Petersburg and of the fear there that Bonaparte would soon be marching towards them. Marfa felt reassured that as long as the tsar stayed in Petersburg, they would be safe. Ostensibly, the implication was that Aleksandr would protect them, but her real meaning was that, as soon as he scarpered, then they'd know they were in trouble. Her understanding of politics was, as ever, remarkably clear-sighted, certainly for a woman.

Dmitry Alekseevich had been a little unwell, but was better now. He had been asking when I would be coming home. I resented being told that. I felt that Marfa was using our son to voice her own desires. Not that it was untrue that Dmitry wanted me home, nor was it unreasonable that Marfa did as well. I just resented the way that she impinged on my desire to have it all. Strange that I resented only Marfa, not Dmitry, but then I did not have a rival son here in Moscow.

She did not write very much on the matter of Maksim's death, but the little that she did put managed in its own way to express much the same feelings as I had. Marfa's approach was simply to ignore the reasons that had led to Maks' execution. She could describe her sorrow without ever facing the unpleasant fact that Maks had been a traitor. She would have written the same words if he had died by a French sword at Borodino. It was of unspeakable comfort to read her words about Maks, as if he had died a decent soldier's death. She was spared, in her mind, the embarrassing subtext of his treason, and I was momentarily spared my own condemnation for my abandonment of him.

The final piece of news was that Vadim's daughter, Yelena, had given birth to a baby boy on 6 September. He had been born a little earlier than expected, but was completely healthy, and was named Rodion Valentinovich. Marfa anticipated that I knew all this already, since I would have heard it directly from Vadim, but I could tell she was hoping that that would not be the case and that not only would she have the pleasure of being the first to tell me, but I in turn would have the pleasure of being the first to tell Vadim.

It would have been a delight to be the two hundredth to tell Vadim, just to have had the pleasure of seeing him at all.

I wrote a quick response to Marfa, saying very little except that I was safe and back in Moscow. I said nothing of Dmitry or Vadim, since to say only that Dmitry was safe would imply that Vadim was not, and I saw no sense in raising undue alarm. For all I knew, he could have headed straight back to Petersburg and be doting over his beloved grandson, cradling him in his arms at that very moment.

I went to Degtyarny Lane to find out what had happened to Domnikiia the night before. When I arrived, I was told she was occupied. I knew she was still working, but the reality of it remained nonetheless unpleasant. That, I suppose, is why she had said we should not meet there. I went back outside and truculently began to throw pebbles up at her window. Soon, her head popped out. I immediately felt concerned that I was intruding on her territory, that she would brusquely send me away, much as I would have done if she were to interrupt me on the battlefield—a bizarre image.

Her face, however, was a portrait of delight at seeing me.

"Are you all right?" I asked.

"I'm wonderful, Lyosha. How are you?"

"What happened to you last night?"

"Things just got busy. I'm sorry." She pulled a sorry face as she said the word.

"I wasn't complaining. I was just concerned."

She smirked. "You're scared of me, aren't you?"

"Scared of losing you. I wish you didn't seem so happy."

"Charming! Shouldn't I be happy to see you?"

TWELVE

"So you were miserable until you opened the window?"

"Wretched," she grinned.

"Good. Now *I'm* happy."

I heard the call of a man's voice from within her room. "I have to go," she said.

"I'll see you tonight?" I asked.

"I'll try." With that she was gone.

That evening, I went to the Stone Bridge, still clinging on to the receding hope of seeing Vadim. Even over the three days that I had been back in Moscow, it was already just perceptible that more people were returning to the city. Like the complexion of a man drained of almost all his blood, but not quite to the point of death, the colour was beginning to return to Moscow's cheeks. Although the hour was late, the bridge was still busy, busier even than in happier times as the amount of work that people found themselves faced with increased the hours that they put into it.

As I stood there on the bridge, it began to snow. This was the first real snowfall of the winter; heavier than we had seen in Yuryev-Polsky and still scarcely settling, but a portent of what was to come. It was another sign that winter was to be early that year, but Muscovites—and all Russians—are well prepared and would take the winter in their stride whenever it came. In retreat, out to the west, the same could not be said of the French.

I waited for over an hour, inspecting every face that passed me, but Vadim's was not among them. I headed north, back to my bed and, I hoped, to Domnikiia. I was just gazing up at the towers of the Kremlin when I heard the voice of someone very close behind me whisper in my ear.

"Murderer!"

I turned, but saw no one near. A few steps away from me, I saw the back of a tall, shabby man who was marching directly away. It could only have been he who had spoken. I followed him. Although he never had to run, his long legs carried him with enormous pace, forcing me to break into a trot. As we headed on to the Stone Bridge, I found my pursuit of him hindered by the crowd, bumping into them in my rush to keep up. For him, the crowd offered no such obstacle, seeming to open before him like the sea before the bow of a ship as he strode purposefully across the bridge.

We were across the river and the Vodootvodny Canal before I caught up with him. I put my hand on his shoulder and he offered no resistance in turning to face me. He was tall and pale, with many small scars on his face. His shoulder-length hair was loose and unkempt. His dark, black eyes looked towards me, but seemed to see nothing. There was no specific reason for it, but I knew in my heart that I was standing face to face with a vampire—moreover, a vampire that was not one of the Oprichniki. I had thought that my task had been reduced to having just five more of these creatures to face, but now—as my grandmother had told me they could, and as I had hoped she had made up—the vampires had bred. And if they had produced this one offspring, then how many more might there be? They would become unstoppable.

The creature looked fixedly into my eyes for a few seconds and then turned away and continued his journey. I stood in shocked immobility for a moment, considering the prospect of the number of vampires that I might have to face; considering that I had helped to introduce them into a city where they might now stay forever, neither noticing nor caring that the language spoken by their food supply had changed from French to Russian. The monster that I had been following might be just one of dozens of innocent Muscovites, picked at random, who had not only been denied life, but subsequently denied a true death as the hideous plague spread.

And yet somewhere at the back of my mind, I recognized the face into which I had just been staring. It was certainly not one of the Oprichniki, nor anyone that I knew very well. It was someone that I had previously seen in Moscow. Then it hit me; a corpse that did not decay. Weeks before, when the dead and wounded of Borodino had been arriving in the city, I had looked briefly into those same dark eyes to verify that the grenadier was indeed dead. The priest had declared it to be a miracle that the body did not putrefy, but I knew now it was no such thing. The corpse did not decay because the body had survived the death of the soul. Presumably one of the Oprichniki, during our first foray out to the west, had transformed him into one of their own. The process must take some time. When I had seen him, he was somewhere between the two states of existence—dead as a human but not yet alive as a vampire. But now he was fully a *voordalak*.

I continued my pursuit of him, but now more stealthily, reenacting how I had pursued Foma, Matfei and then Ioann. This vampire displayed little of their discretion, walking openly down the streets without any show of fear. Indeed, what was there to fear? The city was free again. He had no need to worry about being stopped by French patrols and he could walk about without obstruction, as free as any other Russian. I, too, was in a better position for the French having left. I could once again wear my sword which, though it gave me some comfort, I knew was not the best weapon at my disposal. Tucked inside my coat was the wooden dagger that I trusted would be of far greater use. I reached in and grasped it firmly, reassured and emboldened by the texture of the chiselled wood.

His indirect meanderings about the city might have been put down to his unfamiliarity with its geography, but it seemed to me more that he was merely trying to pass the time. It wasn't until the early hours of the morning that he finally reached his destination and went up to the doorway of a particularly grand house, certainly owned by one of the wealthier families in the city. It was not far from the cellar where I had left Iuda and Ioann to burn so many weeks before. This residence appeared strangely unravaged in comparison with those around it. The area had not been molested by the fires, but no street in Moscow had been left unmolested by looters, be they native or invader. All along the street, windows were smashed and doors kicked in. Rejected booty—and times were harsh enough that only the most impractical of items (books, paintings and so forth) were counted so valueless as to be rejected—lay strewn outside. But this house had its windows intact, its door still a barrier. Even the street outside, though not clean, was at least clear of the debris that lay outside its neighbours. It was as though some faithful servant had remained behind in the house and had—out of habit and oblivious to the tumult around him—kept the building in the tidiness that befitted it. And yet in the chaos that had befallen Moscow, no amount of diligence alone could have maintained such order. A terrifying strength would have been required. The absence of refuse around the house was reminiscent of the absence of insects around the dark corner of a room in which a spider lurks.

The soldier unlocked the door and went inside without fear of encountering the true owner of the residence. Although the rich and the powerful had not yet begun to return to Moscow in any great numbers, many had at least sent servants ahead to reoccupy their property. Perhaps the owners of this place had done so too. Any servant arriving to open up the house would be little expecting to find it infested with vampires and would be quickly dealt with.

Despite the sanitary atmosphere that hung around the building—for which the explanation was all too easy to imagine—I could not in all certainty be sure that this was where the creature planned to sleep. It was still some time until dawn and so I waited a while to see if he reemerged. After about an hour, no one had come out of the house and no one else had entered. Despite knowing what I might encounter within, there was little debate in my mind that I had to go inside.

I went up to the door and tried the handle. He had not locked it behind him. Inside, the hallway was dark, but on a table I found an oil lamp, which I lit and carried with me. It was a large house of many rooms—the vampire could be hidden in any one of them. I drew out my wooden dagger and grasped it firmly, knowing that at any moment I might be called upon to use it.

I went first into the cellar, having learned from experience that that was where a *voordalak* would make its nest, but I found nothing untoward. The only thing of note was that the cellar wall had been roughly knocked down, so that it connected to the cellar of the next building. I glanced briefly in there, but saw nothing. A faint smell of sewage greeted my nostrils. I realized that the street outside must be close to the Neglinnaya, the tributary of the Moskva into which many of the city's sewers flowed. In Moscow's good times—when people were plentiful enough and nourished enough to make the sewers full to overflowing—the stench would have been far stronger, but still somewhere beyond the broken-down wall was an underground path to that public drain.

The rooms on the ground floor too were empty, though they were surprisingly well furnished; surprising in contrast with other houses I had seen in the city. Those houses that had not been cleared out by their departing owners had been cleaned out by the invading French, but this place remained disquietingly habitable; almost homely. It all fitted in with the image that the building was somehow "blessed"—protected from any who would dare to despoil it. Indeed some of the rooms seemed to have too much furniture, as if it had been shifted here to make space in other rooms elsewhere in the house. The only sign of serious upheaval—somewhat incongruous—was that in a number of rooms the floorboards had been removed, adding a challenge for me to pick my way between the joists.

I was suddenly reminded again of my grandmother's house. These rooms, like many of hers, were unlived in, but no serious attempt had been made to close them up or to either protect or remove their contents. For my grandmother, it would have been an admission of her decline to formally abandon the unused rooms of her home. For the occupants of this house, it was probably more a case of laziness than pride. Here, I guessed, as in my grandmother's house, there would be one or two rooms at the heart of the building where its residents dwelt. But unlike another visitor to another grandmother's house—from a story which my own grandmother had told me—it would not be a wolf that I would find living there, but something far worse.

I began to climb the stairs. The shadows cast by my lamp through the balustrade made strange shapes on the walls of the upper hallway as I ascended. Suddenly I heard a rustling noise and something scuttled across the hall into a corner. I held up the lamp and peered in the direction it had gone. It was a rat, frozen in the corner, looking almost pitifully scared, its beadlike eyes reflecting the lamp's flame. Glancing around, I could see by similar reflections that there were dozens of rats up here, each marked out by the same two tiny points of light. This struck me as odd. I had seen no rats on the ground floor, or even in the cellar. Why should they all have chosen to congregate here on the first floor? What, I wondered, had those staring, shining eyes struck upon up here that they could not find down below?

It was then, as I continued to climb the stairs and my head rose above the level of the floor, that I noticed the smell. It was the smell of a charnel-house. I thought instantly of the stench of Zmyeevich's breath, which I now knew to be the stink of the raw, decaying human flesh and blood that rose from his stomach. Holding back the rising need to vomit, I followed the smell into a room to the left of the stairs. I heard the scampering of the rats as they fled out of my way. As I stepped into the room, the stench was stronger and its source was immediately revealed to me. On the floor were laid out ten corpses—all in assorted French uniforms, or those of their allies. They were in various stages of decay. On some, no human features remained recognizable. On others, the telltale throat wounds that betrayed both the manner and the motivation of their deaths were still clear. In between, the wounds had begun to vanish into a formless sponge of decomposing flesh.

I didn't inspect any of the bodies very closely. The light of the lamp was faint, and bending down close was not a pleasant experience. I looked around the rest of the room. In addition to the door through which I had entered, there was another that led to an adjacent room. Before I went through, I glanced back and noticed how, in contrast to the careless way in which the bodies had been desecrated by the vampire's fangs, their actual positioning was rather orderly. The ten bodies were neatly placed across the room in two rows, as though they were in a hospital ward. It was no different from a dining table in a grand house such as the one in which I stood. The crockery and wine glasses and cutlery are laid out with punctilious consideration, but little attention is given by the diner to the messy carcass of the chicken left on his plate once he has eaten.

Here I could see why some of the downstairs rooms had been over-furnished. Space had to be made up here to store these mementos, much as a man might overcrowd one room with paintings to leave room in another for the stuffed heads of wolves and bears that he has hunted, oblivious to the protestations of his wife about having such ugly things in the house. Those stuffed beasts would always be placed in poses so much more terrifying and aggressive than the true state of the creature when it was killed. The same could not be said of the bodies laid out here in so orderly a fashion. If any-thing, it was their defencelessness, not their majesty, that was emphasized in the display. The Oprichniki saw no nobility in their prey, nor did they have wives to moderate their sense of decor.

TWELVE

The orderliness of the layout revealed something else to me. There were only ten corpses in the room because it had reached its capacity. The doorway to the next room beckoned. As I stepped through I heard behind me a rustling sound as the rats returned to the activity from which I had disturbed them.

The next room was larger and had a few vestiges of furniture left in it. In one corner was a high-backed armchair and near it a folding screen of oriental appearance. Elsewhere a table, chairs and a stool all made this room appear a little more "lived" in, though the very word brought a grimace to my lips. A second door led back out on to the landing. The windows, like the windows in all the rooms I had been in, were hidden behind thick, heavy curtains. Again there were bodies in here, but the room was not yet full. Only two of them were in French uniforms and both were less decayed than any in the other room. The bodies next to these were very different. They were shabbily dressed in ordinary clothes. By this and simply by their faces, I could tell that these were Russian. Like an archaeologist, I had found a division between strata which I could use to mark a precise date; the date when the French had left and the Oprichniki had chosen not to follow them, but to remain and enjoy an alternative, plentiful food supply.

There were seven Russian bodies in the room. The soldiers had naturally all been men, but once the Oprichniki had switched to civilians, they demonstrated no discrimination over sex. One of the bodies was small, scarcely bigger than a child. Its head, covered in tight curls of black hair, lay on one side, facing away from me, causing the foul lacerations in the throat to gape open even more. For an agonizing moment, I believed it to be Natalia. I bounded across the room and turned her head to look at her face, the wounds on one side of her neck closing up as I did so. It was not her. It wasn't even a girl, but a boy of about Natalia's age. I stood up, relieved that the suffering of grief was not, in this case, to be felt by me but could be transferred to others elsewhere in the city who knew and loved this boy.

I went over to the oriental screen and pulled it to one side. Behind it, a figure stood upright, its awful, contorted face staring directly into mine. I smelled the reeking stench of decay stronger than ever and I threw myself back, knocking the screen to the ground.

I had been mistaken. The figure was not standing; it was hanging—hanging like a coat casually thrown on to a peg. A long nail had been hammered into the wall behind and the body had been thrust upon it so that the head of the nail could just be seen sticking out of the neck under the chin. It was in a position that would not have much hindered the Oprichniki as they ate. The body was old and almost as decayed as some of those in the other room, but it wore no French uniform, just regular clothes. The wounds in the neck had long ago begun to putrefy, to such an extent that it was surprising it still had the integrity to support the weight of the body from that single nail. Most of the flesh of the face had begun to decay, but the full beard still remained, as did the eyes.

And so, despite the darkness and the hideous putrefaction of his face, the body was not unrecognizable. His clothes and his beard and his eyes—especially his eyes—all gave him away.

It was Vadim.

So it became clear that Rodion Valentinovich would never be held in his grandfather's arms; that their lives had overlapped by only a few hours or days, if at all. Vadim could never even have known of his grandchild's existence, and neither I nor anyone else would have the pleasure of telling him. I could not weep. I had known for a long time that Vadim was dead; known since I had seen Iuda arrive at that house in Kitay Gorod without Vadim in tow. Every time I had tried and failed to meet up with Vadim since, I had felt a little fear and a little sadness and suspected that his failure to appear hinted at his utter inability so to do. And so seeing his body now was more of a confirmation than a revelation. Still I wished, as I had done and still did with Maks, for the chance then to say a proper goodbye and the opportunity now to mourn.

I turned away and my foot knocked against something hollow and wooden. Vadim's corpse had not been the only thing hidden by the screen. I had also found what I had come into the house to look for. It was a coffin, but again, like those of Matfei and Varfolomei, not purpose-built; merely a crate of the conveniently correct size and shape.

I pulled it away from the wall, towards the middle of the room, and

TWELVE

prised open the lid. Inside was the soldier whom I had so long ago seen dead but not decaying, whom that night I had followed to the house where he now slept. His eyes were closed and his hands lay across his belly. I raised my hand, firmly grasping my wooden dagger high above my head, ready to bring it down on the sleeping monster's heart with all my strength.

His eyes flicked open. He engaged me in the same dead stare that I had seen in him before and once again hissed the only word I had ever heard him utter.

"Murderer!"

Chapter XIX

I WASTED NO TIME IN THROWING MY ARM DOWN TOWARDS the creature's chest, but a hand grabbed my wrist, and I could not reach my target. Another pair of hands took hold of my left arm and I was dragged away from the coffin and over to the wall. The Russian soldier climbed out of the coffin and approached me.

The two men who had grabbed me relaxed their grip, and the one on my right said to the soldier, "Hold him." It was a voice I knew and should not have been hearing; the voice of a creature that I thought I had seen annihilated in a burning cellar many weeks before. It was Iuda.

The soldier pressed his hand against my chest, revealing a tremendous strength, and I found myself unable to move. Iuda and my other captor—as he stepped into the light, I saw it was Andrei—walked to the middle of the room.

"You're surprised to see me, I think," said Iuda, with the tone almost of a bonhomous host.

"A little," I replied.

"It must be so irksome," he continued, "when you think that you've murdered four of your comrades—men who have willingly come at your invitation to your country to fight on your side—it must be so irritating to find that one of the four has survived."

I didn't respond.

"It's the same mistake your friend Maksim made," said Andrei, making none of Iuda's faux effort to hide his loathing.

"So how did you get out?" I asked.

"Can't you work it out?" asked Iuda. "My good friend Dmitry Fetyukovich rescued me. By the time you arrived, he had already awakened me and helped me to safety."

"Safety where? You couldn't go out into the daylight."

TWELVE

"No, of course not, but in these big blocks of connected buildings one can move from one house to the next without ever going outside. Having a little greater strength than living humans helps too. It allows us to knock through the odd wall here and there between houses."

I had seen examples of these creatures' strength weeks before, and I felt it in the hand that pinioned me against the wall. I wondered what other powers they might possess, and moreover what their weaknesses might be. "And that's it?" I asked, "Your strength? Is that the only thing you creatures have that gives you an advantage over us?"

Iuda laughed; I had been very obvious. "Perhaps you'd like a written list? Three dozen ways that vampires are better than humans? Well, it won't help you, Lyosha. No, our strength is nothing. I think it's just a side effect of the diet. What makes us superior is not something that we have; it is something that we lack. We lack conscience. When we act we are not bound by any rules of what is wrong and what is right. We have no fear of recrimination either on earth or in hell. We can achieve things that you could never dream of because our dreams are not haunted by doubts about our righteousness and concerns for others."

"And what have you achieved?" I asked him, scornfully.

He chose to ignore the question. "I can do things of which you would never be capable. When I caught Vadim Fyodorovich following me" (he nodded carelessly towards Vadim's hanging corpse) "my scruples might have told me to let him go, but I didn't. When he told me he had just been curious to see how I worked, I might have believed him, but I didn't. When he begged me for mercy, telling me about the wife and family that he loved, I could have felt pity, but I didn't. Instead I hung him up on that nail over there, just to shut him up, not so as to kill him; otherwise we wouldn't have been able to taste the fresh blood that we all so much prefer.

"Could you have done that, Lyosha?" Iuda continued. "Of course not—you wouldn't want to. But you'd like to do it to me now, wouldn't you? And yet still you couldn't. I could just beg you for mercy; tell you about my terrible upbringing in the Carpathians and you'd lose all stomach to do it."

"So that's why you're so hard to kill?" I said, straightening up. The soldier, listening to Iuda, had relaxed his pressure on me a little. "It's not your strength, but our weakness?"

"Exactly. We are certainly quite easy to kill. Sunlight. Fire." He nodded down towards my wooden dagger, which had fallen to the floor. "A stake through the heart. Decapitation. They're all ways that I've seen it happen. Maybe there are others too. I can't say I'm an expert."

"You mean you don't know?" I asked. I was surprised, but also attempting to goad him.

"Why should I know? You're not a doctor, are you? You don't know every detail of how your body works, nor do I of mine. We're not going to carry out experiments to find out new ways of killing ourselves." He smirked suddenly, as if he'd just thought of something very funny. If he had, he did not share it.

"Why not?" I asked. "You're easy enough to replace."

Iuda raised an inquisitive eyebrow. "Easy?"

"Like your friend here," I said, indicating the soldier who had by now, relaxed by my utter defeat, completely forgotten to restrain me. "Just a quick bite and it's one less human and one more vampire."

Iuda chuckled. "If only it *were* that easy, but unfortunately we remain a very exclusive group."

"You have a long list of membership rules, I suppose, to keep out the riff-raff."

"We have but one criterion. The individual in question must want to become one of us. One would imagine that most organizations offering such a relaxed admission would be inundated with applications, but we are not. For us, self-selection is the ideal approach. You, for example, would not wish to join us, would you?"

"No," I said, needing no special effort to inject absolute conviction into my voice.

"And so we would not have you. In fact, this gentleman is the only recruit we've had since we arrived in your deeply pious country. Not that we have the opportunity to ask on every occasion."

"And what happened to him?"

TWELVE

"He ran into Varfolomei. That, by the way, is why he has a particular dislike for you. We're all upset that you murdered Matfei and Ioann, but he regards Varfolomei as something of a father figure. Anyway, there he was, fleeing from—deserting if you will—the field at Borodino and whom should he meet but Varfolomei? They have a little chat and he decides that yes, a life of immortality would be preferable to being a *ryadovoy* in the Russian army, to be sent to his death at the whim of cowardly officers such as yourself."

"And so just by wanting to be a vampire, he became one?"

"No, no. There's a mechanism. First Varfolomei drank some of his blood, just enough so that he would die, but not straight away. He then willingly—and it has to be willingly, I'm told—drank some of Varfolomei's blood. It's traditional to drink from a cut to the chest, but I don't think that matters."

"So you understand that much of how your body works," I commented. "How you're created, but not how you are killed."

He smiled. "We have an advantage over you in that we can remember the moment, and therefore the process, of our own conception. It makes it so much easier for us the first time we come to do it ourselves, rather than all that messy fumbling about that humans go through."

"So how many vampire offspring have you produced in your time, Iuda?"

"None," he replied and then quickly added with a smile, "that I know of. And I would know. What I have just described could not very well happen by accident. Some of us are different, but I am very like you humans. I like the chase and I like the kill, but I don't want to be concerned with any long-term consequences." He thought for a moment. "It's much the same as you feel when you're with that young lady—Dominique. You love the physical experience of her body, but you'd be appalled if your congress with her ever produced a child." He looked into my face enquiringly and then raised his eyebrows. "Or maybe not."

He turned away and the eyes of the other two vampires in the room followed him. I took my chance. I raced across the room towards the window, brushing aside the relaxed arm of Varfolomei's "offspring" and playing hopscotch over the pitiful corpses which were lined up across the floor. My best guess was that by now it was dawn outside. I grabbed hold of one of the curtains and wrenched at it, pulling it away from its fixings high above me at the top of the window. Andrei took a step towards me as I tugged, but he was too late. The curtain rail gave way and the curtain came tumbling down over my head, blocking my sight completely, but revealing the window behind it.

I quickly wrestled the heavy material off me, the darkness of its covering giving way to the still dim, lamp-lit room. Around me stood the three vampires—two of them utterly impassive at the futility of my action, Iuda with the trace of a mocking smile on his lips. I turned back to the window to see that, behind the curtains, it had been boarded up with the floorboards that had been taken from downstairs. Through the occasional chink I could see that outside it was just daylight, but not enough of it could get inside to do any harm to my captors.

In happier times, parties held in a house such as this would have carried on long into the night and on to the following morning. Sometimes the zealous host would ensure that the windows were shuttered and the clocks stopped so that no guests would realize that dawn had broken and spoil the atmosphere by considering that it might be time to depart. My hosts—the new, undead occupants of this house—had a similar desire to obscure the light of the new day, but with very different motivation.

With a flick of his head, Iuda indicated to the soldier that I should be held fast once again. The soldier pushed me back against the wall and pressed his hand firmly against me.

"So," I said, feeling the depressing reaction to my failed action sweeping over me, "I suppose you're going to kill *me* now."

There followed a brief conversation between Iuda and Andrei in their own language. I think that Iuda wanted me to die there and then, but Andrei disagreed. He mentioned Pyetr a number of times. It was odd that they referred to him as Pyetr even amongst themselves. Did they not know his real name, or were they taking caution to the extreme—making sure that no one could ever find out who they were and use that knowledge to track them down? From their discussion, I presumed that they were waiting for Pyetr to arrive. Any delay was a moment more for me to enjoy life, and any moment was time for me to think how I might escape.

TWELVE

"It's going to be a bit cramped for the three of you all sleeping in that one coffin, isn't it?" I said.

Iuda looked away from his conversation with Andrei to answer me. My attempt to escape seemed to have knocked his earlier good humour out of him. He was now quite dismissive in his mood.

"We don't *need* coffins to sleep in, any more than you need beds. How do you suppose we spent all those days out there on the Smolensk road?"

It was a good question. "How did you?" I asked.

"We'd just dig a hole and bury ourselves in it. All we need is to keep the sun off. It doesn't need to be very deep."

Before I could reply, we heard the sound of footsteps coming up the stairs. The door to the landing opened and in walked Pyetr. He was quickly followed, to my consternation, by Dmitry.

Pyetr and Iuda began talking furtively in their own language. Dmitry spoke directly to me.

"You shouldn't have killed them, Aleksei. I know we couldn't help Ioann, but Matfei and Varfolomei—that was just murder."

"I suppose you told them about Matfei and Varfolomei," I said.

"I told them you followed Matfei. They knew he was dead. It didn't take much to work it out."

"How did Pyetr get here?" I asked. "It's light outside, isn't it?"

"We came underground. The sewers run right under this street. With a bit of work you can get into any of the cellars. It's dark as night down there."

"I presume they've agreed to spare your life," I said bitterly.

"And yours, Aleksei. They have no quarrel with us. They understand you killing them. If we'd told you the truth from the start, you wouldn't have overreacted."

He was utterly deceived; deceived by himself as much as by the Oprichniki into the conviction that because their cause—our cause—was right then they themselves must be righteous; deceived into the belief that because they were righteous, anything that they did to support our cause must be to the good. And yet through it all, the thought popped into my head that there was something I had been meaning to tell him next time I saw him. It wasn't relevant, unless Dmitry was in an even greater state of self-delusion than I could possibly believe, but there was little else to discuss.

"Did you hear that Yelena Vadimovna has had a little boy?" As I spoke, my thoughts went to Marfa and an idea began to form.

"That's nice," said Dmitry. "Vadim will be pleased." I was shocked that he did not know, but also relieved that his present attitude was based upon ignorance.

"You have no idea, do you?" I said to him, as I slipped my hand inside my shirt.

"What do you mean?"

"Vadim Fyodorovich is just over there," I said, gesturing towards where the rotting corpse hung, as yet unnoticed by Dmitry. "They . . ."

Iuda had been listening and interrupted me. "We have decided what we are going to do," he announced loudly.

We never heard his plans. As he spoke I withdrew my hand from my shirt with a jerk. I felt the chain snap around my neck, leaving me free to pull out the icon that Marfa had given me. I held it up to the soldier's face and ominously shouted at him, "Keep back!"

In the face of the Saviour's image, the *voordalak*'s entire strength began to wither away. He released his grip on me and covered his eyes, backing away from me across the room.

The reaction of the other vampires was quite different.

"You fool!" shouted Pyetr at the terrified creature.

"Don't be so damned superstitious!" added Iuda. Pyetr gave a brief hand signal to Andrei, who marched across the room and, without fear, grabbed the icon from me and cast it into a corner. Evidently, there was nothing real for them to fear in the religious symbol, but the young, inexperienced vampire believed that there was, and that was enough to make him afraid. Fortunately, the moment's distraction gave me time to place my hand on something which could have a very real effect on them.

As Andrei turned back towards me I grasped my sword and, with a single backhand motion, drew it and struck him across the front of the throat. Ever since Iuda had mentioned it, I had been itching to try decapitation as a method for despatching one of these creatures. It was not, as I knew from battle, an easy thing to achieve. The blade slipped over the top of his Adam's apple and, severing his windpipe, buried itself about halfway through his neck. With a swift tug I extricated it. The wound was not fatal. Andrei bent forward, his hands clutching at the long, deep gash in his throat as a torrent of blood flowed out between his fingers. He was incapacitated, and his death was not my immediate concern. I dashed towards the window once again, this time stepping first on to the seat and then the back of the armchair that stood near to it and leaping as high as I could. I thrust the tip of my sword hard down into the wooden planks to give me a little more upward momentum. My left hand just grasped the top of one of the floorboards that covered the glass and with my two fingers I hung there above the room for five or even ten seconds, viewing the scene beneath me.

On one side of the room, Dmitry, Iuda and Pyetr stood stock still, not in shock, but unable to make any move until they could see what would happen next. On the other, Andrei stood quite upright with his back to the wall. His left hand pressed against the wall behind him for support, while his right was held ineffectually across his throat, having little effect on the flow of blood from it. Near him crouched the soldier, covering his head in fear—fear either still of the icon, or of the horrific injury I had inflicted upon Andrei.

My entire weight was held on my two fingers, and they began to scream at me that they could not hold on. Beneath me, Iuda and Pyetr were almost licking their lips in anticipation of my fall. I felt my body gradually begin to descend. But it was not my fingers that had given way, it was the board itself. With the screeching sound of nails being drawn out of wood, the floorboard I was holding yielded. As its tip etched out a quarter circle across the room, moving horizontally at first and then smoothly bending round to its final, rapid, vertical descent, I fell with it.

I landed on my feet, but immediately fell on to my side, managing to keep hold of my sword. Where the wooden plank had been, now sunlight could penetrate as a beam which sliced across the room, bisecting it with an area of light about the thickness of a brick wall. For the vampires, it was just as impassable. I had landed on the wrong side of the division, being at the feet of Iuda and Pyetr, but for me the barrier was as impenetrable as mere air. I rolled across to the other side of the room and got to my feet.

Iuda was enraged. He leapt towards me with a look of unutterable malevolence on his face, and it took the combined strength of both Pyetr and Dmitry to keep him from crossing through the intrusion of light that would so certainly have meant his death.

I smashed the hilt of my sword into Andrei's stomach and he doubled up in pain, his hands leaving his throat to clutch at his belly. The back of his neck was now fully exposed to me and I brought the blade of my sabre down on it with the strength of both hands. Still it was not enough to sever it. I could feel my sword trapped tightly between two vertebrae, unable to move forward or backward. I flicked my wrist and gave the blade a sharp sideways twist. I heard the popping sound of whatever ligaments remained to hold Andrei's head upon his shoulders and felt the blade come free.

Andrei's head was dust before it ever hit the ground. His body straightened up and his hands went to where his face had once been. They too never made it, desiccating and then crumbling to nothing as his body fell to its knees. It was a falling motion that was never stopped. By the time he had reached his knees, his whole body was no more than a fine powder which settled, rather than fell, to the floor. At some moment during the descent his coat, his shirt and his breeches ceased to be carried down by his body and began to fall of their own accord as a heap of laundry—as a marionette whose strings had been suddenly cut.

The looks of horror on the faces of Pyetr and Iuda were nothing compared with that of Dmitry. Theirs were angry and vengeful. His was a genuine shock to see his friend Andrei slaughtered before his eyes and to see his friend Aleksei carrying out the butchery with such evident satisfaction.

"Take him, Dmitry Fetyukovich!" growled Pyetr. "You're the only one who can."

Dmitry approached the wall of light, but even he seemed reluctant to cross it. There were tears in his eyes as he spoke.

"Why, Aleksei?" he said. "You of all people are an enlightened man. You don't have to wallow in the prejudices and superstitions of our grandparents. They came here to help us, to fight against our enemies as though they were our brothers. Throughout their lives they've had to face the hatred of the ignorant and now you—even after they helped us to throw out the French—even you can offer them no thanks but death."

He drew his sword and took a step towards me, standing in the middle of the very barrier that split the room, his face and his scars and his tears illuminated by the sunlight.

"Kill him, Dmitry!" snarled Iuda from behind.

"I don't want to fight you, Dmitry," I said, dropping my sword to my side, but not being so foolish as to sheath it, "but I will if I have to, and if I do, I will win."

"I don't believe you would kill me, Aleksei, but having seen what you did to Andrei, what do I know of you?"

"Take a look around you, Dmitry," I insisted. "Look at the corpses on the floor. They're not French; they're Russians—innocent Russians. These creatures don't kill to help liberate our country. They kill to eat, and they'll eat whatever they find there is the greatest supply of."

Dmitry began to look about him, taking in the truth of what I said. Almost beneath his feet lay the body that I had briefly mistaken for Natalia. With his boot, he turned its head to one side so that he could see its face. If he had suspected it was Natalia, he showed no sign of relief on seeing that it wasn't. Perhaps like me he realized that it might just as well have been.

Behind him, Iuda came to the conclusion that Dmitry was losing the argument. He took a step towards Dmitry, but at the same time Dmitry took a step forward and entered my side of the room.

"We have to live, Dmitry," Pyetr called plaintively after him. "These few peasants were just so that we could survive until we left the city."

"And what about Vadim?" I called out to Pyetr.

"Vadim?" asked Dmitry.

"Over there," I said with a jerk of my head.

Pyetr and Iuda could find no more words to say as Dmitry inspected the remains of his commanding officer, comrade and friend. He put a hand to Vadim's face and let out a cry of deepest sorrow. Vadim's dead eyes stared back at him and offered no forgiveness.

Dmitry raised his sword and began to advance upon the two vampires who stood on the other side of the room from us. I restrained him before he could cross back into their half.

"You promised you'd control yourselves this time," he said, addressing Pyetr, whom he had known longest.

"I did," replied Pyetr ambiguously.

"It's too late to pretend to be surprised, Dmitry," said Iuda in a more determined tone. "You chose to sup with the Devil. You knew what we are—what we do."

I think his words were directed more at me than at Dmitry, and I agreed with them. If the reality of the deaths of innocent Russians and of Vadim had come as a surprise to Dmitry, then he had only been fooled by himself, not by the Oprichniki. It could never be said that Dmitry was one to see only the good in people, but in this case he had only seen the benefit to himself, and to his country, that could be gained from working with them.

However, if Iuda's words were intended to make me mistrust Dmitry, it was also clear that Dmitry would no longer be wise to trust the Oprichniki. They might have had better reasons to kill Vadim or to kill me, but if he stuck with them, Dmitry's time would eventually come.

"I'm sorry, Aleksei," muttered Dmitry. It was hopelessly inadequate, but it was all that could be said.

"I think you had better go," I said, addressing the two vampires.

"Go?" said Pyetr. "Why should we go? It's you that's trapped." This was ostensibly true. The two doors to the room were both in their half. While they could leave if they wanted, we would not be able to reach an exit without crossing the divide and risking attack from them.

"All we have to do is wait until it's dark again," continued Pyetr. Iuda, however, was glancing nervously around at the narrow window, at the ray of light and at the doors.

"I'm not sure," I said, "whether you creatures still believe that the sun revolves around the earth or that the earth revolves around itself. Either way, the sun travels from east to west once a day. And that means that that beam of light is going to travel from west to east—towards you. By noon, you'll only have one door to exit by. By midafternoon, you'll have none. You'll slowly be backed into the corner, until the sunlight hits the corner, and then you'll be gone." Unless, of course, it turned cloudy. I didn't know whether the indirect sunlight of a cloudy day would be enough to kill them. That's why I played my card then, hoping to force them to leave, rather than risking the scenario being played out.

"Or we could just pull down all the other floorboards from the window right now," suggested Dmitry. It was practical, but somewhat less elegant.

Either way, it was enough to persuade the Oprichniki. Pyetr was already out of the room. Iuda clicked his heels together and gave a mocking formal bow. "We shall meet again, Aleksei Ivanovich," he said, and then left.

Dmitry made to pursue. "We had better wait a little," I told him. "Give them time to get out." Dmitry nodded. "Let's get some more light in here," I suggested, going over to the window.

Before we could start work on any of the remaining boards, we both heard a whimpering noise emanating from underneath the oriental screen that I had knocked over. I drew my sword and used it to lift up the edge of the screen and flick it aside. Underneath was the crouched figure of the soldier-vampire, curled almost into a ball, his hands covering his head. He was shaking with fear. He had been there all the time, forgotten by us and, had he been capable of it, he had been in a position to reach out and kill us. Perhaps Iuda and Pyetr had been counting on that, or perhaps they, like us, had forgotten him.

I poked him with my sword and he looked up, his eyes showing that he was still inexperienced enough as a vampire to remember the sensation of terror.

"What's your name?" I asked him.

"Pavel," he stammered. In his eyes I saw a new emotion; hope—the vaguest conception of the possibility that this day might not be his last.

Iuda, it turned out then, was correct. I did have scruples which held me back from killing. If Pavel had resisted, or simply remained bravely silent, I might have had the stomach to kill him. But now, though I knew him to be a vampire, he had such shades of his recently lost humanity about him that I found myself incapable of any action against him.

The decision was taken from me.

With a whoosh of displaced air, my wooden dagger came down upon Pavel's curled back, driven by Dmitry, who clutched it with both hands. The dagger buried itself deep between the vampire's ribs. Pavel let out a gasp and knelt upright, his hands reaching behind him to try to pull out the weapon. Dmitry gave it another thrust and then twisted it. The wooden blade broke in two, leaving Dmitry with only the handle. A trickle of blood appeared at Pavel's lips and his eyes became glassy as he slumped forward.

I nudged the body with my foot. It still felt like flesh and blood. Unlike the others, there was no instant collapse to ashes and dust.

"He hadn't long been a vampire," said Dmitry, reading my thoughts. He evidently knew, as I had already deduced, that a vampire's body could only decay to the extent that it would have if he had never become one.

"What shall we do now?" I asked.

"Pyetr told me they would be leaving Moscow."

"Back the way they came?"

"No. Just like the French, they won't retreat by the same lines that they advanced along," explained Dmitry.

"So which way will they go?"

"Southwest. Pretty much the same way that Bonaparte is going—at least for a while. It will give them a food supply of French soldiers."

"Or Russian," I added. Dmitry did not reply. "Do you believe what Pyetr said about them leaving?" I asked.

"I think so. It's what I would do."

"So we follow them?"

"I suppose," said Dmitry, nodding thoughtfully, "or just let them go."

I went over to the corner of the room and bent down.

"What are you doing?" asked Dmitry.

"My icon," I said. I tied a knot in the broken chain and put it back over my head. It felt a little unusual, resting against my chest slightly higher than its accustomed position, but I would quickly get used to it.

I turned again to Pavel's body. Though slower than in the other vampires I had seen, his body's decomposition was still quicker than that of any human. As we had been speaking, he had decayed enough to be indistinguishable from one of the older corpses in the adjacent room, whose deaths must have occurred only a short time after his. Only the untidy placing of his body distinguished him from them.

We went down into the cellar, carrying Vadim Fyodorovich's body with us. The broken-down wall into the next cellar I now realized, and Dmitry confirmed, was part of the route that he and Pyetr had used to get to the building without venturing out into the daylight. It was then also the exit through which Pyetr and Iuda had left. I peered through and once again caught the polluted stench of the sewer below, a stench which I now realized consisted of not just a miasma of human waste, but also that of bodily human decay. I could just hear the sound of water flowing somewhere down there, but the darkness was total. It was the habitat of the Oprichniki and I chose not to follow them.

Fear begged me to just leave Vadim's body where it was and get out into the light as soon as I possibly could, but that would not have been decent. He needed to be buried and this cellar was as good a place as any. Even so, we worked quickly, and as we first dug and then filled in the grave, it was with a wary eye over our shoulders towards the dark breach in the wall, in case the vampires returned the way they had left.

Chapter XX

W E RETURNED TO THE INN. THE INNKEEPER WAS, IN keeping with the hospitability of his profession, overjoyed to see Dmitry. He showered him with questions as to where he had been and what he had been doing—questions which I too hoped soon to have answered. Dmitry's responses were noncommittal.

"Oh, Captain Danilov," called the innkeeper after me as I made my way up to my rooms.

"Yes?" I replied.

"Your young lady was round last night. I had to tell her you weren't here."

"What time?"

"Gone midnight, sir."

"Did she say anything?"

"Nothing, sir. She just went home again."

"Thank you."

I was abominably tired and my first thought was that a few hours' delay in seeing her would not be too significant. I continued up to my room and lay on my bed. My head had scarcely hit the pillow when I realized what Domnikiia must be thinking. She knew what creatures I was up against and that I was out looking for them. Coming here to find I wasn't back at that late hour, she would have concluded either that I had found them or that they had found me. (I still wasn't too sure myself exactly which had been the case.) The longer I delayed seeing her, the more worried she would be that they had been the victors. I hauled myself off the bed and set out to find her.

It was still early, and the brothel was not yet open for business. I hammered on the door and it was answered by Pyetr Pyetrovich.

TWELVE

"We're closed," he told me.

"I've come to see Dominique," I said, pushing my way in.

"Oh, it's you," he said. "This is a place of business, you know. You can't just call when you please. Not without paying."

I walked past him, pulling my coat to one side to make sure he got a clear view of the sword I was wearing, and headed up the stairs.

"If you like Dominique so much, we could come to some more permanent arrangement," he called after me.

Domnikiia was still in bed, but awake. She sat up as I entered. I sat on the bed beside her. She looked intently at my face, but said nothing, her eyes searching my expression for some clue as to what had been happening.

"We found Vadim," I told her.

"Really?" She sounded pleased. For a moment I didn't realize how ambiguous I had been.

"No, it's not like that. He's dead." I rested my head on her shoulder and tears ran down my cheek, though I just about managed to keep my voice steady. "Dead since just after I last saw him."

She stroked my hair and murmured soothing words. Though it had not been my intention when I entered the room, I pushed her down on to the bed and made very selfish love to her. There was little pleasure in it for me, and less for her, but it fulfilled in me merely the need to obliterate for a moment every higher thought and every human emotion, to descend to the level of an animal where nothing but the moment matters. Considerations of the future, of my responsibilities, of those around me, all could be forgotten just briefly—all too briefly. It was the way a soldier screws a woman he has never met before and knows he will never see again. He might pay for it—he might not have to. Although I had paid Domnikiia many times before, I had never had such disregard for the person beneath me. It was not about her. It was about allowing me to forget her along with everything else.

For her part, I can only suppose she was used to such things, though, I hoped, not from me. I think she was happy enough to perform it as a service for me, as a wife might prepare her husband's dinner or wash his clothes. For me, it had nothing to do with her, and any woman in the building could have taken her place. But she would have seen that as a betrayal, much the same as if a husband got another woman to make his dinner or wash his clothes—a betrayal not of the heart, but of the partnership.

"What's to become of us, Lyosha?" she asked a little while afterwards.

It was the question every faithless husband must dread.

"I've no idea."

"Neither have I," she said. "That's the problem."

"Is it a problem?"

"Not at the moment."

"There's still a war. I could be dead tomorrow." I decided to give myself a little leeway. "Or the day after that."

"I know. That's why it's not a problem, but one day it will be."

"Only if we both survive," I said with a mirthless laugh.

"Or if the war never ends."

"So you want an unending war, with us both under the threat of death, but never actually dying, just so we can stay together without our consciences bothering us?" I asked lightly, though the very mention of conscience almost made me shiver at the memory of a different, recent conversation.

"That would just about do it," she said with a grin.

"I'll have a word with the crowned heads of Europe, then. See if they'll help us out."

"They seem to be doing pretty well already."

It was a silly conversation, as trivial as many we had had before, allowing us daily to forget reality, but today it could do little to lift our mood.

I sat up on the side of the bed and glanced towards the table. On it was a letter. I could not see the content, but the single word of the signature screamed out at me: Iuda.

"What's this?" I asked, picking up the letter.

"Ah, yes," said Domnikiia. "I was going to tell you about that. Very mysterious—especially from a man you told me was dead."

"You should have mentioned it," I snapped.

"I was going to," she insisted, upset by my tone, "if you'd given me the chance. Polya—one of the girls—found it when she opened up this morning.

TWELVE

It was slipped under the door, addressed to me. Read it. It's more for you than for me anyway."

I opened the letter and read it silently.

Mademoiselle Dominique,

As I am sure you will have heard from our mutual friend Aleksei Ivanovich, our mission in your country has not gone according to the plans that were originally conceived. It is to my utmost regret that this has led to deep misunderstandings arising between myself and Aleksei Ivanovich, for which I must immediately acknowledge my share of blame. Sadly, affairs have come to such a state between us that it is now impossible for us even to communicate the simplest of requests to one another and, as I'm sure you will readily comprehend, this is no basis from which we can easily find any remedy to the situation.

I therefore entreat you, Mademoiselle Dominique, as Aleksei Ivanovich's close friend (and, I dare to flatter myself, as mine) to act as an intermediary, that you might help to heal this melancholy rift between two formerly hearty and successful comrades. If you would desire to help in this matter, then my simple request is that you convey to Aleksei Ivanovich my petition to meet with him at seven in the evening on the twenty-eighth day of October at the crossroads to the south of the village of Kurilovo. He will know this location better, perhaps, as Г4, although I shall not bore you with details of why it is so designated.

Please express to Aleksei Ivanovich the utter sincerity of my wish to meet with him and my fondest hope that with a few minutes of conversation, we can resolve any confusion that may have led to the distressing rift that now exists between us. If Aleksei Ivanovich cannot or chooses not to attend, then please assure him of my continued devotion to both him and his country, and please also, Mademoiselle Dominique, appreciate the heartfelt affection that I hold for you personally.

Your devoted friend,
Iuda.

"He does gush," I said scornfully.
"I think it's nice that he makes the effort."

"You are joking, aren't you?"

She put her chin on my shoulder and I felt her arms around my waist. "Yes, Aleksei Ivanovich, I am joking."

"I mean you only met him once, and that was for five minutes."

"Absolutely," she said in heartfelt agreement. "And of course on top of that, he *is* a vampire."

"Are you teasing me, Mademoiselle Dominique?"

"Well, you sound like a jealous husband going through my correspondence."

"When did you get this?" I asked.

"I said, this morning, when Polya got up."

"When was that?"

"About ten o'clock. We work late here."

"And when did you close up last night?"

"Around two."

"So this could have arrived any time between two and ten?"

"Yes," she replied, with emphasized patience. "Does it matter?"

It mattered a lot. If Iuda had delivered it before our meeting the previous night, then that presented a number of possibilities. Our encounter that night might not have been as premeditated as it had seemed, at least not on Iuda's part, or it might have been that he had all along expected me to escape. A third possibility was that the letter was not intended for me at all, but was solely for the benefit of Domnikiia, to whom, after all, it had been addressed. Could this be to persuade her to attend the meeting in my place? It seemed unlikely. Could it be to give Iuda a veneer of innocence in Domnikiia's eyes once my death was discovered? That was more believable.

On the other hand, if the letter had been delivered this morning, after I had seen him, then it would make more sense, but since Iuda would have been unable to travel in daylight, he must have had human assistance in delivering it. Was this some errand boy he had simply hired for a few copecks, or did he have human servants of a more devoted nature? The obvious suspect would have been Dmitry, but Dmitry had been with me all the time.

"Are you going to go to the meeting?" she asked.

"I think so."

TWELVE

"Won't it be dangerous?"

"I'll have Dmitry with me."

"You mean Dmitry's in Moscow? I thought he went back to the army."

"No, he had other things to do."

"Do you trust him?"

"I do now."

"You mean you didn't before?" she asked.

"I did before, but I was wrong."

"And now you're right?"

"Dmitry's run out of options."

She paused for a moment before asking, "How far is Kurilovo?"

"Not far," I replied. "We'll set off the day after tomorrow. I'd better go."

We made our goodbyes and I left, taking Iuda's letter with me. I went back to the inn and slept for most of the afternoon. Early in the evening, there was a knock at my door. It was Dmitry. I showed him the letter.

"Well, you're not going, are you?" he asked dismissively.

"Yes, I think we are."

"We?"

"Yes, Dmitry, we."

"But it's so obviously a trick," he insisted.

"Do you know the crossroads he mentions?"

"No, I don't think I do."

"It's a very good place to meet someone you don't trust. There's a clear view all around. We'll easily be able to see if he's brought anyone with him."

"Do you think he knows that?"

"Possibly," I replied. "They may have come that way as they made the last stretch of their journey here from Tula. I think he's chosen the place so that we'll both feel safe."

"You think he's afraid of you?" asked Dmitry, betraying by the edge in his voice the fear he felt for the Oprichniki—a fear which had been in him all the time, but which only gained substance when he discovered they had become his enemies.

"I hope he is," I replied.

"I still don't think it's a good idea. They've left Moscow and soon they'll have left the country. Enough of them have died so that they won't come back. Let someone else deal with them. Let the French deal with them."

"You think they won't come back?"

"Why should they?"

"Revenge. Look what they did to Maks. He'd killed three of them. I've killed four—even you've killed one."

"They're practical—not spiteful."

"Most of them maybe, but why would Iuda try to entice us into this meeting if his only plan was to get away? If we don't go, then he'll just have to come back here. He's already suggesting that Domnikiia might be at risk by sending the letter to her."

"I suppose," replied Dmitry contemplatively.

"Have you tried to track down Boris and Natalia at all?" I asked, ostensibly changing the subject.

"I went back to where they were staying," said Dmitry, "but the French had torn it all down."

"I found out that their shop burnt down on the first day of the fires."

"I know," he said. "Boris told me."

"But I met someone who has seen them since Bonaparte's departure."

"Really? Where?"

"Just around."

"In that house this morning, I thought that one of the bodies might be . . ." Dmitry could not bring himself to say it.

"I know. I thought so too for a moment."

"So when shall we set out for Kurilovo?" asked Dmitry, after a moment's pause.

"We'll leave the day after tomorrow, on the twenty-sixth. That will give us two days to get there."

Domnikiia did manage to join me that night. On my instructions, her arrival was soon followed by that of the innkeeper, who brought us some supper and a bottle of wine. We sat at the small table in my room and talked of things of little consequence. Eventually, there was no option but to raise the subject of my journey to Kurilovo.

"So what time will you and Dmitry be setting off?" she asked.

"First light. We should be there by Sunday and then we'll have a whole day to check things out before the meeting on Monday."

"Do you mind if I don't come over tomorrow night then?"

"Why? Don't you like the idea of being woken up so early?" I joked.

"I don't like the idea of waking up to see you go—or to find you gone."

"OK," I said, though the prospect struck me more harshly than I would have imagined.

"It's selfish of me, I know."

"It's all right. If you were here, I probably wouldn't be able to leave."

"You can have me all day tomorrow, though. I'm not going to work."

"Can you? Just like that?"

"I can do what I like. Pyetr Pyetrovich is terrified of you."

"Really?" I was surprised. "I've barely ever spoken to him."

"Yes, but I've said a few things, about what a great soldier you are and so forth—all exaggeration, of course."

"Thank you."

"Anyway, he needs me on his side. I'm his most popular girl."

I felt a knot in my stomach as I was presented with a reality of which I was already fully aware.

"Is that meant to make me feel good?" I asked, trying to keep it lighter than I felt.

"Don't you deserve the best?" she smiled.

I stood up and started to clear the things from the table. Then I noticed her face drain of its colour. I followed her gaze to the replacement wooden sword that I'd been working on, lying half-finished on the desk in the corner of the room.

"What happened to the other one?" she asked.

"Dmitry broke it," I said.

She sensed my desire not to give her any more detail, and did not ask. "They must break very easily," she said simply.

"It's never a problem to make a new one," I told her.

*   *   *

We spent the following day wandering around the city. It was below freezing and a layer of snow coated the ground—nothing compared with what was to come. We both wore heavy coats to keep warm.

"I hate to see Moscow like this," said Domnikiia after we had been walking for a little while. "So devastated—so empty."

She didn't see it as I did. Although I saw the burnt-out houses and the empty streets, what stood out for me above that was the appearance of growth. Like the first green shoots of spring, it was not obvious, but for those who had eyes to see it, it was ubiquitous and unstoppable. At every turn, someone was repairing some damage to their home or reopening a shop. Even the winter cold could not spoil my optimism. Recovery would take time, but it would inevitably come.

We had come to a churchyard in Kitay Gorod that I knew well.

"This is where we stayed after the fire," I said to Domnikiia, "with Boris Mihailovich and his daughter."

"That reminds me. One of the girls at work knows her."

"Knows Natalia?"

"Yes, I was going to tell you."

"Tell me now. Are they all right?"

"Yes, yes. She saw her a few days ago."

"Have they found somewhere to live?"

"They're sharing with another shoemaker on Ordynsky Lane, in Zamoskvorechye. Shall we go and see them?"

"No," I replied. "Not today."

"You'll tell Dmitry about them, though?"

"Yes, yes." But I wouldn't tell him straight away.

We said goodbye outside her door in Degtyarny Lane. The square was covered in snow and I couldn't help but be reminded of the scene the first time I had laid eyes on her, just under a year ago. I scooped up a handful of snow and made a snowball, which I hurled across the square at no particular target. She smiled, remembering, and held my hands.

TWELVE

"My saviour," she said, but then she became more serious. "How long will you be gone?"

"Two days out there—two days back."

"You will come back then?"

"Of course I will," I smiled.

"Straight back?"

"I can't promise that. It depends what happens. But I will be back."

"And then we can be together forever?" She smiled wistfully as she spoke, knowing that the dream was unrealizable. My only answer was to kiss her. As I walked away, I looked over my shoulder and saw her watching me all the way to the end of the street.

The following day, at dawn, Dmitry and I mounted our horses and rode south, out of the city. It was not difficult to be reminded of another departure from Moscow, months before, when four of us had set off with our hearts full of optimism that the then twelve Oprichniki with whom we were working would help us to rid Russia of the French invaders.

Now there were only two of us and there were five of them—their losses, as a proportion, marginally greater than ours. If we continued at the same rate, then we would be the victors, but only just—and at what cost to ourselves?

As we rode, we talked.

"So tell me, Dmitry," I asked him, "what were you doing after you left Yuryev-Polsky?" It was asked innocently enough, but he knew as well as I that it was a debriefing, if not an interrogation.

"Well, obviously I didn't go to join back up with the army. I skirted round Moscow to the south and then went in to find Pyetr."

"They're not easy to find if they don't want to be."

"Pyetr and I had made some other arrangements. The meetings with you were more for show as far as they were concerned."

"I see." I had suspected as much. "But why should they be concerned about us at all?" I asked. It had been puzzling me for some time. Their whole motivation for travelling to Moscow still evaded me.

"You may not accept it, but they genuinely believe in the cause. Zmyeevich does, anyway, and they're all afraid of him," explained Dmitry. His mood swung, almost sentence by sentence, between self-pity and self-justification.

"They seem to believe more in satisfying their own hunger than in any cause," I said.

"They're like any soldiers. Like you and me. They like to fight, but they like the idea that they have a just cause to fight for." I snorted in disagreement. "Oh, come on, Aleksei," continued Dmitry. "Would you be fighting this war if it wasn't for something you believed in? They're the same."

"They've made it very clear that they are not the same as you and me. For them, killing comes above all things. You can't persuade me that they're just a gang of latter-day Don Quixotes looking for a noble cause for which they can employ their knightly skills. Have you forgotten what we saw in that room?"

"No, I haven't," said Dmitry, sombrely. "There are two factions amongst them—Pyetr versus Iuda. The ones I knew before—Ioann, Andrei and Varfolomei—all stuck with Pyetr. Now that there's only Pyetr left, I think he's pretty much fallen in with Iuda."

"As easily as that?" I asked.

"None of them has the strongest of personalities, as I'm sure you've noticed. I think the self-selecting nature of vampires tends to prevent that. Pyetr was under Zmyeevich's thumb for a while, now he's under Iuda's. I don't suppose seeing his last ally so ably decapitated by you in front of him would have done much for his independence of spirit."

"And so it was only Iuda who made them turn on innocent Muscovites?"

"I like to think that." But he had reached the limits of his own credulity. "I *would* like to think that," he added, "but I don't." It marked the end of a prolonged transformation in his view of the Oprichniki that had begun back at the house in Moscow where he had first seen the mutilated corpses of his fellow countrymen. Perhaps—I hoped, though I had seen no sign of it—it had started even earlier.

"So, what happened when you met Pyetr?" I asked.

"They had already pretty much worked out that it was you who killed Matfei and Varfolomei. Pyetr explained to me what happened in the fire—when you locked me in."

TWELVE

"I didn't know you were there," I said, more apologetically than was really necessary.

"No, I know that—despite the way that Iuda tried to tell it."

"So Iuda saw the whole thing?"

"Apparently."

"Apparently?"

"He had already gone by the time I got there. His coffin was empty. He must have hung around to watch."

That was not the story that Iuda had given me, in the house in Moscow as I stood beside Vadim's rotting corpse. It was interesting that Iuda should choose to lie on so minor a point. Perhaps it was to make me doubt Dmitry. On the other hand, perhaps it was Dmitry who was lying. If I thought that, then clearly Iuda's plan was working.

"Why didn't he help?" I asked.

"It was Ioann. Iuda's position was better without him."

"So what else did Pyetr say?"

"He said he thought that they could probably let you get away with murdering two of them. It wasn't like with Maks, he said. Maks killing them was treason. With you, it was just instinct." Or perhaps Maks' instincts were better tuned than mine.

"And you believed him?"

"It was what I wanted to hear," Dmitry explained with uncharacteristic self-awareness. "*I'd* have killed Maks, but I wouldn't have killed you."

"How comforting."

"Pyetr said they'd get you to a meeting somehow where we could talk it out. He came and found me that night—told me that they'd managed to persuade you to talk to them. So I went with him."

"But he must have known," I said, thinking aloud, "or at least worried, that seeing those Russian bodies—and seeing Vadim, for heaven's sake—you wouldn't stay on their side for long."

"The location was all worked out by Iuda. He must have wanted me to see that."

"To test you?" I wondered.

"Maybe. Or maybe his plan was exactly how it all turned out. He got rid of Andrei, after all."

It was the same thought that had occurred to me earlier, when I first read Iuda's letter. Beyond that, though, Dmitry was pretty much allowing himself to be duped. There may have been disagreements within the Oprichniki, but I could not give credence to the idea of there being noble vampires and ignoble vampires. Pyetr and Andrei had survived for over two weeks in Moscow after the French had left. What, I wondered, were they supposed to have been eating in that time? Borshch?

More worrying to me than any of the details of what had taken place, was the new light in which I had to view Dmitry's character. That he could be ruthless and that he judged himself superior enough to make his own decisions on moral issues—such as whether it was conscionable to work alongside the Oprichniki in order to get rid of the French—I had never doubted. But that he could be so blinded by his own desire for success as to not see the truly malevolent nature of the Oprichniki and be so gullible as to believe what they had told him—that was the surprise. On the surface, he portrayed himself as the most hardened cynic of us all, but every cynic must, as well as doubting the motivations of others, always doubt their own.

By the afternoon of our first day of travel, we had come to a village that I had known we would pass through, and I suspected that Iuda must have known it too when he chose the rendezvous. From Dmitry, however, I saw no sign of anticipation.

I dismounted and tied up my horse outside the familiar woodsman's hut, from which leaked a stench that I could not distinguish as being real or part of my guilt-ridden imagination.

"What town is this?" asked Dmitry, still utterly ignorant of where we were.

"Desna," I said, conveying by both tone and look the significance of what I was saying.

He pulled a face to indicate that the name meant nothing to him, but he saw by my expression that he should think more deeply. Then it dawned on him.

TWELVE

"Oh, I see," he said, respectfully.

We went into the hut. Little had changed since I had last been there, two months before. The French had been this way on their retreat, but the hut had nothing inside that would be of use to them. The stove still stood against the far wall. The chair that had been in the middle remained as well, knocked over on one side.

Maks' body was slumped in a corner of the room, leaning against the wall as if he sat, wearily, his head tilted back, watching Dmitry and me as we looked around. Whether it had been placed there or fallen like that by chance I could not tell. His legs were bent almost up to his chest and one arm rested upon his knee; the other hung loosely by his side. Thankfully, his body was too far decayed to leave any clear residue of the wounds that had been inflicted at his death, although I was now familiar enough with how the Oprichniki operated to be able to make a pretty good guess. The cloth of his breeches hung close to his shin to give a hollow impression of what remained of the withered flesh beneath. Only his hands and his head could be seen outside his clothes. His hands were shrivelled and old. His face was decayed beyond recognition. Unlike Vadim, Maks had had no beard to remain after the rest of him had rotted away. Only his spectacles gave any evidence that confirmed for me what I knew to be true—that this was Maksim Sergeivich. They hung off his nose and one ear—the other having long since lost the integrity to support them—the metal rim sinking into the yielding, dead flesh of his cheek.

We stood in silence for a few moments. More than once I sensed that Dmitry was about to speak, but each time he thought better of it. He was wise to do so.

"We should bury him," I said at length.

"Yes," said Dmitry in a way that expressed strong agreement, where none was needed. "I'll see if I can find some tools." He walked away, leaving me a few more precious seconds with my abandoned friend. Moments later he gave out a hushed shout.

"Aleksei! Look at this." He was kneeling down looking at the wall just by the doorway, an area that would be covered when the door was open. I knelt beside him to see what he was looking at. It was textbook positioning for a message. A shaky hand had scratched the following into the wood:

8-27-20-M-Π

Maks had been here and left this mark on the evening of the twenty-seventh of August. I had known as much—that had been only the day before I had met him here. The "Π" was, however, the more interesting part of the message. "Π" meant that, somewhere nearby, Maksim had hidden a letter.

Chapter XXI

IT DIDN'T TAKE US LONG TO FIND THE LETTER. THERE WERE not many places where it could be hidden in such a rudimentary structure. Maks had slipped it between one of the beams supporting the roof and the wooden roof itself. One had to be looking for it to find it.

It was addressed to me—dated the twenty-seventh, the same as his scratched message. There were about half a dozen sheets, covered on both sides with Maksim's small, precise handwriting. I read it aloud.

"My dear Aleksei,

"If you are reading this letter, then I must apologize for not having waited longer for you to arrive. As you will understand once you have read this, I am very much in fear for my life and perhaps for even more. In communicating the circumstances specifically to you, Aleksei, and (I hope soon) in committing myself to your custody I intend at least to ensure that I die with some vestige of my reputation intact and also to die by a method whereby my soul might be saved. I can see your expression of surprise to learn that either of these should be of concern to me, but let me assure you that the former always has been. The future of my soul is a question that I have only recently begun to realize is worth asking.

"I shall remain here for four days. I have told Dominique where I am and she will, I hope, tell you and only you. If you have not arrived within that time, then I shall be forced to move on. The possibility that either Dmitry or the remaining Oprichniki should find me here is too dreadful to risk. I shall head south to Tula and on then to my mother's. You know where she lives. I shall not write here where that is in the hope that my omission may protect me from any others who might read this. Once I have seen her and, with luck, my sisters, then I shall attempt to leave the country forever. I shall not be happy to make my home in France. It has become less and less the country I thought it to be.

TWELVE

"You are, I know, well aware of my interest in the republics of both the United States and France. We have happily discussed the matter often and I know that, at least on general principles, your views and mine have often coincided. Where I am certain that you will find no sympathy with me is that as a result of these principles I decided some years ago to make an active effort to support republican France. It was when I was captured at Austerlitz that I first began to work for France. I see the cynical curl of your lip, knowing that you would tell me that at that time the republic was no longer a republic since by then it had an emperor. Though Napoleon had indeed become emperor, though Austerlitz was fought on the anniversary of his coronation, I still believed that he and those around him did what they did for the sake of enlightened, republican ideals. Even today I still believe it.

"After my capture I was persuaded—willingly persuaded—by, in partic-ular, a French colonel (whose name is best kept secret), who convinced me that by helping them, I could ultimately be helping Russia itself to become a republic as great and as powerful as France or America ever could be. I was returned to Russia as though I were a freed prisoner of war. In reality it was an act not of liberation, but of infiltration.

"So you see, Aleksei, for almost the whole time that I have known you, I have been a French spy, but believe me, that is the only matter on which I have deceived you. You may regard that as small consolation, if consolation at all, but in everything I have ever said to you, in every matter of opinion, of strategy and of friendship there has been no veil of pretence between us, nor between me and Vadim or Dmitry. The Maksim you have known has been the true Maksim in all aspects except this one tiny issue of allegiance. Men of different political colours and even of different nationalities do not have to be at war with each other, and even when they are they become ene-mies not out of choice but out of circumstance. Their friendship can be rekin-dled once the smoke of battle has cleared. If I had been born French then, although we might not have become the friends we once were—that I hope we still are—I would at least have retained your respect. That is not to say that I am blaming my treason on an accident of birth. I would not choose to have been born French rather than Russian. My affiliation has always been to ideas rather than to states. My hope was to take an idea born in France and see it flourish in Russia.

"Whether I have in practice been of very much use to France, I have to doubt. The only work of significance that I have undertaken has been alongside you, Vadim and Dmitry. I count my allegiance to you three higher than any and so I could never have handed over any information that would have directly put you in jeopardy. As to the more general picture of the state of our armies which I have conveyed, I doubt whether any of it has been of much assistance.

"I write this not in any attempt to exonerate myself or to make some plea for clemency that may help me avoid my execution as a traitor. I will attempt to avoid death by flight, but not by denial of what I truly believe. I write it simply in the hope that, though you may rightly condemn me in your own heart to death, you will at least regret that it had to be so.

"However, I would have no scruple that urged me to tell you the truth about myself had it not been for the fact that you most certainly already know the entire truth. It is of the circumstances of how this truth came to be revealed that I must give you every detail I can recall, in the hope that what I tell you may help in some way to defeat these despicable creatures whose war on humanity casts into unmistakable relief the petty squabbles of petty nations."

"So he did know about them," I said, half to myself, half to Dmitry, though I had been convinced of it almost from the start.

Dmitry did not respond. He sat with his back to the wall, almost mirroring the posture of Maks' lingering remains. The two sat at opposite corners of the same wall, like naughty schoolboys who have been told to sit apart. Neither, for very different reasons, could raise his eyes to look at me as I continued to read.

"When we returned to Moscow from Smolensk, I had had no opportunity for several months to make any report back to my superiors in the French camp. (By the by, when you see Vadim, tell him that in the French army I also carry the title of major, so he can no longer pull rank on me. To be honest, I think they bump up the ranks of agents just to flatter them. I hope that, despite what I have done to him, Vadim will be able to smile at this. I know I have no right to be flippant, but I cannot tell you how much I long for just five more minutes of the times when we used to sit beside the Moskva and drink vodka and tease one another—but mostly tease Vadim.)

"Our return out west with the Oprichniki gave me a fine opportunity to get back behind French lines and report what I knew. I looked for every chance to separate myself from Andrei, Simon and Iakov Alfeyinich, but it transpired that they were even more keen to be rid of me than I was of them. The very same night that we set out from Gzatsk—the last time, in fact, that I saw you—first one, then two, then all three of them had made some excuse to separate from the rest of the party and scout around on their own.

"I took full advantage of the solitude and headed straight off for the French encampments to the west of the town. I told them all I knew—again, I must assure you, nothing of our personal work, nor even of the Oprichniki, although on that latter point I wish I had—and after a couple of hours of debriefing I was treated to the wine, food and good company that is bestowed on any patriot who has been so long away from his confederates. It meant little to me. I seek little more from food than nourishment and the company was not as good as I have known.

"It was after sunset on the evening of the next day, as I was preparing to leave, that suddenly the camp that I was in came under a ferocious attack. Screams came from all around us in the darkness. I looked out of the tent, in which I had been talking with three other officers, to see two figures that I recognized as Andrei and Iakov Alfeyinich creeping towards the sentry who stood guard outside. I could only see the sentry's back. He could see the two Oprichniki that approached him and his head turned from one to the other in disbelief. Eventually, he fired his musket at Andrei and without doubt the musket ball passed through his chest, but hindered him no more than would a brief gust of wind. Iakov Alfeyinich dived for the soldier's legs. The soldier responded by stabbing his bayonet hard down into Iakov Alfeyinich's back. It was as ineffective as the musket ball had been.

"Iakov Alfeyinich's attack brought the sentry to the ground and in the same instant that he fell, Andrei launched himself upon his throat. What I saw then is beyond any comprehension of a civilized man. My upbringing never allowed any of the myth and folklore that is the staple for so many of my contemporaries. From what little I heard in the schoolyard of vampires and werewolves and other such abominations, I was glad to have been spared such nonsense. Even those who did hear those stories as children do not grow up to believe them. But any man must believe the evidence of his own eyes.

"Andrei sunk his teeth deep into the man's throat and tore off a sliver of flesh. The soldier was still alive and struggling for freedom beneath Andrei's firm grasp as Iakov Alfeyinich fell upon him and took a similar bite from the other side of his neck. Then the two lay there beside him, their mouths to his neck, lapping away at the blood that seeped out of him. It was only when the sentry had ceased to breathe that the two Oprichniki raised their heads from his throat and exchanged between themselves a glance of pride and self-satisfaction.

"Before they could rise, three more soldiers were upon them. Again, the damage inflicted by shot and by blade had little impact. They killed by the same method—with their teeth—but now they did not linger to drink the blood of their victims. Time had become too pressing for them to enjoy the aftermath of the kill.

"I turned back to speak to the other officers in the tent with me and was horrified by what I saw. Two of them lay dead upon the floor. The third remained upright, showing on his contorted face a look of agony that was matched only by the terror revealed in his staring eyes. Over his shoulder I saw the face of Simon, looking down to where his teeth were sunk into the man's neck. Behind his teeth, Simon's tongue flicked back and forth between the man's sinews, to taste every drop of blood he could find, much as a dog's tongue probes every crevice of his bone in search of the last tasty morsel of marrow.

"Behind them, I saw the rip in the side of the tent through which Simon had entered. Before Simon could look up and see that I had observed him, I felt a heavy blow to my head from behind and I collapsed into unconsciousness.

"When I came to, it was still dark. I saw Andrei's face looming close to mine, and I feared that it was now time for me too to become a meal for these creatures. Instead, Andrei displayed concern. I feigned amnesia until I had heard enough from them to understand what they thought had happened. It turned out that they were under the impression that I had been captured by the French. They had attacked the camp by chance, but when they recognized me, they transformed their attack into a rescue mission. I played along with them, and also managed to convince them that I remembered nothing of my liberation—that the blow to my head had wiped away all images of what I had seen of their methods of killing. Their concern was so much concentrated on finding out whether I knew their true nature that they showed no inquisitiveness whatsoever into my true nature. The fact that I had been captured by the French was universally accepted and the possibility that I had voluntarily walked into the French camp was never even mooted.

"They suggested that I should rest and recover from the head wound that—it turned out—Andrei had inflicted upon me, while they would continue to harry the French as best they could. The plan was that we meet again in Goryachkino in four days. I agreed, happy that this would give me plenty of time to engineer their downfall.

"Once it was daylight, I returned to the camp where the previous night's events had taken place. Not a soul remained alive. The Oprichniki had made some effort to cover their tracks. Many of the corpses had bullet wounds or bayonet wounds which, it was clear to my eye, had been inflicted after death. A number of fires had been started, but these too only superficially hid the stomach-churning throat wounds which I found on every carcass.

"The Oprichniki had not killed the horses at the camp, but had released them from their pens so as to add to the general impression of chaos. I got hold of one, and so my journey to Goryachkino was rapid. For a few days I attended the meeting place—the farm building—that we had arranged there, but neither you, nor Vadim, nor Dmitry, nor any of the Oprichniki showed up. By the twenty-fourth of August—the night when I had arranged to meet my three Oprichniki—the French were almost upon the village and were preparing for the great battle at Borodino. I left a brief message for you, simply saying that I had been there, and then went back out to the French lines to prepare the trap that I had planned for the Oprichniki.

"I told the guards at the camp that I would be sending three enemy spies to them that night. I described what they would look like, what direction they would come from and even the incorrect password which they would use when challenged by a sentry. I instructed the guards simply to capture them, bind them hand and foot and then hold them until my return. I told them to make sure that the captives were not held in a tent, but outside next to the fire. You may be surprised, Aleksei, at how easy it was for me to issue orders, but once my *bona fides* had been proved, the men in the camp were all too eager to help capture the Russian infiltrators.

"I went back to Goryachkino and waited. Soon after dusk, Andrei, Iakov Alfeyinich and Simon arrived. With them, they had brought Faddei, whom they had met somewhere along the way. My enthusiasm at seeing the opportunity to destroy four of these creatures, rather than the three that I had originally planned, was, I suppose, my undoing. I told them that I had found an isolated French camp that was perfect for them to attack. I told them the weakest points in the perimeter and even what the day's password was (which, incidentally, I said you had supplied for me, Aleksei).

"Faddei was not keen to join the raiding party. He felt he should get back to Vadim and the other Oprichniki under his command. I persuaded him that the French camp was a sitting duck, and that he would be a fool not to go. The description I gave of all those young, innocent, healthy soldiers must, I think, have whetted his appetite. They departed and I lay back and waited until dawn.

"Soon after the sun rose, I returned to the French camp into which I had sent the four Oprichniki. My instructions that they should be tied up and left in the open air had been a test of them and a test of my own credulity— something akin to the trials of witches in the Middle Ages. Despite my blinkered education, I had gathered some slight knowledge of the legends of the *voordalaki*. It seemed preposterous to me that mere sunlight could have such a devastating effect on their physical being, but no more preposterous than what I had already discovered to be irrefutably true. If the legends proved correct, then I would enter the camp to find four dead vampires, otherwise I would find four live ones, tied up and ready for death by firing squad. Either way, the twelve Oprichniki would be reduced to eight. A third of the battle would be won.

"Already, before my arrival, there was much commotion in the camp. A lieutenant, who recognized me from my visit the night before, dashed over to me and took me to the remains of the Oprichniki—three scorched patches of grass. They had been sitting, I was told, on wooden stools, of which only a few charred lumps remained. Some scraps of shoe leather and fragments of material were all else that was left to see. I asked what had happened to the fourth. He had escaped, I was told. They had been expecting only three and so the fourth had been able to get away almost before anyone saw him. As someone who has been lying throughout my adult life, Aleksei, I have long become used to disguising the fear of discovery, but there was little I could do to suppress the fear I felt then that one of the Oprichniki was out there, somewhere, aware of the trap into which I had sent them. I managed outwardly to retain my composure, but inside me every voice shouted that I should flee. I have been fleeing almost ever since.

"The lieutenant told me that they had followed my orders. They had done better than tie the three spies up, they had put them in irons, from which there would be no escape. As dawn had approached, the three had become more and more agitated, had pleaded to be released and had even tried to run—to any extent that they could—for freedom. At around dawn there had been three terrific explosions, so close together that they sounded as one. Two of the sentries guarding the prisoners had been slightly burnt, and all that remained of the three was the ash that I now saw.

"All the soldiers who had witnessed the events were keen to discover what had caused the explosions. A Russian in the same circumstances might, I suspect, have made some connection between the violent and unusual deaths of these men and their first contact with the sun's rays. The French are, however, not as superstitious as we foolish Russians. The most popular theory was that the men had come into the camp with gunpowder hidden in their clothes, hoping to get close to Napoleon himself and ignite the powder, but it had accidentally gone off too early. Some doubted that this could be so, that no Christian—not even a Russian—could commit the sin of suicide, however much he believed in his cause. I glibly assured them that, while the Catholic Church was strong on the point, the Orthodox had no such qualms about sending young men to their deaths. And so this was the version of events that became accepted.

"I departed as quickly as possible and set out eastwards, back to Moscow. I was in unprecedented fear for my life and so I stayed away from the main roads; thus my progress was slower than it would have been if I had taken the direct route. That night I made camp in a clearing in the woods. I had slept for a few hours when I was awakened by the sound of voices. I opened my eyes to see in front of me one Oprichnik and one man—Andrei and Dmitry.

"It was Andrei, clearly, who had escaped the raid on the French. He had obviously worked out that I had betrayed them. I could make no attempt to deny it. Instead, I told Dmitry what I had seen, what the Oprichniki had done, that they were vampires, but his only reaction was that he was well aware of it. I asked him how he could live with that knowledge, and he said that he would use any means he could find to defeat the French. Andrei was after my blood, but Dmitry—to his credit—held him back. He asked me to swear that I would take no more action against the Oprichniki. He seemed to think that now I understood what they were, I would let them get on with their work in the way that they did it best. I refused to go along with him.

"I believe at that stage, Dmitry only thought I had betrayed the Oprichniki because they were vampires; he had not perceived that I was working for the French. Perhaps, even if Andrei had told him, he hadn't believed it. But it was sometime during our conversation there that the realization came to him that I could not have set up the trap without being able to walk freely across the French lines. It was pointless for me to deny it. He took it like a physical wound—a shock to him far greater than had been the shock to me that the Oprichniki were vampires. He muttered that he did not relish the prospect of telling you and Vadim, and then he left me with Andrei.

"I tried to talk with Andrei, but he was as uncommunicative as the rest of the Oprichniki. His only intent was my death. Both he and Dmitry had an enormous faith in his abilities, since they had made no effort even to disarm me of my sword. When attacking by stealth, the Oprichniki were successful assailants, but Andrei's chances were less good here in an evenly matched contest. I drew my sword and he showed no fear of it. It did not seem right to use it on an unarmed man, so I told him to keep back, but he kept advancing. When he was just over the sword's length away from me he leapt towards me. I had no option but to bring the blade between us, and I felt the pressure on my hand as my sword met and overcame the resistance of his body. His face was up close to mine and I could smell his foul breath, but although the wound from my blade did not seem to hurt him, the physical impediment of the guard of my sword itself prevented him from getting close to me. After persisting for a little while, he stepped back and I heard and felt my sword slide smoothly out from under his ribs. There was a slight stain of blood on his coat, but little other damage seemed to have been done.

"I suspect that at that point, most of Andrei's victims give up in the face of his invincibility, for he laughed and suggested that I surrender to the inevitable. He did not realize that there is more than one way in which a man is trained to use a sabre. On his next advance I chose not to stab but to cut. With every step he took, I slashed the blade across his torso. On a normal man, each blow would have broken several ribs. Whether they did on him, I do not know. He showed little sign of weakening, but the very force of the blows did begin to push him back, away from me. The energy I was expending in every blow would not have allowed me to continue for long, but as he stepped back, he stumbled over something and found himself prone and helpless on the ground. I lifted my sword to give what I hoped would be a debilitating blow to his head, and he raised his arm to defend himself. The blade made contact with his arm and drew blood. I brought my sword down again and again, knowing that my attack now was only on his arm. I made no attempt to inflict a fatal blow, for I knew that such an attack would be unsuccessful. I cannot tell you, Aleksei, and if I could I would be ashamed to, the feeling of elation I felt with every blow as it cut further and further into the bone. Eventually, even the supernatural matter of which Andrei was made up could not resist me and his arm became detached from his body, leaving a bloody stub just below the elbow.

"The wound was clearly not fatal, but at least seemed to have incapacitated Andrei enough that he was no longer an immediate threat. I had never paid enough attention to even the little I had heard of the legends to know the various ways in which a creature like this might be destroyed, and I did not want to remain there trying to find out, for fear that Dmitry or some of the other Oprichniki might return. It is my hope that I disabled him enough so that he was unable to find shelter and so perished in the first light of dawn.

"For my part, I once again took flight. I stopped briefly at Shalikovo, hoping I might meet with you there, but I was afraid to wait long, so I chalked a message for you and continued to Moscow. I felt certain that I was being followed, either by Andrei or by the other Oprichniki, but the days are still longer than the nights, so the advantage was with me. Once in Moscow, I could think of only one way to contact you and to be sure of Dmitry not finding out. I went to see Dominique at the brothel. I told both her and Margarita the briefest of details of where I would be, and that you and only you should meet me. In that you are reading this, I must assume that you have spoken to Dominique. She was very concerned for your safety, Aleksei, and interrogated me for information about you—anything and everything about you—much as she has done in the past.

"I headed straight out for Desna and arrived here today. I travelled through daylight, so I don't think that the Oprichniki could have followed me here, but still I fear that they will find me. I do not want to die, but if I must, I would prefer it to be with the relative honour of a Russian firing squad than at their hands. Perhaps it is for the better that I never listened to the stories I was told about vampires as a child, otherwise I might fear even more what is to become of me now.

"If you are reading this, Aleksei, then it must be that I could not wait long enough for you and have moved on. Perhaps I am already in France by now. My hope is to settle in Paris, although I have learned that fate has little inclination to consider what my hopes may be. Should you one day come to Paris, either at the head of a conquering army, or as a visitor in more pacific times, then perhaps you will try to come and find me.

"To anyone else who finds this letter (or to whom you, Aleksei, choose to show it) I must make a plea that no suspicion of treachery should fall upon any of Vadim Fyodorovich, Dmitry Fetyukovich or Aleksei Ivanovich. Just because I am a French spy, it in no way follows that they are. I am reminded of a discussion we once had, Aleksei, about the Bible. Just because some things in it are true does not make the whole of it true. And (you will see that

I stick to my guns to the last) just because there are vampires doesn't mean there is a god. I may soon know for sure.

"Please convey my apologies and regards to Vadim and Dmitry, and also my warmest affection to Marfa Mihailovna and young Dmitry Alekseevich.

"I remain, I hope, your friend,

"Maksim Sergeivich Lukin."

Though some were more explicit than others, Maks' letter contained many condemnations. Most obvious was Maks' condemnation of himself in his confession of treachery against his tsar and his country. What it told of Dmitry and of the Oprichniki was once shocking, but by now it was nothing new. To that, though, there was one exception—Andrei's arm. I was not surprised that the flesh and blood of a vampire was close enough to that of a human that it was possible to sever one of their limbs. I had myself already seen that I could sever Andrei's head. And that was just the point. When I had destroyed Andrei, both his arms had been intact. Somehow since his meeting with Maks, Andrei had recovered.

But that was a minor distraction. The worst thing in Maksim's letter was its condemnation of me. When I had spoken to Maks in this very building, all those weeks before, I had given him no chance to explain what he had now told me so clearly in his letter. I had been so blinded by my rage at his betrayal of our country that I had never even paused to consider that there might be some issue of greater importance which he had to tell me. I could blame Maks himself for not forcing me to listen to him and I could blame the Oprichniki for arriving to cut short our conversation, but I was the true culprit. With the Oprichniki there I might not have been able to save him, but at least he could have died knowing what he wanted to know above all— that I was still his friend.

CHAPTER XXII

I LOOKED OVER TO DMITRY. HE HAD RISEN TO HIS FEET AND was eyeing me suspiciously, calculating whether there was anything I had read in the letter that might tip the balance of my trust away from him. With self-defensive instinct, his hand reached for his sword.

"Don't worry, Dmitry. There's nothing much in there about you that I didn't know already." I spoke with the intention of being more dismissive than comforting. There were a few details of Dmitry's involvement that had not been clear to me earlier, a few he had twisted to avoid revealing the nature of the Oprichniki, but nothing that substantially changed the nature of his attitude towards them or to anything else.

"He was an enemy of Russia. I knew that. That's what he died for," Dmitry pleaded.

"You're a patriot, Dmitry," I told him—a patriot and nothing more.

We found a few old tools behind the hut and between us we dug a grave for our fallen comrade. Two shards of wood formed a simple cross to mark his final resting place. For reasons that I am unable to explain—certainly not to Maks' level of satisfaction—I took off his spectacles before we placed him in the ground and slipped them into my pocket. One of the lenses was shattered, no doubt from a blow to Maks' head, but the other remained intact. Apart, perhaps, from the metal buttons on his jacket and his ancient, unidentifiable bones, they were all that would remain of Maksim, long after the rest of him was consumed by the earth in which we had buried him. I preferred that they would survive in the possession of someone who remembered the man who had once worn them.

It was dark by now, and so we decided to spend the night in the hut. It was cold. Once the sun had gone down, the temperature began to plummet. At the coldest during the nights at that time there were several degrees of frost, and it was usual to discover a covering of snow on the ground each morning that could be stirred up into a blizzard when the wind was high. We lit a fire in the stove, which would keep us in some comfort through the night.

"The difference this time is that it's *my* country," said Dmitry. It broke a silence which had descended upon us after we had turned away from the grave of our friend.

"Your country?" I asked, failing to comprehend what he was saying.

"Our country, obviously, but I meant as opposed to theirs—the Oprichniki's—where I first met them."

"So they were better behaved when they were at home—smart enough not to piss on their own doorstep?"

"No, not that," said Dmitry resignedly. "I just meant that my perception of it was different. They were just the same."

Dmitry paused, but it was evident that he had more to tell. "The same?" I prompted.

"When I told you before, about Wallachia, about meeting Zmyeevich, there was something I missed out."

He stopped again. "So tell me now," I said.

"You remember I said that Pyetr, Andrei, Ioann and Varfolomei were the only ones still left from when I first met them."

I nodded.

"Well, that wasn't quite true. After that first night, when Zmyeevich and the others had saved us from the Turks, we began to work together. We'd search the mountains by day, finding out where the Turks were and then telling Zmyeevich so he and the others could deal with them at night—just like we did in Moscow.

"But then after a few days, one of the Wallachians went missing; two days later, another. In less than a fortnight, there were only two left, from almost a dozen originally. I never saw the vampires take them, but somehow I knew—things they said; things Zmyeevich said. I couldn't really be sure, until this year back in Moscow when I first met Foma. I knew I recognized him, but I knew that he hadn't been one of the vampires who rode alongside Zmyeevich back then. Then I realized. He'd been one of the Wallachians who'd ridden alongside *me*; the one that went up to the castle door and called out to Zmyeevich. He'd been turned into one of them. I don't think any of the others were lucky enough to join the predators—they were just prey."

"I'm not sure you should call either fate 'lucky,'" I said bitterly.

"No. No, you're right, of course. But as I said, it didn't seem so bad then. Who was I to argue if Wallachian vampires chose to kill Wallachian peasants? Mind you . . . when I left Zmyeevich and rejoined the army, the last thing I remember as I walked away was the look of fear and betrayal in those last two Wallachians' eyes."

I was horrified. Until then, I had thought that Dmitry had been deceived, that despite what *I* knew, *he* had never had reason to suspect what they were doing behind our backs. Now I knew that he had been deceiving himself.

"Why didn't they leave too?" I asked. It was a mundane question.

"I don't know. They respected Zmyeevich as well as fearing him. Who knows, maybe they're alive and well even today."

I let out a short laugh.

"Maybe not," he muttered.

Dmitry was up before me and I was woken by the sound of him harnessing his horse.

"You're in a rush to get going," I said to him.

"I'm not coming with you."

"I see," I said.

"I'm scared, Aleksei." His voice quavered as he expressed the terror inside him. "They'll not show any mercy to me—or to you. Come with me, Aleksei, back to Moscow. You don't have to face them. We can't bring back Vadim or Maks. All we can do is die like they did. They wouldn't ask us to."

His diffidence was quite reasonable. Maks would not have seen the logic in taking revenge—in threatening it, yes, but not in taking it. Vadim would have understood the instinct, but would have counselled restraint. But I was motivated not by reason, but by hatred. I could no more rationalize the passion which drove me to pursue and erase the surviving Oprichniki than I could that which drove me to make love to Domnikiia when I had a loving wife at home. Hatred is a most powerful emotion. Leaders use it to stir up aggression in their armies and men use it to force themselves into actions that they would not contemplate without it. Hatred was the inseparable companion of the very thing that Iuda had said made me weak. While scruple could make me spare a man when every rational voice screamed to kill him, so hatred could make me kill when the arguments and reasons for doing so had long been forgotten. To divide them was impossible. Iuda might despise me for having one, but he would learn to regret my possessing the other.

"Do as you wish, Dmitry," I said. "I'm going to face them."

"If they were French, or Turks, you know I'd be with you," he tried to explain.

"We owe each other nothing, Dmitry. You know it doesn't work like that."

"I want to help you, Aleksei, but I know them better than you do. I've seen what they do."

"So have I. Remember?"

"You've seen nothing. What they did in Moscow? A fragment of what I saw them do to the Turks. Even side by side, the two of us could never beat them." There was an edge of panic in his voice as he tried to convince both me and himself that what he intended to do—to desert—was in some way less than totally dishonourable.

"If it helps, Dmitry, I'm not convinced that I'd want you by my side." It was more hurtful than I had intended it to be. Dmitry fell into an immediate silence. There was truth in what I had said on two counts. One was that, even after his apparent change of heart, he was still too close to the Oprichniki for me to trust, and the other that in his state of panic he would be of little use to anyone in a tight situation. But I had said it to try to help his decision; to make it me that decided he should not stay, rather than him.

"Thank you for that, Aleksei," he said at length, without bitterness. "I'm not much of a soldier anymore, I know. Better to hear it from you, I suppose." He was like a spurned lover, holding back his tears and clinging pathetically to the last vestiges of his pride. I took a step towards him, to embrace him before he left, but he raised his arms to fend me off. "I'll just go," he said with attempted nobility. "You have things to do."

He mounted his horse and began back towards Moscow at a gentle trot. Standing in the place where I had last seen Maksim alive and watching Dmitry depart, I was filled with the premonition that this would also be the last time I saw Dmitry. I recalled the miscommunication of my last words with Maks and the casualness of my farewell to Vadim. I knew that I could not let Dmitry leave quite like this.

I climbed on to my own horse and caught up with him. Perhaps if I had pleaded with him then, I would have been able to persuade him to stay with me. His joy at knowing I wanted him would have overcome his fear. But the truth was, I didn't want him with me. I just wanted him to leave on better terms.

"Take this," I said, taking the icon from around my neck and handing it to him.

"It's no protection from them," he said. "You know that."

"Do you think I'd be giving it away if it were?" I laughed, and was pleased to see something of a smile in him. "It's a symbol, not a talisman."

"A symbol of what?"

I did not have an answer. He put the chain around his neck and tucked the pendant into his shirt. "When you're in Moscow, go to Ordynsky Lane," I told him.

He looked puzzled. "And why's that?"

"That's where Boris and Natalia are."

He raised an eyebrow and then smiled at me. "Thank you, Aleksei. I hope to see you soon."

"You will," I replied. We shook hands, and then he departed with the same steady trot of a few minutes before, but with his head held inestimably higher.

I rode back to the hut and packed my few possessions; then I turned and headed south towards Kurilovo.

It was around noon the following day, the twenty-eighth of October, when I finally reached the village. The blizzards of the past few days were beginning to abate, leaving the whole landscape as a desert of white. The crossroads where I was due to meet with Iuda that evening was a little to the south of the village. The sun was already low on the horizon by the time I inspected it. Already I could see a narrow crescent moon in the sky and even that would be following its brighter cousin round to the other side of the world before long.

As I had remembered, the crossroads was at the top of a slight hill. To the north, the buildings of the village were small and distant. To the east and west, I could see down the roads even further. The fields between the roads were smooth, blank and white. Anyone attempting to approach the crossroads by them would not only be hampered by the deep snow, but would also be seen long before they got anywhere near. The closest cover was to the south—a small coppice of trees which spanned the road almost a verst away—still far enough so that any approach from there would be seen long in advance of its arrival.

The crossroads itself was undistinguished, but for one thing—from a makeshift gibbet hung the gently swaying body of a hanged man. It was stiff from the cold and caked with snow, but I only needed to brush a little of the snow aside to discover beneath the dark blue uniform of a French infantry captain.

I went back to the village and sat in the sole hostelry, drinking vodka until the appointed hour.

"I judge from your sword that you're a military man," said a voice from a nearby table. I turned. It was just a couple of peasants, bored with each other's conversation and looking for an alternative. The one who had spoken was in his forties, with straggly, long red hair and bloodshot green eyes. His friend—possibly his father—was well past sixty. He had few hairs left on his head and even fewer teeth left in it.

"That's right," I replied brusquely. My thoughts had been happily settled upon the image of Domnikiia, and I was irritated to be distracted from them.

"A bit of a forgetful one though," said the older man.

"How do you mean?" I asked.

"Forgot your uniform and turned up two weeks late for the battle," he laughed.

"You know—the battle. At Maloyaroslavets," the first man explained, eager to start a conversation. Maloyaroslavets was the site of the first battle between the Russian and French armies after the latter had quitted Moscow.

Like Borodino, it had been an encounter in which Bonaparte's tactical victory was to assist his strategic defeat. Though they were the victors, the French were turned back north, to retreat west along the road down which they had advanced—a road which they had already sucked dry of supplies. The town of Maloyaroslavets was almost forty versts away from Kurilovo, but it would be the closest to actual conflict that they had ever come, so it was not unnatural that it should become to the locals "the battle."

"I'm afraid I didn't fight there," I said. "I haven't been in a battle since Borodino."

"Well, Bonaparte's probably back beyond Borodino by now," laughed the second man. "Maybe you should get back over there and relive your glory days." These were the men for whom I had spent my adult life fighting. They had probably never left this village, certainly never gone outside the oblast, and yet they could criticize me for what they saw as my cowardice. That is the cross that must be borne by every spy, I heard Vadim's voice silently tell me. He is never given laurels—he must wear his medals inside his tunic. And what choice do they have? They're serfs, Maks now joined in. If they have fought, it was at their master's command. If they stayed home, it was that their masters preferred farmers to fighters, not that *they* preferred life to death.

There was no madness in my listening to the voices of my departed friends, only pleasure. Even when they were alive, I could at any time have conjured up their voices and their opinions. I had encountered few problems that could not be alleviated by a simple question along the lines of "What would Maks think?" or, just as often, "What would Marfa think?" Now, with Maks and Vadim at least, it was the only chance I got to hear them. Even if it was madness, it was a madness I would gladly choose.

I slammed my bottle of vodka down on their table with my left hand, making clear for them to see the wounds that I had earned on the Danube. "Have a drink on me, why don't you?" I suggested. Whether it was my generosity or my manifest war wounds I do not know, but their mood towards me warmed a little.

"Where did that happen?" asked the older one, once he'd poured himself a vodka, indicating my missing fingers.

TWELVE

"In Bulgaria—Silistria."

"In a battle?"

"That's right," I lied, but I couldn't prevent the true story from forcing its way into my mind.

It had not been in a battle, but in a gaol. After Prince Bagration had decided to abandon the siege of Silistria, myself and a few others were sent into the city to spy. We'd split up, and I found myself staying in a hostel, with half a dozen or more men to a room, all of them locals. It was handily located right against the city wall, so all I had to do was drop messages out of the window at an appointed time—midnight each night. One of my comrades had simply to creep over, pick up the message and take the precious information to Bagration.

I don't know if it was me or the courier who got sloppy, but on the third night, it wasn't his hands that the small piece of paper, covered in Cyrillic and wrapped round a stone, fell into, but the hands of a Turkish patrol. There was nothing of much interest in it, even if they could break the simple code and then read the Russian, but they had seen which window it fell from.

Minutes later, Turkish soldiers—Janissaries—rushed into the room. It was easy enough for me to work out from their conversation what had happened, but the problem for them was that there were seven of us in the room. Any one could have dropped the message—and I'd made sure that none of the others had seen me go to the window.

So the Turks rounded us all up and took us to the gaol and used their best methods to persuade the spy to confess. I didn't, despite losing two fingers.

I forced myself back to the present. That much of the story I was happy to tell to most people. That's what I'd told Boris and Natalia. The details of what went on in the gaol, I never told. But to these two and today, I didn't even feel the urge to tell the basic story.

"I don't suppose you saw much of the French round here," I said instead.

"No, not many," said the younger man. "The only Frenchman you'll find around here is old Napoleon, up at the crossroads." They both laughed.

"I saw him," I said. "How long has he been there?"

"Since just after the battle," the redhead continued. "He wandered into town and we showed him some true Russian hospitality."

"Was he a deserter, or just lost?" I asked.

"How would we know," replied the old, bald man. "We don't speak their language. We were just happy to do our bit for Russia."

"So that's been what—two weeks?" I asked.

"Nearly," said the younger. "Now that the cold has set in, he'll be up there till spring."

"Won't anyone cut him down?"

"Not while he's doing his work," said the older.

"His work?"

"He's keeping the plague off us. They had it terrible in Tula." His withered lips were sucked into his toothless mouth as he spoke.

"That was in the summer," said the other man, evidently more thoughtful. "It had died down long before we hung up Napoleon."

"Are you going to take him down then?" came the reply, to which there was no response. Leaving the body hanging there kept away the plague, along with, no doubt, tigers, Turks, elephants and Englishmen, none of whom would have been seen in these parts since "Napoleon" began his vigil at the crossroads. The one creature which it would not keep away was the very thing that I was due to meet that evening.

I set off back to the crossroads, leaving my horse in the village, with the plan of being there well before the appointed time. I trudged back along the road, listening to the creaking snow beneath my boots and feeling the cold wind in my face. The low crescent moon cast just enough light to see the whole landscape around me. Looking back over my shoulder, the little village glowed warm and inviting out of the darkness. I would have loved to stay and natter away the evening over a vodka with those two locals, to stay out of the cold and forget why I came to the village in the first place, but I could not. A serf can sit and remain in one state until his master tells him what he must do next. A freeman must be his own master.

Occasionally, the wind blew up a tiny snowstorm and I could see nothing beyond the scrabble of whiteness before my eyes. It would only last a moment. No new snow was falling and so, in the dim moonlight, I could see nearly as far as I had done during the day. At the crossroads, the snow showed traces of a few more pairs of feet having passed that way, but little else. The body of "Napoleon" still hung from its noose and swung gently in the breeze, warding off all those alien terrors that might otherwise have dared to visit the little village of Kurilovo. There was less snow on his body than there had been earlier. Presumably the waning heat of the sun had been attracted to his dark uniform enough to melt a little of the snow that covered him. Any such thawing could only be superficial. After two weeks of the Russian winter, this Frenchman would forever remain frozen to his heart—or if not forever, at least until spring.

I walked around in a wide circle, keeping respectfully distant from the corpse at its centre. My movement was partly in order to keep warm, but also to patrol each of the four roads that approached me. All of them remained empty for a long time. It must have been a little before seven that I saw the figure of a man approaching from the south. He first became visible next to the coppice I had noted earlier. I could only assume that he had been concealed somewhere within it.

As he approached, I continued to keep an eye on the other three roads which fed the crossroads. This was the most dangerous moment, when I could be blocked off along all four paths, leaving my only escape route across the impassable, snow-covered fields where I could easily be run to ground. There was no sign of anyone else. Each time I looked back towards the coppice, the figure approaching me was a little closer. Soon, it was clearly recognizable as Iuda.

"When he arrived, I was a few steps away from the centre of the crossroads. He stood still, looking directly towards me, right beside the hanging man whose feet swung lazily in the breeze at about the level of Iuda's waist. Looking into Iuda's cold grey eyes, it was not difficult to believe that he was just as dead as the cadaver that hung beside him and that what now animated him was not the soul of a man, but the will of the devil.

"Good evening, Aleksei Ivanovich," he said.

Chapter XXIII

"GOOD EVENING," I RESPONDED, STEPPING TOWARDS HIM.

"I see you have come alone. Did Dmitry Fetyukovich not care to join you?"

"This is between you and me," I replied.

"That is indeed true, Aleksei Ivanovich, although some of the others do have issues with Dmitry. But I agree with you—it is best to save those separate squabbles for a separate occasion. You will see that I too came alone. We will only be able to talk if we trust one another."

"I don't trust you, Iuda," I said bitterly.

"I'm sorry, my friend," said Iuda with a sincerity that anyone who did not know him would have taken for genuine. "I am unfamiliar with the nuances of your language. Of course you don't trust me. Why should you? I have not earned that privilege. But you do trust your eyes. I have chosen this place well, I hope. You can see that there is no one else here."

"I can see that." The wind blew up a little more fiercely. A light shower of snow had begun which, combined with the wind, reduced the distance I could see down the roads. As we spoke, I rarely looked directly at Iuda, keeping my eyes instead always prowling for signs of a distant attack. "So what do you have to say?" I asked.

His face pulled an expression of mild anguish, as though what he had to say was distasteful, but had to be discussed—like a man about to confess to his wife his infidelity. "You have now killed three of our comrades—the same number that Maksim Sergeivich succeeded in destroying."

"I've killed more than three," I said, attempting to twist the knife.

He pressed his lips together as though he had tasted something sour. "We have chosen to be gracious over the death of Ioann in the cellar. Though you were there at his death and did nothing to attempt to save him from the flames, he was probably beyond salvation. To kill by omission cannot be counted as murder. As for the Russian soldier—Pavel, I believe he was called—I would not count him amongst our number. He was a useful foot soldier, but not a loss to grieve over. So we will leave the tally at three.

"We cannot but be impressed by the martial skills that you have shown as you have killed," he continued. "I do not know precisely what you did with Matfei and Varfolomei, but they were strong fighters, so you did well to defeat them. I saw in close detail what you did to Andrei. That was truly inspiring—not just in the skill you showed with your sword but in the relish you displayed in finishing off an already incapacitated victim. It was a pleasure to see your hatred surging forth in that way—so much more manly than your friend Maksim, sending his friends off to a remote death in which he need not participate directly."

"I'm glad to have you as an admirer," I said, "but if you wanted to compliment me, you could have done it all by letter."

"I could. I could. And that would have meant that dear Dominique could also have read my praises of you and then she would warm even more to the image of her dashing hero. But perhaps I will yet have the chance to tell her in person. The poor girl must be in something of a quandary. On the one hand she sees your bravery and heroism as you do battle with us. On the other she must see that we with whom you do battle were once your friends. She must wonder if she will ever make some similar tiny mistake that will turn you against *her*."

"The only mistake you made, Iuda, was not a tiny one," I said, responding with the anger that he had clearly hoped to instil. "Your mistake was to willingly turn your back on humanity when you became a vampire. It was foolish of you to let me know that only willing victims become vampires. It erased the last trace of pity that I might have had for any of you." Behind him, back along the road he had come from, I thought I saw a slight movement through the buffeted snow. "I presume there is a point that you're going to come to? Some sort of deal between us?" I asked, trying to move things along.

"A man of directness, I see," smiled Iuda. He began to walk as he spoke, almost as if trying to outflank me, and I realized that he was moving my attention away from the road down which he had come. I stepped closer to the centre of the crossroads, ensuring I still had a good view in all directions.

"But you are right," he continued. "We must come to some sort of accommodation. When one comes up against a strong and powerful enemy there are two possible ways to deal with it. The first is to attempt to destroy it, to wipe it off the face of the earth so that it can never again irritate one with its persistent aggression. We have both already attempted this; we have both failed."

"I don't seem to be failing too badly. There's seven of you dead already."

Iuda smiled, not unlike a father delighting in the premature wisdom of his child. "Such camaraderie, Lyosha. You are right, you personally are doing well—you are alive. But taken as a group, I think the four of you have fared little better than the twelve of us."

The flurry of snow had subsided and whatever movement I had perceived in the distance behind Iuda had gone. For as far as I could see in the silver haze of the moonlight reflected by the glistening snow, there was only stillness. I looked around again at the other roads. They too were empty. Behind me, the hanged French captain continued to swing gently with the momentum picked up from the earlier breeze.

"But there is also a second way," continued Iuda. "That is accommodation. A creature does not need to be an enemy just because it is powerful. Wolves do not attack bears and bears do not attack wolves. It is not that the wolf loves the bear, it is that he knows he has little chance of winning. So which would your choice be, Lyosha? Shall we continue to fight and see which of us survives, bloodied and maimed? Or shall we leave each other to go in peace and continue the comfortable lives we enjoy?"

I remained silent. I had known my answer when I spoke to Dmitry just before we parted. Such a deal would fail because I did not trust the Oprichniki. And even if they were to keep their side of the bargain, I would not have kept mine. Iuda read my thoughts.

"But I do us an injustice to make comparisons with wild animals. If the wolf and the bear seem to trust each other, it cannot be because they are wise, so it must be because they are fools. The path to personal safety does not come by hoping that one's enemies will not attack one. It comes by ensuring it—by destroying those very enemies. We both know, Lyosha, how much each one of us yearns to kill the other—how much we dream of the pleasure we will take in it. Neither of us could walk in safety with that knowledge. The only safety lies in knowing that the other is truly dead, in being sure that he can never rise again to harm one."

His voice was rising now. The patina of civility fell away and his every expression was filled with wrath and hatred. "Much as one can be sure that a hanged French captain, whose body one inspected in the afternoon, cannot come back to life and attack one." He stared into my eyes just long enough see that I had fathomed what he was talking about. "Unless of course one goes away to drown one's sorrows in vodka, allowing one lifeless carcass to be exchanged for another."

At the same time as he spoke, I was grabbed from behind. The arms of the body hanging behind me wrapped themselves around my neck and the legs around my waist.

"You remember Filipp, of course, don't you, Lyosha?" asked Iuda, his overplayed politeness returning, but accompanied now by a look of maniacal victory in his eyes. I heard a snigger from Filipp, and he held me tighter as he continued to hang, unharmed, by the noose around his neck.

Over Iuda's shoulder I saw movement. A coach emerged from the coppice from which Iuda himself had earlier come into view. Iuda turned and saw it too.

"And soon the others will be here, and then we can all go away to some nice, quiet, secluded retreat and have dinner. Oh, I know you're a brave man, Lyosha, and your own painful death will mean little to you, but it will give me the deepest satisfaction to know that you understand exactly how much Vadim and Maks suffered as they died."

The coach was moving only at a canter and would take several minutes to reach us, but if its driver chose to break into a gallop, it would be with us in less than two. I had to act there and then. I lifted my feet into the air, so that Filipp now supported my whole weight, and kicked hard at Iuda's chest.

The impact merely caused him to take a step backwards, but it sent me and Filipp swinging back on the rope. Filipp could do little but hang on to me. He tried to tighten his grip around my neck, but his initial aim had been to hold, not to throttle, and so it was to little effect.

I managed to free my sword from its scabbard and we swung around in a wide ellipse with Iuda at its centre. He was crouched and ready; in his right hand he held the double-bladed knife that once, long ago, he had been so keen for me not to see. He made a few thrusts at me as I passed, but could not seem to get the measure of the irregular motion of the human pendulum confronting him. I had no control over where we were going, but I waited until we swung close enough for me to strike. In the distance, the other Oprichniki had seen what was happening, and the coach broke into a gallop.

One swing brought us close enough to Iuda, and I struck. I knew from Maks' experience that stabbing would be to no avail, so instead I used the edge of my blade. I caught Iuda across the upper right arm and he yelled as he put his hand up to the wound. At the same moment, I heard the sound of splintering wood and Filipp and I came thudding to the ground as the gallows above us gave way under our combined weight. As we hit the snow, Filipp lost his grip on me and I felt the coils of the rope which had supported us snaking down on to me. I rolled aside just in time to avoid being hit by the wooden beam to which the other end of the rope was tied.

Filipp was not so lucky. The heavy beam hit him hard in the chest, knocking the breath out of him, but doing him little serious damage. Still clutching my sword in my right hand, I now took my wooden dagger in my left and began to back away, looking to see which, if either, of the two Oprichniki would pursue me. Iuda was hanging back, unable now to use his knife because of the wound to his arm. Filipp, however, was almost instantly on his feet and advancing towards me, the noose still trailing from his neck.

The coach was less than a minute away now. I backed behind the vertical post of the gibbet as Filipp came towards me. Iuda shouted something to him and he replied scornfully, clearly not needing advice in the matter. He lunged at me to one side of the post and I dodged round the other, running for all I was worth until a depression in the ground, hidden beneath the snow, tripped me and I fell. I quickly rolled on to my back and saw Filipp's bulky form looming towards me, his jaws wide open in readiness for the attack.

Suddenly his head jerked back and his body came to a halt. His hands reached up to his neck. The broken beam at one end of the rope had become embedded like an anchor in the snow. Wrapped round the post, the rope had become taut and Filipp could move no further. I sheathed my sabre and, grabbing the other end of the rope, began to pull. Rather than let himself be hauled off his feet, Filipp trotted along with the rope. Meanwhile, as well as pulling the rope, I began to cut across in front of him. Iuda was screaming instructions at his fellow Oprichnik, but Filipp was in no position to obey. As his back thudded against the wood I jerked the rope fast across his chest and ran twice more round him, pinioning him against the post.

Realizing the imminent danger, Iuda began to approach through the snow. The rope would not hold Filipp for long, but it was not my intention that he should be alive for long. I lunged at him with the dagger, straining hard on the end of the rope so that he was squeezed still tighter against the post and giving me even greater force against him. The wooden blade paused momentarily as it came up against his overcoat, but the cloth soon yielded and I felt the blade separate his ribs and slide into his heart.

I took no time to linger over his decaying body, but withdrew the dagger and turned to face Iuda. This was my golden opportunity to destroy him at last. The blow to his arm had weakened him and he seemed in no mood to fight. He backed away from me cautiously. I had little time to think. The coach was now only seconds away from us. Though I might take Iuda's life, it would be at the cost of my own. I turned and fled towards the village.

The snow-covered road was not easy to run down. Once I had built up speed then maintaining it was feasible enough, but to turn, stop or even slow down would risk me slipping and falling to the ground. Behind me I heard the coach come to a stop. There was shouting between its occupants and Iuda and then I heard the rattle of the harness and the wheels turning once again. I had managed to cover perhaps a tenth of a verst in the time they had taken to set off after me, but now it would be only a few moments before they caught up with me. I glanced over my shoulder and saw that they were still distant, but gaining. The black silhouette of the coachman stood upright against the sky, whipping his horses furiously.

I kept on running, swifter than I had ever done before, but still I knew that the coach would soon be upon me. I heard its clattering wheels, partly muffled as they cut through the snow, coming closer and closer. I was lucky they had chosen a coach, not a troika or any kind of sled, which would have run faster, but even so, they were faster than me. The coachman's whip cracked again and again as he urged the horses towards me. They came so close that I could feel their breath on the back of my neck. I felt sure that the Oprichniki planned to run me down and let me be crushed to death in the snow under hoof and wheel, but that would have been too pleasant a death for them to inflict.

Rather than let the horses trample me, the coachman steered them to one side and the coach began to pull level with me. I looked over my shoulder again and saw the coachman—it was Foma—leaning out from his seat towards me, precariously balanced and leering like a gargoyle from the side of a western cathedral. In his hands he held his whip loosely so that the leather formed a long loop. He tossed the loop towards me and I felt it brush against the back of my head. He was trying to lasso it around my neck, so that he could drag me into the racing coach.

Foma was almost parallel with me. I was running level with the hind legs of the horses. I drew my sabre, knowing there was little I could do with it to fight the Oprichniki, but with one hope in my mind. I slashed at the hind leg of the creature that was racing alongside me. My sword bit deep, just above the hock, and with a startled neigh, the poor, lame animal instantly pulled up. As the heavy coach ploughed on into the two unfortunate horses, I lost my balance and fell to the ground, rolling over off the road and then into the adjacent field.

I turned to see what had happened to the coach. It had tipped over on to one side and was just coming to rest in the ditch on the far side of the road. One of the horses lay motionless in the road; the other was in the ditch, trying to get up under the weight of the coach to which it was still harnessed. Foma had been thrown off and lay dazed in the field beyond. The side door of the carriage, now facing upwards, flipped open like a trapdoor and Iuda emerged. He hauled himself out and then bent back in to help those remaining inside.

I left them to it and ran across the snowy field. The edge of the field was not far away, marked by a hedgerow. Once beyond that, I felt I was safely hidden, so I turned to look back at the Oprichniki. Through my spyglass I could see them making attempts to right the coach. Iuda was taking a supervisory role, evidently issuing instructions to the other three, but not himself participating. They soon abandoned the idea and began to remove from the coach a number of items of baggage. They then started to trudge purposefully through the snow, back towards the crossroads, Iuda still clutching his arm where I had cut him.

I shadowed them from a distance. The moon had now set and at times it was almost impossible to see them, but they were talking loudly and angrily to one another and, although I could not make out any of the meaning of what they said, it was enough to let me know where they were without ever getting a clear sight of them. Back at the crossroads they paused for a while. Stare as I might, I could see no sign of Filipp. I had not had a chance before to make certain that he was dead, but the fact that there was no sign of a body left me happy that I had indeed killed him. Pyetr knelt down in the snow next to the post where I had tied Filipp and lifted up a handful to examine. I inferred that he was holding the dust that was typical of a *voordalak*'s earthly remains.

They continued over the crossroads, back along the road from which they had come. I continued to follow, though the snow in the fields was waist deep in places and my trousers were by now cold and sodden. Eventually, we came to the coppice from which the coach had emerged. To go round it would take me too far from the road, so I had to cut into the woods to keep close with them. While the voices of the Oprichniki had carried clearly across the open fields, once we were amongst the dense trees, they became muffled and soon faded to complete silence. I knew that it was from somewhere around here that they had set out in their coach towards the crossroads, so if they stopped and I continued on parallel to the road, as I was heading, there was a good chance that I would overtake them and lose track of them completely.

I changed direction, heading now towards the road instead of keeping level with it. In the dense woodland, there was no light at all. Looking up, I could just make out the stars through the canopy of branches which, although denuded of leaves, were clung to by sufficient snow to ensure that only patches of sky were visible. Without being able to see the pole star, it was difficult to know whether I was heading the right way. I had turned left to head back towards the road, but even after a few paces, I could have wandered a long way from that chosen path. Vampires are creatures of the night, and although I did not know for sure, I could only presume that they would be able to see far more clearly than I in this light. I could walk straight into the waiting arms of any one of the four of them and not know it until I saw the gleam of their fangs.

At least there was in that some morsel of comfort; there were now only four of them—one fewer than there had been when the night began. A part of me insisted that it was achievement enough for the evening; that I should return to rest and safety and leave the others for another day. It was an academic issue. More in question was whether I would make it out of these woods at all. Vampires were not my most pressing enemy. Wolves or even the icy cold itself were a more present danger.

I pushed on in the direction that I hoped would lead me back to the road. When I had entered the coppice, I had been only half a verst away from the road, and yet I had now been pacing through the woods for over a quarter of an hour without finding it again. Clearly I had not been sticking to a straight line. At last, a little way ahead of me I saw a light through the densely packed tree trunks. As I drew closer, I saw that I was coming to a clearing, opening onto the road but hidden by the trees so that I had not seen it from the crossroads. In the clearing was a small farmhouse and next to it a barn. The light I had seen was coming from the barn. There were no lights at the windows of the farmhouse. The sight of those lonely, snow-covered buildings looming out of the dark woodland gave me the sensation of being the child protagonist in some gruesome fairy story.

I crept close to the barn and listened. From within came the guttural, laughing voices of the Oprichniki. They seemed to be in a good mood again. Something had cheered them after their defeat at the crossroads. I quietly worked my way round to the door, looking for some crack in the woodwork through which I might observe them.

TWELVE

I put my eye to the narrow gap at the door's hinge, but before I could look in, the door was flung open, outwards at a huge speed. I would almost have been crushed as it slammed against the side of the barn had I not rolled out of the way. I pressed my back to the barn, coiled to fight, but not knowing whether the door had been opened because of my arrival or for some other, coincidental reason.

From the open doorway, something was hurled into the snow outside, carrying almost as far as the trees. It was large and bulky and sank into the snow where it landed. I glimpsed the two Oprichniki who had thrown it, but they did not venture outside and saw nothing of me. Having completed their task, they went back in. I heard more laughter and chatter in their language and what I made out to be a Russian cry of "*Niet!*" in a voice that certainly did not belong to any Oprichnik. Then Iuda's voice barked some instruction, and the barn door was closed again.

Rather than going straight over to the object that they had thrown out, which would have taken me straight past the door and hence possibly through the vampires' line of sight, I went back into the coppice and skirted around the edge of the clearing until I was as close to it as I could be. I crawled out to examine what the Oprichniki had so carelessly discarded.

It was, in accordance with the expectation that I had desperately tried to deny, a body. I wiped the snow away from the face and recoiled in brief shock, raising my hand to cover my mouth. It was a woman, middle-aged and most certainly dead, but none of that was of especial horror to me. Clearing more snow from her naked body, I saw repeated almost everywhere what I had seen on her face. Beyond the usual wounds to the throat, the Oprichniki had gone far further with this victim.

There were bites everywhere. Not just bitemarks, but actual missing pieces of flesh, torn away by the vampires' hungry teeth. Both her cheeks were missing, along with parts of her throat, her breasts, her belly, her buttocks, her thighs and her calves. They had not been thorough in their devouring of her. There was plenty of flesh still remaining. From the look of torment on her face, I could imagine only one reason why they had decided to stop eating. It was that she had died.

Chapter XXIV

THE OPRICHNIKI HAD NOT HAD LONG IN WHICH TO capture their victim. I had lost sight of them as I entered the woods, and that had been barely twenty minutes before. The only conclusion was that they had come across the woman earlier and left her imprisoned in the barn as they came after me. They may even have found her in the farmhouse just there. If she was the farmer's wife, then there must also be a farmer. I remembered the Russian voice I had heard from inside the barn.

I stole my way back over to the barn and peered through the crack at the side of the door. The scene within was unspeakably gruesome. The farmer was in the centre of the room. His wrists were tied together by long rope which had been slung over a beam in the ceiling. His arms stretched up above him, leaving his near-dislocated shoulders to take his full weight. His toes barely brushed against the floor as his body swung from one side to the other. Of all the devices medieval torture invented in the west as Catholic and Protestant each tried to bring the other closer to God, the rack was the most famously effective, but manacles were just as agonizing to their victim and far simpler. But this was only the first level of the suffering that the Oprichniki had created.

The man was stripped to his waist. His head hung limply backwards, but occasionally he tried to raise it. This, and the alternating groans and screams that emanated from his throat, told me that he was still alive. More importantly, they told the Oprichniki that he was alive. In what could be considered a twisted sexual parallel, the vampires' pleasure came not simply from the sensations which they experienced, but in the knowledge of the pain that they bestowed upon others.

Pressed close in around his body stood three of the four Oprichniki. They too were naked from the waist up—their appetites evidently requiring satisfaction through touch as well as taste. The three were Pyetr, Foma and Iakov

TWELVE

Zevedayinich. Iuda stood a little way back from the action. He remained fully clothed and I saw on his bloodstained lips a sadistic smile that both shared and despised the gratification of the other three.

Iuda spoke. I could not understand what he said, but I could make out that it was addressed to Foma, and it had the tone more of a suggestion than of an instruction. Foma turned his head towards Iuda and grinned in pleasurable agreement. The other two watched Foma as he raised the palm of the man's right hand to his mouth and bit hard into the fleshly part at the base of the middle finger. The man screamed, not the shrill cry of shock that I would have expected, but the low weary howl of a man for whom pain has all too quickly become the only sensation he has left in his existence. The other wounds that I could see on his body told me that the Oprichniki had already indulged their appetites to quite an extent that night.

Foma pulled his mouth away from the hand and swallowed what he had bitten off displaying the same extravagance with which I might swallow an oyster in front of a charming dinner companion whom I wanted to impress. As he did so, the others all let out sounds that I took to be not part of their language but simple vocalizations of appreciation that could be understood in any tongue.

Foma moved to the next finger and took a deeper bite. This time, as well as the farmer's scream, I heard the crackle of splintering bones. The tip of his finger dropped to the floor, but Foma still managed to get a mouthful. He spat something out across the room, which bounced off a wall and fell to the ground. I could not see what it was, but it must have been in some way significant, since it got a tremendous laugh from the others; tremendous, but not hearty. It was the same laugh I had heard from them when I had first met them, the dirty laugh of those who want to be seen to laugh by those around them. Iuda joined in convincingly, but it was obvious that he mocked as much as he partook. Even later, when I discovered what Foma had spat out, it was difficult to fathom where the humour lay.

It is not easy to say now, nor was it then, why I stayed to watch the scene played out before me. But it was inevitable that I would. The fact that the farmer had just lost two of his fingers took me back to that prison in Silistria, three years before, but the strongest resonance was not with the farmer, not sharing his pain, but with those who stood and watched—with myself today, peering through a crack in the door and, worst of all, with Iuda who watched, smiled and, like me, did nothing.

The Turks had known that at least one of the seven of us was a Russian spy. They could just have killed us all, but they wanted information, and they could only get that if they could identify which one of us to concentrate their efforts on. They had kept us awake until late into the night, asking us questions, laughing at us, jeering at us. Eventually they lined us up; made us face the wall. I was in fifth place. Then they took the first man. I heard a strange crunching sound that I could not interpret, accompanied by a scream. It was the same sound I had just heard as Foma's teeth splintered the bones of the farmer's finger.

I had still not been able to see what was happening as our Turkish captors worked their way along the line, but each time I heard the same unfathomable combination of sounds. Then they came to me. I saw the blood on the table—not a huge amount, but four small, separate stains. When they grabbed my wrist and held it down I thought I understood what was happening—that they were going to sever my whole hand. I tried to pull away, but couldn't. The blade was a mundane thing, not one of the *palas* with which they fought, just a meat cleaver they had found somewhere. They tucked my other fingers in and the blade fell. I don't know whether I screamed. I don't really remember the pain, but I do remember feeling the blood that ran from the stump of my little finger dripping off my other fingers to the floor.

Those of us who had already visited the table were returned to position, but facing away from the wall. Once the element of surprise had been lost, it was far better torture for us to see what was going on. They explained to us it would stop if the spy confessed; that it would end not only his suffering, but all of our suffering. I was unmoved. I had little concern for my fellow captives—Bulgarians who had been happy to fight with the Ottomans against fellow Slavs—and I had no doubt as to just how permanently our captors would end our suffering.

TWELVE

Then they went round again. The fear in all of us was greater this time. Even though I cannot remember the pain, I can remember being afraid of it. The sound was the same as before as each man in turn lost a second finger. Most of the men against the wall turned their heads away to avoid seeing what was happening—what would soon happen to them—but I did not. I stared at the table, saw the cleaver fall each time, saw the agonized face of the victim and saw the indifferent faces of the Turks as they brushed the severed finger aside. I don't know why I looked; perhaps it was the hope that I would become numb to it by the time my next turn came. It worked, but it worked too well. The numbness persisted—increased over the years. It was that numbness, I realized, that meant I was now able to—needed to—stand at that barn door near Kurilovo and watch the torture that went on within.

In Silistria, only one of the other victims had looked on as I did. He was the second in the row—a young man, scarcely more than a boy. He too did not scream as the blade came down and took away his finger. When they came to me, I certainly did scream. I have no idea why the second cut hurt so much more than the first. Perhaps it was the anticipation. I was not at the point of confessing, but I wondered how many fingers I would be prepared to lose before I did give in. I could face, I thought, the loss of my whole left hand, but how many fingers of my right could I lose before I became useless as a man? But why did I care?—they would kill me anyway.

Again I felt my own blood running over my other fingers. It would not be fast, but the blood loss itself would eventually be enough to kill me. One of the soldiers indicated that we should hold our hands above our heads. It reduced the flow, but it was not an act of kindness. They had done this before, and this was experience showing. Raising our arms to reduce the blood flow prolonged our lives, and added a new, throbbing pain as our numbed arms began to ache. I felt the warm trickle of my own blood now running down my arm and on to my chest.

It was after they had moved on to third fingers that the confession came—but not from me. It was from someone who, to all my knowledge, had no connection with the Turks' enemies at all: the boy who was second in the line, who had not turned his face away from the table. There had been silence after he spoke; relief on the faces of the captives—even of the boy—satisfaction on those of the captors. I remember hearing the quiet chirping of birds through the high window. We had been in the prison all night.

The odd thing was that the boy had confessed just after, not before, it had been his turn to have his third finger severed. Had the pain broken his spirit? It didn't look like it. I could only guess that he had done what I would not have dreamed of—he had decided to spare the rest of us. If that was the case then he was a noble fool, but a fool nonetheless. If he'd made up the fact that he was a spy—as he surely had, unless there were two of us—then they would soon work it out. And then the torture would resume for the rest of us—perhaps some new, even worse torture. Only at that point was I truly tempted to confess, but even then I did not.

All seven of us were led out into the early, predawn light, to be thrown back into the two small cells where we had been previously kept. It was at that point the boy made a run for it. He was up on to the prison wall in a flash and about to jump over when a shot rang out. I just saw him fall, but then I was off in the other direction. My left hand first stung as it gripped the top of the wall, and then slipped on the greasy blood that still oozed from it. But by then, my right hand had got a grip, and I pulled myself over. The Turks had now realized their mistake in all pursuing the one escapee, and shots whistled over my head, but they were too late. I was lucky to escape the city and lucky not to bleed to death, but I survived. I do not know what happened to the others whose torture I had both witnessed and shared, and at the time I did not care.

Now, staring into a similar scene inside that barn, I did care. But there was nothing I could do. To engage in a fight that pitted the four of them against just me would have ended in such a pointless death as to be immoral. I knew that I had to wait for better chances—to wait for the Oprichniki to become separated and to wait for daylight—before I could risk an attack. But the more difficult question was why I stayed to watch. I did not need to see any more to appreciate the vile nature of the Oprichniki, nor to find any aspect of their behaviour which might reveal a weakness in them. Part of what I needed was fuel for my hatred. It was a facet of myself of which I had long been aware. I am, or at least I perceive myself to be, a man of many passions, but all of those passions are difficult to kindle. I arrive at them in small steps, not in giant bounds. I would not go to the trouble of taking a lover, unless that lover was so available that her selection cost me but a few roubles. Moreover, I would not go to the trouble of falling in love unless it was with someone who was already my lover; it was only through the intensity of sex that I had discovered my depth of love for Domnikiia.

And similarly, it was only through the nauseating wrath of seeing what the Oprichniki actually did that I could stoke the fires of loathing enough to know that I would carry to the end my determination to destroy them. Iuda's words to me had struck home. I was a shallow, fickle, comfort-loving man. Desensitized by what had happened in Silistria, and by what I had already seen of the Oprichniki, I had to remain there with my eye glued to what went on within the barn in order to corral the strength and determination that I would later require to defeat the accursed creatures. And yet, though it would give me that determination, would watching also not desensitize me further? The next time—though I prayed to God there would be no next time—I saw such horrors, would I dismiss them as commonplace, needing ever greater depths of corruption to raise my righteous passion? Whatever the risk, I stayed and watched.

Iuda issued another suggestion; this time it was to Iakov Zevedayinich. The vampire knelt before the man's stomach, gazing at it as if preparing to bite. The man already had several wounds to his belly. One on the side was long and deep and still bled profusely. Into this Iakov Zevedayinich swiftly jabbed his fingers, and the man's whole body convulsed with pain. Again a wave of laughter rippled through the Oprichniki. Foma grabbed the man's feet and Pyetr his chest so that he could not move. Iakov Zevedayinich twisted his fingers in the wound once more and this time the man's contortions, though more intense, were absorbed by the two vampires that held him fast.

Iakov Zevedayinich poked the wound again and again, learning from each jab how to make his victim's pain more intense. Each time, he exchanged glances with the other two, seeking their approval and relishing with laughter the approbation that he found. Pyetr called out to Iuda in a tone that might in normal life have said, "Come on in, the water's fine." Iuda strolled over to them. He had in his hand a small stick of wood. He may have picked it off the floor or ripped it from some tree or bush as he passed, but it was long and probing and had a jagged, uneven point. Iuda rammed it into the wound in the man's side and at the same time turned it like a gun worm. The man screamed in agony and Iuda spoke to him in Russian.

"I think your wife enjoyed it more than you when I did that to her."

The man raised his head and attempted to meet Iuda's eyes. Had he the strength, he might have spat at him, but his head merely fell back as the exhaustion of his suffering overcame him.

Foma asked a question that could only be interpreted as "What did you say to him?" Iuda's reply was, I presume, an honest answer to the question. The Oprichniki laughed again that same laugh.

Iuda took a step back and made a further suggestion. This time it was to Pyetr. I did not need to understand the details of it to comprehend that Pyetr complied readily. Whatever power struggles Dmitry might have perceived within them, it was clear that at this moment Pyetr was utterly subservient to Iuda, as were both of the other surviving Oprichniki. There was no laughter at Iuda's latest idea, but an intake of breath and an anticipatory licking of lips on the part of the two vampires who were not to be its implementers.

Pyetr opened his mouth wide and put his lips to the man's chest, totally encompassing his nipple. He left himself there for a moment mimicking a suckling baby and glancing slyly sideways at Iuda. Iuda smiled an appreciative smile and the other two exchanged their own glances, communicating solely in appreciative grunts, like a couple of dogs who knew that their master was about to feed them a titbit.

With a cocky smile, Iuda uttered a single word of encouragement to Pyetr to which Pyetr's response was simply to bring his jaws together and then to pull back, shearing away the flesh that he had clasped between his teeth. The man's scream, momentarily so loud, exhausted him, fading into a croaking plea. Pyetr lay on his back on the floor of the barn with his hands behind his head, chewing contentedly at the flesh between his lips. It was as a red rag to the other two.

They pounced upon the farmer and began tasting the blood of old wounds and creating new ones with their sharp, probing teeth. Iuda's voice became firmer and his utterances became orders rather than ideas. He took a step forward and jerked Foma away. On seeing this, Iakov Zevedayinich meekly stepped away from the farmer as well, but it was too late—too late for them, but nothing like soon enough for their victim, or indeed for me. The farmer was dead, whether through the accumulation of unendurable pain or the happy accident of a thoughtless bite at a vital artery, it did not matter. He was released to join his so recently departed wife.

I slipped back into the surrounding woodland just in time to see the farmer's body ejected from the barn to lie alongside his wife in the snow. Crouched behind a tree in the freezing cold, I waited. If all four chose to sleep there through the following day, then it would be their last sleep. In daylight I had no qualms about confronting them and disposing of each as I had done others before them. But I would not go and face them in the dark. The fear that I had seen in Dmitry now became a solid presence in my chest. It stifled me and stiffened me, making me incapable of either advance or flight. It was as a conduit for the cold around me to enter my heart and freeze every sensation, every concept except for the most volatile instinct of all—that of self-preservation.

But at least the cold and the terror combined had one positive side effect—they kept me awake. Much as I would have liked to surrender to oblivion as I stood sentinel outside that barn, I could not. I waited and I wondered, thinking of all that had taken place since I had first met the Oprichniki, thinking of my memories, both happy and sad, of Vadim and Maks, thinking of Marfa and Dmitry Alekseevich, and thinking most of all of Domnikiia. The most ridiculous thing was the way that I attempted to combine my thoughts of those last three together—to see Dmitry playing happily with Domnikiia and to see the youthful Domnikiia chatting carelessly with the wise Marfa. I did not want them to merge. I did not want a single creature with the best aspects of both any more than I wanted a single great city of Russia, combining all that was fine in both Petersburg and Moscow. The result would be nothing—a synthetic perfection that could appeal only to the blandest of palates. I would enjoy it no more than if I were to take half a glass of red wine and another half of white and mix them together to produce the ideal beverage. My task was not only to keep them separate, but also to keep them balanced—to ensure that neither bottle became empty and also that neither came to taste so good to me that I would forget the other.

I may not have been at my most lucid, but at least I was wakeful when, some hours after their hideous feast, Iuda and Foma emerged from the barn. At the roadside they exchanged a few words and then Foma headed south while Iuda turned north. Foma's journey south would not have taken him far. He would soon hit the main road that could take him either east to Serpukhov or west to Mozhaysk. The latter seemed more likely. That would take him back to the path along which Bonaparte was retreating. As for Iuda's course, there was only one major city to the north.

I waited. There were good reasons for me not to rush in and surprise the two remaining vampires in the barn. One was that Iuda and Foma might yet return. The other was that, under the veil of night, even two Oprichniki might prove to be able opponents. I knew that I should wait—wait until midday when they would both be at the nadir of their consciousness and would be able to offer no opposition to the wooden stakes that pierced their chests. But in their consciousness lay the only satisfaction I could derive from their deaths. I had seen that they loved to keep their victims alive—that their only pleasure came in the pain of others. My reasoning went beyond that. I wanted them to suffer, but moreover I cherished a desire for them to know why they died, and at whose hand. In all honesty, I felt the same desire in myself. To perceive and comprehend the moment of one's death must be the final act of understanding, be the perception good or ill. I had failed to be present at the moment of Maks' death and before that, at my father's. I did not want to miss the occasion of my own mortality, nor did I see why these two vampires should miss theirs. Thus, even if it had not been to punish them, I would have wanted them to be sentient of their own deaths. It was merely that that was how I felt it ought to be.

TWELVE

Hence it was not long before dawn, but most certainly before it, that, to the sound of the first birds welcoming the new day, I crept back up to the barn and looked inside once more.

It was empty. I slipped inside. Two lanterns, hung from beams in the ceiling, lit the space within. The rope by which I had earlier seen the farmer suspended was still there, both ends roughly severed where his body had been cut down. Beneath it, the ground was stained with blood; two patches, side by side—one for the man, one for his wife. There was little else. In one corner was a collection of farm tools, and near to them an overturned manger, not big enough to hide a man. A ladder led up to the hayloft. There was no sign of any Oprichniki, not even of their coffins.

Above me I heard the sound of rats scuttling across the hayloft—their tiny claws clattering and their tails slithering over the wooden floorboards as they either scoured for food or clambered to see if I was any threat to them. Or was it rats? Was it a different breed of vermin? The hayloft provided a low flat ceiling for about a third of the length of the barn. From it sprouted a thick beam that ran across to the far wall. This was the beam from which the rope still hung. Smaller shafts sprung outwards from the central beam to support the walls and upwards at angles to hold up the roof.

I walked backwards to the far end of the barn, keeping my eyes on the hayloft. As I moved, I heard the sound of their movement. When I stopped, they stopped. I could not see them, but I knew that Pyetr and Iakov Zevedayinich were up there. Then, between two bales of hay, I saw the glint of a pair of gleaming dark eyes. I fixed my gaze on the eyes and began to approach. They made no move, nor any indication that they knew I was looking at them. My hope was to get back underneath the hayloft, directly under whichever of the Oprichniki those eyes belonged to and to stab at him upwards from below. I knew that I could not kill them that way, but I had seen how disabling the wound to Iuda had been the night before and I hoped it would give me enough of an advantage to move in for the kill. I glanced occasionally toward the ladder and along the edge of the hayloft. There was a second vampire up there as well, and I did not want my attack on one to leave me vulnerable to the other.

With a start, I felt something land on my cheek. I brushed it away and looking at my hand saw that it was a spider, curled up into a defensive ball. I glanced upwards to where it had fallen from and came face to face with Iakov Zevedayinich. He himself was perched much like a spider, his limbs spread across the oak roof beams without any visible means of purchase. It was the same climbing skill that I had seen Foma display once in Moscow. Iakov Zevedayinich dropped down towards me from the ceiling, and though I had enough warning to take a step back, he still knocked me to the ground.

The vampire was immediately looming over me, ready for the kill. Over his shoulder I saw Pyetr emerging from the hayloft along the central beam, managing to crawl on all fours along a path no wider than his hand. I slashed wildly at Iakov Zevedayinich with my sword and he held back, giving me a chance to get to my feet. I swung the sabre sharply back and forth in front of me, aiming for his neck. On one stroke, I felt a tiny impediment as the sharp tip made contact with his skin. He put his hand to his throat. It was a trivial wound, but enough to make him wary. He backed further away and I looked up to see Pyetr now even closer to me, climbing his way deftly through the web of beams as though he had spun them himself.

I made a few upward jabs at him, but he easily dodged them, emitting a feral snarl. Iakov Zevedayinich made another lunge for me, but I was not so distracted by Pyetr that I could not connect the blade of my sword with the back of his hand. He snatched it back. Pyetr swung down from above, his legs hooked around a beam, and grabbed at my sword, holding the blade tightly with both hands, oblivious to any pain that the action might cause him. I tried to shake the sword free from his grasp, but he held firm. Iakov Zevedayinich approached again, more slowly now, not out of fear, but to savour the moment of my death. With Pyetr holding my sword, I had nothing with which to fend him off. My wooden dagger, though a fine device to despatch the creatures, was no weapon for engaging them in open combat.

I grasped the handle of my sword and lifted my feet, as though trying to drop to my knees. Pyetr managed to sustain my full weight for a fraction of a second, before the sharp blade of my sabre sliced its way out of his grip and I fell to the ground. I lashed out with the sword at Iakov Zevedayinich's ankle and landed a blow which made him leap sideways. Pyetr was still hanging upside down from the beam, examining his injured hands, his head dangling like a ripe plum ready for the harvest. I swung at his neck and only a cry of warning from Iakov Zevedayinich told him to raise his body back up to the roof as my blade whistled inches beneath his head.

Pyetr retreated back across the rafters and I followed, jabbing at him with my sword. Iakov Zevedayinich too had retreated back under the hayloft. I soon discovered why, as a pitchfork from amongst the tools I had noted earlier flew towards me, flung like a trident from across the barn. I sidestepped and parried it with my sword, but still it caught my upper left arm, tearing through my coat and drawing blood before continuing to the ground, where its tines sunk in deep. The battle was not going my way and I decided now was the time for departure. I raced to the door, but Iakov Zevedayinich beat me to it. He now held a scythe in his hands and swept it in front of him, keeping me away from both himself and the exit. With a leering smile he slid the bolt across the door. It was not a serious impediment, but it would delay me.

"Just like you locked Ioann in," he said, still smiling.

Behind me I heard a thud which I took to be Pyetr dropping to the floor of the barn. With the two of them now on my level and with Iakov Zevedayinich armed, the fight was most definitely going away from me. Iakov Zevedayinich was the closer of the two and I knew he had to be removed from the picture before Pyetr could take the few steps needed to reach me. Despite all that I knew of the inefficacy of the traditional use of the sword against these creatures, years of training and experience had built up in me so strongly as to make it almost an instinct. I attacked Iakov Zevedayinich as though he were a mortal man.

As he swung at me again with the scythe, I took a step back. He followed my movement and became slightly off balance. I grabbed hold of the shaft of the scythe and pulled him closer towards me and towards my sword, wincing even as I did at the pain it caused to my wounded arm. In fear, he let go of the scythe, and took a step away from me. The door was at his back and he could go no further. At that moment I lunged and the tip of my sabre pierced his chest, went through his heart, out of his back and through the wooden door behind him. So great was the force of my thrust that the blade continued, stopping only when the guard came to his chest. I let go the sword and took a step away. Any human would have died in an instant, his heart rupturing as the blade penetrated it, and with its rupture would come the withdrawal of that force which supplied blood so vitally to the body. But vampires had different means of supplying their bodies with blood and had no need—in any sense—for a heart. I heard Pyetr's laughter behind me, and a broad grin spread across Iakov Zevedayinich's brutal face.

"You should stick to fighting against men," said Pyetr, mockingly. "You'd be good at that."

Iakov Zevedayinich prepared to take a step forward to resume the attack, but found that he could not. Although my sword had done him no serious injury, it had pinned him to the door like a butterfly in a collector's case. He put his hands to the handle of the sword and tried to pull it out, but he had no leverage. Pyetr's laughter ceased.

I turned to face Pyetr, drawing my only remaining weapon—my wooden dagger. Pyetr backed away in what struck me as unnecessary fear, but I took full advantage of it. I began to run towards him, and he backed away faster. Behind him, the handle of the embedded pitchfork jutted out of the ground towards him like a spear. It would be a lucky chance if he fell on it at the correct angle.

In the event, Iakov Zevedayinich foresaw the danger and shouted to his comrade. Just in time, Pyetr twisted his body to one side and avoided falling on to the handle of the pitchfork. Instead he fell on to his back on the ground beside it. I wrenched the pitchfork out of the earth and thrust it back down on to Pyetr's throat. His flesh offered only a momentary resistance before yielding deliciously to my pressure and allowing the sharp points to penetrate through it and deep into the ground beneath. It did not kill him; it didn't even appear to hurt him, despite the blood that oozed from the punctures in his neck, but it kept him from moving. His body writhed and arched as he tried to get free and he could even raise his head a little, his pierced neck sliding up and down the tines of the pitchfork, but unable to escape them.

Now I had two captive Oprichniki in my collection, but I needed only one. I turned back to Iakov Zevedayinich. He was still struggling to free himself from the door. It would take a few minutes, but he would have worked himself free. I kicked at the door's bolt with the sole of my booted foot. It gave a little, but not completely. Iakov Zevedayinich stretched out towards me with flailing arms, but could not reach me. At a second blow, the metal bolt splintered away from the wood and the door swung open into the early daylight outside, taking the vampire with it like a jacket hung on a peg—like Vadim Fyodorovich hung on a wall.

Only then did Iakov Zevedayinich realize the implication. His scream was not of pain, but of fear, and it was soon cut short by the sound of an explosion as the sunlight hit his body. It was not the tight, sharp explosion of a gun or a cannon, but a slower, broader whoosh, as when gunpowder ignites in a bowl. The door opened as far as it would go and then bounced closed again. My sword still remained protruding from the back of the door at the height of a man's chest. Of Iakov Zevedayinich there was no sign, save a few scorched rags drooping from my sword and a slight singeing of the wood, roughly forming the shape of a man.

I turned back to Pyetr. He was still struggling to try to free himself. I pulled the pitchfork out of him and held it to his face. He crawled backwards away from me with a crab-like motion, heading towards the door as if it could bring him some escape. I thrust the fork back into him—this time through his shoulder, laying in with all my weight so as to pierce the tough bone and sinew—and he was immobile once more. He stared at me with a face that revealed no fear; only hatred and contempt.

"More Russian hospitality?" he sneered. "You invite people into your country and then kill them off one by one."

"We may have invited people," I replied, "but that's not what we got."

I glanced around the barn and saw the two pools of blood, reminding me of what I had witnessed just hours before. Part of me wanted to forget it, but a stronger part had to know more.

"I watched you," I said, my voice scarcely above a whisper, "watched what you did to that man. I saw the body of that woman. Animals eat, but that was. . . . *What* was that? *Why* was that?"

Pyetr smiled. "You really want to know?"

"No," I lied instinctively. "But tell me anyway."

Within the constraints of the metal shafts that pierced his shoulder, Pyetr adjusted his posture, as if settling in to tell a long story.

"We each start off just by drinking," he began, "and that in itself is a pleasure, when one is young at least, and inexperienced. But as we grow older, merely drinking becomes dull, so we eat. Then eating becomes what drinking was, so we play. Then playing becomes as dull as eating, so we torture. Then to satisfy, torture becomes worse torture. The older the vampire, the further he has to go."

They were, it seemed then, like me. I needed ever more intensity of experience to raise my anger; they needed it for their pleasure.

"Your beloved Zmyeevich is pretty old," I said. "He must do . . ." I dared not even imagine what he must do.

"The master is too old. He told me once, he has gone beyond physical pain. There is more pleasure to be had from people's minds. But humans realize that far quicker than we do. It's beyond me. The physical will do for now."

"I'm surprised you have the imagination to find new . . . ideas."

"It can be troublesome." He smiled again. "But Iuda must have been a vampire for a very long time—not as long as the master, for Iuda's interests are still physical, but he has such ideas." He nodded an acknowledgement of the word he had taken from me. "For instance," he went on, smiling more broadly, "had the man not died, we were going to—"

I jogged the handle of the pitchfork. In a human, that slight motion would have sent agonies through his wounded shoulder. For him it meant little, but at least it shut him up. I didn't want to help him indulge in a vicarious pleasure through his retelling, much as—to my shame—I was eager to hear. I moved on to more significant matters.

"Where have Iuda and Foma gone?" I asked.

"Gone to screw your mother," he replied charmingly. I kicked him hard in the armpit, just next to where the pitchfork transfixed him.

"Tell me," I growled, but again he seemed to feel no pain. I had no urgent need for the information. I felt sure that I would be able to track them down and that, even if I didn't, Iuda would not be able to resist the temptation of coming after me once again. I took a step back and picked up my wooden dagger, readying myself to kill the defenceless monster. Outside, the distant sound of a cockerel belatedly heralded the dawn. I turned back to Pyetr and saw that his expression had changed from a look of resigned malevolence to one of utmost fear. It was as though the sound of the cockerel had terrified him. Perhaps it had. It was a signal of the danger that he would have known every morning since he first made the repellent choice to become a vampire.

But it was not the sound—or at least not only the sound—that caused him this new unease. His breathing was short and shallow and he flicked his nervous gaze between me and his right hand, which he had snatched up from the ground in pain. On the ground where his hand had lain, a small patch of sunlight had been allowed in through the door by the damage I had done when I kicked off the bolt. A wisp of smoke arose from the centre of the patch, where a fragment of fingernail was shrivelling to nothing.

I looked at Pyetr's hand. The cuts to his palm where he had grabbed the blade of my sword had already vanished. The nail of his middle finger was missing where the sunlight had hit it. Even as I watched, it began to grow back. Pyetr was now gripped by a fearfulness that I had not seen in any of the Oprichniki before. He tugged his whole body against the pitchfork, trying to get free, and he looked up at me with a meek, frightened anxiety.

I placed my foot on his forearm and pushed it back down towards the ground, forcing his hand back into the patch of sunlight. His scream was high-pitched and continuous. The mild sunlight burnt the flesh of his hand in a way that would require the heat of a fire on human flesh. The skin of his fingers quickly blackened and split open, peeling back and curling like the skin of a rotten apple. Through the splits in the skin oozed red blood and yellow pus, some of which dribbled to the ground, while the rest boiled away into the atmosphere. The stench was nauseating—a mixture of the most pungent mildew and burning human hair. Soon his four fingers and the top half of his hand were stripped of all flesh and all that remained were bones which themselves began to smoulder. The tip of his middle finger caught fire and then fell off on to the ground below. The edge of the beam of light left a neat divide across his hand. All that was in darkness was untouched. The surviving skin ended in a thin black fringe across his palm, where the flesh had begun to burn and then receded into the safety of darkness. From the back of his hand, like a torn glove, hung a large flap of charred skin which had similarly slipped out of the sunlight as it fell away from the bone.

I lifted my foot and he snatched his hand back towards him. His screams stopped, but his breathing was irregular. He breathed out with hard, grating pants, but his in-breaths were short and snatched. He was coping with both pain and fear.

"Where have Iuda and Foma gone?" I asked again, shouting this time. He made no reply. It was hard to tell whether he had even heard my question. I was about to press his arm back into the light when, just as I had glimpsed with his nail, I saw the whole of his hand beginning to regrow. The bone that had fallen from his middle finger had already been replaced and lumps of healthy new flesh were forming before my eyes around each of his fingers. A new layer of skin was smoothly advancing from the undamaged half of his hand. Within five minutes the whole thing would be back to normal. This explained why there were no lacerations on his hands from my sword, and even further, explained why Maks could claim to have severed Andrei's arm when I had subsequently seen Andrei with the full complement of limbs. These creatures were (in this and in other ways) like spiders. The loss of an arm or a leg could be a temporary inconvenience, but they could be sure it would grow back. I shuddered as a thought crossed my mind that made me hope that they *were* merely like spiders. For a vampire to grow back an arm was one thing, but I prayed that the arm, once detached, could not grow back a new body, as is the case with an earthworm or a sorcerer's broomstick. If that were the case then there could still be another Andrei out there to deal with.

To my more immediate ends, however, this was an interesting turn of events. The aim of the torturer is to inflict the greatest pain on his victim whilst doing the least damage—the Turks had taken fingers, not arms or legs. The motivation is not out of any sympathy for the victim, but simply lies in the understanding that, once a body has been damaged too much, it is no longer able to feel pain—or indeed much of anything. But the vampire was a torturer's dream. Continuous pain could be inflicted because the body would be continually refreshed. I could take Pyetr up to the very point of death and then let him revive, only to do the same thing again the next day and the next. It was tempting, but I was not that much a follower of de Sade. I could not be sure it would work, anyway. When I had been tortured, although the physical pain had been excruciating, half of the terror had been in the knowledge that I *would* be maimed, that I would forever be missing those two fingers. Had I known that, whatever the degree of pain, I would still leave with my hand as intact and whole as it had ever been, the physical pain might perhaps have been bearable.

Pyetr did not seem to view it so philosophically. The pain to him was very real. And yet still he had not answered my question. I stamped my foot down on his arm again. The sun had moved a little and so this time the whole of his hand was exposed to the light. He screamed again as the centre of his palm split and peeled open to reveal the roasting flesh beneath. I held it down there until his entire hand was almost gone, and even then, I only let go to alleviate the sickening smell.

"So are you going to tell?" I asked.

He nodded, trying to catch his breath. "Yes," he panted. "Yes."

"Well?"

"They've gone after the French. They're trying to get back home to the Carpathians, but they'll stick with the French as far as they can—for food."

"Both of them?" I asked.

Pyetr nodded. I placed my boot on his arm again, but did not push down.

"So why did I see Iuda heading towards Moscow?"

"I don't know," he replied, trying to shrug his shoulders. I pressed his arm down once more, just briefly letting his raw, bleeding wrist touch the light before releasing him.

"All right," screeched Pyetr. Then he smiled the self-satisfied smile of a man who in death foresees the ultimate retribution that will befall his killer. "He's gone to see your whore. Dominique—that was her name. He's going to make her into one of us. He thinks she is just the sort who could be persuaded. And if not—well, you can look outside if you want to see how much we get out of a single human body. Either way, you won't get to fuck her again." He forced out a laugh that reflected no amusement in him, but which he hoped would contribute to my pain.

I marched purposefully to the door. As I approached it, something glinted at me from the floor. Seeing what it was, I wondered how it might have got there. Then I realized. This was precisely the place where Foma had spat something after biting off the farmer's finger the previous night. I could now see what the thing was that had caused so much mirth amongst the Oprichniki. It was the man's wedding ring.

I continued to the door and flung it open. Behind me I heard the broad, whooshing explosion that had accompanied the destruction of Iakov Zevedayinich. I turned to see no sign of Pyeti but only the pitchfork tottering to the ground now that its support had vanished. A rectangle of light shone through the door casting a shape akin to a coffin around where Pyetr had been lying, the lingering smoke his only memorial.

I wrenched my sword out of the door and set off on my way.

Chapter XXV

MY HORSE WAS STILL IN KURILOVO. THAT WAS ALMOST two versts away. I ran for all I was worth down the snowy road, slipping and stumbling as I went. I paused at the crossroads, exhausted, gasping for breath. The rope still lay coiled around the broken post where I had tied Filipp, but otherwise there was no hint of the previous night's adventures. I carried on, so out of breath that I ran probably slower than I could have walked. When I came to it, the coach still lay overturned in the ditch. The dead horse remained in the road, but the other one was gone, cut free from the wreckage either by some Good Samaritan or by some horse thief.

I carried on to the village. In the street I passed the red-haired man I had spoken to the previous evening. He recognized me and called after me.

"Hey! Was it you who stole Napoleon? Did you see what happened to that coach?"

I didn't pause to answer. I carried on back to the tavern, paid the ostler and, without waiting for change, mounted my horse. It had been almost fifteen minutes since I had left the barn. I spurred the horse into a gallop and allowed myself my first real opportunity to think.

My one hope lay in the fact that Iuda could not travel by day. He had left about three hours before dawn. That could never be sufficient time to reach Moscow. I had eight hours of daylight—slightly less now—to overtake him and get to Domnikiia before he could reawaken into the darkness and reach her. The journey ahead of me was around eighty versts over treacherous icy roads. It was achievable but it would be tight. I would not manage it at all if I killed my horse. I reined him back a little and we continued at a less breakneck speed.

If I did not get to Moscow in time, then my outlook was bleak—that of Domnikiia hopeless. The prospect of her suffering as she died, in the way that I had seen that farmer and his wife die, in the way that I now knew Maks and Vadim and so many others must have died, filled me with a nauseating rage. Were that to happen, then there would never be any peace for me until Iuda was destroyed. I would hunt him across Russia, across Austria, across the whole of the Ottoman empire if need be. I would climb every damned mountain in the Carpathians if I had to, but I would find him and he would die. I would not make him suffer physically too much—that would be to descend to his level—but he would know that it was I who took his life and why it was I who had done it.

I filled my journey with fantasies of discovering him in the dungeon of some mysterious Wallachian mountain castle, perhaps ten or twenty years from now; of pulling back the heavy stone lid of his coffin and raising my lantern to see the still-youthful face of the monster I had been stalking for so many years; of seeing his eyes open wide and peer into my world-weary face; of seeing the look of recognition in those eyes as he saw in me the face of the man he once confronted years before; of the memory returning to him of what he had done to Domnikiia at the very instant my stake plunged into his heart and terminated his putrid existence forever; of seeing his earthly body collapse to dust under the weight of the corruption that it had borne over his long, repellent life.

There was more than self-indulgence in my desire to fill my mind with these thoughts—it was to keep other thoughts out. There was another possibility that Pyetr had mentioned—another side to the coin. Iuda was going to try to persuade Domnikiia to join him. It was a laughable concept, but it struck a cold terror in my heart. Domnikiia was a woman and a vain woman at that. She had already spoken of the delight she thought it would be to live forever. How easy might it be for Iuda to persuade her that her sugar-coated vision of the life of a vampire was close to the truth? What lies would he conjure up to influence her—lies not only about him but about me as well?

But it could not happen. Although she might be romantic and fanciful, Domnikiia was a clever and a good woman. She would never choose such a path, no matter what worm-tongued falsehoods she was spun. And yet if she did, what would I then have to do? My vengeance upon Iuda would remain much the same, but what of my vengeance on Domnikiia? Vengeance it would be, for she would be beyond all hope of salvation. The moment she shared Iuda's blood, her soul would be condemned to hell. Whether it went there immediately or with the ultimate destruction of her mortal body, I knew not. I knew now many ways that a vampire might be killed. Which, I wondered, would I have to use on my dear, sweet Domnikiia?

I spurred my mount to a fast gallop, expelling from my mind all such thoughts and instead concentrating on riding across the slippery ground. The movement caused a sharp pain in my arm where the pitchfork had hit me. I had forgotten about it until then, and now I dared not look to see how serious it was, for fear that it would delay my journey. My arm was still strong enough for me to hold the reins—that was all I needed for the moment. We galloped on for several minutes through the chill winter air, my heart racing with the excitement of the ride. I cast my mind back to the more trouble-free days of my youth when I rode freely across the hills and fields around Petersburg, days when the name Bonaparte was rarely heard outside Corsica—never outside France. Could I really blame all of my present misfortunes on that one man? He had not transformed the Oprichniki into vampires, nor had he asked them to come to Moscow. The former was down to Satan and the latter to Dmitry, and with the willing agreement of the rest of us. And yet it had to be remembered that the Oprichniki, for all their ability to kill, were at heart scavengers, not predators. To flourish they had to exist in a matrix of death and fear. To be sure, at times of peace they might eke out an existence in Wallachia, killing just enough peasants to survive without drawing too much attention to themselves, but in war, where death was commonplace, they could indulge their most carnal of inclinations. War created an atmosphere in which all other evils could thrive, appearing trivial by comparison to the daily toll of death and carnage. A war is a fine place to hide any crime—another tree in the forest—and who could be so trite as to focus on perhaps a hundred deaths caused by the Oprichniki compared with the hundreds of thousands killed on both sides in the war? Bonaparte was not just responsible for those hundreds of thousands, but also for belittling every other death and every other tragedy that occurred in Russia, if not the whole of Europe throughout his era. When so many die as heroes, who remembers those who die frightened and alone?

TWELVE

I changed horses at Troitskoye. They did not have one shod and I had to wait almost half an hour before I could set out again. It was tempting to continue on my old horse, but he was tired and could barely manage a trot. Once I got going again, the delay was soon made up. Even so, the sun was already setting as I rode into the outskirts of Moscow. I continued across the city and tied up my horse just a little way from Degtyarny Lane, so as to approach on foot.

I banged impatiently on the door. It was Pyetr Pyetrovich who opened it. He ran his eyes up and down my bedraggled body, curling his lip with a degree of disdain that hardly befitted a man of his profession.

"Mademoiselle Dominique is not available tonight," he told me before I had even uttered a word.

"Who is she with?" I asked.

"By 'not available,' I mean she is not here. You should try again tomorrow."

"Where is she?"

"I have no idea. I should have thought *you* would be the man to know where she goes on an evening." I could have forced my way past him and rushed into Domnikiia's room, but there was no reason to doubt that he was telling the truth. Whenever previously Domnikiia had been busy with a client, he had notified me outright, taking pleasure in the fact that I had to share.

"Is Margarita around?" I asked, hoping she might have some better idea of where Domnikiia had gone. Pyetr Pyetrovich's attitude changed slightly. I was no longer a possible threat to his livelihood—the single-minded suitor who might take away his star attraction—I was once more merely a customer like any other, prepared to accept in Margarita an alternative when my first choice was unavailable.

"Ah, I see sir has an eye for the brunette. But I'm afraid that Margarita too is unavailable. Raisa is free, but please, captain, do go and change your clothes first. And perhaps a wash as well? If not for the sake of Raisa, then at least for the other customers."

I smiled a quiet, contemplative smile which I hoped gave the impression that I was about to break his nose, then turned and walked away. I had no idea of where I might start to look for Domnikiia. There was a slight chance that she had gone to find me at the inn, but she had no reason to expect me back in Moscow so soon, and even if she went there, she would not wait once she had discovered my absence. My best hope was to wait and watch the brothel. That was the one place that I could be sure Domnikiia would return, and also the place where Iuda would eventually show up. Given that Iuda could not travel by day and assuming that, when he did travel, his progress was at best at the same rate as mine, then I could expect him in about five hours, some time towards ten o'clock.

I glanced around the square for somewhere to wait, watch and hide. Several of the houses opposite the brothel appeared to have not yet been reoccupied. It was no effort at all to break into one—that had already been done weeks before by the pillaging French—and I went upstairs to get a better view over the square. As I climbed the staircase of the dark, abandoned house, I could not help but cast my mind back those few days to the house where I had found so many dishonoured corpses—Russian, French and others, Vadim among them—part eaten and then discarded like old chicken bones. But here there was no stench, no sound of rats. This was just an empty, looted house; one of the fortunate ones that had survived the fires.

In an upstairs front room, I was even lucky enough to find a little furniture. I sat on an old dining chair and watched the square below, in expectation of a long vigil.

I was taken by surprise. Scarcely had I sat down when across the square I saw a lamp come to light in Domnikiia's room. I took out my spyglass and focused it on the uncurtained window. Domnikiia and her client came into view. Evidently Pyetr Pyetrovich had lied to me. She was naked and had wrapped herself around the man. As he walked across the room towards the window, her arms held him tightly round the neck and her legs clasped him about the waist so that he could move freely as he held her whole weight. Her head swivelled from side to side, obscuring his face from view as she kissed his lips. Her shimmering, dark hair hung down over her neck and then disappeared over her shoulder, between their two bodies, leaving her elegant white back in plain view.

Less than twenty-four hours before, I had been the clandestine observer of another scene from which others might perhaps have turned away. Then I had stayed to watch out of the memories of how I myself had suffered, despite the nausea that rose within me. Now my motivations were far more mixed. Certainly I had to keep watch over Domnikiia to ensure her safety, but many men would have chosen to turn away on seeing the woman they loved in the arms of another. Although I had long been reconciled to the fact of Domnikiia's profession and though I truly believed that these men meant nothing to her, surely I should still have looked away and attempted to quell the jealous monster rising within me.

Instead, I felt only excitement, not just at seeing two other human beings engaged in so intimate and private an activity, but specifically to see the woman that I loved behave so utterly unlike how I had been brought up to believe a woman should—so much like a base animal. It pleased me also to see the man so deceived, to see him so overpowered by his own primitive instincts and to know that while for a moment he had all that he could care to have, in the long run he had nothing. It was I that had Domnikiia's heart, Domnikiia's love and Domnikiia's soul. Though they might queue for her all the way around Saint Vasily's and back, I would still mean more to her by a gentle touch of my hand than they with all their sweaty exertion ever could.

The man was already naked to the waist, save for a bandage on his arm. As he walked across the room with Domnikiia wrapped around him, he slipped his hands under her buttocks to support her. Together they came all the way over to the window, and the flesh of her back was pressed smooth and flat against the glass panes as he leaned against her. They pulled away from the window slightly and stood for a few moments, their mouths inseparable, his fingers meandering up and down her spine. Then he stepped back and Domnikiia dropped to her feet, looking upwards towards his face, which I could now see for the first time.

It was Iuda. He stared down towards Domnikiia with a look of dreadful tenderness and bent his head lower as though to kiss her, but I knew instantly what was his real intent. I leapt to my feet, but there was nothing I could do. If I shouted, I would not be heard, and even if I was, it would not stop him. It would take over a minute for me to go back down the stairs, cross the square and get to them. Had I brought a gun, I could have shot at him, but even that would have had no effect on a vampire.

I could only stand and watch as he parted his lips and prepared to plant them delicately on Domnikiia's throat. He brushed her long hair back over her shoulder and pulled it to one side with his hand, so as to make the flesh of her neck clear for his bite and also—or so it seemed to me in my numbed terror—to make it easier for me to see. His lips descended and Domnikiia's head arched back slightly as he made contact with her. Over her shoulder I could see only his devilish, grey eyes staring out into the night towards me. He did not drink for long, but soon raised his head and took a step back from her. She sat back unsteadily on the windowsill, her hands reaching out sideways for support. Her head was raised to look into his face, but I was unable to see whether the expression on hers was of terror, submission or ecstasy.

Iuda drew his knife from his pocket. My sudden, laughable fear that he might harm her was immediately quashed by the knowledge of the harm he had already done. He put the twin points of the knife to his own chest and, briefly closing his eyes, drew them across, etching two neat, red lines below his right nipple. Drizzles of blood seeped out of the wounds and ran down his firm stomach. Domnikiia rose to her feet and approached him, bending her knees slightly to lower her mouth to the level of the lesions. She placed one hand on his left breast and the other on his shoulder, pulling herself towards him as she pressed her mouth against his chest and, only moments after he had drunk hers, drank his blood.

Iuda placed his hand on the back of Domnikiia's head, pressing her into him. He closed his eyes and raised his head to the ceiling with a smile of sexual elation on his lips. Then his head dropped and his eyes flashed open, gleaming victoriously out of the window and across the square.

And though the room I was in was in utter darkness, and though there was no way that Iuda could be aware that I was there, I knew he was staring directly at me.

Chapter XXVI

I FELL BACK INTO MY CHAIR. I HAD BEEN WARNED WHAT IUDA had intended to do. I had flown from Kurilovo to Moscow to make it in time. I had stood at the very door of the building in which it had happened. And yet I had quietly and without intervention watched as Iuda had done everything I had feared, as he had destroyed yet another creature that was dear to me, as he had taken first Domnikiia's life and then her soul.

I dashed from the building and across the square towards the brothel. Halfway across, I glanced up at Domnikiia's window. Light still shone from it, but inside I could see no sign of either Domnikiia or Iuda. Even as I watched, the light was extinguished. I paused. If I went into the brothel, there was nothing that I could do. I was in no state to kill. If I went in there, I would be easy prey to Iuda and even to . . . I could not face thinking about it. I could not face anything. I turned and fled into the dark city streets. I would kill her tomorrow, and let her live tonight.

I do not know where I wandered that night. Every waking nightmare I had experienced on my journey during the day had come true. I felt a strange sense that Iuda had cheated. I had carefully worked out that he could not be in Moscow for several hours—certainly that he could not have arrived before I did. And therefore, if he could not have done so, it followed that he did not do so. Hence he had not just intermingled his blood with Domnikiia's and thereby transformed her into a creature as hellish as himself. It was an argument of perfect logic, except that I had witnessed the occurrence which I had just concluded could not have occurred. Domnikiia had become a vampire, and no amount of appealing to the gods of reason was going to change that.

And after all, it took only a little imagination to come up with a dozen ways in which Iuda could have made it to Moscow before me. How could I apply any physical laws to such a creature? By some legends, he could transform himself into a bat. How fast can a bat fly? It doesn't matter; a vampire in bat form may travel much faster. He could have reduced himself in size to some minute homunculus and been carried to Moscow in my own saddlebag. Preposterous? Who was I to say? Moreover, it did not matter. Somehow, Iuda had got to Moscow. In some way, it had been possible. I had smugly calculated that he could not make it, but I had observed rules to which Iuda had no need to conform. It was like playing chess against an opponent who could suddenly announce that his queen can move in a way that I had never been taught.

Even to invoke the supernatural was unnecessary. All Iuda had needed was another coach and a human driver. He could lie in the back, slumbering in his coffin, protected from the daylight by blackened windows, while his accomplice drove him pell-mell to his rendezvous with Domnikiia. I had already suspected that he might have some human servant, who could perform those daylight tasks that he could not.

There was no need to choose the correct explanation. The problem was that I had not considered the possibilities earlier. If I had not been so arrogant in my belief that I had beaten Iuda, then I could have stopped what had happened. I was horrified by my own stupidity.

But the real horror came in knowing that there had been no coercion on Iuda's part. Domnikiia had willingly done what she did. She did not love me, or God, or even life enough to resist the temptation offered to her of the prospect of eternity, even if that eternity came through eternal damnation. She knew that the Oprichniki were vampires—I had told her. She knew that they were evil. All the times that we had spoken of it—when she had said that living forever was just a fantasy, when we had laughed together at Iuda's pompous letter—each time she had been hiding something away from me, some secret notion that in reality Iuda was right and I was wrong.

It was that betrayal that was so hurtful to me. If it had been some stranger who had chosen the path Domnikiia had taken, or even someone I knew and even loved, but whom I didn't expect to love me, then it would have been different. I would have felt some passing sorrow that the person was so foolish or so corrupt as to want to become a vampire, but that very revelation of their true nature would obliterate all genuine sympathy. Just as

Iuda had said the desire to be a vampire was the only qualification required to become one, so that desire is also a sufficient disqualification from any expectation of the love of the rest of humanity. The convicted murderer cannot expect to be pitied for being what he is, except perhaps by his mother. Even then, is she not asking herself the question, how am I to blame? And so the sorrow I felt was not really directed towards Domnikiia. It was for myself that I wept. As in so many circumstances, my own self-interest was the matter at the front of my mind. It was *I* who had been betrayed. Domnikiia had chosen Iuda over *me*. *I* had failed to do what I could to prevent it. It was vanity, pure and simple. My pain came from my humiliation and from Iuda's ascendancy. Domnikiia was part of the mechanism of it all, but she was not the beginning or the end of my emotions.

And yet none of that was true. It all hinged on the fact that Domnikiia could not be worthy of my sympathy and therefore did not have my sympathy and therefore any sorrow which I felt could not be for her. But it was for her that I felt. I knew her. I knew that her decision must have been some tiny aberration and that somehow the one fragment of her mind that whispered "yes" had spoken louder than the thousands which had screamed "no." Those thousands were now silenced forever, I knew for sure. I knew because I had stared into the eyes of Matfei and Pyetr and Iuda and others and seen how little was left of them. It had been one, tiny, vociferous part of my mind that had originally persuaded me to visit Domnikiia for that first time, a year ago. The other voices that in unison shouted "Marfa" had been drowned out then, and by now had been brought round in their way of thinking. From then on, until now, no part of me had seen my relationship with Domnikiia as anything but good and right. Was that how Domnikiia now felt about her newfound state? Did that one taste of Iuda's blood persuade her instantly and completely of the joy of the existence ahead of her, much as my first taste of her flesh had persuaded me?

It was a dangerous path to follow. I might allow myself during that night the indulgence of thinking fondly of Domnikiia and of looking for reasons not to judge her, but in the light of tomorrow I knew that she had to die and that I must be the one to kill her. Hard as it had been to drive out all sympathy for Maks when I had found out he was a spy, it would be so much harder for me to steel my heart enough to plunge a wooden shaft into Domnikiia's own heart—a heart that had so capriciously turned against me. True, a vampire is infinitely more deserving of death than a French spy, but then my love for Domnikiia was infinitely greater than my love for Maks. Not greater—different. Subsequently I had harboured, and still did, doubts as to whether the way I had treated Maks was right. Days, months and years after tomorrow I would wonder whether I had been right to kill Domnikiia. That was why tonight was a time to build up my hatred, enough to ensure that when the moment came, it would be the moment of least indecision. Once I had destroyed her then I could lie back and bathe in the luxury of doubt. It would be too late then to do anything more than to regret.

I found myself back in the churchyard in Kitay Gorod where Dmitry and I had stayed so briefly with Boris Mihailovich and Natalia Borisovna. I was sitting on the ground, the dampness of the snow seeping into me, with my back against a gravestone. I could not remember arriving there or how long I had been there. I was certain I had not been asleep and yet somehow the whole night had passed. The eastern sky had imperceptibly transformed from starry black to a dark, glowering blue, noticed only by me and by the waking birds who began to hail the rising sun. This time, my nightmare did not end as the birds sang to the dawn. It became worse. The horrors I had seen in the night were merely an overture to the horrors that the day would bring. I was going to kill Domnikiia. It was a horror made so much more dreadful in that I would not merely be an observer, but a participant. I could back away at any point and the horror would go away, only to be succeeded by the unthinkable prospect that she would live on. The price of my inaction of the previous night would be paid in the action of today.

But the day was long. There was no reason for me to go now, just as the sun rose. Yesterday I had had eight hours of daylight in which to race from Kurilovo to Moscow in order to save Domnikiia. I had failed. Today I had the same amount of daylight, and all I had to do was wander along a few Moscow streets, climb into a room and embed a wooden blade in a heart that was already dead. I could wait until lunchtime before I set out, complete the task, and still have most of the afternoon to myself.

I set off immediately. Domnikiia may not have been in any state to appreciate her hellish existence, but out of any love that remained in me for her, it was my duty to end that existence without a moment of undue delay. I scooped up a handful of snow to rub into my face, then noticed that it was stained red. All around me the snow was bloodstained. It was my own blood. The wound to my arm had reopened at some point during the night and had marked the snow beside me. I moved away to find some cleaner snow and bathed my face in it. I was cold enough already, but the icy contact refreshed and awakened me. I took a mouthful of the snow and let it melt on my tongue. Then I set out to do what I had to do.

I was scarcely out of the churchyard when my conviction failed me once again. I set off not towards Degtyarny Lane, nor away from it, but instead I followed a path that seemed simply to circle it, as if I were trying to trick myself into arriving there. My orbit was neither circular nor, like a comet, elliptical, but spiral like a meteor. Each turn I made took me closer to Domnikiia, but I never headed directly towards her. Just as when I had first arrived back in Moscow, after Smolensk, I was tricking myself into falling upon the brothel as if unintentionally. Then it was so that the thief of my desire could slip past the sentry of what I knew was right and wrong. Now my morality had to follow a path that was unnoticed by my sentiment.

Before too long, I was standing beneath her window once again. The ground-floor window below hers opened directly into the salon. It was easy enough to slip the catch and climb into a room in which but a few hours later I would have been welcomed through the front door as an honoured guest. The open window lay in front of me and beyond it the stairs that led to Domnikiia's room and hence to Domnikiia herself and so to Domnikiia's death, and now was my chance to leave.

I went in.

The silence and darkness inside were unfamiliar and unsuitable. This room above all in the brothel was where the sales pitch was made. Always before, it had been a happy, bright and noisy place. I had rarely wanted to linger here in the past, having in my mind a specific and singular objective in the room upstairs, and so the shopfront of the salon had scarcely been a distraction for me, never holding any allure. This time I almost burst into tears at the memory of it. I recalled the anticipation I had always felt on entering; the timid flick of my eyes from one girl to another until they fell upon Domnikiia; sometimes not seeing her there and having to wait until she floated down the stairs to greet me. Even in its darkness the room held those associations. I could hear the light chatter of the girls and the quiet, unnecessarily seductive murmurings of their suitors that had once filled the room. This would be the last time I entered. In its darkened, silent state I would, I feared, remember it always as the anteroom to a very different occasion. In holding back, I was attempting not only to relive happier times, but also to delay my journey upstairs to do what I had to do.

Though it was light outside, the heavy curtains over all the windows kept the inside in a state of muffled dimness. On a table was a candle, which I lit. The looming shadows cast by the flickering flame did little to rekindle in the room the vitality with which I had always associated it. I began to ascend the stairs. The third and the fifth step both squeaked loudly as my foot fell upon them. It was after half past eight, but I knew that no one in the building would yet be preparing to rise. Business hours extended long into the night and so almost the entire morning was spent in sleepy recuperation. The sound of my approach awoke no one.

I crossed the landing and put my hand on the knob of Domnikiia's door. I listened before turning it. Inside I could hear nothing. What I had expected, I did not know. Somewhere in me there had been the urge to knock. This slight pause of apparent politeness served as some form of substitute for that. I turned the knob and entered.

Inside, all was familiar. Across from the door, Domnikiia's dressing table was filled with her cosmetic paraphernalia. To one side was her window; the bright light of day barely glowed through the shutters and thick curtains. Opposite was her bed. I could hear her light breath and saw the blankets rise and fall in time with it. It was a cold night and she was heavily wrapped in bedclothes. Only her beautiful face peeped out. Her long, dark hair, plaited into a ponytail, adorned the pillow beside her.

It would have been easy to just fling open the curtains and shutters, and let the day outside cascade through the window and onto her bed, destroying her bodily remains as I had seen it destroy both Iakov Zevedayinich and Pyetr, but I remembered the look of terror in Pyetr's eyes as the sun had first caught him and the fearful scream that Iakov Zevedayinich had expelled as he had swung out into the light. This, it seemed to me, was the death that they found most terrible and most painful. It was not what I wanted to inflict upon Domnikiia. With those two, and with all the Oprichniki, I had wanted them to be aware of their own deaths—wanted them to understand that I was the cause of their demise. That was why I had gone to the barn before dawn, to be sure that they would still be awake. With Domnikiia, it was just the opposite. There was no need for her to be aware of the brevity of her life as a vampire, or that it was I who had terminated it. Her real life had been ended by Iuda the previous evening. I was simply tidying up the mess he had left.

I placed the candle on the table next to the bed and sat gently beside her. The candlelight illuminated an apple nearby on the table, with two, perhaps three bites taken from it. The flesh had already begun to brown in the time since Domnikiia had eaten. It was surely the last meal she had eaten—the last palatable flesh that she would ever eat. I tried to look at her, but could not. I turned away from her and cradled my head in my hands, silently sobbing. Once again, I attempted to summon up my hatred. It was not a hatred for her, even though it was she who had willingly become this monster. It was a hatred for vampires and specifically a hatred for Iuda. The creature which now lay on the bed behind me was not Domnikiia; it was a creation of Iuda's—a body that he had consumed and then corrupted by making it a continuation of himself. It was as if Moscow had been under the French occupation. The streets and the buildings were beautiful and familiar, but they were nothing without the people who had built them and who lived in them. If destroying the French meant destroying the physical city of Moscow along with them, then amen to it. If destroying the monstrous spirit that lay on the bed beside me meant destroying the beautiful, familiar body that it had stolen, then amen to that too. The body was only a memento of the soul that had once occupied it. Governor Rostopchin (if in fact it had been Rostopchin) had proved himself a true patriot in instigating those fires which, though they destroyed so much of the city, made it uninhabitable for the marauding French. He had understood that the essence of the city was not in its structure but in its people. No true Russian would disagree with him.

But now I had to display the single-minded righteousness of Rostopchin. I had to destroy the physical for the sake of a greater good. The greater good was not Domnikiia's soul—that was lost forever. It was her memory. If I could limit her existence in this altered state to a mere few hours, then at least the creature she had become could do nothing to debase the years of goodness of her life.

I pulled back the bedclothes to reveal her body, clothed in a simple nightgown. The silver crucifix which, despite all superstition, would have done nothing to protect her still hung around her neck. She murmured softly and raised her hand to her face to brush aside a straying hair, but she did not awake. Her hand fell back across her chest and lay as if cradling her heart. I gently nudged it and it fell lazily to the side of her body, leaving no obstacle that would distract my aim. I took out my wooden dagger and held it in both hands. I remembered our conversation when I had first been making it—in fact, making its predecessor. I remembered the look of fear in her eyes when I had waved it at her and shouted at her. Had she decided even then that she would choose this path and become a vampire? Or was that a decision that had come to her more recently?

I kneeled over her, resting the tip of the dagger on her chest, just above her heart. It merely required that I should drop my weight on to my hands and through them to the dagger and I would have ended the accursed existence of another of these creatures. How long, I wondered, would it take for Domnikiia's bodily remains to decay? For her there would be no collapse into dust as there had been for the others. Her death had occurred but twelve hours ago. That was scarcely any headstart at all. Once I thrust the blade into her and extinguished her life, her body would remain almost as perfect as ever, decaying only over a period of days and weeks just as though she had been a mortal woman. I closed my eyes and whispered a prayer for strength in what I was about to do. It would take only the briefest of action from me to shift my weight and plunge the wooden blade into her. I waited for the moment when strength and hatred would fill me and I would carry out what I had to do. And I waited.

I was no Rostopchin. I was no more capable of destroying something so beautiful as Domnikiia as I would have been of burning down Moscow if I had been handed a flaming torch and pointed towards the quarters of Bonaparte himself. I was a pathetic cousin of Othello. For me the victory of my love over my wisdom meant that I could not kill when all sense dictated that I should. It was beyond me, as if some power greater than I could not stand to see Domnikiia depart the face of the earth at this time; that all the love that had been poured into her creation could not be so easily cast aside.

And yet if I could not kill her, then what was I to do? Should I leave now and never see her again, hearing only occasionally of the strange death of some innocent that I would suspect had been caused by her? The regret would crush me. Every terrible death would be my fault for my inaction today. By choosing now not to destroy the creature that had come to inhabit Domnikiia's body, I would take on the responsibility for each death that she went on to bring about. Were I to die tomorrow in battle, or even today by my own hand (the thought had occurred to me), then the deaths of all those future souls would still be reckoned against mine at my judgement. To not plunge my dagger into Domnikiia was to damn my own eternal soul, and yet I could not do it. So I was damned. The very certainty of it opened up a new vista of possibilities. A new liberty was endowed upon me that allowed me to take any action, regardless of its moral consequences. Like a man sentenced to hang for a petty theft, I was now free to commit any crime I chose—freer, in fact, because the thief would still have to fear what came after his death.

It was conceptually thrilling, but as I contemplated it, I could not think of many immoral acts that I desired to perform—certainly none that I hadn't already committed even before my newfound ethical liberation. I would never have considered myself an especially good person, but it seemed that somehow in my life I had lost—or had never acquired—the urge to be bad. My behaviour was not imposed upon me through a fear of ultimate retribution, but was somehow an innate part of my character, created perhaps by the accumulation of a lifetime of those fears. But did having no desire to be bad make me good? Surely goodness must come from the resistance of dark urges, not from their mere absence? It is only the weak who beg the Lord not to lead them into temptation. The strong need temptation to test their strength. I had been presented with but one temptation—to let the vile creature that Domnikiia had become live—and I had yielded to it without a fight. I knew that it was not too late, that I still only had to raise my hand and let it fall again to bring about my own salvation, and yet I knew too that I could not and nor would I ever be able to.

There was only one conceivable advantage that could be taken from my decision to damn myself. If I was to walk the remainder of my days on the earth in the knowledge that, when I departed it, my subsequent path would be precipitously downwards, then at least I did not have to walk alone. I could be with Domnikiia. I would let her take me and create me as a vampire in the same way that she had so recently become one, and then at least our journey to hell would be made hand in hand. I knew that I was clinging on to one last gleaming thread of self-flattery—that she would want me beside her. If she did not, then I would die at her hand with no subsequent rebirth as a vampire. It would be apt punishment for my vanity.

I set down my wooden dagger at the side of the bed and took one last look at Domnikiia's beauty, then I licked my fingers and put out the light of the candle beside us. I took off my boots and my coat and my scabbard, discarding them on the floor, and lay on the bed beside her. Beneath my coat I saw the bloody mess of my wounded arm, but it did not matter. When I awoke—if I awoke—it would be to become a creature of the same ilk as Domnikiia and we would have an eternity of togetherness before us. A wound such as that would mean nothing to me. I had not shut my eyes for two nights and, as the rush of sleepiness came over me, I began to wonder whether I was in any state to make such a profound decision about my life. What did this mean for how I felt about my wife and my son? Even if my soul was bound for hell, did they not deserve my company and my support at least while I was alive? They were questions which I was too weary to answer.

It struck me that one of the interesting aspects of what I was about to undertake was that I would have the opportunity of looking back on my own death. I had observed death from the outside on many occasions—although there were other times when I wished I had been there to observe it—but it would be a rare privilege to be able, as a vampire, to recall what it was like actually to die. And yet, I thought, all souls, whether they end up in heaven or in hell, must have that same opportunity. If I didn't appreciate that, then I had to question whether I believed in heaven and hell at all, in which case, how could I be so certain of my own damnation?

But the speculation was unnecessary. Soon, I would have knowledge. I fell asleep.

Chapter XXVII

WHEN I AWOKE, I WAS INSTANTLY UNEASY. MY
surroundings were vaguely familiar, but I was aware of some pressing issue
that had to be resolved. Memory quickly returned. My first, perhaps unre-
markable observation was that I was alive. I reached out to my right, but
Domnikiia was no longer beside me. She must have awoken. She would have
seen me. Surely I would have to have been awake to have drunk her blood and
become a vampire. Had I woken to do that and then gone back to sleep, forgetting what had taken place? I considered myself, trying to determine
whether physically or mentally I felt any different. I could find nothing.

I glanced to the window and looked outside. As far as I could judge, it
was late morning. The snow shimmered in the light of the sun. The reflected
light shone into my face and cast a shadow of my hand on to the empty
pillow beside me. I was no vampire. As I had thought, I needed to be conscious to become one of those creatures, so that I might imbibe the blood of
the one who created me. Domnikiia had not yet transformed me into a creature like herself, but she soon would. I heard a footstep outside and the door-
knob began to turn. My earlier conviction that I would become a vampire
had completely left me. I found it impossible to retrace the line of reason that
had led me to it. Now, the prospect of letting Domnikiia sink her teeth into
my neck and of my drinking her blood in return was both sickening and
frightful. I would gladly kill her in order to save myself from such a fate.

I reached over the side of the bed to where I had dropped my dagger the
previous night. I felt a twinge of pain, but at the same time I noted that the
wound to my arm had been bandaged while I slept. The dagger was not
there. I glanced around the room and saw it. It was on a chair, sitting on top
of my neatly folded coat. My boots were beside it and my sword hung from
its back. I would have no time to reach it before the door opened. Then my

panic abated. It was daylight. Whoever was entering the room, it could not be a vampire. If it *was* Domnikiia then she would be quickly destroyed without any need for my intervention. Even so, I could not help but cower against the bedstead, clutching the blankets up to my chin.

It was her. She was carrying a tray on which I saw some bread and some cold meats and a pot which, from the smell, I immediately knew to contain coffee. She walked across the room, past the window, and put the tray down on the dressing table.

"Good morning," she beamed. I said nothing. She came over to the bed and sat beside me. Even though it was now clear to me that she was no vampire, still I shrank from her. There was no sign that she noticed. She put her arms around me and laid her head on my shoulder, kissing my neck and squeezing me tightly.

"That was a nice surprise," she said.

"What?" I managed to whimper.

"Waking up with you, of course!" She sat up and slipped her legs underneath the blankets. "I did know you were back in town, though. Pyetr Pyetrovich said you'd called. Even so, I didn't expect you'd go to quite such lengths to see me. I don't know how you're going to get back out without anybody noticing. You could have bathed first, too." She rose and went over to the dressing table.

"I'm sorry," I mumbled, simply as an instinctive response. My heart was pounding and I felt a heady relief. It was like the resurgence of reality after a nightmare—a nightmare that has contained a horror so dreadful that there is no solution to it but to turn back time and discover that the horror never existed. What I had seen at Domnikiia's window the previous night had been no nightmare, but it was just such a horror. And yet, somehow, its inevitable consequence had not taken place. Domnikiia was human. In all my contemplation through the night I had found no sensible course of action to take, and yet now the solution came in a simple, inexplicable fact. She was not a vampire.

"Oh, I'm sorry, Lyosha," she said with genuine distress. "I was joking. You know I'll always love you however much you stink." It felt cruel not to smile and acknowledge her humour, especially on seeing the disappointment in her face, but I was too deep in thought to react in any way. She came back over and handed me a cup of coffee. "How's your arm?"

"Where were you last night?" I asked.

"I was visiting a client, if you must know. I don't do all my work here."

"What time did you get back?" My voice was hushed and passionless as I tried to disguise my shock and fear.

"What is this, Lyosha?" she said, rising to her feet in anger. "You know what I do. Do you want details all of a sudden?"

"Tell me!" I moaned with a pleading intensity, leaning across the bed towards her. She knelt down beside the bed and put her hands to my face.

"What is it, Lyosha?" she asked, staring into my eyes to discover what had brought this on in me. "Why are you like this?"

"I saw you with Iuda last night," I told her simply.

"What?" Her incredulity appeared genuine.

"Through that window," I explained, pointing. "I was watching."

"You were spying on me?" She was more disappointed than angry.

"It's too late for that," I said, taking her by the wrists and rising to my feet. "I saw the two of you together and I saw what you did."

"Lyosha, I saw no man in this room last night." She was icy calm, perceiving that her life might depend on what she told me.

"Ha!" I snorted. "You should be a lawyer. You saw no man, but you saw Iuda."

"I didn't return here until almost midnight, and then I went straight to bed. Tell me what it was that you saw."

"I saw what happened. I saw you and him, together. I saw him when he carried you over to the window. I saw when he bit you. I saw when you . . ."

Domnikiia put her hand to the collar of her nightdress and ripped it away to expose her neck. "If he bit me, then where are the marks?" She arched her head first to one side and then the other, stretching her neck so that I could clearly see that there was no sign of any contact with a vampire.

Dumbstruck, I put my hand to her throat and stretched the skin, peering closely to verify what was already quite evident. I sat back down on the bed, bewildered, and she sat beside me. I lay my head in her lap and stared vacantly at the ceiling.

TWELVE

"I think perhaps you dreamed it, Lyosha," she said soothingly, reminding me, for the first time, quite specifically of my mother. I shook my head miserably.

"No. It was no dream. I saw it. I saw something."

"And you thought I had become a vampire?" There was a mocking tone in the question.

"Yes," I said, and a tear came to my eye. I took her hand in mine and pressed it to my lips. She thought for a moment before the obvious question came to her.

"So what were you doing here this morning?"

"I came to kill you."

She took it well. "I see."

"But I couldn't," I explained.

She thought for a moment longer. "So . . ." She didn't complete her question. Instead I felt her hands on my chest, pulling my shirt open, searching for something. "You're not wearing it," she said. "The icon—you've taken it off."

"I gave it to Dmitry."

"But it would have protected you. If I had been . . . If I had been a vampire, I could have killed you—or worse. Are you mad? You gave away your only protection."

"It doesn't work as protection," I explained. "They're not superstitious."

"*I'm* superstitious," Domnikiia shouted. "It would have kept *me* off you." She thought for a moment more. "Is that what you wanted?" she asked, incredulous. "You're an idiot, Aleksei Ivanovich; a sentimental idiot." She paused before adding quietly, "But thank you."

"As if anything could keep you off me," I muttered. She smiled and then bent forwards to kiss me.

"We still don't know what you saw," she said, returning to the point. "Perhaps they can do that—change their faces to look like someone else."

"I never saw her face," I confessed. I had realized already that my reasons for supposing it had been Domnikiia at all were scarcely substantial.

"Well, it looks like I had a lucky escape. I wouldn't like to have been killed by an idiot while I slept. So what did you see?"

"Just her back—her hair. It was so like yours." I had already realized the implication.

"Oh my God!" whispered Domnikiia. "Margarita! She sometimes uses this room when I'm not here. It's bigger than hers. The connecting door's never locked." She sprang to her feet and went over to the door.

"Wait!" I called. "Given what I saw, she'll be a vampire too by now."

"So what am I supposed to do, just leave her?"

"Let me go first."

"What if she is a vampire?"

"It's daytime," I explained. "She won't be able to do much."

I picked up my dagger from the chair and then went over to the door. I felt Domnikiia, behind me, pressed close to my body. For all that I feared for her safety, it was reassuring to have her there. As I turned the door handle, I felt a debilitating weariness within me. I had no more stomach to be chasing around Moscow killing vampires, or even killing Frenchmen. I just wanted them all to go away and leave me to enjoy my life. But I knew I had to go on. I opened the door.

Inside, it was dark. The curtains were closed and in the little light that there was, I could make out a figure on the bed.

"Stay there," I whispered to Domnikiia, and I began to edge my way towards the window, keeping my back always to the wall. When I got there, I wasted no time in pulling the curtain to one side and flooding the bedroom with light.

Iuda had not changed his attitude towards offspring. He remained, as he had once told me in that room of rotting corpses, free from the responsibility of long-term consequences. The purpose of the previous night's theatricals had not been to convert Margarita into another vampire who could accompany Iuda across the centuries. It had been purely a charade for my benefit, so that I would believe that Domnikiia had become a vampire and would then, as I so nearly had, kill her. For me to know that she died at my hand would make a vengeance upon me far sweeter than anything that Iuda could have done to her.

But once the performance had been acted out, Iuda had no further need for the bit players. On the bed, Margarita lay naked on her back. Her legs were together and straight and her arms lay limply stretched out on either side of her, in a grim mimicry of our crucified Lord. Her long, dark hair radiated from her head across the pillows like a halo, surrounding a face from which her dead eyes gazed blankly at the ceiling.

To her right side, sheets and pillows were drenched in vivid, red blood, which was also smeared over her stomach, breasts and cheeks. The right side of her throat was ripped open in a style that only a *voordalak* could achieve.

Domnikiia screamed.

Domnikiia did not stay at the brothel after that. None of them did. The authorities began an investigation. A brief look at my papers was enough to persuade them not to pester either myself or Domnikiia, although I doubt whether it did much to convince them of my innocence. I could have told them to terminate the investigation with all possible haste, but I chose not to. I wanted the nature of Iuda and the other Oprichniki to be known by everyone, but it was something that the police would have to find out for themselves. A simple account of the truth from me would not be believed.

As it was, they showed little interest in the history of one more body amongst the thousands. They were more concerned with identifying those in Moscow who had collaborated with the invaders. If they had chosen to speak with Domnikiia, they might well have perceived a discrepancy between her description of Margarita's body and what they found. An additional wound would have appeared.

After I had guided Domnikiia out of her colleague's room and into her own, but before summoning the police, I had returned to see Margarita once more. Her body was lifeless. Her dead eyes gave no reaction to changes in the light. Her flesh did not burn when it came into contact with the sun. For all anyone could tell, Iuda had caused her death, not begun her transformation. But I recalled another body that I had once seen in a not dissimilar state— the body of a young Russian soldier named Pavel, carried on a wooden cart through the streets of Moscow. He too had seemed dead. He too had been able to lie unaffected under the gaze of the sun. But his body had not decayed, the reason being that he had exchanged blood with a vampire and so had, within days or weeks, become one.

I could not let that happen. It took a single, swift, undebated thrust from my hand to rupture her dead heart with the wooden shaft of my dagger. How much easier it was for me to do that to Margarita than it ever could have been with Domnikiia.

Domnikiia stayed with me at the inn. It was not the best of times in our relationship. Domnikiia may have kept her soul, but her spirit had been dealt a heavy blow by the death of Margarita. Her vitality had faded to almost nothing. She didn't smile; she didn't joke; she didn't even hate. All those reactions were, I was sure, quite natural under the circumstances, and those qualities would return with time, but for now she was not even a shadow of the Domnikiia I had known and had loved. Worse, though, than losing those things I admired in her, I now found her dependency upon me stifling. Again this was no more than a temporary reaction to her shock, but it was a reminder to me that, whatever might happen to us, while we were together she would be my responsibility. I already had responsibilities—Marfa and Dmitry. It was not that I could not cope with another; it was simply that I didn't want to. Domnikiia was supposed to be my irresponsibility—the person with whom I need have no concern for the future or for the world out-side. Now, more than ever, that was what I needed. The carnage that I had witnessed in those autumn months of 1812 had left me as an old man. I had lost the three people closest to me; Maks and Vadim by their very lives, Dmitry by the insuperable mistrust that had grown up between us. Dmitry's cowardly retreat from what faced him had turned out to be a wise response, one which now, only a few days later, I followed. The terror that had consumed me in Moscow after the fire had returned. Then safety had seemed to lie in flight, now it lay in immobility. Yet I would have liked Domnikiia— the real Domnikiia—to have been there to distract me from the reality of my inaction; either to fill my days with trivial frivolity or to stand up to me in a way that would either force me to justify my torpor or would shatter it.

Instead, she was simply meek. She could have goaded me into chasing west after either the French or the two surviving Oprichniki, or she could have begged me to stay with her in Moscow. As it was, I stayed, but not because she begged—she hardly spoke at all. The excuse for staying was my wounded arm, but it was well on the mend and I had ridden into battle with worse injuries. The reason for staying was fear.

Margarita's funeral took place three days after her death. She proved to have many friends and acquaintances who had taken the time out of their lives to attend, though few spoke to one another—particularly the men. Of the nine uniformed officers who attended, I was surprised to see that four outranked me. What was truly remarkable was that Margarita should have a funeral at all. The fires in Moscow had not killed many, but subsequent starvation had eradicated thousands, both native and invader. Most were still to be hauled into mass graves. From what I could gather, it was Pyetr Pyetrovich who had paid for the ceremony. His diligence in looking after his property now proved to stretch beyond simple good business.

Most significantly, the funeral marked a turning point in Domnikiia's mood. Having bid a formal farewell to her friend and colleague, some hints of her former charm began to reemerge. Even so, the memory of her at her lowest always haunted me.

A few days later, as we sat in my rooms at the inn, she made an announcement.

"I'm going to get a job."

"You have a job—or you will when Pyetr Pyetrovich reopens," I told her. It sounded odd even as I spoke. Most men in my position would be delighted for their mistress to be giving up such a profession, but I had grown used to it.

"I can't go back there. What happened to Margarita . . . well, even if it hadn't been Iuda, it could have been someone else. It could happen to me one day."

"Will Pyetr Pyetrovich let you leave?" I was not trying to place obstacles in her way, but it must have come across as such.

"If he doesn't, he'll have you to answer to."

I went over and kissed her cheek. "He certainly will." I sat down beside her. "So what will you do?"

"I could work in a shop, or go into service."

"I might know people who would take you on as a maid."

"Here or in Petersburg?"

"Some here; mostly in Petersburg though."

"I'd prefer Moscow," she replied. I'd prefer you in Moscow too, I thought, but didn't say it.

"On the other hand," she asked thoughtfully, "wouldn't your wife like a new maid?"

A momentary image of the convenience of such an arrangement was quickly banished by the unending riskiness of its reality. A wife in one city and a mistress in another was a comfortable arrangement. To have both in the same city would add spice. To have both in the same household was the stuff of Moliere. It could never be. I knew she would understand that in the long run, but in her present mood a blunt refusal could be damaging.

"Wouldn't you like that?" she went on. Still I could find no response to give to her. "*Prostak*," she murmured softly.

It was a word that one heard a lot in the army, especially among card players; an insult that they applied to anyone who was an easy mark.

"I beg your pardon," I said with mock offence.

"You heard," she replied. I don't know whether she had been trying to trick me all along, or whether this was just to save us both embarrassment. Either way, it was a joy to hear her speak again with that easy impertinence. "I'm not surprised Iuda found it so easy to fool you," she added slyly.

Sometimes her humour could be less of a joy.

"Captain Danilov!"

I had just walked out the door of the inn. It was a week now since Margarita's death; a month since Bonaparte's departure. Snow lay thickly on the ground. I turned my head to see where the call had come from.

I smiled broadly, recognizing the familiar face that emerged from a doorway across the street. It was Natalia.

She ran over to hug me. I held her tightly for a few moments, clinging to her as the only person in my world who had not become terrifyingly unfamiliar over the past days and weeks.

TWELVE

"And how are you, my dear Natasha?" I asked.

"I'm good. Well, better than when you last saw us. We have a roof over us. Father has work. What about you?"

"I'm well—a little war weary. I meant to come and see you."

We walked along the street as we talked, as Muscovites habitually do in winter, avoiding the cold that would penetrate our bones if we stayed still.

"That's all right," she said. "Captain Petrenko said you'd be busy fighting the French."

"You've seen Dmitry?" I asked, surprised that he had been in Moscow.

She nodded. "He said he's going after them too."

"After the French?"

"No, after the English," she said with heavy sarcasm. And why not? She had no reason to suspect that Dmitry or I had any enemy other than Bonaparte.

"When did you see him?"

"Um . . . five days ago."

"How was he?"

"Like you—exhausted, but he still carried on." I wondered if this was meant as a jibe at me. "I told him not to go—said the French would leave without his help. But he said he owed it to you. Did you make him go?"

"Not on purpose."

"Are you going to go after him?"

I thought for a while, but with no conclusion. "I don't know," I told her.

"Then today, I got a letter from him," she continued. I was taken aback by the fact that a girl of her status could even read, but the possibility of news from Dmitry was far more consuming.

"What did he say?" I asked urgently.

"That's between him and me," she replied, with a proud smirk. "But he did enclose this for you." She handed me a small envelope. "He said it was safer than sending it to you. Does that mean there are still French spies about?"

I looked at the package in my hands. The word "Aleksei" in Dmitry's hand was all that was written on the outside. It was very thin—it might only contain a single sheet, but I was desperate to read it.

"Do you think?" asked Natalia.

"Think what?"

"That there are still French spies in Moscow."

"Probably not," I said distractedly. "But Dmitry is always cautious."

"You want to read that, don't you?"

I nodded.

"I thought you would. That's why I brought it straight here. I'll let you get on with it."

"Thank you," I said with a smile. I kissed her hand and said goodbye.

"Will you come and visit us?" she asked.

"Of course."

"That's what Mitka said."

"Then that's what he'll do." And that was one thing concerning Dmitry of which I felt sure.

I opened the letter as soon as I got back to the inn. It was dated the third of November, three days previously, and was typically succinct.

Aleksei,

I think I have tracked down Iuda and Foma. They have infiltrated the French army and are retreating with them. While my every instinct is to leave them to it, I know you will disagree, and I think it is time that I deferred to you on this. I am staying in Smolensk, at the hostelry by the Dnieper where we stayed last time we were here (Я8). Please join me here with all speed,

Your friend and comrade,
Dmitry Fetyukovich Petrenko.

I no longer had the excuse of my arm to keep me in Moscow—it had almost healed. I no longer had the excuse of not knowing where I should go—Dmitry's letter told me. There was no way that I could avoid setting out once again, nor did I want to.

I showed the letter to Domnikiia. She read it swiftly. "How long do you think it will take?" she asked.

TWELVE

"Who says I'm going?"

She pulled a face to tell me that I was fooling her no more than I was fooling myself. My fear required excuses, and the letter left me with none.

"You think I should go, after all Dmitry's done?" I asked her.

"No, but you think you should."

"And you don't mind?"

"Would it make any odds if I did?" She was probably right.

I rushed downstairs and ordered a horse to be prepared, then returned and began to pack, with Domnikiia's help. I was soon ready. I wrote down a list of names of people that I knew in Moscow who might employ her, along with a hasty letter of recommendation. I held both her hands as I stood at the doorway. It suddenly felt more like *adieu* than *au revoir*.

"You'll have a job by the time I get back," I told her.

"Maybe," she said quietly, then she gazed intently into my eyes. "Please don't go, Lyosha," she implored. I considered for a moment, but no longer than that.

"I have to."

She smirked. "You see," she said. "No odds whatsoever. You're so easy, Lyosha, you *prostak*."

I smiled broadly and embraced her tightly.

"I will be back," I whispered.

I went out into the winter street, mounted my horse and set off westwards once again, this time in pursuit not of the French, but of the last two remaining Oprichniki.

Chapter XXVIII

THE SMOLENSK ROAD WAS SCARCELY RECOGNIZABLE compared with when I had last seen it. The hot, hazy warmth of summer had been replaced by a deep blanket of snow. The road itself was well trodden and the snow often gave way to slush and in places even to mud. I too had changed. Twelve weeks before, four of us had set out, confident and comradely, eager to defend our land and trusting of our new allies, the Oprichniki. Now only Dmitry and I were left, and the trust between us was fragile. Vadim and Maksim both lay silent in anonymous graves. The French had come to Moscow and they had gone. Had we or the Oprichniki played any significant part in that? I doubted it. Bonaparte's fate was sealed the moment he stepped across the border from Poland. In the west they simply don't understand how much east there is. Warsaw is a long, long way from Paris. If Bonaparte could get that far, could Moscow be much further? In reality, it's as far from Warsaw as Warsaw is from Paris, and the journey is a hundred times more dangerous.

Along the road were various signs of the devastation brought by the armies that had marched back and forth over the past weeks. In villages along the way, buildings had been destroyed by fire or, sometimes, by simple, brute force. This may have been caused by the French as they advanced, but more likely by the Russians as they retreated—not just the Russian army but also the very Russian peasants who lived in those villages. The policy of destruction that had been so effective in Moscow was also enacted wherever Bonaparte's army chose to march.

Beyond Mozhaysk, a new and horrible feature began to decorate the landscape, increasing by degree with every verst that I covered. Bonaparte's original plan had been to return by a different route from that by which he came, travelling to the south of the main Moscow to Smolensk road. But at Maloyaroslavets, the battle from which the French captain hanging at the cross-roads at Kurilovo had fled, General Kutuzov had forced Bonaparte to turn from that path, back to the north. Mozhaysk was where the French had rejoined the main road, and there began the debris of an army in flight.

Horses—French horses—lay dead beside the road in their hundreds. Exhaustion, starvation and the freezing cold might have been to blame for some of them, but many were down simply to the ignorance or laziness of the French blacksmiths. The horses' shoes lacked the three calkins that a Russian smith would have instinctively added in winter to stop the shoe slipping on ice. Once a horse had lost its footing on the ice-covered road, there would have been little that it, or its rider, could do to raise it. I heard later that the starving French soldiers fell upon each stumbling horse even as it struggled hopelessly to regain its footing, hacking it to pieces in order to feed themselves. Only a fraction of the horses' bodies exhibited the kindness of a bullet to the head.

Even so, men succumbed to the same environment as did their mounts. The reason that the bodies only of horses and not men lay abandoned in the snow was probably not so much that men were dying in any few numbers, but that their comrades had made some effort to bury them. As their journey—and, following in their footsteps, my journey—continued, they had begun to forget such sensibilities. The bodies of men lay ever more frequently beside the bodies of fallen horses.

As I passed each body—be it of a man or a horse—a flurry of birds would launch themselves into the air, frightened by my passing. Once I had gone by, they would return to peck at what flesh still remained. Soon after Mozhaysk, I caught sight of huge flocks of crows circling some way in front of me. While the sound of birds may herald hope—the new dawn—the sight of them is so often an indicator that death is nearby. I soon realized that I was approaching the field of Borodino. I had seen little of the main battlefield on the day, though I had heard much of its horror from survivors. But now as I approached, almost three months later, I saw for myself for the first time how great the death toll had been.

There had not been a moment to pause for breath—certainly not for my country—since that battle, and so little effort had been made to clear away the dead; at least, little human effort. Dogs, wolves and scavenging birds had picked what they could from the thousands of bodies, yet still enough remained to make it clear where each man had fallen. The road ran for about eight versts through the battlefield, with the village of Borodino itself marking the midpoint. On either side, the bodies of the dead spread outwards as far as I could see. The French, from what I could see, had at least made some attempt to bury their dead after the battle, but they had not been thorough; many that had been hastily buried had subsequently been disinterred by the heavy rain. It was impossible—not to say repellent—to count, but the carcasses numbered in their tens of thousands. It was as though some extraterrestrial giant had chosen to slap his hand against the surface of the earth at that point, flattening with one blow all those men who stood beneath it. But no such unworldly explanation was needed. Each man that had died here had died in the way that most men die—at the hands of others. I spurred my horse and rode through as quickly as I could. Even beyond the battlefield, there was no letup in the accompaniment of the dead. Now, though, it was once again not the bodies of those who had died in battle but of those who had died in retreat. It was not worth a debate as to which was more sickening.

From people I spoke to along the way, I learned that it was not just frost and starvation that was killing the retreating French; it was the Russian peasantry as well. When the French passed through a village they were welcomed with open arms, given food and brandy and put into a warm bed, only to have their throats slit or receive a bullet to the head as they slept. I recalled the hanging body of the French captain who had been lynched at Kurilovo. There was no reason that the serfs should have any sympathy for the invaders. Even if they did, they would still follow their master's orders and kill them without pity.

It took me three days to get to Smolensk. Fresh horses and accommodation were not plentiful along the way, but they were sufficient. It had been two weeks since the French had passed along that road. What had been a hostile trail through an unfriendly foreign land for them had, of necessity, become a vital supply line for the Russian forces that pursued them. Horses and victuals that had been moved away from the road during the French advance had surged back in after their retreat, as though Napoleon were Moses leading his army of Israelites across the Red Sea, except that what was drawn away in advance of him and returned behind him would have brought life, not death to his army.

Smolensk was changed in much the same way that Moscow had been— it was ruined and burnt. And whereas Moscow had been freed from French hands after only five weeks, Smolensk had been held for three months. The final days of the occupation had seen a complete breakdown in discipline as the cold, beleaguered, frightened remains of Bonaparte's army had ransacked the city that they passed through in their retreat. There had been less than two weeks for rebuilding to take place. It was in a worse state than I had ever seen Moscow.

I went to the inn from where Dmitry had sent his letter. I had stayed there earlier in the year, but I did not recognize the proprietor. A brief conversation with him revealed that his predecessor, a cousin of his, had been killed in the first French attacks. There was a letter for me from Dmitry, dated two days before.

Aleksei,

Sorry for not staying to wait for you. It's not that I'm impatient or doubt you will come, but I have discovered the precise whereabouts of Foma. He and Iuda had been together, but now I cannot find any trace of Iuda. If I can capture Foma alone, then I may be able to use him as bait to tempt Iuda into the open. If not, I will have at least reduced their numbers by one. In either case, I would appreciate your help. Out here, our list of places to meet has become very sparse. I will try to make it to the farmhouse north of Yurtsevo (Г1) and wait there as long as possible.

As ever,
Dmitry.

Yurtsevo was another two or three days' journey to the west. I was cold, tired and saddle sore. I spent a long, well-earned night in Smolensk before continuing after Dmitry. His plan was at best foolhardy. Capturing Foma might not be impossible, but were I to catch him, I would not keep him alive for long enough for Iuda to come to his aid. I would kill him within seconds. Better yet, I would kill him before he even knew I was there. Whatever desire I might once have had to allow these creatures to be aware of their deaths was now lost in the pragmatic expediency of my own fear.

The idea that Iuda would put his own life at any risk for any of his fellows was the most laughable part of Dmitry's scheme. Of all the Oprichniki, Iuda was the least human—the least likely to be swayed by any sense of camaraderie or partnership. But Dmitry had asked for my help, and I had to give it. I had little interest in small fry like Foma, but if he or Dmitry had any clue as to where I might find Iuda, then that would be of help to me.

Early the next day, I set out west once again. The ground was still frozen to iron and the wind still blew a blizzard that would cover with snow anything or anyone that remained unmoving for more than a few minutes. Yurtsevo was only a few versts north of the city of Orsha. The going that far was relatively easy, always downhill along the Dnieper valley, with plenty of places along the way to get a meal and a fresh horse.

The road to the west was still lined with the bodies of horses and men. Many of the men had been stripped of their possessions and even their clothes. I was not chauvinistic enough to believe that such desecration of the French dead could not have been perpetrated by Russian peasants or even by Russian soldiers, but it would have been their fellow Frenchmen who had the first opportunity to plunder the bodies of their fallen comrades, and they too who were in the direst need of extra clothing.

I was in Orsha in two more days, and after resting the night there, I set out on the final leg of my journey, to Yurtsevo. This was no longer a route of well-trodden roads between large, populous towns. When we had drawn up our list of meeting places, we had had little idea whether we would be meeting under the benign reign of Tsar Aleksandr or under the occupation of the invader Bonaparte. Moreover, it had been under a glorious summer sky that we had made our plans. Then the road from Orsha to Yurtsevo would have been a pleasant one through verdant woodland. Had we known the eventual circumstances, we would have chosen to meet by the largest fire-place inside the warmest tavern in Orsha. As it was, we had chosen a place where a man could die in November and be discovered in a state of perfect, frozen preservation the following March. But at least the road was no longer one that had been trod by the French, and so too it was no longer paved with carcasses of horses and of men. Even so, this slight recompense was soon forgotten in the face of the gnawing cold.

I began to doubt whether there was any point in my continuing when the depth of the snow reached up to my knees—and taking into account that I was still mounted on my horse. I had tried dismounting and leading my horse through the great drifts of snow, and for a while we had made swifter progress. But in places the snow was so deep that it would have been above my head. The prospect of me reaching the rendezvous was bleak, and even if I did, I was in grave doubt as to whether Dmitry would have made it there too. On the other hand, I believed that I was now nearer to Yurtsevo than I was to Orsha, and so to advance was the most sensible option.

The snow grew deeper. There were times when the drifts were so high that we had to plough through them like a ship frozen fast in the icy Baltic. The top of the snow was higher than my horse's head and it was only down to the sense of either trust or fear that she held for me that I was able to coax her to walk onwards along a path she could not see. Through half a dozen layers of clothing, the cold bit into me with a carnivorous aggression. How my horse bore it, I cannot tell.

It was after nightfall when I first saw the lights of the village. On any normal night they would have been a beacon to guide us home, but through the blowing snow they were but a glimpse, to be seen one moment and gone the next. Having first seen them, though they then disappeared, I headed towards them. Five minutes later I saw them again, this time to the left and further away. I spurred the horse and she grudgingly turned towards the lights. The wind and snow lashed against the tiny gap between my hat and my collar from which my face peeped out. It would have been more comfortable to be whipped across the eyes than to endure that frozen blast.

It was another ten minutes before I saw the lights of the village again.

This time they were closer, but still to the left, at right angles to the direction in which we had been heading. I tried to turn my horse once again, but she would not move. It was no stubbornness on her part, she was simply stuck fast. She tried to neigh, but the sound was muffled by the insinuating snow that filled her mouth and nostrils. I dismounted and found that I could no longer see the village lights. I was in a snowdrift of which the top was way above my head. I scrabbled through the mountain of snow before me, tearing out handful after handful and casting them aside, but new snow built up far, far more quickly than I could disperse it. Soon, I could move neither my legs nor my hands. With each movement I made, the snow froze even harder to ice and tightened its grip upon me. I would be moving no further that night, and if I did not move that night, I would never move anywhere again. With hope gone, the cold seemed to double in its intensity, and I knew that I would quickly succumb.

I chose in my last moments to turn my mind to pleasant things. Images of my wife and my son came to me, but were quickly dismissed by thoughts of Domnikiia. My mind's eye became detached from my body and flew back to Moscow to observe her. It dwelt on her large eyes, her lips, her pale earlobes. I observed her closely, though she was unaware of my presence. I brought to mind the chatter of her voice, and even though I could make out no individual word, the sound of it was a perfect rendition of the real Domnikiia. It would have been hard to discover a more contented frame of mind in which to die.

Through the whistling of the wind, I heard the howl of a wolf, which was soon accompanied by a second. I prayed that the cold would render me insensible before the wolves got to me. At the same time, I remembered the folklore that the *voordalak* could transform itself into a wolf. I modified my prayer. If the cold could not save me, at least let the howling come from regular, respectable wolves.

I remember being dragged across the snowy ground, and the sound of voices shouting all around me. I also remember the impression of mouths and sharp teeth close to my face, the repellent smell of half-digested flesh rising from a

TWELVE

carnivorous gullet and the curiously pleasant sensation of my face being licked.

When I awoke, the one concept that cut its way through an abundance of feelings was that of warmth. I was wrapped in a heavy fur, and near me a fire blazed in an iron stove, filling the room with heat. I tasted brandy on my lips, which must have been forced between them while I was unconscious. Beside the fire, breathing heavily, their tongues lolling from the sides of their mouths, lay two huge dogs. They could well be mistaken for wolves. Their fur was a mixture of grey and white and their grey eyes looked towards me with a blank curiosity. One of the dogs raised an eyebrow as it turned its gaze away from me towards the source of a sound.

"Drink some more brandy!"

The voice came from just behind me. A tall, bulky man stood a little away from the fire, staring into its dancing flames, breathing in its warmth through large, hairy nostrils. On the table beside me was a glass of dark liquor, with a bottle beside it. I drank and the man refilled it for me.

"Thank you," I said, drinking again from the replenished glass.

"You're a long way from the rest of the troops," he said.

"How did you know I was a soldier?" I asked.

"You carry a sword, even though you wear no uniform."

"How did you know I wasn't French?"

"I didn't until you spoke," he explained, placing a cocked pistol gently on the table beside him, "but I do now."

The fact that we both spoke Russian was as reassuring to me as it was to him. This far west, I could just as easily have found myself in a Polish household, where a Russian soldier might have encountered a less friendly welcome.

The dogs turned their heads across the room to the door. Another man entered, younger than the first, but still of the same powerful build.

"He's awake then," said the newcomer.

"Yes," replied the other, "and he seems to be on our side, although he still hasn't told me what he's doing here."

"I'm supposed to be meeting someone," I explained. "This is Yurtsevo?"

"It is," said the older man.

"There's a farm about a verst north of here," I went on, "towards Mezhevo."

"Not any more. It burnt down."

"The French?" I asked.

"Not even the French. It burnt down more than a year ago."

"I see. I think my friend will still try to meet me there."

"We haven't seen anyone. Mind you, in this weather, they could walk past the village and never see it—or walk through the village and we'd never see them. You were lucky the dogs caught your scent."

"There was that smoke we saw from over there the other day, Pa," said the younger man.

"When?" I asked.

"Yesterday, or the day before."

"I must go and find him," I said, rising from my chair.

"Not tonight, you don't," said the older man. He put his meaty hand on my shoulder and pushed me back into my seat with an enormous, casual strength that reminded me of the force that the vampire Pavel had used to hold me against the wall. As the man moved, his dogs rose swiftly to their feet and silently bared their teeth. "You go in the morning," he told me firmly.

I spent the night in the chair where I had been sitting, revelling in the warmth given to me by the furs and the fire. I was woken early when a woman—I presumed from her age that she was the older man's wife—came in to refuel the fire. Later, she beckoned me into another room, where I shared a silent breakfast with her and her husband and son.

Soon after dawn, the head of the household turned to me.

"You're still planning on going out to the farm?" he asked.

"I have to," I replied.

"Well, I won't offer to come with you, but I'll show you the road. It's not far, but in this weather it's treacherous. You should leave your horse here and go on foot."

TWELVE

"My horse is alive?" I asked in surprise. I hadn't even thought to consider it.

"Why shouldn't she be? She was in a lot better state to survive the weather than you were when we found you."

I put my overcoat and hat back on and we went outside. The village was not large and the buildings seemed to huddle together for warmth in the winter cold. It had stopped snowing and the wind was lighter than it had been, but it was still bitterly cold. We walked along the single main street to the edge of the village.

"That's the road to take," the man told me, pointing to a path that could only be discerned as a vague gap in the trees. "It's only about a verst. There's still enough of the buildings left for you to recognize it, unless the snow's covered it."

"Thank you," I said.

"If you're not back in three hours, I won't be coming to look for you, because you'll be dead. I'll bury you in the spring, if the wolves leave anything of you."

I offered him my hand, but he preferred not to take his out of his deep pockets. I headed along the road he had indicated. I turned back to wave to him, but he had already turned and I saw only his stooping back as he trudged towards the warmth of his home.

The wind blew up again soon after I set off, directly against my direction of travel, making each step more tiresome and whipping sharp flecks of snow across my face. It seemed preposterous that Dmitry had ever got here, let alone that he would have stayed here, and yet being so close, it would be ridiculous for me to turn back. The same thought might well have passed through Dmitry's mind. If he had got this far, he would have gone further, and that could be said of him even if "this far" had only been a single step. Besides, there had been smoke, so someone had been there and that was most likely Dmitry, though it was still improbable that he had stayed.

It was thanks only to a lucky break in the wind that I didn't walk straight past the ruins of the small farmhouse. The snow had not completely covered the charred remains, which still bore some resemblance to the basic shape of the building, but shrouded in the blizzard they would have been hard to spot. Walking through the blackened timbers, I saw on the far side of the structure the remains of a more recent fire—this time a campfire. The gnarled shapes of snow-encrusted logs that had been pulled up to sit on partially ringed a wide patch of burnt wood and cinders. I put my hand to it and felt that the fire was now completely cold. It had been more than a day since it had been burning. However, I was now certain that Dmitry had been here. No one would cast more than a passing glance at this cold, deserted place, let alone stop and make a fire, unless they had reason to be there. I too had made it to the appointment, but I was too late.

I searched around the ruins of the farmhouse, looking for a message from Dmitry in the code that had served us so well, hoping to discover where he had moved on to. It did not take me long to find it. A blackened, half-burnt tabletop had been leaned against what was once a door post. It was plastered with drifted snow, but as I wiped it clean I found Dmitry's message scratched firmly into its surface:

11-9-21-Д

Three days ago. Unquestionably, it had been too long to wait in this overwhelming cold, but there was no further message to indicate where he might have gone. I brushed off the rest of the snow from the tabletop and then did the same on the other side, but there was nothing more. I went back over to the place where Dmitry had made his fire and sat on one of the logs. Its hard, twisted knots dug into me and its coldness seeped into my flesh.

What was I to do now? Dmitry clearly had been here, but where had he gone? Had his plan to capture Foma succeeded, or was he yet to carry it out, or had Foma somehow turned the tables on him? Worse still, had Dmitry's plan gone even further? Had he successfully used Foma as bait, only to find himself defeated by Iuda? That could mean that Iuda was still somewhere hereabouts, waiting for my arrival. I thanked the Lord that I had arrived in the daytime.

I could only act on the assumption that Dmitry was still alive, otherwise anything I did would be futile. If I were in his circumstances, then what I would have done would be to attempt to join up with the regular army. From what I had heard in Orsha, they were heading for Borisov in an attempt to prevent Bonaparte from crossing the Berezina. That was only a couple of days' ride away. My best guess was that that would be where Dmitry would go, and so that was where I would follow.

The decision made, I drew in my feet to stand up. As I did so, I disturbed the snow beside the log I was sitting on, revealing something that glinted in the sunlight. I bent forward and cleared away more snow to discover that it was a fine silver chain, of the sort used for a necklace or bracelet. I pulled it out of the snow and found that it was caught under one of the stunted branches that protruded from the log. As I cleared the snow further, I suddenly leapt to my feet with a startled gasp.

This was not a branch; it was a human hand.

I had not been sitting on a log, but on a frozen, rigid, human corpse.

Chapter XXIX

EVEN BEFORE I HAD CLEARED THE SNOW AWAY, I KNEW that it was Dmitry. His body was, in fact, lying alongside the log on which he must have been sitting. Once he had collapsed, the blowing snow had covered them both, making them appear as a single object. I brushed the snow from his beard and hair and eyes to reveal his face. His lips and his eyes were tightly shut and his expression revealed no agony of death, just the solid determination of a man facing up to a night in the cold.

The silver chain that had first hinted at Dmitry's presence still trailed from his tightly clasped hand. I prised his fingers open one by one and found within the icon that I had given him the last time we had spoken, just after we had buried Maksim. I had been proved right and Domnikiia wrong. It had offered him no protection from death. I decided against exposing myself to the cold by putting it back around my neck. Instead I wrapped the chain around the small image of Christ and put it in my pocket.

There were no wounds on Dmitry's body that I could see; none, certainly, to his neck. Dmitry had, like so many of the fleeing French invaders, succumbed to no more terrifying an enemy than the Russian winter—an enemy more powerful, more reliable and far more ruthless than the Oprichniki could ever be.

One question remained. Had Dmitry captured Foma, as had been his plan? I glanced around the other logs that lay beside the burnt-out fire with new eyes. Each one could be interpreted through the thick snow as a twisted corpse, crawling across the ground in the agonies of death. When my eyes finally fell upon Foma's body, the form of a man became irrefutably clear. Once the idea that it might be a body had been put in my mind, what I saw could be interpreted in no other way.

Foma was lying on his front. A nodule which protruded from his back at about the level of his hips I took to be his hands, tied behind his back by

Dmitry when he was captured. It surprised me that his body could exist at all outside in the daylight. I had seen the effects of the sun on Pyetr and Iakov Zevedayinich, and knew that little should remain. I could only surmise that the snow provided sufficient protection for his body from the sun's rays, or alternatively that once he had died of the cold and his body had frozen solid, then it was impossible for the sun to have any further effect upon it.

The body was some way away from Dmitry's, back towards the burnt-out house. It looked as though Foma had been crawling—or rather wriggling, with both his hands and his feet bound—away from Dmitry and towards relative safety. Perhaps Dmitry had yielded to the cold sooner than Foma and he had been taking the opportunity to escape, though to where he could escape I did not know. It did not matter. Foma too had become a lump of solid, icy flesh before he had got any distance.

I poked Foma's remains through the snow with the tip of my sword. He was quite solid, like stone or ice. Two days outside in this weather could turn to rock any living thing that did not keep moving. I rolled the lifeless corpse on to its back and leaned over it, wiping a little snow away from the face to verify that it was indeed Foma. It most certainly was. He had died with his eyes open, and looking into them I recognized the blackness that in life had been no more expressive than it now was in death.

The eyes flicked suddenly to the left and then to the right. I started with surprise and then looked again. He repeated the action twice, with a pause in between. Foma was not human, he was a vampire. Just as a stab wound that would kill a mortal man had no effect on a vampire, so it was impossible that a vampire could freeze to death. Though his whole body had cooled to the temperature of the world around him at tens of degrees of frost, though every fluid that had once flowed within him had now turned to solid ice, still life, or the vampire equivalent of life, could not be extinguished.

Only his eyes remained movable, though they themselves must have been tiny, hard balls of ice. They now moved rapidly in all directions through the only gap in the outer skin of snow that he had acquired, like the eyes of a man peering through a frosty window at a cosy, warm, firelit room. I was reminded of how I had seen him once before, standing frozen against the wall of an alleyway in Moscow, only his eyes moving as he inspected the potential prey that walked past him. Then his immobility had been voluntary, to help him in his concealment. Now it was forced upon him.

I do not know what it was, if anything, that Foma had been trying to communicate to me. Perhaps he had not been thinking at all, or had not even recognized that it was I who had discovered him. Perhaps they were just the eye movements of his dreams, revealed to the world now that he was unable to shut his frozen eyelids. He could be harbouring no hope that I would save him, but he might perhaps be hoping that I would kill him quickly, that he would die now rather than remain in this state of limbo until spring, when the warmth of the strengthening sun would obliterate both the winter snow and the vampire that lay shrouded within it.

As it was, his death was immediate, but by no intent of mine. I cleared a little more of the snow from his face, to see if he was capable of any further movement beyond that of his eyes. My shadow may have protected him before, but as the first blush of sunlight hit his cheek, it began to smoulder. I leapt back away from him, realizing what was about to happen. What I witnessed was strangely beautiful, not just in that I could take pleasure at the death of another of these creatures—I was becoming too jaded for that—but also in the spectacle of the display. It was as good as any show of fireworks I have seen in Moscow or Petersburg. Through the small patch of skin that I had cleared, the sun began to burn the vampire. This in turn melted more snow and even incinerated his clothes, exposing more flesh for the sun to work upon. A sparkling line of flame radiated out from Foma's head and ran in seconds down the length of his whole body, the heat melting ever more snow and the melted snow revealing ever more fuel for the combustion. A sound like the roaring of a fire combined with the whistling of the wind was emitted, following the line of flame down his body. For a moment, there was only a glow of blinding white in the shape of a man's body—reminiscent of the image I have always had of our Lord's ascension—but it quickly faded.

Soon, nothing remained but a pool of melted snow, some of which was warm enough to steam slightly. Within minutes, the winter had reasserted itself and the pool had frozen back to a gleaming sheet of ice.

TWELVE

I would have liked to bury Dmitry. He had been a friend for a long time; seven years. We had never been as close as Maks and I had been, but that was merely a result of our personalities, not of our hearts. He and I had trusted one another— we all had—and though, as with Maks, my trust had faltered for a moment, it had returned. I was blessed to have had the opportunity to be sure that Dmitry was aware of that. I hoped that somehow Maks was now similarly aware.

But to bury Dmitry was impossible. Even if I had had tools, the frozen earth was as hard as rock, and I would not have been able to dig deep. The best I could do was to cover him with snow and make a cross out of a couple of charred pieces of wood from the house. I hoped I would have the opportunity to return before spring and lay him to rest more properly.

I headed back to Yurtsevo. The wind, which had been against me as I had travelled away from the village, had contrived to change direction so that it was still against me as I went towards it. The snowy gale once more bit into my face, but the return journey was easier for the fact that I knew how far it was to my destination.

Once in the village, I knocked on the door of my saviours. The younger man answered.

"Did you find him?"

"No," I replied, keeping it simple.

"I told you," said his father, coming up behind him. "I suppose you'll be wanting to stay here tonight as well?"

"No," I said. "I think I should be able to make it back to Orsha today."

"You don't want to get lost like you did last night."

"I'll try not to."

"Show him his horse," the man said to his son. The son, accompanied by the two huge wolf-like dogs, padding faithfully by his side, led me to a stable, where I found my horse fed and rested. We walked back to the house and the father handed over my bags.

"Thank you for your help," I said to them both, as warmly as their gruff demeanours allowed.

"We're Christians," said the father, the implication being that it was a duty, not a pleasure. I handed him some money. He looked at it with contempt—whether because it was too little or because I offered it at all, I could not tell—and then slipped it into his pocket. Their door was closed even before I had mounted my horse.

The journey back to Orsha was easy enough in daylight. The snow had already covered any traces of my journey the previous night, and though I tried to see where I had gone off the road, I could not. The sun was beginning to set as I entered the town. I gazed at it in the western sky, knowing that in that direction lay what was left of the French and with them, to the best of my knowledge, Iuda—the sole remaining Oprichnik. Back in the other direction, along the same road, was Moscow and in it Domnikiia. To the north was another road that stretched all the way to Petersburg—to my wife and my son. I returned to the same inn that I had been in two nights before. Any decisions about the day—and the days—to come could be deferred.

I ate and bathed and sank into an untroubled sleep.

When I awoke, I had come to a decision. The fine decision, the one in which would lie soul-searching and angst, was between Moscow and Petersburg, and so I chose the third path, to head west and rejoin the body of the army. It was the basis on which I knew many other soldiers had made their decisions to join up—to escape the complexity of trying to live their lives by opting for a world where they could simply pass the time trying to avoid their deaths. There was little chance, I thought, that I would be able to find Iuda (though some chance that he would find me), but even so, I could do some good helping to rout the French using the traditional methods of soldiery with which I felt the need to be reacquainted.

Still the refuse of the retreating French lay by the roadside, and became ever more sickening. Even before Orsha, I had noticed more and more that the dead horses had not simply died; they had been butchered. I could not blame the starving, desperate soldiers for turning to eating their faithful former companions in order to save their own lives. It would have started out with the horses dying of cold or of starvation; only then would they have been seen as meat. Later, though, even healthy horses had come to be regarded as a source of food, and were slaughtered deliberately. Again, I could not blame the men who did that. It was some slight respite that, as I carried on along the road, the bodies of mares and stallions became fewer and further between.

But as I headed towards Orsha, those telltale signs that I had seen on the carcasses of horses now became evident on the bodies of men. As the last horses died, so one food supply dried up. The living, who had already learned how to extract something nourishing from the body of a horse, had switched to applying the same skills to the bodies of their fellow men. Starvation had led to cannibalism. As with the horses, it would have begun with the violation of the bodies of those who were already dead. It would not have gone on to killing men for their meat—surely.

Was this the beginning of the path down which the Oprichniki, or their ancestors, had once, long ago, embarked? But no. As I had seen in the barn, and as Pyetr had told me, the Oprichniki ate not for sustenance, but for pleasure. They could not be compared with the degraded, starving men who had turned in desperation to the flesh of their comrades. But then, I too ate for pleasure. Nourishment is a requirement, but it was only the tiniest fraction of the motivation behind any meal I had enjoyed in the lowliest tavern in Moscow. Was there some parallel moment in the histories of vampires and humanity when consumption was transformed from a necessity into a vice?

I was closing now on the rear guard of our own Russian armies, and the road became busier with stragglers trying to catch up and with couriers ferrying messages in both directions. Still no one bothered even to begin to clear up the mess that the Grande Armée had left in its wake; and nor did I. Bonaparte had not yet been vanquished. There would be time for clearing up later.

Two days out of Orsha, and still some way east of Borisov, I came upon a fairly large encampment of Russian troops. I rode up to the sentries and dismounted. It had already been dark for some hours, and they were wary of a man who did not wear a uniform.

"Password?" one of them barked at me.

"I've no idea, I'm afraid," I told him, "but here are my papers." I handed over my credentials, which he inspected. They were clear enough to convince him of my rank and also gave him some idea I was not a part of the regular army. Beyond that, he judged it better not to ask questions.

"Can you take me to your commanding officer?" I asked him once he had returned the papers. He ran to a tent and returned with a young man of about twenty, in the uniform of a sublieutenant of the imperial guard infantry.

"Captain Danilov, I take it?" I acknowledged his greeting. "My name's Tarasov. Pleased to meet you. So what brings a man in your line of business to the front line?" There was no sign of resentment in his words. He was a professional soldier, and understood there are many ways in which a man can serve his country. With a gesture of his hand, he indicated that I should follow him through the camp.

"I've come to fight," I explained as we walked.

"I see," he said, with a hint of disbelief. "Fed up with the spying game then?"

"There's no one left to spy on."

"There'll be no one left to fight soon, either, thank heavens. If I'd been in your shoes I'd have given it another couple of weeks and Bonaparte would have been long dead."

"I need to feel the sword in my hand once again."

Tarasov laughed the laugh of a man who did not, in his heart, understand my sentiments. "Well, good for you," he said.

"So what is the French disposition at present?" I asked.

"They're pretty much trapped at Borisov," he explained. "They were hoping to cross the Berezina there, but Admiral Tchitchagov got in before them from the west and burnt the bridge."

"Do they need a bridge?" I asked. "Surely the river must be frozen pretty solid by now."

"Ah, no. They may have Bonaparte, but we have God on our side. Haven't you noticed the thaw?" I looked at him in his heavy greatcoat, hat, scarf and gloves. He was more sensitive than I if he could notice any thaw. "The river was frozen, but it's flowing again now. They'll never get across."

"So we're going in for the kill?"

"Well, we can't leave them there, can we? Kutuzov is coming in from the south as well. They're trapped."

"And who's in charge here?"

"Wittgenstein," said Tarasov proudly.

"So will Bonaparte fight?"

"He doesn't stand a chance. He'll have to surrender."

"That doesn't sound like him. Maybe he'll head south."

"It won't help him. The river just gets wider downstream. He won't find anywhere to cross."

"Until it freezes again," I put in.

"Then he'll freeze too."

We had come to a tent. Tarasov went inside and then soon returned to beckon me in, announcing me at the same time.

"Captain Danilov, sir!"

"Thank you, lieutenant," said the lieutenant-colonel who sat behind a makeshift table inside the tent. Around him, a number of other officers were standing or sitting. The relaxed atmosphere of the officers' mess filled the tent. "Sit down, Danilov," he continued, indicating a bench opposite him. "I'm Lieutenant-Colonel Chernyshev, by the way." I saluted him before sitting. "Drink?" he asked.

"Thank you, sir," I responded.

"Wine or vodka?"

"Vodka, please sir."

"Good man." He handed me a glass of vodka and also offered a cigar, which I took and lit from the candle on the table.

"So tell me, Danilov, who's your commanding officer?" asked Chernyshev.

"Major Savin."

"Savin? Vadim Fyodorovich, you mean?"

I smiled. "That's right. A friend of yours?"

"Oh, yes. A great friend—Petersburg man, like myself."

"Me too," I told him.

"Really?" His interest seemed to waver a little. "Splendid." Then, returning to the subject that interested him more, he added, "So how is Vadim Fyodorovich?"

"He's dead, sir."

"Ah!" Chernyshev took the news with the numbed resilience that I have seen in many experienced army officers. Through all his bluster and bonhomie, the death of each man under his command was felt deeply. The accumulation of deaths made it more painful, but gave him more experience of hiding that pain. Some feel they can never leave the army, for fear that the sorrow of all those accumulated deaths will be released if they do. For those who do leave, the failure of civilians to understand what they have been through can be the cause of even greater pain.

"So tell me, Captain Danilov," continued the lieutenant-colonel, his brief mourning absorbed into the mass, "why have you come to join up with us?"

I took a deep breath in preparation to give an answer that I did not know myself. Before I could begin, one of the other officers bent down and whispered into Chernyshev's ear. Chernyshev whispered back and nodded at the reply he got.

"Well, Captain Danilov," said Chernyshev, "it seems we have been struck by something of a coincidence." He waited for me to respond, but there was little that I could say. "I am told that there is someone in this camp who claims he knows you. A prisoner, no less. A Frenchman, no less!"

He seemed particularly aghast at the fact that the prisoner should be French, though it was well within the realms of likelihood. It suddenly struck me why he should have got on so well with Vadim.

"Did he give a name?"

"No. Tell him the details, Mironov."

The officer who had just whispered to Chernyshev now addressed me. "He came in about an hour ago. They caught him up on the hills to the northeast. He didn't bother to put up any kind of a fight at all. He gave no name. He's wearing a French uniform, rank of *chef de bataillon*. All he would say was that he wanted to speak to Captain Aleksei Ivanovich Danilov."

"He knew I was here?" I asked.

"Evidently," shrugged Mironov.

I had been in the camp less than an hour myself. It could only be that I had been followed. "What does he look like?" I asked.

"I'm afraid I haven't seen him myself," replied Mironov. "Do you want me to take you to him?"

"No, not yet," I replied, taking another sip of vodka. "What time is it?"

"Just gone midnight," Mironov told me.

TWELVE

"And when's sunrise?"

"Around eight."

"I'll speak to him at seven. Where are you keeping him?"

"He's with the other prisoners."

I thought for a moment before saying, "Keep him apart from them. Make sure he's bound hand and foot. Put him outside somewhere, by a fire— keep him warm—but definitely outside." I was imitating Maks' plan of months before. "And be very, very careful with him. He's dangerous."

"You know who it is then?" asked Lieutenant-Colonel Chernyshev.

"I believe I do," I replied, puffing at my cigar.

Once again, I slept well. I was woken up around six o'clock and had time for a leisurely breakfast before Lieutenant Mironov led me to where the mysterious prisoner was being guarded.

"I hope you're not going to spend too long with him, Captain Danilov," the lieutenant told me as we walked across the camp. "The word is that Bonaparte is heading south. The French are trying to build a bridge."

"And we're to follow?"

"Absolutely. Admiral Tchitchagov is shadowing him, on the other side of the Berezina. We're already beginning to break camp. We'll be on our way within four hours."

"I assure you, lieutenant, I'll be finished with the prisoner by dawn."

"I hope so, sir."

We were now some way away from a large campfire which warmed me even at a distance.

"There he is," said Mironov, nodding towards the fire.

Beside it stood two guards, weary from their night's vigil, but still alert enough that their prisoner had not escaped. Between them, sitting on a bench next to the fire, a tall man with his wrists bound was slumped forward, his elbows on his knees. His long blond hair, straggly and dishevelled, hung forward to cover his face. Even so, he was unmistakable.

"Is it who you thought it was?" asked Mironov.

"Oh, yes," I replied.

Chapter XXX

"GOOD MORNING, IUDA," I SAID, SOFTLY.

Iuda lifted his head. He looked decrepit. His hair was unwashed and matted, his chin was unshaven and his complexion was sallow—I doubted whether he had "eaten" for days. His jaw was swollen with the bruise of a recent, heavy blow. Yet still he smiled.

"Good morning, Aleksei Ivanovich."

"Has he tried anything?" I said to one of his guards.

"Nothing, Sir. He kept asking when you would come, but I shut him up." He mimicked the action of a blow with the butt of his musket. Iuda winced at the appropriate moment, joining in the mime so as to mock it. He glanced momentarily up at the guard's face, then averted his eyes.

"Was he armed?" I asked.

"Just this." The guard reached into his knapsack and handed me the double-bladed knife that I had seen in Iuda's hand before. "It's an odd thing, don't you think, sir? I can't see the practical use for it."

"That's one of the things I intend to find out."

"Do you want us to stay close, sir?" he asked. It was refreshing to be once again amongst men who were so trustworthy and so steadfast, though his suggestion might also have been motivated by self-interest. Keeping close to us would mean keeping close to the fire. Both guards looked pale and deathly cold, their greatcoats buttoned tight up to their chins to keep in what warmth they could. Even so, my own concerns overcame my sympathy for them.

"Not too close," I said. "For reasons you'll understand, it's best that you don't hear what we discuss." He nodded earnestly. I had no doubt that he would stand just on the far side of earshot, but I would speak to Iuda in French to be on the safe side. "But if he does turn nasty, you'll need to be ready—for your own sakes as well as mine."

TWELVE

All around us, the camp was in turmoil. Tents were being taken down. Horses were being harnessed to guns. Baggage was being loaded on to wagons. The activity of all was enough to keep them warm despite the frozen night air, but for Iuda and myself, and the two guards who stood apart, both at some distance from us, the fire provided the only heat.

I sat down opposite Iuda as his guards moved warily away. I pondered how to start, hoping that he might say something, but he remained silent, looking at the ground. Despite his circumstances, he still had an air of victory about him. Then I realized why. As far as he knew, his trick with Margarita had worked—I had believed Domnikiia to be a vampire and had killed her.

"Aren't you going to tell me that Domnikiia was never a vampire?" I asked him. He frowned briefly. The name was unfamiliar to him. Then he made the connection to Dominique.

"It seems you're already aware of it," he replied.

"She's alive and well, you know."

"I don't doubt it," he said, nonplussed.

"Oh, come on, Iuda. I'm sure you have your pride, but I think you can be honest now. These are your last moments on earth—don't waste them. I know you intended me to see your performance with Margarita."

"I won't waste them, Lyosha. Neither should you. You're right, though, I did know you were watching at the window."

"And you expected me to march right in there and ram a stake straight through Domnikiia's heart, and then regret it for the rest of my life."

"Do you play chess at all, Lyosha?" he asked.

"Some," I replied.

"When you form a plan of attack—equally, when you plan an attack in a real battle—do you see it through (in your mind) to a single end, or does your plan branch with the varying assumptions about how your opponent might react?"

"It branches, of course—though I'd always assume it most likely that my opponent would make the best move." I was surprised at how quickly Iuda had managed to take the reins of the conversation.

"Exactly. And it's disappointing, isn't it, when he doesn't play the best move—when he falls into some trivial trap you threw in his way, not with any real intent of entrapping him, but simply to force him along the path you had chosen? He doesn't in the end rob you of the victory, but robs you of the pleasure of demonstrating the full brilliance of your plan."

"I think that depends on whether you're the sort of person who prefers the game or the victory," I said.

"Clearly, without the victory, the game is nothing," he replied, nodding in agreement. "But the reverse is also true. And don't tell me that you don't enjoy the game, Aleksei Ivanovich. You've had many opportunities to go for the swift conclusion, but you've not taken them."

"Haven't I?"

"Perhaps it's just caution on your part."

I felt the same sense of unease in myself and the same confidence in him that I had done during our meeting at the crossroads. Here, though, I could see no reason for him to be confident. This was my territory. There was no hanging cadaver that was going to spring to his aid. Perhaps he was expecting something of the sort. Perhaps he was unaware that Foma was dead. That was it. This was part of a plan where Foma would come to his rescue. It would be a pleasure to see how he reacted to news of Foma's death, but for now I chose—as one cannot in the game of chess—to keep that card up my sleeve. In chess one can disguise one's plans, but not hide them.

"And so your scene with Margarita was just a sideshow—one of these little traps that I didn't fall into?" I asked.

"You have always played the better move when you've been given the choice. Only an idiot would kill the woman he loved without being sure she was a vampire." It was the very word Domnikiia had used. As he spoke he smiled as if he knew how close I had come to doing what he described.

"So what's your real plan, from which that was just a diversion? To get captured here and to die in the morning sun?"

"There are more moves to make before you will see it."

"Chess isn't a game of bluff, Iuda. A gentleman will resign once he sees he cannot win."

"I am, I assure you, a gentleman."

"And all your pretence at planning," I went on, realizing that much of what he said could be only bravura, "it all relies on so much luck. How could you be sure I would come back to Moscow to see Domnikiia that night?"

"Because I told Pyetr and Iakov Zevedayinich I was going to see her," he said simply.

"And you asked them to tell me, I suppose?"

"No, I instructed them not to tell you."

"So you knew I would get it out of them?"

"There were two of them in the barn, you outside. Either they would defeat you—which would have been a disappointment, but still a victory—or you would defeat them and probably get the information from them. Which one was it that talked, by the way? I would suspect Iakov Zeve-dayinich."

"It was Pyetr. I didn't give Iakov Zevedayinich the opportunity. How did you know I was there?"

"Where else would you be? I never saw you after the coach crashed, but I knew you wouldn't run away. We were not particularly stealthy in our return to the barn."

"And no concern at all for the others. You set up Pyetr and Iakov Zeve-dayinich for me to kill, just to further your own ends. Are all vampires like that, Iuda, or is it just you?"

"They all had as little concern for each other as I did for them. Clearly, there are times when it is convenient to work as a pack, and sometimes it's worth making an issue over the fate of one's comrades, as we did with Maksim Sergeivich, but it's mostly for show. There is no brotherly love that would make one sacrifice himself for another."

"It's hard to see why there's any need for your soul to be damned," I said contemplatively. "To feel like that must be a living hell."

"On the contrary, it is one of the vampire's most desirable attributes. I have no idea why it is that most humans possess these feelings of affection for other humans, nor why vampires suddenly lose them. I'm sure one day some great scientist will explain it. Myself, I suspect it's something to do with the different methods of reproduction."

I looked at him blankly. He still did not believe that these were the last minutes of his life. I picked up his knife, which I had jabbed into the snow between my feet, and inspected it. It was a simple construction—precisely as I had conceived it to be when I first saw it. Two identical, short knives had been fastened together at the handles. The handles were bound up with a long strip of leather. The bond was very firm—I could not make the blades move relative to one another. Beneath the leather there must have been something that fixed them more solidly. The blades were smoothly sharp on one side, and serrated on the other—the teeth pointing slightly backwards towards the handle—ideal, in a single blade, for cutting the fur away from an animal's carcass. Each ended in a sharp point that could be used to stab. The gap between the blades was wide enough for me to comfortably fit two fingers.

"You don't all carry these, I noticed, do you?" I asked Iuda.

"No, just me."

"Why do you need it? Your teeth no good? Too much sugar in your diet?"

He smiled, but did not grin, and it occurred to me that I could not recall ever seeing him grin. Perhaps I was right. Perhaps he was that most pitiful of creatures, a vampire with rotten teeth.

"Not quite," he said.

"Useful, I suppose, for cutting your chest open when you create another one of you."

"Then, and at other times." He was more reticent on this matter than he had been on others. Another question raised itself in my mind, and the image of my own hand driving a stake into a young woman's chest.

"Did I need to kill Margarita?" I asked. "Was she dead when we found her, or had you made her . . . one of you?"

"She was dead," he said calmly, his eyes fixed on mine. "I killed her."

"But why? Why waste the chance of turning her into a vampire?"

"I killed her because I enjoy it. But as to turning anyone into a vampire, I am sadly incapable of that."

"And why is that? I'm sure you must far outstrip the others in your ability to persuade people to willingly take the step." I didn't like to compliment him, but as I had long ago discovered, he was the only one of the Oprichniki who showed any real personality.

"Certainly—and that, for me, is one of the most pleasurable parts. The problem, though, is a physical one."

"What do you mean?"

"As we have discussed before, I am not a doctor. I cannot explain how these things work. I can go through the motions but it simply does not happen, any more than it would if you were to attempt it."

"Except that I wouldn't even want to attempt it," I added vehemently.

"That may be the difference between us," he smiled.

"So in the end, despite what you both did, despite her willingness, Margarita did not become a vampire. When you killed her she died as a mortal human."

He nodded thoughtfully and then looked towards me with an intent gaze, pinching his bottom lip between his fingers, indifferent to the inconvenience of his bound hands. I was reminded of the discussion of chess he had introduced earlier. He was a player who had made a move and was now trying to determine whether I, his opponent, had seen the full ramifications of it.

"What were you doing when you were captured?" I asked.

"Spying for the French."

"Really?" I laughed.

"Really. I need to leave Russia. They are leaving Russia, or at least trying to. I can help them while our interests coincide."

"It can't help you or them much for you to be captured. I presume that wasn't part of the plan."

"No, you're right, it wasn't. Not until I happened to see you trotting down the road towards the camp. Then I knew I just had to see you one more time."

So—assuming that he was telling the truth—he had not been following me. It had simply been luck that we had found each other again, though a luck that we had both been trying to manufacture. That he had not been following me made it all the more likely that he did not yet know about the death of Foma. I felt sure now that there was no escape for him.

"One more time before you died," I added.

"One more time before I left your country," he countered. "Being the only one of us left, I feel it my duty."

"The only one left?"

"Well, you've told me about Pyetr and Iakov Zevedayinich, and I presume that Dmitry has killed Foma by now."

I nodded. "Foma's dead." I was deflated, but I had to hide it. If Foma was not part of Iuda's escape plan, then what was? I recalled the possibility that he might have some human collaborator. If he did, and he was a Russian, then the man would have had little trouble infiltrating this camp. Was that the basis of Iuda's confidence, or was it mere bluff? He glanced at the two guards, some way away on either side of him, as if judging how far he could run before they could catch him.

"Dmitry Fetyukovich proved to be a startlingly brave man," Iuda continued. "To kill a vampire is one thing, but to take one alive is quite another."

"You saw it happen?"

"Oh yes."

"And you did nothing to help Foma?"

"Why should I? It wasn't worth risking my life. Dmitry believed that I would come and rescue Foma, but he really didn't understand. As I said to you, even a vampire would not risk his life to save another vampire. I take it, then, that you've seen Dmitry. Is he here with you?"

"No, he's not here," I replied. "Just tell me, Iuda. How do you plan to escape?"

He deliberately misinterpreted the question. "Well, as far as I understand it, Napoleon's move to the south is a feint. Already Tchitchagov has set out to follow him on the far bank of the Berezina, and Kutuzov will soon be heading that way too."

Although it wasn't what I had been trying to find out, it was vital information nonetheless. I followed the line that Iuda had begun. "Whereas Bonaparte's real plan is what?" I asked.

"Ah!" said Iuda with a smile. "See how the wily interrogator tricks his quarry into revealing all!" He leaned forward and winked with an air of conspiracy. "Between you and me, Lyosha, he's found a ford, upstream at a place called Studienka. It'll still need bridging of course, but it should get them across."

"Get *him* across," I responded cynically.

"How do you mean?"

"There's not much of the Grande Armée left compared with what came. Thirty thousand out of half a million? It's about the emperor, not the army now."

"And why not? Napoleon is a great man."

"You think so?"

"He makes my life a lot easier."

"So Dmitry was quite wrong. You were never on our side?" I asked, feeling more vindicated than shocked by the proposition.

"Not at all. If Napoleon had defeated Russia it would have meant French hegemony over the whole of Europe. And that would have meant peace—a peace you and I would have despised for different reasons, but nonetheless inimical to both of our lifestyles. True, there would still be war with Britain, but I've never been much use at sea."

"So you just always support the underdog?"

"I like to help maintain the balance of power."

"So now you switch sides to France when she is weak?"

"Exactly."

"How long have you been doing this?" I asked with genuine curiosity. "How many times have you switched sides? How many wars have you tried to perpetuate for your own ends?" I was prevaricating unnecessarily. "What I mean is, Iuda, when did you become a vampire?"

"An interesting question," he replied, but one which he was not going to answer.

I had not noticed it begin, but as our conversation paused, I heard that the few birds which for some reason chose to remain in the trees during the winter months had begun their daily song. The pre-dawn dark blue of the sky was only just becoming visible, but already they had noticed it and reacted to it. I felt a little sorry. There was so much more that I wanted to ask of Iuda and discover from him, but I could not afford to be sentimental. I could so easily learn to regret any opportunity for survival that I might offer him.

"Might I be allowed to smoke?" he asked politely.

I could see no harm in it. I shouted to the guard, "Have you got a pipe? Or a cigar?" He came over and handed me a cigar. It was a thin, withered offering—much like the man who offered it—made à l'Espagnole, with just paper to wrap it. It was possibly all he had. I gave a coin in exchange, paying—in my sympathy for his instinctive willingness to hand over even his personal possessions at a senior officer's behest—a similar price to that I would have received during my days as a tobacco vendor in occupied Moscow.

Again Iuda eyed the guard, looking for a chance to flee. I lit the cigar from the fire and offered it to Iuda. He gestured to me with his bound hands and gave an expression of humble entreaty. I placed the cigar between my lips and then cut his hands free with his own knife, before handing the cigar to him. His feet were still tied, and I had the guards with me. Besides, it would soon be dawn and Iuda would be no more threat to anyone. I felt safe.

"Thank you," he said, inhaling deeply. I sat back down and threw the knife once again into the snow between my feet. Knowing that time was short, I searched my brain for any other questions I could put to him. One immediately occurred to me.

"How was it that you managed to get from Kurilovo back to Moscow so quickly?"

"By horse," he answered simply. "The same as you."

"But it took me eight hours, and you got there ahead of me."

"Well, I left before you did."

"What I mean is," I asked, annoyed that he was, quite sincerely, missing my point, "how did you travel in daylight?"

"Ah, I see. One of the many curses that the vampire must put up with. I often wonder whether there are any advantages to it at all."

"The immortality, surely," I said. It was Domnikiia's voice that had put it in my head.

"Ideally, yes, but not in practical terms. Did Pyetr prove to be immortal?

TWELVE

Or Matfei? And what about that boy—Pavel? His vampire existence spanned only a few weeks. Vampires are so easy to kill."

"I've not found it so easy."

"Oh, you have, Lyosha! Once you know what to do. And even if you don't, the daylight thing must be a misery. Thousands must die by accident just because someone happens to open the curtains." He failed to conceal the smirk that broke on his face, pleased at his own ridicule.

"So why do people willingly choose that path?" I asked.

"As you say, some are fools who do it for the immortality. Others do it for the liberty."

"Liberty?"

"Yes, liberty. I doubt vampires have any desire for equality and I know that they have no conception of fraternity, but isn't liberty what all men seek?"

It was as though he had been reading my mind as I had lain beside Domnikiia, waiting to join her in that world of immoral immortality. Still I was compelled to hear what Iuda had to say—to understand what the appeal was that could turn a man willingly into a monster. "Liberty from what?" I asked.

"Most men want liberty from many different things, but all seek—and few achieve—liberty from themselves. That is what the man who drinks the warm, fresh blood of a vampire seeks. That is what I too have found—to be unconstrained by conscience or by God—to revel in the ultimate pleasure that lies in the pain of others, both as its witness and its instigator, without the clammy undertow of one's own . . . sentiment." He spoke the final word as though it tasted of rotting fish, then he smiled. "You of all people, Lyosha, know that."

He glanced pointedly at the scars on my left hand as he spoke, but I knew that he could not be aware how much his words rang true.

"And that makes becoming a vampire worthwhile?" I asked, both fascinated and repelled by what he had said.

He paused and bent his head forward. Its shadow, long and distorted in the low sun behind him, reached as far as my feet.

"I don't know," he said wearily. "There are so many restrictions—so much that they must miss out on. The desire to kill is so much intermingled with the desire to eat—much like in humans. The first kill of the night delights both predilections, but as they become less hungry, they also lose (to an extent) the urge to kill. By surfeiting, the appetite sickens. How much better it is to separate the two; to eat for hunger and to kill for pleasure. Do you hunt, Lyosha?"

"Occasionally," I said.

"Then perhaps you will understand what I mean. More than that, though, there are straightforward, mechanical problems that make the life of a vampire so unappealing. For instance, have you ever considered, Lyosha, that a vampire can never look into the eyes of his victim as life departs? *You* can, and I'm sure you have. You know the experience of seeing a man's face as, thanks to you, he breathes his last. Whether you count it as a pleasure or not, you know the experience. A vampire must bite at the neck, and so can never take that pleasure.

"Now, with my knife . . ." He leaned forward, casting his cigar aside, and reached forward for the knife. I was so enthralled by what he was saying and his movement was so appropriate to the conversation, that I almost let him. Only at the last moment did I kick his hand to one side. He sat back upright and raised his palms to me in apology. The guard I had spoken to glanced towards us at the movement, but did nothing.

"With my knife," Iuda continued, "I can inflict all the pain that a vampire can with his teeth and so much more, and yet I'm still free to gaze into the face of my companion and see every exquisite reaction to every excruciating action I perform. And by joining up with the others—the Oprichniki, I believe you called us as a group—I had eleven other so much more brutal weapons whom I could let get on with inflicting the pain, whilst I sat back and experienced the pleasure."

As he spoke, I found myself confronted with the memory of the scene in the barn near Kurilovo. Each of the Oprichniki had bowed to Iuda's every suggestion of what they should do. He had scarcely touched the man or ever tasted his flesh, and yet he had been the one who had taken the most pleasure from the situation. The sun, now risen in the east behind Iuda's head, made to seem larger by its low declination, formed an ironic halo.

TWELVE

"What freedom, I wonder, do they really have—the vampires—that I have not also achieved?" asked Iuda.

"Achieved?"

"You are right, as ever, Lyosha. I cannot claim it as any achievement. It is something I have always had—something I was born with—something that most men can only gain by becoming a vampire. I have the best of both worlds. I can bask in the sun. I can eat a normal meal. I could even father a child if I wanted. Yet still I can indulge in the ultimate bliss that lies in the unutterable, absolute, unfettered suffering of another human being."

"Did the other vampires never recognize you for what you are?" I asked.

"For what I am? I could ask the same question of you. You had no idea that the twelve of us were vampires at first. And then when you did, you had no idea that I was not. There's no magic to it. I act as they do. I feel as they do. I kill as they do. They're not going to notice that occasionally I like to go outside during the day—not without killing themselves in the process. Zmyeevich, of course, is a different matter. He's been a vampire for a long, long time. But whatever his suspicions about me may have been, he has his own reasons for not pursuing them."

I sat in silence, facing him. Still today, I cannot determine exactly when during the conversation the truth had come to me. It was astonishing, but not revolutionary. Iuda was exactly what he claimed he was. He was not a vampire in much the same way that Maksim was not French. He aspired to be a vampire. He behaved like a vampire. But occasionally he was able to benefit from the fact that he was not a vampire. Maks himself had known that he deserved to be treated as though he were French. Similarly, though he might in some minor, legalistic way be human, Iuda deserved to be treated as though he were a vampire. The problem was that the light of the sun could no longer do the work for me. It was a problem and a pleasure. I would be happy to see him die in a more traditional manner.

I rose to my feet and faced him. "I think we should be able to arrange a firing squad before we break camp. You are, after all, a French spy." I began to raise my hand to summon the guard.

Iuda frowned and turned away from me with a look of impatient disappointment on his face. He shook his head and tutted to himself quietly. "So, you see, there was never any prospect of her becoming a vampire," he said. There was some point on to which our conversation had not turned, and he wanted it to.

"Margarita, you mean?"

"I wonder when it was she realized that she was unchanged—that she would remain mortal."

"I think you demonstrated her mortality pretty quickly," I snapped.

"What do you mean?"

"By killing her straight after."

Iuda smiled a tight, knowing smile that barely resisted breaking into a laugh. "Tell me, Lyosha," he asked. "What was it that first made *you* believe that it was not Dominique you had seen me with at the window?"

I thought about it for a moment, but there was no trick to it—the answer was obvious. "The fact that she hadn't become a vampire."

"Which means . . ."

"Which means?"

Iuda sighed. "It's really no fun for me if you can't be bothered to work it out for yourself." I looked at him blankly. "You concluded that Dominique had not been with me because if she had been with a vampire she would have become a vampire," he explained, like a schoolteacher.

I don't know whether I had been dull witted or whether it was a conclusion that I wanted to avoid coming to, but now Iuda had brought it to a point where I could not ignore it. I sank back on to my seat. Could it have after all been Domnikiia that I had seen with Iuda at the window and not Margarita? Of course she had not become a vampire; Iuda had no ability to make her into one.

She could have sucked every last drop of blood from the wound in his chest and it would have had no effect.

But she had believed that it would. Had she awoken that morning with exactly the same sense of surprise that I had later felt, as she discovered there had been no change in her? Had she found to her horror that she could stand comfortably in the bright morning sunlight and begun to cry as she realized that it meant she would still one day die a mortal death? She would have had to think quickly to then pretend that it was Margarita that I had seen. No, that was impossible. She must have decided to say it was Margarita beforehand. Either Iuda had told her to, or they had planned it together. There had been a great deal of careful choreography to ensure that, watching from across the square, I only ever saw Domnikiia from behind. Had Margarita known about the plan? Domnikiia had seemed genuinely shocked when we had found Margarita's body. Genuinely? How could I now regard anything about her as being genuine? A woman who would gladly become a vampire would hardly baulk at the death of her best friend being a part of the process.

It could not be true, and yet I could not see any fault in it. I myself had been sure it was Domnikiia that I had seen with Iuda right up until the point I had discovered she was not a vampire. Now I had a better explanation for that. Was I really fool enough to mistake Margarita for Domnikiia just because their hair was similar—I who knew every inch of Domnikiia's body? There must have been something more that I had seen, without consciously registering, that had told me it was Domnikiia, and now I knew it to be true. All her sorrow and anguish in the days that followed had been very convincing, but then, that was her speciality. I heard Domnikiia speaking to me, but she only repeated one whispered word over and over. How much she must have been laughing to herself when she had first said it to me. *"Prostak! Prostak! Prostak!"*

Iuda placed a consolatory hand on my knee, saying, "She did it for you, Lyosha. She thought she could be with you forever." He was standing now. At some point, unnoticed by me, he had retrieved his knife and had cut the ropes around his feet with it. I heard a shout from one of the soldiers guarding us to the other, but he was too late. The other had momentarily turned his back on us and Iuda was now behind him. A brief stroke from Iuda's toothed blades across his neck and he fell to the ground, the pure, white snow around him sullied by an ever-growing stain of red as blood haemorrhaged from his wounded neck, unhindered by the grasping of his dying hands.

The other soldier had raised his musket, but had been hesitant to fire while he might hit his comrade. Now he fired, but it was too late. Iuda was on the move again, keeping low and changing direction again and again. I set off in pursuit. The remaining guard did likewise, some paces behind me. The rest of the camp, consumed by their preparations for departure, did not at first notice what was happening, but soon our shouts alerted them to the fugitive. Those who threw themselves in Iuda's way offered little impediment to him. He was far more brutal and effective with his knife than any vampire could have been with its teeth. Some men tackled him with swords and bayonets, but he showed no fear, and though some of the blades hit their mark, he seemed to show little discomfort either. None of the wounds was deep enough to cause serious injury, and while posing as a vampire he had clearly learned to control his pain—along with so many other feelings—lest his humanity should be discovered.

We were now beyond the edge of the camp, almost at woodland in which Iuda could easily hide himself. The guard who had been pursuing a little way behind, younger and fitter than I was, had now caught up and overtaken me. Having discharged his musket, he had found no time to reload, and so now had only his bayonet as a weapon. He was within striking distance of Iuda when Iuda stopped and turned. The soldier had no time to stop himself. He had not been aiming his bayonet and so it glided harmlessly past Iuda's side. As he turned, Iuda brought forward his hand and the soldier ran straight on to Iuda's knife. It penetrated just below his breastbone, embedding itself deep behind his rib cage. With the force of the blow, the soldier was lifted off his feet, his back arched in agony and his limbs splayed out limply as life began to retreat from them. With a jerk of his arm, Iuda threw the man off his knife and I heard the tearing, rasping sound of its teeth making the wound even greater on exit than it had been on entry.

Iuda turned and continued to run, but I was already upon him. I launched myself towards him and grabbed him around the waist. We both fell to the ground and my face was filled with snow, blinding me. I knelt up and wiped the snow from my eyes, just in time to see Iuda's hand scything towards me, the toothed blades presented, not to stab but to slash. I flung myself backwards, flicking my head away from him. As I fell, I felt a searing pain in my left cheek where the blades connected. I fell to my back, breathing deeply, and noticed as I breathed that air was coming in through my wounded cheek as well as through my mouth.

I pushed myself up in preparation to avoid Iuda's next blow, but it did not come. A shot rang out from behind me, hitting Iuda in the arm. He turned and fled into the woods, leaving me to live with the misery that he had created for me.

CHAPTER XXXI

THE WOUND TO MY CHEEK WAS NOT AS SERIOUS AS I HAD first thought. The cold weather became a brief friend as it numbed my face while the surgeon closed it up with a suture. I went back to Lieutenant-Colonel Chernyshev to tell him what had happened.

"Escaped?" he thundered.

"I'm afraid so, sir," I replied.

"I'll have those guards flogged."

"It's too late for that, sir."

He glanced up at my face and understood. "I see," he said. "Well, it's only one man, I suppose. All a bit of a waste of time, though."

"Bonaparte's move south is a ruse, sir. The prisoner told me. The real crossing is to the north, at Studienka."

"That's something at least. So you'll soon be joining us in action there then?"

"No, sir. I'd like to pursue the prisoner."

"Is he worth it—just one man?"

"I believe so," I said.

"Well, I suppose you people know your job. I can't lend you any men."

"I don't ask for any, sir. Just a French uniform, if you have one."

"We have dozens. Lieutenant Mironov, see that he gets what he needs."

Mironov provided a dragoon uniform and a horse and some provisions, and I was soon heading out of what remained of the breaking camp. At first, I had to make my way alongside the advancing Russian troops (fortunately, I had not yet changed into my new uniform), but soon I headed off to the north of their path and the sound of marching faded behind me.

The only trail that Iuda had left was that he had planned to cross the Berezina with Bonaparte at Studienka. It was quite possible that this had been a lie, or that he would now change his mind, but my only option was still to try to intercept him there. I had not had time to properly consider what Iuda had said to me, but now as I rode through the quiet, frozen woods, I began to think.

The less painful matter to deal with was that Iuda was not a vampire. I had already concluded that this made little difference to my opinion of him. If a man chooses to become a vampire so that he may behave like a monster or if he finds himself quite able to behave like a monster anyway, he is still a monster and still happy so to be. Iuda remained a danger to all those he came into contact with. One question that had to be asked was whether any of the other Oprichniki was also not a vampire. Iuda had implied that they all were, but was Iuda to be trusted? The evidence of my own eyes convinced me of most of them—after their deaths I had witnessed their immediate bodily decay. I had not seen what became of Ioann or Filipp once they had perished. The deaths of Simon, Iakov Alfeyinich and Faddei had, if Maks was to be believed, been caused by sunlight. I felt confident that all eleven had indeed been vampires. If not, what was I to care? Just as it did not fundamentally matter with Iuda, neither did it with any of the others.

But what of Domnikiia? The idea of being tricked—of being betrayed—by her of all people was the true nightmare from which I saw no prospect of awakening. When she teased me it revealed her wit and her spirit, but to play games with me like this over such issues showed in her what almost amounted to insanity. "I'm not surprised Iuda found it so easy to fool you." Those had been her words. She and Iuda both delighted in playing me for the fool, and I had so far been gullibly eager to oblige them. But I also remembered what Maksim had once said, about the best place to hide a tree being in a forest, the best place to hide a lie being amongst the truth. Why had Iuda allowed himself to be captured? To speak to me. What was it that he wanted to tell me? Not about Bonaparte's plans. Not about his views on chess. Not even to tell me he wasn't a vampire. It was to put the thought into my head that Domnikiia had chosen to become a vampire. Amongst that forest of truth, that was the single fact that he had wanted to convey. It was not even a fact—it was a piece of information that might be true and might not be. The truth could never be known and so the doubt would haunt me forever.

Iuda's game, either through planning or through extemporization, had unfolded layer by layer in front of me, like a journey up a mountain when every false peak, once conquered, reveals another higher peak behind it. First I believed he had turned Domnikiia into a vampire. Then I discovered that, even so, I could not kill her. Then I discovered that she was not a vampire and that, had I killed her, it would have been as a mortal woman. This morning he had convinced me that she had all along wanted to be a vampire, even though he could not make her one. He could not go on forever pushing on one side of the scales and then the other and switching my view from one side to the next, but now he did not need to. He had found a perfect balance point. I could never know the truth and so, whatever I chose to do, I would spend half my life regretting. If I abandoned Domnikiia, then I would worry that I had done her wrong, that I had believed Iuda's final lie about her when she had behaved throughout in perfect innocence. If I stayed with her, I would be forever looking at her, wondering what happened between them that night in Moscow.

My perception was so battered by my constantly changing view of the truth—not just over Domnikiia, but over Maksim, over Dmitry, over the Oprichniki and over Iuda himself—that I was no longer able to find certainty in anything. Vadim's advice, I knew, would have been to go back to Petersburg, to go back to Marfa. She was someone in whom I had never had any doubt, nor had I any reason to. With her I would find a safe, content retreat. But then even Vadim's advice became ambiguous. How he would have despised any concept of retreat.

I was nearing the village of Studienka. I dismounted, tied up my horse and, despite the freezing cold, changed from the outer layers of my clothing into my French uniform. Skirting around the village, hidden by the woods, I made my way to a small hillock that overlooked the river itself. There I lay, concealed almost instantly beneath the falling snow, and observed the tattered remains of the Grande Armée.

Tattered and yet magnificent. There must have been fifty thousand before me; half of them soldiers, half noncombatants, all desperate to get across that river, to get out of Russia and to get home. Bonaparte's great campaign lay in ruins, the conquering ambition of every man transformed into self-preserving terror. None could have dreamed that the largest army ever assembled in the world would be reduced, in scarcely six months, to such a shambles. And yet it had happened, and I was thrilled to witness it.

But for an army slashed to less than a tenth of its former size, beset by the hellish cold of a foreign winter and caught between three Russian armies, each on its own the size of theirs, they had performed a remarkable feat. Two bridges had been built across the river. Even now I could see sappers and pontoniers up to their armpits in the icy water, strengthening and repairing the bridges as thousand upon thousands of men broke step to march across. Every building in the village had been torn down to provide timber. On the high ground on the far side of the river, the advance guard had already set up a defensive position. They were being engaged from the south. Tchitchagov, realizing his error, had travelled back north to the real crossing point. The French deployments already across the river were holding him off and allowing the remainder of the army to slip away to the west unmolested once they had crossed.

On the eastern bank, an innumerable multitude waited to cross along the two narrow, man-made isthmuses—not just soldiers, though of those there were many, but the entire entourage that any army requires to survive, particularly one so far from home. Men and women waited to cross the river, and those whose duties, however vital they might be, did not require them to carry a sword or a musket found themselves reckoned least in the pecking order. Cooks, washerwomen, smiths and armourers were among those who waited to cross and, even amongst them, an order of merit would be established. Would an army in hopeless, frozen retreat favour those who maintained its weapons or those who filled its belly?

My intention of spotting one man amongst the tens of thousands was not as futile as it could have been. Though it would be impossible to scan the crowds of weary-faced troops that milled and bustled on the riverbank, the bridges themselves were narrow and all had to cross by one or the other.

Indeed, most crossed by the smaller bridge, the larger being used for guns, wagons and cavalry. When I had last seen him, Iuda had no horse. Whether he had acquired one by now, I could only guess.

Although, with the help of my spyglass, I could inspect the face of each man as he approached the bridge, I was so far away that Iuda would be across the river by the time I could get down to the bank. My only prospect was to get down there amongst the French.

However determined the French were in getting as many men across the river as possible, it was at the expense of every other feature of military discipline. I was not challenged for any password or credentials as I picked my way first through the crowds of casualties and camp followers who would be the last to cross the bridge, if at all, and secondly through the teeming infantry who waited impatiently for their turn to cross. I looked out of place; any idea of uniform had been abandoned by the majority of the Grande Armée, in favour of more practical clothes—any clothes—that might keep out the cold. Even so, nobody paid me any attention.

As I got close to the bridges themselves, I received a few angry shoves from those who thought I was trying to jump my turn, but it was easy to assure them that I was not planning to cross the bridge, but to guard it. I joined the exclusive band of truculent sentries who stood at the entrance to the smaller footbridge.

"What did you do to get posted here?" asked one.

Evidently, this thankless duty was assigned as a punishment, not an honour. "I misheard an order," I said.

"Lots of soldiers have been hard of hearing today," he laughed. We said little more to one another. There was nothing to do but watch the lines of men as they jostled to get on to the bridge, giving them the occasional shove when they got too much out of shape. I inspected every face that went past, as well as trying to keep an eye on the mounted men that crossed by the other bridge, but there was no sign of Iuda. What I would do if I saw him, I was not sure. To kill him there and then—one French soldier killing another, apparently unprovoked—would mean almost certain and instant execution for me. Despite the fact that I had voluntarily walked into the midst of a desperate enemy, I was in no mood for suicide. Iuda's death was now a secondary issue to me. What I needed from him was certainty. If I was lucky, I would have the opportunity to see him die afterwards, but now I had to know, one way or the other, what had happened between him and Domnikiia.

I could think of no other way to determine it. I could ask Domnikiia herself, but I would not believe her answer; at least not if she denied it. I would believe her only if the answer she gave was the one I did not want to hear. I could find the man she claimed she had been with that night, but he would, for the sake of his reputation, instantly deny ever having heard of her. Iuda was the only other person who knew for sure. He had already told me that it had been Domnikiia, but he had previously allowed me to believe that it hadn't. I would go through hell—and this frozen exodus seemed to me a pretty close thing—to get a definitive answer from him.

That afternoon, I was bestowed with an unexpected privilege, if that is the correct word for it. For the first and only time in my life, I saw Bonaparte himself in the flesh. Accompanied by the once mighty Imperial Guard, he made his way across the larger bridge to the west bank of the river. He was not the man I had imagined him to be. My image of him was formed from engravings and paintings and stoked by his reputation. It was no surprise if today he was not at his best. He was both older and fatter than any picture I had seen of him. His nose was not hooked, as is often portrayed, but of normal size and with a slight, hardly noticeable bend. His hair was not black, but of a dark reddish-blond. I wondered if the images I had seen of his empress, Marie-Louise, were as inaccurate and whether Domnikiia in fact looked anything like her. Though he tried to ride upright and erect, he had a tendency to slouch in his saddle. His mouth held the grimace of a man in pain. Despite all this, his blue eyes still burnt with a fury. Was this the look of the intense desire for conquest that had brought the whole of Europe under his heel? Or was it the glazed shield of defiance of a man despairing at his humiliation?

For those tired remnants of the Grande Armée, it was still the former. A cheer—with which I instinctively joined in—went up as he passed by, even from those men still in the water, working to ensure that the bridges would hold up long enough to get not only their emperor, but every one of his subjects across to safety. For at least an hour after his crossing, there remained a stir in the atmosphere, an increase in conversation and a general feeling that all would survive and make it back home. Looking out across the mass of those still waiting to cross, however, I could see that the enthusiasm was not felt universally. But around me, the feelings were genuine. Only when he was long gone did some sense of reality return to the men with whom I stood.

"I'm surprised they're still bothering, now he's across," said one, his eyes flicking back and forth between the men who continued unendingly to file past.

"He'll get us out," said another.

"Why so sure?"

"Because it's another two hundred leagues to Warsaw. He needs us till then."

"But do we need him?"

"Could you have got the bridges built?"

That night, to my astonishment, the horde that had been filing in unbroken procession across the bridges petered away to nothing. Tens of thousands still remained to cross, but they sat around huge campfires, roasting the flesh of fallen horses and waiting to recommence the crossing in the morning. With hindsight of the number that failed to make it across before the full Russian forces fell upon us, this was a ridiculous waste of time, but no one gave the order, and so no one crossed.

The quiet darkness would be a perfect opportunity for Iuda to slip over the bridge, avoiding the crowds, and I tried to stay awake and so prevent him, but I could not. Had Iuda come by that night, I would not have noticed. Had he seen me, he could have killed me with ease. But he did not come that night.

I woke at about seven. I could hear the sound of artillery, closer than it had been the night before, but I do not think it was that which woke me. I looked and saw a solitary figure crossing the river via the smaller bridge.

TWELVE

There was no question of it being Iuda, although his hat and clothing completely obscured his face; he was far too short. He was dressed in a bearskin—at least, that was the outermost layer—with a hole cut in it from which his head protruded. It was practical, if inelegant. I could only guess that he was that rarity of a French soldier who had the independence of mind to cross the river when the opportunity was there. I felt sure he would be one of the few that made it safely back to France.

Soon the sun rose, and the crossing of the Berezina resumed *en masse*. The indolence of the previous night now forced an additional urgency during the day. All had heard rumours that the Russian forces were closing in on our side of the river, and we began to hear to the north and east the sound of battle which was not so far distant when it began, and grew ever nearer as the day went on.

Later in the day, when the first Russian cannonballs began to fall on the riverbank itself, any remaining vestige of orderliness evaporated. The crowds around the entrances to the bridges became more disorderly, and those who failed to angle themselves on to the bridges began to be pushed into the water by the crowds behind them.

Laden with too many horses and too many carts, the larger bridge began to sag in the middle and soon, with a wrenching and creaking of splintering wood, a section of it crumpled into the river. Horses, wagons and men were swept downstream. Those on what remained of the bridge on the far side dashed to safety with an alacrity they had not shown when it was intact. The crowds on the bank at first did not realize what had happened and continued to push on to what they thought was a bridge but was now a jetty. Dozens were forced off the bridge's broken end and into the river—soldiers becoming sailors as they were obliged to walk the plank into which the bridge had been transformed by its collapse—before any order was restored. As people realized what had happened, there was a rush to the other bridge, where I was standing watch. By now all the other guards had abandoned their post, either voluntarily or simply swept away by the crowd. A French marshal—I think it was Lefebvre—stood at the end of the bridge and tried to restore order, but the crowd ignored him and in the end he was forced to cross with them, rather than resist and be trampled underfoot. I retreated behind one of the piles that supported the bridge, my feet lapped by the river water as it scurried over the ice, and continued my vigil.

As darkness fell there was still no sign of Iuda. I had always known it was a long shot, but now I realized that, unclear as I was what I would do if I found him, I had no idea whatsoever of what to do if I didn't. If the evacuation continued then I would soon be swept across the bridge with the rest of the troops. Somehow, I would have to get away from them. Doing so on this side of the Berezina would be preferable, but I could foresee the possibility of having to creep back across this bridge or another, somewhere else along the river, to return to Russian lines.

Whatever plans I might have been able to formulate, I was interrupted by the sound of cannon fire. To the east, the Russian forces were much closer now. The French rear guard, which had been holding off the main body of the Russian army, was beginning to disengage. New swarms of men came down the banks of the river and tried to get on to the bridges. From the far bank, shells from French cannon were now screaming over our heads to rain down on the unseen Russian troops beyond the trees. With the fall of darkness, there was to be no cessation in the flow of people across the river as there had been the previous night.

As more and more soldiers crushed on to the narrow bridge, a sense began to fill the air that the end was coming; that if we did not get across now, then the Russians would be upon us and there would be no further chance to escape. Officers and men all around, who had been maintaining some slight degree of order, abandoned their posts and joined the mêlée that pushed and shoved around the bridges. Others decided to forget about the bridges and risk the river itself.

Close to the bank, the water remained frozen, and men began gingerly to walk out as far as they could. One reached the edge of the ice sheet and leapt into the water. Because of the thaw, the river was full and fast. He was swept away downstream. Others were luckier. I saw two or three who stripped themselves of guns, swords and boots—anything that weighed them down—and who thereby managed to swim across. How much further they would get without boots, I had to wonder, but on either side of the river there was a plentiful supply of dead men who had no further requirement for their footwear. One man who jumped in was again swept away, his head disappearing instantly beneath the turbulent water, only to emerge way, way downstream on the far side of the river and scramble thankfully on to dry land.

Upstream of the bridge, a group of a dozen or so were edging out across the ice. The man at the front turned to the others and began screaming at them, urging them to go back because their weight would break the fragile shelf. The vigour of his gesticulation unbalanced him and he slipped over on the ice. With the impact of his fall I heard a cracking sound as the whole sheet splintered away from the bank. Almost immediately it capsized, tipping the men into the water. The current took them rapidly downstream and dashed them into the side of the bridge. Some began to climb up on to the structure and were kicked back by those already desperately scrambling across it. Others remained in the water, clinging to the piles that supported the bridge until the sheet of ice itself slammed into the bridge, crushing those who clung beneath it and knocking several who were on the bridge into the water.

Memories of Austerlitz and the horrible mass of men drowned at Lake Satschan came rushing to me—memories that I had been fighting off ever since I had arrived at this place, ever since winter had begun to fall. At Austerlitz it had been Russian and Austrian lives, but now the score was evened. This time there had been no need to fire upon the ice to break it, as Bonaparte had at Satschan. That is not to say that there was no Russian cannon fire, only that it killed by more traditional means.

Terror finally overcame my desire to confront Iuda. It was time for me to leave, but even that was not going to be easy. Close to the bridge I was protected from the crowd, which travelled with a single mind and in a single direction. It would have been easier for me simply to get into the crowd and let it carry me across the river, but the bridge was now so swelled with bodies that I doubted whether more than half those who got on to it made it to the other side without falling into the water. I remembered crossing the Moskva Bridge, back when Moscow was being evacuated and when I again had found myself the only person wanting to travel against the flow. That had been an easier bridge to cross than this, but then the French crossing here were a hundred times more certain of their defeat than those Russians had been. I started out away from the river, against the direction that every other man on the bank was heading. They were not concerned or inquisitive about the direction I was going, they did not deliberately try to take me with them, but however much I pressed onward away from the icy water, still I found myself carried closer and closer towards it.

I grabbed men's arms and their coats and tried to push them aside to get past them, climbing against the flow of human bodies. As I grabbed one man's lapel to throw him out of my way he looked at me with cold, familiar, grey eyes. For once he had not been looking for me, and I had only just then abandoned my search for him, and yet still Iuda and I had found one another.

Chapter XXXII

It was almost a waltz that we engaged in as we made our way through the morass of panicking men to the edge of the crowd. Each of us had grabbed hold of the other, not in the conventional pose to dance but holding tightly so that the other would not escape. We each pushed the other, neither realizing it, but both with the same intent; to be free of the crowd so that we could deal with one another alone.

As we emerged, we were released from the supporting pressure of the men and women around us and fell to the ground. We rolled down the steep bank towards the river's edge, with first one man on top and then the other, coming to rest in an icy puddle, which the tread of thousands of feet had kept liquid despite the freezing temperature all around. By luck, I ended up on top of Iuda, and gave him a blow to the jaw with my fist which I hoped would subdue any further fighting spirit in him. He was still in the uniform of a *chef de bataillon*, whereas I was a mere *soldat*—each of us overdressed in comparison with the multitude around us—but no one around seemed to question whether I should be treating my superior officer in such a way. On the far side of the river, the military hierarchy might reassert itself, but here, each man's soul was his own.

"I presume by now you're beyond believing me," shouted Iuda, striving to be heard above the chaos around us.

"I've long been beyond that," I lied. Suddenly a body of men erupted from the main throng like a hernia, redrawing the arbitrary lines that partitioned the crowd from the empty space around it. Hundreds surged through us and past us and out on to the ice, knocking me over and knocking Iuda from my grasp. I hauled myself up to my feet and, feeling the slippery surface beneath them, realized with dread that I too had been forced out on to the frozen river. Seven years ago, on Lake Satschan, I had felt the same terror.

TWELVE

Today, supported above the waves not like Saint Peter by the will of God, but by a flimsy layer of frozen water, I stood my ground.

I looked around to try to recapture Iuda before he could disappear into the mob, but, through the thinning veil of frightened men and women who slipped and slid their way to the shore, I could see him, facing me and approaching me.

"But are you yet beyond disbelieving me?" he shouted through the crowd. He had not read my mind; he had simply understood it perfectly. I once heard a story of a chess player—who was said to have studied under Philidor—who could write down his opponent's play for five moves ahead, but only if that opponent was a great player. Against a weaker opponent, he was consistently wrong. In truth, it was the opponent who was wrong, the master who was right. Iuda knew that at some point I would have come to the conclusion that his word was valueless in terms of the truth it represented, and therefore all the more powerful in the ideas that it suggested.

"I have to know," I said. We were now face to face.

"I can't tell you," he replied, with a smile of mischievous delight.

"You will!" As I spoke I grabbed his wrist and swung my foot against his shin, knocking his legs from under him. He writhed as he fell and succeeded in pulling me over too. The ice sheet dipped under our weight and we both slid towards the water. My grip on Iuda's wrist was now reciprocated by his on mine, but there was no grip that either of us could find on the glassy surface beneath us to halt our descent. A swathe of powdered ice sprayed into my face, sheared from the surface as Iuda dug in the teeth of his knife to slow our motion. He came to a halt on the very lip of the ice, but my impact into him knocked him a little further over, so that his legs dipped into the water.

Wriggling on my back, I kicked at the knife in his hand and it skated across the ice and over the edge, disappearing into the water with a plop. Iuda spread his hands and arms wide across the surface of the ice, trying to find purchase, trying to prevent himself from slipping into the cold, turbid water. But he was no *voordalak*, and did not have their ability to find a grip on the most polished of surfaces.

I regained my feet as he hung limply off the edge of the ice, now up to his chest in water and, with every movement he made, slipping in a little deeper.

"You can't let me die," he said, not as a plea but as a statement of fact.

"Why not?"

"That way you'll never know."

I stamped my foot firmly beside his hand. He grabbed it and clung to it, his arm wrapping around my leg like a serpent's tail.

"So," I asked, breathing deeply and trying to calm myself now I had the upper hand, "was it Margarita or Domnikiia you were with?"

He looked up at me with his head cocked slightly to one side. "It was . . ." He paused in thought, as though he had been asked whether he would prefer beef or mutton for dinner. "Margarita!" he announced with an air of decision. Then he yanked firmly on my leg, throwing me once again on to my back on the ice. As I began to slide once more towards the river, Iuda too had lost his only anchorage and his head disappeared beneath the surface.

The ice sheet beneath me began to tip and I found myself sliding even faster towards the water into which Iuda had just disappeared. I rolled on to my stomach and splayed my arms out wide, but just like Iuda, I could find little purchase. My right hand found a momentary grip, but the fingers of my left could do nothing. Within seconds I splashed into the water, going under and feeling a new coldness that infiltrated those last few parts of me that had been protected by my clothing. By the time I bobbed back to the surface, so had he.

"I can't lie to you anymore, Lyosha," he said, spitting out some of the water that had filled his mouth and swallowing the rest. "It was Dominique."

Once again he disappeared beneath the waves. I might have dived down to pull him back to the surface, but my concern now was more that the current was hurtling me towards the pillars of the bridge itself. I put my arms and legs out in front of me, but even then I could not protect myself entirely from the force of the impact. The wind was knocked out of me as my chest collided with the wooden support and my head bashed against it, almost knocking me out. Only some instinct told me to hold on to whatever I could grab, otherwise, weighed down by my wet clothes, I would have sunk straight to the riverbed.

TWELVE

Moments later, I was again fully conscious. I hauled myself up out of the water and entwined my legs around one of the beams. Looking to my left, I saw Iuda also climbing out of the water on to the substructure of the bridge. His motion was like that of a newt, dragging itself from the slime of its watery habitat on to dry land. He paused for a moment, panting, and only then looked around to see me advancing on him, stretching from pillar to beam across the wooden web that comprised the bridge's foundations.

Iuda ducked inside, crossing underneath the bridge. I followed, but made better ground, managing to get both to the other side of the bridge and closer to him. We were now dead centre in the river, about as far from one bank as from the other. Above our heads, hundreds of French were trampling one another in an attempt to get over to the right bank. Russian cannonballs splashed into the river around us. Stretching away from us to the south, the river flowed fast and free. Beyond this bridge, past what little the current had left of the shattered other bridge, there was nothing for miles. Somewhere, way downstream, there would be some other bridge against which all those dead who fell here would eventually congregate. If not, the Black Sea awaited them, far, far away.

Iuda leapt out into the water and I made a grab after him. With my left hand I just managed to get a hold of a clump of his filthy blond hair, whilst keeping myself anchored to the bridge with my right. With only two fingers and a thumb, it was hard to get a good grip, but his hair was long and soon I had it entwined. He was at my mercy, up to his neck in the water. I could duck him beneath it, pull him to safety, or let him go.

"Tell me the truth!" I screamed at him.

"I have told you the truth," he replied, laughing despite his predicament.

"When?" I demanded. It was not a rhetorical question and he knew it. What I wanted to know was which of his two contradictory statements was true.

"Often," was his only reply, again accompanied by a laugh.

I pushed him downwards under the water, counting the seconds to myself to be sure that he would not die. I pulled him back up and he gasped for breath, but never lost his smile.

"Tell me!" I screamed at him again.

"You can't torture me, Lyosha." He raised his hand to clear the wet hair from his eyes. "I have the ultimate protection that you'll never believe me. I've told you everything—not just everything that's true, but everything else as well. All I can offer you is the ultimate enlightenment; not just what is but what could be. To know everything is to know nothing. What's the point in asking anymore? What's the point in forcing it out of me? You might as well torture a coin and expect it to turn up tails."

I pushed his head back under the water. He was right. Many people choose to live by their reputation; Iuda chose to live by the lack of it. With my help, he had put himself in a situation where I could lend no credence to anything he said. However many times I dipped his head beneath the waves, he could change his answer. The final answer would never be the definitive one, because another different answer could always follow. I could put Iuda through the agonies of hell and he could scream "Margarita" nine hundred and ninety-nine times and I would still not believe him, for fear that on the thousandth he would mutter "Domnikiia."

I pulled him back up to the surface, tightening my grip on his hair as though to pull it out of his scalp.

"You're slow today, Lyosha," he said. "Do you still think you can get the truth out of me?"

Silistria had taught me more than one thing about torture. It had taught me about being a victim, but I had also learned about being a perpetrator. I'd learned that it's not always about gaining information; sometimes it's an end in itself.

I shook my head and waited for the look in his eyes that showed he realized that the torture was over. The instant I saw it, I pushed his head back under and began to count again. He knew that, this time, I was not intending to pull him back up again. He had chosen a game that led to his own destruction; chosen to lose with a clever move rather than survive through a mundane one. As I counted the seconds, he struggled to break free; past ten, past twenty, thirty and forty. Then he quietened. It was not long enough for a man to drown—I knew he was bluffing. My hand was so cold I could scarcely feel his head beneath it. I squeezed tighter, unable to feel even pain and wondering if I might be breaking my own fingers by gripping so tightly. After about a minute he began to struggle again and then a convulsion ripped through his body. Had that been his final, irresistible, instinctive attempt to breathe, when the urging of his lungs overcame the knowledge that he was surrounded not by air but by water? Afterwards, he moved no more.

I waited for a further minute with my numbed arm plunged deep into the river before I raised it to look into his face. He was gone. A clump of trailing blond hairs was left curled around in my insensible fingers, but of the rest of him there was no sign. His body had been ripped from my numb, frozen hand by the torrent of the river. I looked out downstream, but it was an impossible task to distinguish one lifeless, floating corpse from another. Amongst them, a few swimmers even now made it to the safety of the western shore, but I did not see Iuda amongst those either.

I pulled myself back in, underneath the bridge, my knees hunched up against my chest as I listened, troll-like, to the tramp, tramp, tramp of feet above my head. I began to shiver. The layers of clothing that I wore were all wet through. If I were to leave my hand at rest for too long against some piece of the bridge's structure, it might freeze there. I crawled back along under the bridge to the eastern bank of the river. Thousands still remained to cross, but it was now unlikely that many more would. The Russian troops under Kutuzov and Wittgenstein were closing in.

I headed south along the riverbank, quickly discarding my French great-coat. The choice was between death from the cold or from a Russian bullet. I chose not on the basis of preference but of likelihood, and it was a close-run thing. As I continued downriver, those few Russian patrols I encountered were convinced by a few words from me. The even fewer French I met were just as easily convinced when they heard their own language.

Before long, I came to Borisov, the town abandoned by Bonaparte but a few days before. Now Bonaparte was heading back west. How much of his army made it with him was open to question, but he himself would surely get back to Paris. I had no further desire to chase him, nor to chase any other Frenchman. And if Iuda were somehow still alive, I did not have the desire to pursue him, or even find out for sure if he was dead or not. He was out of Russia, or very soon would be—whether swept south, downriver to the Black Sea, or swept west with the Grande Armée to Poland and beyond. He was no longer my problem. My problems were those that he had left with me.

Though it was still dark when I reached Borisov, I was lucky enough to be able to find a horse, left forgotten as the French rushed north. I mounted it and headed out of the town.

Bonaparte would struggle on for a few more years and would even, it would transpire, rise as a brief phoenix before his ultimate finale, but here in Russia his defeat had begun. It was not a defeat that I had taken any part in. I had fought Bonaparte at Austerlitz and we had lost. I had fought him at Smolensk, and we had lost. After Borodino I had found another battle to fight. If my grandchildren one day were to ask me how I helped in the downfall of Napoleon, I would be unable to tell them the truth. I could tell them of Maksim and of Vadim and Dmitry and of how we had fought together in unorthodox ways on and off for seven years, but I could never tell them how it had ended. I could never tell them how Dmitry had frozen to death and how he had been lucky compared to Vadim and how even Vadim had been lucky compared to Maksim. For although both Vadim and Maksim had died a similar death, Maks had the added weight of knowing that he had been sent to it by those he thought to be his friends.

The doubt about Domnikiia which Iuda had so guilefully insinuated into me was, I now understood, easy to cope with. It was Maks who had suggested the solution to me. It was a matter of faith. Faith, Maks had said, allows us to feel certain about things that we can never know for sure. I could never discover whether it had been Domnikiia or Margarita with Iuda—that was knowledge that could never be known—but it was clear what I wanted the truth to be. All I had to do was have faith in my chosen view of reality. It would not be easy, certainly not for a man like me, to maintain such faith, but the fact that it meant I could be with Domnikiia would make the effort worthwhile. Every day on which my faith was rewarded would in its turn strengthen that faith—and strengthen my need for that faith. I would not, however, be seeing Domnikiia quite every day.

TWELVE

The town of Borisov holds an interesting geographical position in Russia. It stands on one corner of an equilateral triangle, of which the other two vertices are Moscow and Petersburg. From here it was as far to Petersburg as it was to Moscow, and it was as far again from one to the other.

I could weigh myself down now with the choice of which one to go to, and I would not even attempt to fool myself that it was a choice between two cities—it was a choice between Domnikiia and Maria. It did not matter which road I chose now—Moscow or Petersburg—I would still be able to travel at will between the two. I knew that I could never give up Domnikiia, simply because I did not want to. I knew that I would never abandon Marfa, not only because I would never abandon my son, but because I knew that my love for her was always inside me, waiting to be rekindled whenever I chose to let it. I spurred my new horse and headed off under a red sky, just beginning to be lit in the east.

Birds began to awaken to the new dawn and, to the sound of their song, the nightmare began to fade. My country had faced five hundred thousand invaders. I had faced just twelve. We had both won. We would both recover. But, unlike Russia herself, when I was to look back on the events of the autumn and winter of the year 1812, I would not feel the blood coursing in my veins, my heart swelling in my bosom and my lip quivering at the recollection of honours past. Oh, I would shed a tear for my fallen friends. But, unlike my country, I would feel no pride.

ABOUT THE AUTHOR

Born in 1968, Jasper Kent has a degree in natural sciences from Trinity Hall, Cambridge, and works as a freelance software consultant. He has also written several musicals. He lives in Brighton.

For more information on Jasper Kent and his books, see his Web site at www.jasperkent.com.